UNBRIDLED PASSIONS

"Lord, you feel good," Maggie sighed, rubbing her hands briskly up and down Wager's bare back. "It's been so long. . . ."

She stirred when his hand slipped down between them and her hips seemed to arch of their own accord; she moaned as he slowly came into her, his lips pressed to her cheek. She heard him whisper, "I love you, Maggie Barth," and she smiled into the dark and tightened her arms about him. The warm, exquisite sensation of his moving loins caused her mouth to open, gulping in cold air as she matched her movements to his. How she needed him!

Maggie had gone into the relationship with Wager wondering how long it would last. The bonds that kept them apart still existed and might never be broken, but that was a bridge they would one day have to cross. Now she reveled in his lovemaking, giving herself over to the ecstasy that he brought to her, the precious release that made her strong. . . .

It was a strength that Maggie would need in the days ahead when the loyalties of the Lynn family are put to the test of fire in this torrid tale of men and women divided by love . . . damned by desire.

* * * * *

THE STRONG AMERICANS

A sensual saga of tender romance and lusty adventure in the thunderous dawn of the Revolution comes alive in . . .

THE RAGING HEART

ATTENTION: SCHOOLS AND CORPORATIONS

PINNACLE Books are available at quantity discounts with bulk purchases for educational, business or special promotional use. For further details, please write to: SPECIAL SALES MANAGER, Pinnacle Books, Inc., 1430 Broadway, New York, NY 10018.

WRITE FOR OUR FREE CATALOG

If there is a Pinnacle Book you want—and you cannot find it locally—it is available from us simply by sending the title and price plus 75¢ to cover mailing and handling costs to:

> Pinnacle Books, Inc.
> Reader Service Department
> 1430 Broadway
> New York, NY 10018

Please allow 6 weeks for delivery.

____Check here if you want to receive our catalog regularly.

The Raging Heart

ARTHUR MOORE

PINNACLE BOOKS   NEW YORK

This is a work of fiction. All the characters and events portrayed in this book are fictional, and any resemblance to real people or incidents is purely coincidental.

THE STRONG AMERICANS

Copyright © 1981 by Arthur Moore

All rights reserved, including the right to reproduce this book or portions thereof in any form.

An original Pinnacle Books edition, published for the first time anywhere.

First printing, May 1981

ISBN: 0-523-41144-8

Cover illustration by Bruce Minney

Printed in the United States of America

PINNACLE BOOKS, INC.
1430 Broadway
New York, New York 10018

*For Gaye Tardy,
who is beautiful . . .*

In the year of our Lord, 1761.

The force of life, the deliverance of
laughter, the raging fire that consumes,
the tears and despair . . . love is constant,
love is tomorrow, and love is all.

Chapter One

Canaan, Connecticut

It was the end of summer, a day of low, drifting clouds and clammy fog writhing in from the gray Atlantic, shortening the streets in the middle of the morning. Maggie Barth Lynn hurried from the house, bound for the boatyard with a parcel of hot food for her husband, Azariah, and her son, Morgan.

She glanced at the sky and decided it would not rain, no need to take a cloak. She would do with the heavy blue-figured shawl across her shoulders and would go across the old footbridge that spanned Canaan Creek. It was a shortcut that lessened the walk by five or six minutes, and that way it was unlikely she'd meet anyone who would take up her time with chattering. She must hurry to the yard and back; there were so many things to do. . . .

Sniffing at the fog, Maggie glanced toward the ocean where a mournful horn sounded. Her long auburn hair swirled in the light breeze and she brushed it back with an impatient gesture, tucking in the ends under the tight black wool cap her daughter, Becky, had knitted for her. She had hazel-brown eyes; all the Lynns were dark-eyed and so were the Barths, not a blond among them. Her father, John Barth, had been black-haired to the day of his death in his seventy-third year, only ten months ago. Maggie was only a few inches shorter than

Azariah, who was six feet; she had a full ripe, carmine mouth, and cheeks pink from the chill wind. She moved with the sinuous grace of a deer, her slender body encased in a faded blue-gray dress with a long-waisted bodice that came to a point in front and had a simple round neck without lace. It had seen better days, but she was not one to discard anything that could still serve. With seven in the family she had to make do. Clothes bought in the stores were expensive.

Holding the skirt inches off the damp ground, she walked quickly to the corner and turned west. Pulling the black cap firmly down over her ears, she tied the shawl, thinking she might have worn a cloak after all. It was colder than she'd expected and the sky promised no relief. Well, she would go as quickly as she could and the walk would stir her blood.

She looked neither to right nor left, her mind busy planning the tasks of the day. As soon as she returned it would be necessary to wash a bowlful of black beans and put them to soak. The family loved black bean soup. She had also to pound corn in the mortar for bread, then stir the meal into milk and let it sit overnight. After that there was a list of the week's staples to be made out, which Becky or Marie would take to Goodman Eli Burley's store, and it would be a good idea to add lemons to it, if Eli had them. Azariah was very fond of tart lemon bread.

When she came in sight of it, the gangly footbridge was half hidden by fog. It was a long, rather ugly affair put up by the men of the town more than five years past when the stout wood and stone one had been washed away by an uncommon winter's end flood. Every year in the meeting hall there was talk of building another permanent structure, but nothing had been done because every year there were more pressing needs, and the rickety bridge *was* serving, after all.

Azariah had lately suggested that she and the girls go round through the town as he and Morgan did because the creek was running fast with storm water, and Maggie bit her lip looking down at it. She stepped onto the wet planks, grasping the single handrail. The bridge creaked as she took the first halting steps, but it seemed firm enough. Fog swirled about her and the round rail was cold and wet. The creek, muddy and brown as chocolate, ran swiftly eight or nine feet below, with weeds and brush tumbling along playfully.

As she approached the middle she saw Wager Tanfield hurrying toward her along the weedy path, holding his coat collar with one hand. His tall form was still indistinct in the fog but she recognized his walk instantly, his long strides and his way of swinging his arms. Wager was a draughtsman and designer of boats whom Azariah frequently employed to draw plans. She had known him for nearly ten years and he was often in their home when he and Azariah talked or worked on drawings. Wager had a patrician-looking actor's profile, of which he was extremely conscious, having been joshed about it all his life. He had broad shoulders and powerful arms, having worked as a carpenter in his youth.

He saw her and paused and she smiled at his wave. Then he stepped onto the bridge.

At his first step the bridge moved perilously, creaking and groaning, swaying to one side. Wager stopped instantly and beckoned to her. "Run!" he called. "Run—it's giving way!"

Grabbing her skirts, Maggie took another step. The bridge suddenly slanted. She dropped the food parcel and held onto the handrail with both hands. Wager shouted as the bridge twisted and slid to the right with an ominous creaking and splintering of timbers, and she felt herself falling.

In the next instant she hit the brown water, felt the icy bath of it and struggled as it closed over her head. The breath went out of her, the shock paralysed her being—then a sliding timber brushed her shoulder and she pushed at it and grabbed another. A pole gave her a hard rap alongside the ear as she came up, breathless. The world smeared red and black and she went down gasping and dazed as the water roared in her ears.

Dimly she heard the crash as the bridge fell. Heaving water tossed her about; loose planks tumbled and caught at her clothes. Despite the icy water she was nearly unconscious from the hard rap. Ruddy images and dazzling white lights spangled her consciousness, and she felt herself being pushed down. She touched the rocky, slimy bottom and her arms flailed as she was dragged—then a strong hand closed round her wrist.

She choked and sputtered as Wager pulled her up, cursing. His words shocked her even as she coughed up the foul-tasting water. He was waist-deep in the creek, fighting to drag her onto the sand, both arms tight about her body, holding her under the arms, hands about her breasts. He heaved and almost threw her down and she felt grass and wet earth.

"Maggie! Maggie! Are you all right?"

He turned her over and she looked at him wearily, breathing hard, gasping for air. He was only a fuzzy shape before her eyes, and she was exhausted. Slowly her eyes focused and she saw his anxious face and managed to nod. She heard him say, "Thank God!"

Her head was on fire. She lifted her hand to the place but he pulled it away. "You're hurt . . ."

"I hit my head."

"Yes, it's bleeding a bit but I doubt if it's serious." He touched her gently. "It doesn't look badly cut."

"Cold," she said, hugging herself. She stared at the

place where the footbridge had been and there was nothing, only the splintered ends of the posts on the opposite side. His coat came round her shoulders.

"You're soaked to the skin. We've got to get you dry or you'll catch your death."

"Must get home . . ."

"It'll take too long. Can you stand?"

"I think so . . ."

He helped her up and she gazed again at the fallen bridge as if at some vanquished enemy. It was a jumble of timbers in the gorge with white water splashing and curling over. How had she gotten out of that alive? If Wager hadn't come along—she shuddered.

He slid an arm about her. "There's a hut close by. Come on. Let's get you inside out of the wind."

She leaned on him, feeling dizzy, not thinking straight. Her shoes squelched as they walked to the hut. Wager pushed the door open and grunted. It was a small, square shack once used by herders, but the land was all taken up and partly fenced now and the herders had moved on to other pastures. A few dull-eyed cows stared at them and Maggie clutched the edge of the door. The hut smelled abominably. It had a dirt floor and one tiny window with tacked-over skin half torn away. The door sagged and protested its every move but Wager forced it open and brought an upended keg for her to sit on.

He said, "I'll get some wood and make us a fire." He went out and she heard him tearing boards from the rear of the shack. Her teeth chattered uncontrollably and she pulled the coat more tightly about her. Thank goodness Wager had doffed it before jumping into the creek after her, so it was dry. The dizziness persisted and the hut reeled when she closed her eyes; she put a hand out to the near wall, beginning to feel sick.

Wager returned with an armload of sticks and boards, glancing anxiously at her. "You look awfully pale."

She felt round the bump on her head. It was the size of a hen's egg and her hair was sticky. He said, "Don't touch it or you'll make it worse."

He built a small pyramid of splinters and sticks and got on his knees with flint and steel striking showers of sparks into a bit of charred linen rag, but it took ten minutes to get a fire. The dry splinters caught with a rush and he carefully placed more, then larger sticks. The smoke curled out through the door as the fire crackled and popped sparks onto the floor.

With the fire going well he examined her head, gently pulling the hair from around it. "It's a good hard bump. I expect it hurts like blue blazes."

"It's sore. Throbs . . ."

"I don't wonder. You'll have a headache."

"Yes, it's beginning."

"Well, the bleeding's stopped anyhow. You'll just have to suffer it for a bit. You shouldn't allow bridges to fall on you. It almost always leads to a bump on the head."

Maggie smiled wanly. "I was lucky you came along." She put out her hand to touch his, thinking instantly of the way he'd pulled her out, holding her breasts. "I would surely have drowned."

"Let's not think of that."

"It's true all the same. I owe you my life."

He put more wood on the fire and spoke lightly. "It's only neighborly, saving lives. But getting you dry is the important thing." He took the coat from her shoulders, unwrapped the soggy woolen shawl, and arranged it near the fire to catch the heat. Smoke swirled about the little hut and he coughed, fanning it away. Maggie took off her shoes and held her wet stockinged feet to the growing blaze. The girls would wonder where she'd got to.

Wager went out again and came back with more wood. The fire blazed merrily, so hot she had to move back. The door of the hut faced away from the ocean and away from the town. There was little chance anyone would see the fire and come to investigate; even the smoke was caught up in the rising fog. When she was dry she'd have to walk seaward along the creek to the wagon bridge, cross it and go back through the town to home.

Wager had been soaked from the waist down. He removed his shoes, shaking his head ruefully. "That footbridge should have been replaced a year ago. What was the bundle you dropped?"

"Food for Azariah and Morgan. They'll go hungry now, or walk home for something." She combed her hair with clawed fingers, careful to avoid the bump. "I must look a fright!"

"Not at all. A bit of mud on your cheek—" He brushed it away, smiling. "Feeling better?"

"A bit." The reaction was setting in and she felt cold inside. How close she'd come to the hereafter! She'd never thought about death before, not applied to herself, and now today it seemed the Reaper had grinned in her face. And been thwarted by Wager.

He asked, "How's the head?"

"A steady throb, I'm afraid." Maggie shuddered again. "I can still feel that bridge giving way. It just seemed to slip sideways out from under me . . ."

"It's all over now. Don't think about it. Easier said than done, I know, but push it out of your mind."

"I know I'll have nightmares."

"I hope you don't." He rose and turned the shawl,

7

smiling at her. "Now the war's over, you'll be the biggest topic of conversation in town. The one who knocked down the bridge."

"Oh, my goodness! I hope not!"

"Can't keep people from chattering." He put the last of the wood on the fire and rose. "I'll have to get some more." He went out and she slumped wearily. The shock was wearing off and tiredness taking its place. Her cotton stockings were dirty. She curled her toes, toasted by the heat. She folded her skirt up to let the petticoats dry. Wager came back with more wood and knelt, placing boards on the fire. He was tanned and very handsome, with long fingers and thick wrists like a workman's. His white shirt was drying but still clung to his arms—the arms that had held her so tightly not very long ago. More tightly than Azariah ever had.

He noticed her gaze. "What is it? Am I muddy too?" He looked at himself.

"No, I was just thinking it'll take forever to get dry."

"Better than to walk about and take a chill." He glanced through the open doorway and she followed his look. The gray fog was definitely lifting but the overcast still kept the sun from them and probably would all day.

Azariah would wonder about it if she or one of the girls did not appear at the boatyard, but it had happened before. He might worry if he went home and she wasn't there; but he'd probably assume she'd stayed in the village with some of the women. And maybe someone would come along and report that the footbridge was down. If Azariah heard about it he'd have half the town along the creek searching for her body!

But no one knew she had taken the bridge that morning; she hadn't mentioned it to the girls. They'd probably figure too that she was somewhere in the village.

Wager put more wood on the fire. The coals were glowing red and the tiny room was cozy, if a bit more smoky than necessary; her eyes smarted, but it was better than the chill. She turned her shoes, finding them almost dry. She was growing used to the steady ache of her head. When she stood she found the dizziness had gone. Wager jumped up and slid an arm about her waist.

"Are you sure you're all right? I thought I saw you sway."

"I think I'm better . . ." She did not protest the arm. It tightened as he gazed at her anxiously. Maggie turned and shook out her petticoats. They felt damp and she wished she could remove them, but of course that was unthinkable. She was a married woman with five children.

Wager was married, too. His wife, Melanie, was a placid but not unpretty woman who had borne no children. Azariah had mentioned that Wager had several times voiced his disappointment. He was doomed never to have sons. Azariah, of course, said it was the Lord's doing and advised him not to fret about it. Wager had dared to say that the Lord was fickle in some things.

It was several hours before they were both dry enough to walk home. The thick wool shawl was still a little damp but Wager had already torn away all the wood from the hut he could manage with bare hands and had gathered up an armful of twigs and branches from the ground around the hut. There was nothing left to burn unless he could find an axe, he said. He looked closely at her head again before they set out, and she arranged her hair over the bump. The black knit cap had been lost in the creek.

Wager offered to go for a horse and rig but Maggie declared herself perfectly strong and they started across the rocky field alongside the rushing creek. When she stumbled he put his arm about her again. "Let's go more slowly."

She was very conscious of the arm, and slightly surprised to find her thoughts hurrying into turmoil. Of course she had always known Wager was exceedingly attractive! Her daughters, Becky and Marie, always were eager to serve him whenever he was in the house, and Wager treated them gravely.

But she, Maggie Lynn, was not a sixteen-year-old full of giggles and whispered secrets with her sister. Still, her heart seemed to flutter just the same, something that had never happened to her before. It was a strangeness that made her shiver. She saw his look of concern and made a remark about the chill wind, but it was not a chill she felt. It was something different, something she'd never experienced . . . not even with Azariah when they were courting!

She leaned against him and, as they came in sight of the gray sea, hearing the booming surf, they halted. The fog was still obscuring the horizon, though a weak and watery sun was doing its best to push through. There was a dreamy, almost ethereal glow on the undulating waters of the Sound. The waves shone like old silver and the few bobbing boats in sight were bits of bark strewn carelessly on a vast carpet. A ketch with brown sails moved along silently, a dusky and half-mysterious form far out toward Long Island. Gulls wheeled near the beach, crying and piping, and the noon gun fired from the foot of Main Street.

Wager said softly, "This is a day I'll remember, Maggie Barth."

She gazed at him in surprise that he called her by her maiden name, something he'd never done before. "The day the bridge fell in the creek?"

He smiled. "Yes, of course. The day the bridge fell in the creek."

* * *

When they came to the Canaan wagon bridge, a large, sturdy structure of square-hewn beams and road planking, strong enough for the biggest wagons and teams, they walked side by side, not touching. Maggie was very conscious of her wrinkled clothes. She must look as if she'd dunked in the surf or fallen off a boat. People were sure to stare if they saw her.

The village had only three proper streets that led toward the ocean and they turned into the first, High Street. It was a tree-shaded lane with houses mostly along the east side. Wager halted at the first turning and removed his hat.

"I'll leave you here, Maggie. Be sure to put something on that wound."

"I will. And thank you, Wager, for everything you did. I—"

"Please. Anyone would have done the same. I'm grateful you're not hurt."

She stepped closer. "Many others wouldn't have acted so promptly. I know I owe you my life."

He smiled and shook his head. "You would have gotten out. I know you, Maggie. A little thing like a fall in the creek—"

"Make light of it if you will, Wager." She smiled and touched his arm. "I know what I know."

He bowed. "I hope to see you very soon."

She watched him stride away toward the stores, still feeling his arms about her. It was a very troubling thought and yet everything he'd done could be explained by logic and expediency. He'd jumped in and pulled her from the roiling water as quickly as possible, not caring where he happened to touch her because it was more important to save her life. She walked on more slowly, holding the shawl close about her shoulders.

And he'd slid his arm about her because he feared she might still have an attack of dizziness.

Or did it mean more than that? Was she feeling something that wasn't there at all? Was it all in herself? Of course she was very fond of Wager and had been for a long time. Azariah was fond of him too, as were the children.

Wager was an easy man to like. But also he was the only man she knew who treated her like a woman. . . .

When she arrived home she went immediately into the kitchen to find that Becky had already washed the beans and put them to soak.

"Where have you been, Mother? My goodness, what happened to you?"

Maggie draped the shawl over a chairback and placed it near the hearth. "The footbridge collapsed and I—"

"The bridge! You fell into the water?" Becky rushed to her, dark hair flying. She wore an old brown dress buttoned almost to the neck and it was obvious that she was rounding out, straining the buttons. The sleeves rode up on her brown arms; she would soon have to give the dress to her younger sister, Marie. She had a grace of step very like her mother's, though she would never be quite as tall. She looked her mother up and down, lips parted in astonishment.

"Are you hurt?" She turned Maggie about, feeling the skirt. "How did you get dry?"

"Wager came along and pulled me out. He was walking the opposite way." She told Becky how they'd built a fire in the old hut. She glanced toward the stairs. "Has your father been home?"

"No, he and Morgan must have had their bite at the ordinary." Becky pulled a chair from the wall. "Let me see the bump."

Maggie sat down and lowered her head. With her

eyes closed she felt as if she could sleep for hours. Becky's deft fingers explored her head and she clucked her tongue. "Ohhh, you were lucky, Mother."

"Put a bit of cold water on it with a towel. Is it still bleeding?"

"No, but there's blood in your hair. I'll wash it." She poured water onto a bit of cloth and lightly pressed the compress to the wound. "Does that hurt? You know you might have been killed!"

"I was fortunate Wager was there."

"I'll say a prayer for him."

Maggie felt even more tired as the warmth of the fire reached out to her. Becky busied herself pounding corn. Little Marie was upstairs, sewing, she said, putting the finishing touches on the fancy handkerchief she'd been making for Junius. It was his birthday tomorrow; Becky had knitted him a yellow scarf with tassels on the ends.

When she went upstairs she had to go through the entire story again for an astonished Marie, who was alarmed at the danger she'd faced. Why coudn't it have been one of the boys who ran pell-mell across the bridge every day? They were doubtless the ones who'd weakened it.

Becky brought her some hot tea and Maggie changed clothes, pulling on a dress with a full bodice and round skirt, blue with small white flowers and circling vines. Lord knew she'd been lucky. Yes, Providence must have something important in store for her.

Chapter Two

Azariah Lynn was a big man, black-haired and stooped, with one leg off at the knee. He wore a hand-carved wooden peg and harness; grunting with annoyance each day as he put it on or took it off. The accident had changed his life, and changed his outlook on it.

He was a man whose size was of bones; he sometimes appeared awkward and now that the leg was gone, frequently shambling. He was an unhurried man with deep lines about his mouth; his eyes were dark with coppery lights and hints of gray and he was usually even-tempered and thoughtful. Men liked him for that solemn temper; he had left the wild passions far behind and seldom even thought of the pranks a two-legged man might do.

The terrible accident had happened on board ship in mid-Atlantic. Azariah, a man of twenty-nine and not long married, was one of the crew. A gusting storm had washed him, shouting, into the scuppers, and a falling block had smashed his leg. The captain had coolly sawed it off by the wavering light of several hanging lanterns, a scene that Azariah, drunk as a man had ever been, partially remembered and likened to the anteroom of hell. He'd suffered months of nightmares and thought in daylight of slipping silently over the side, and sometimes even as he sat in the crosstrees staring at a misty horizon he recalled the terrible screaming of that fateful night, knowing that it was he who'd screamed.

When the voyage ended he'd left the sea and floundered for two years, attempting this and that, losing all his store of saved-up pounds, then going to work for day wages. It had not been easy, competing with two-legged men.

He'd heard of the boatyard up for sale then, and Maggie had pushed him into buying it. When they went to look it over she'd been the enthusiastic one, saying that people always needed boats and repairs and that no one could do it better than he. The boatyard had a short pier, plenty of seasoned timber, and half a boat on stocks. Canaan was a town that lived by the sea, fish and trade, and one day his sons would join him. . . .

But until they were half grown he could not run the boatyard by himself, though he tried. The first year had been a terrible struggle, and he'd barely paid off what was due and fed the family. However, Maggie promised, brighter times were ahead. Azariah was a good and fair man who got on well with everyone, and when he did a job it was done properly and no excuses. It was his best advertising.

Enoch Quant had come along then, just at the propitious moment, when things looked blackest. Enoch was willing to work, he said, and he had a few pounds to put into the business. Enoch smiled those first days and made himself agreeable. But he was a dark, wiry man with deep, angry lines in his face; he seemed very shortly to find scowling more to his liking. Azariah soon found him quarrelsome and resentful and they began to draw apart. A month after Enoch bought into the yard, Azariah told Maggie that one day he'd have to buy him out. He could feel it in his bones.

It was a feeling that Maggie shared. She had been less than eager to see Enoch come into the boatyard, and Azariah knew he should have listened to her. But somehow he made himself get along with Enoch, learning the man's sidelong ways and his evasive mind.

For twelve years he managed to put up with Enoch, and then Morgan came to work at the boatyard. At fifteen, Morgan had been a husky, big-boned lad with thick wrists and smiles for Enoch's scowls. He was a willing, quick-to-learn boy who had been listening to stories about Enoch all his life. The reality was no surprise to him. But now Enoch had to deal with Azariah and son.

In a very few years Morgan could do all that Enoch was capable of and do it better because his mind and hands were uncluttered by the resentment and anger Enoch constantly allowed himself to feel.

Azariah explored all the avenues he could think of to rid himself legally of Enoch, and the only way was to buy him out. Enoch was a fact, a man to reckon with; he owned half the boatyard.

And of course Enoch complained about Morgan from the first day, possibly seeing a rival. The boy did this or that wrong, took too much time . . . nothing was ever exactly right. Usually Morgan listened, looked at him, and smiled. Enoch raged to Azariah that the boy never sought his opinion or approval, and when he grudgingly accepted a job Morgan had done, the boy smiled and the veins in Enoch's neck enlarged.

Of course there were times when Morgan doubled his fists in anger, but usually Enoch never knew about them.

The boatyard only ran smoothly when Enoch was away on errands or at home with the ague, and these were the times when Azariah got out the ledgers and studied them with an eye to somehow scraping together the money to buy Enoch's share. If Enoch would sell;

there was always that. He might refuse just for meanness.

But Enoch had a constant need for money, was in debt to everyone, and spent too fast what he gained because his wife, Tabitha, a gossipy woman, everyone said, usually came to the boatyard on the days when the partners divided what they'd taken in. On those days she and Enoch would quarrel and shout and after a bit she would go home clutching what money she'd been able to wring from him.

Then Enoch went off to the ordinary to nurse his rum with the hangers-on. Enoch liked his rum. He was a hard-drinking man.

Morgan suffered Enoch and his bitter tongue, however, for a different reason. Morgan was no forgiving saint with smiles for those who wronged him. He put up with Enoch because of Enoch's daughter, Sharon.

Azariah was aware of his son's interest in the girl, and despite his feelings for Enoch could not bring himself to lay a stick in the lad's way. Sharon was a flower, completely unlike her parents in any way. Azariah had often studied her—he'd known her since birth—and had never been able to discern a trace of resemblance to either of them. Sharon might have been left at their door in a basket, a thing he'd said to Maggie more than once when they were alone. How was it possible that Enoch's flesh and blood brought forth such a lovely girl? Maggie agreed that the girl had none of Enoch's stubbornness and guile nor her mother's evident failings. Sharon was beautiful and demure and soft-spoken, and it was easy to see that Morgan was far gone with no turning back.

Azariah stumped along High Street with Morgan beside him, hands in pockets. They turned right on Summer Street, then north on Pearl to their home. It was a daily journey of slightly more then a mile each way, rain or shine, snow or wind, and Azariah often said it gave him time to think.

His life had been unfulfilled, he considered, all stemming from the tragic accident that had cost him his leg. The pain was nothing. It was his loss of wholeness, the feeling of being crippled, that seemed to eat at him, though no one had ever said such a thing to his face—certainly not Maggie.

His dream had been to work his way to master, to sail his own ship, a dream dashed in minutes but lingering in his hopes for Morgan. One day Morgan would do what his father had never been able to accomplish. And Azariah would rejoice in it.

Most of the shops of the town were on Main Street, from the warehouses near South Beach to Fort Street and a little beyond. Many times he and Morgan took that route to stop at the tobacconist's or at the ordinary for a pint and a talk about politics with whomever was holding forth or listening or simply opinioning. Azariah was a man who liked to listen; he was always eager to hear the news, if any was available. The British forces had recently captured Quebec in Canada, in what was being called the French and Indian War and that war was over. All of Canada was now British, although there was a large French population, and the English language was the proper tongue to be spoken in America, save for the Frenchies who swore they'd never change, and a few Spaniards far off to the south. The Boston *News-Letter* arrived weekly and each copy was scanned and passed from hand to hand; the news was always a week or two late.

It was the feeling in Canaan town that the British troops would be going home soon. Even the soldiers were of the same opinion. Who needed regiments to protect them against the French when the French were beaten? And, as everyone said, if the Indians made trouble, why couldn't they protect themselves? They always had, and better than the damned redcoats who were dolts in the woods. Remember Braddock? That terrible defeat had occurred only a few years past, and it would have been a real massacre if the Virginian, Colonel Washington, had not saved the day.

But there was one nagging thing—the Navigation Acts. The British were increasingly sticky about them, more so every day it seemed. The Acts had been around for a hundred years without being enforced. But new and active policies were being evolved in England, or so the talk went. It was said on every side that the British intended to keep the colonies completely dependent on the mother country. That was the rub that galled everyone.

And now that the war had ended the British would be able to meddle even more in colonial affairs. And they were expert meddlers, with long noses poking into everything, taxing and fining.

The house on Pearl Street was two stories with rooms clustered about the central chimney, in the usual fashion. It had a parlor, stairs, hall and closet at the front, a large, square kitchen with a huge fireplace and hearth, and a chamber to the rear on the lower floor. There was a large woodshed behind the kitchen, a yard with trees and grass in spring, two privies and a small stablehouse. Upstairs were three bedchambers and closets for clothes and items to be packed away. The house had cornice-hooded windows and clapboarded sides and front with a scrollwork in wood, painted white, over the door, and a fine brass knocker.

Azariah rapped twice with the knocker as he opened the door, and Maggie came from the kitchen to greet them. "You're home and it's just getting dark."

"It cleared a bit this afternoon," Morgan said. He hung his hat and coat in the closet.

Becky hurried in. "Did you hear about the bridge?"

"The bridge?" Azariah looked around. "What bridge?"

He and Morgan were both astonished on hearing of Maggie's adventure and how Wager had saved her. They trooped into the kitchen, Azariah shaking his head. He leveled a finger at her. "I warned you about that damned bridge!"

"I'm not harmed," Maggie said, "not really. It was only uncomfortable." She motioned to Becky. "Set out the spoons and trenchers. Where's your sister?"

"Upstairs."

"Well, set the board, then go after her. Morgan, are your feet wet?"

"No, Mum."

"That's good." She hugged him quickly. He was getting taller each day, she thought, muscular and handsome in a dark way like his father. He wore a checked shirt and dirty breeches and with his hat on in a crowd one would think him a grown man, probably with a family. His features were regular, with level brows and interested eyes that saw everything, and a mouth that smiled easily. But he had a stubborn jaw like his father's, and he probably wouldn't back away any easier from trouble than Azariah ever had.

He asked, "Is anything left of the bridge?"

"It's all in the creek now, and good riddance. It should have been repaired long ago. Penny wise and pound foolish. Wash your hands, Morgan, and call in your brothers. They're in the yard splitting kindling."

She looked after him as he went out and Azariah said, "That damned Enoch tried to pick a fight with the boy today, Maggie. I think Morgan would have flattened him too, but I could see he thought better of it at the last minute. He's a good, level head, Morgan."

"Something's got to be done about Enoch."

A sigh. "Yes."

"There'll be trouble in the future. Enoch gets worse every year, and I hear he's drinking too much."

"He always drank too much." Azariah shrugged. "Junius is seventeen tomorrow. Did you bake something?"

"I will in the morning." Maggie ladled out the black bean soup into wooden bowls. "You promised he'd start at the boatyard on the day he was seventeen."

"I haven't forgotten. I know he hasn't."

"He's expecting to hear it." She took a twig and lighted another cadle. "Enoch will be outnumbered, poor man."

"He's made of tallow, Enoch, for a fact. But he'll pick on Morgan one too many times. I've seen the boy's jaw tighten up, and I shouldn't wonder he'll run out of patience one day—Sharon or not. And if it's God's wish, I'll have a front seat."

She faced him, hands on hips. "You know how Enoch loves money."

"We've got no money! Well, not enough to matter. A few pounds and my mother's gold chain that's worth maybe ten."

They had talked of this many times. They knew the money to buy Enoch out would have to be borrowed, and there were very few men in Canaan who might lend it. Jeremiah Chace was one. But Azariah hated to go into debt.

"It'll have to be done," Maggie said, "now that Junius will be there too. It'll have to be borrowed, Az. There's no other way and you know it."

"Lord knows I'm sorry I took him in . . ."

She went across and put a hand on his shoulder. "You thought it a blessing at the time—we both hoped it would be. Don't worry yourself, Az, no one could tell what he was. You did what you thought was right."

He sighed deeply, thinking she was a good woman to put it that way, since she'd been dead against Enoch. Others would have thrown it up to him. "I'd a lot sooner it was Wager Tanfield a partner." Azariah shook his shaggy head. "I'd change for Wager in an instant if the Lord was willing. In an instant."

"Come and sit," she said, "the soup'll get cold."

Thoughts of Wager Tanfield, since the morning's adventure, were disturbing, but they were safe inside her head. No one could ferret them out or even suspect them, least of all Azariah. He was not a divining man, not even as reflective or attentive as she would have wished. He was kind to her and to the children; that was the most of it. He was a good man at heart.

Unfortunately, he had not ever been particularly loving.

There were times, when she had a moment's respite to sit with a cup of tea, when she'd wondered about their marriage. Her father had arranged it, of course, but if she'd protested loudly enough he might have withdrawn the contract. There had been others seeking her hand.

What had she seen in Azariah? The goodness, perhaps? He'd been younger then, with two good legs, not the stump that she knew took the life and spirit out of him. The loss of his leg had altered everything. When he'd come home from that fateful voyage he'd been a different man, and it had never changed except to grow steadily worse. Though he was only forty-seven, Azariah was an indifferent husband. Now that the children were growing up he seemed to want her less and less.

He was often tired from the long day's vexations when he returned home, usually after dark, and his leg pained him more as the years passed, still aching and gnawing at him though he'd lost it a long time ago.

Now and then, from the things he let slip, she realized that he considered himself much less a man, and of course she'd done her best to tell him—to show him— that it was not so. But he was moody now, and he lacked ambition. There had been a time when he would have done something quickly about Enoch Quant, got it over with. But he'd let it drag on for twelve years. Now he seemed to live in his sons.

The kitchen put to rights, Maggie sat by the dying fire with Azariah and took up her knitting. There was always something to knit, mittens, caps, or gloves, especially since winter was at hand. She'd have to ask Marie to sketch a design or two. The girl was deft and quick at such things, better than anyone else in the family. Azariah read a month-old newspaper he'd read before, grunting over the columns in annoyance.

Several times during the evening he looked toward the door and even got up once to stump into the parlor to peer out. When she asked him he said it was likely that Wager would come by; they needed to discuss several boats.

It was not unusual that Wager came to the house, and Maggie watched her flying fingers, her thoughts far off. Each little sound from outside seemed magnified, a horseman passing or a wagon clattering by with wheels bumping on the half-frozen ground. She wanted him to come. How dreadful that she, a married woman, should anticipate his arrival with so much interest!

And when he did not come, with so much disappointment.

Later, leaving Azariah to bank the fire, she went up to bed and gazed into her small round mirror, examining the strange woman's face that stared back at her. What was she thinking? A man had pulled her from a rushing stream, where she might have been killed, and now of a sudden there were troublesome images in her mind and her thoughts were swirling out like free and untrammeled wraiths—and she could not prevent them.

And the worst of it was, she did not want to.

She sighed, noting the lines about eyes and mouth, the marks of poverty and worry, some called them. But she was past the age of dreaming. Girls of Marie's age, and Becky's, dreamed of knights on chargers, not mature women of thirty-five, as she was.

But there were no fetters on dreams. No disparaging hand would delve into her brain to pull out the hues and colors, the songs and lilting images she conjured up; no one could know they were even there. She smiled at the wavery mirror, and the lines disappeared. How astonished her daughters would be to know how their mother kicked over the traces—in fancy. How astounded Azariah would be!

She listened to him stomping up the uncovered wooden steps, pausing at the top for breath. He was twelve years older than she, very nearly old enough to be her father—but she must not let herself think like that. It would surely lead to unhappiness. He was a good man, the father of her children, and would always be. He was good, and kind to her.

He climbed into bed beside her, gave her a perfunctory kiss on the cheek, and lay back with a deep sigh, coughing slightly. Maggie stared at the ceiling, living again the moment when the bridge slid away from under her; when Wager's arms closed around her. How long had it been since Azariah had put his arms about her? Surely months . . . she could not recall the last time. Did her mind dwell so on this because she had a hunger for love, for the love she no longer received?

But it was foolish to think of Wager. She would be wise to banish such whirling thoughts for they could lead to nothing. He was married, too, and he was a fine and responsible man; he had probably not given her another thought since they'd parted on the street. No doubt he had gone home to Melanie and was even at this moment in bed with her.

Azariah stirred and said, "Why are you squirming?"

"I—I didn't realize I was."

"Are you quite all right?" He turned toward her. "You must have fallen a good distance."

She patted his shoulder. "I'm quite all right, dear. Go to sleep."

"I thought you might be having bad dreams."

"No, I haven't been asleep."

He grunted and coughed and turned again. "Very well . . ."

Maggie lay very still and focused her mind on the various daily tasks of the house, and only when she drifted off did she feel herself lifted from the ordinary routine . . . and sleep claimed her.

She saw Wager the next day. She was sweeping out the hall and opened the door to pound the broom against the boards. He came along the street with Azariah in a feathery drizzle. They both walked with heads bent away from the wind, shoulders dark with wet. They hurried up the steps, Azariah's peg rapping the treads, and she slammed the door behind them. She took Azariah's hat and damp coat and Becky rose at once from her carding and put more wood on the fire, then glided out of the room so her elders might talk.

Morgan had remained at the yard. He'd put up a canvas and was eager to finish fitting ribs to a keel. A bit of drizzle was nothing to him. As for himself, Azariah said, the leg was a damned bother with this kind of weather, aching like a live one being chewed on by an alligator. He plopped by the fire with the stump outstretched.

"I'll put the kettle on," Maggie said, doing her best to avoid Wager's eyes. He was dressed in a brown coat and darker breeches, his straight brown hair caught in a queue in back. Wager seldom wore a wig and had never shaved his head as the gentry did. Azariah wore a tiny little queue.

Wager said, "I talked with Marcus Carnon and Jeremiah Chace yesterday about rebuilding the footbridge."

She thought he was speaking to her and glanced at him, catching his eye. She looked away instantly to fumble with the cups.

"They think nothing can be done until spring, though I believe a jury rig could be put up. Don't you think so, Az?"

He grunted and eased his leg. Maggie hung the kettle on a pot hook that swung from the lug pole, pushing the fire under it. She blinked at the smoke seeping out and brushed by Wager to get the spoons for sugar. Azariah mumbled something about spring, and fished for his pipe.

"A simple rope bridge would do," Wager went on, "until we could sink more piles and do the job properly. The footbridge is so handy. . . ."

Azariah coughed. "Of course it could be done, but it means doing the job twice." His voice was grudging. "And I'd hate to go across a rope bridge in the wind or rain—or Maggie either." He loaded the pipe and reached for the small tongs to capture a live coal.

Maggie set out earthenware cups and measured the tea. There were enough seamen in Canaan town to put up a dozen jury-rig bridges if they wished. Wager was right, but she thought the older men would wait, saying it wasn't pressing.

Azariah puffed his pipe and they began talking about the plans for a schooner. Jeremiah Chace wanted a fast craft, Wager said, the fastest on the Sound. "Fast enough to outrun a British sloop of war, I think."

"Ahhh, smuggling."

"I expect so. But I don't ask questions." Wager had some drawings, which he rolled out. Az held one side of the paper and peered at the lines, squinting through his glasses.

"You've got 'er flat-bottomed!"

"Well, there's a chance she'll be faster that way. It's worth trying."

Azariah shrugged. "After you build her there's no way to tell."

"Well, no, but I think I've got Jeremiah talked into it." He winked at Maggie over her husband's head, and she smiled.

When the kettle boiled, she poured water into the cups and passed them around. As the men talked, she went to the rear window and stared out at the rain, sipping the hot tea. It was well known in the village that Jeremiah had been running cargoes past the British blockade, but he was only one of many. The British had no right to refuse the colonies their God-given talents. What good was knowledge if one could not use it? Even her son, Morgan, had talked now and then of somehow squeezing into the smuggling trade because of the money to be made. Morgan wanted to build a boat in their own yard, and probably would have started it except for Enoch Quant, who was known to drink with redcoat soldiers.

Morgan argued that it would be easy for him and Junius, or maybe Brayton and another man or two, to slip past the Lobsters down to the Bahamas and come back richer. After all, how did Jeremiah and the others get their gold?

But Brayton was only fifteen, though he looked grown and strong. She'd never forgive herself if she let them go and they were caught. . . .

Thank God the war was over and none of her sons had been forced to go, though Morgan had spent many a weary hour marching and shooting with the militia. A few boys of the town had run off to join up with the troops, but Morgan's thoughts always turned toward the sea; he was not interested in becoming an infantryman.

Wager thanked her for the tea and picked up his three-cornered hat. He said good night to Azariah and she walked with him to the front door. When she opened it he looked at the rain and said it was a nuisance that Europeans had not yet taken up that excellent Oriental invention, the umbrella. One would come in so handy. . . .

He thanked her again and touched her hand—she made it easy for him to do so, and she thought his fingers lingered on hers. Then he went down the steps to the street.

Maggie sighed deeply, watching him hurry along bent over as the wind came sweeping off the ocean and blew up the skirts of his long coat. Closing the door, she leaned against it. What ridiculous ideas circulated in her head! Wager had probably forgotten all about his holding her. . . .

Chapter Three

Morgan spent the morning at his father's direction, sorting timbers. He selected the most seasoned for Mr. Jeremiah Chace's new schooner. Jeremiah was a man who paid well. Most of the timber was marked with daubs of paint in a simple code telling where and when the tree had been felled. Morgan was interested in those chopped down in the winter months because then the rot-inducing sap had been dormant, still in the lower trunks or roots.

And as he worked he whistled and thought of Sharon. He had seen her only a few days past when she'd brought her father's meal to him and he'd circled through the yard out of Enoch's sight and stolen a moment alone with her. A much too brief moment; not long enough to say anything important, not even long enough to steal a kiss.

She had dark reddish hair, darker than his mother's, and black eyes that often seemed all pupil. Her skin was soft, so delicate that he hardly dared to touch her with his work-hardened hands. She appeared fragile compared with his sister Becky; she was slim and dainty and easily the most beautiful girl in all Canaan and the surrounding countryside. He had looked at every one, of course.

But she wore hand-me-down clothes, made over from her mother's—a not unusual thing, his sisters did the same—and usually looked like a small girl in a too big dress. He knew she was conscious of it.

Naturally he had an eye for beauty, and all the others his age thought the same. Morgan often discussed the girls of the village with his peers, in places where no one could overhear. His father would be astounded and probably outraged if he ever heard their talk! And his mother . . . !

Of course the chatter got around to Sharon in due course; they left out not a single girl; and Morgan was secretly astonished that his friends did not consider Sharon as desirable as some. She was not rounded enough, they said, did not have roguish eyes, did not promise enough—or anything—with her glances.

There were many kinds of girls, he knew, and when he listened to the talk of rough and seasoned sailors who had been everywhere, he realized there were things he would never see in Canaan. He was genuinely shocked by what he heard and scarcely able to believe them. There was no way he could reconcile such incredible information with Sharon's image. Nor did he want to.

But talk was only talk, idle chatter to while away the idle minutes. Not one of his friends had really *been* with a girl, though they implied much. He had not either, and the idea was frightening because it was common knowledge that the awesome consequences were never absent. But even if it were possible to lure a girl to a secret place there was no chance under heaven that she would enter into anything more than ordinary kissing. He could forget consequences.

To have a child out of wedlock was so enormous a crime that it was difficult to contain in the mind. Such an event would ruin the lives of all it touched, likely for all eternity. Or so it was thundered from the pulpits.

But that very heinous crime had its fascinations and raised questions. When he looked at the married women of the town, especially in church, he could hardly believe that any of them acceded to the carnal demands of their husbands. Did they undress, right down to the skin, and get into bed together? The sailors said so, and laughed at his ignorance. Girls were just as eager for the joys of bedding as men, they told him, winking and cocking heads.

Alone, Morgan thought about it and decided it must be foreign women they meant.

Why did his mind dwell on those uneasy matters? He tried to fill it with others, but for the life of him could not altogether banish the thoughts from his head. They crept in, taking up his time sleeping or waking without his leave, encroaching and sliding in even when he furrowed his brow to bend his mind to his father's work.

And occasionally he was startled to discover his own Satanic mind busy doing its level best trying to imagine what Sharon looked like stark naked!

He had seen his little sister Marie completely naked one evening, only for a few seconds. She was changing into a night dress with Becky's help as he'd walked past the door. It was some kind of relief to find out that girls had bodies with skin all over, like his own, and were much the same. He has assumed so, but it was good to learn the truth.

Why were boys cursed with these moments? It was not to be believed that girls had the same thoughts. Everyone knew that was ridiculous.

His daydreaming was interrupted when Enoch Quant came through the yard, an adze in his hand. A dark, wiry man with suspicious eyes, he was dressed as usual in dirty leather jacket and apron. For several minutes he paused and watched Morgan's every move, scowling as if none was to his liking. He seemed on the point of saying something, then turned and walked off to the boat being built and Morgan heard the adze thudding against the timbers as Enoch smoothed the ribs.

Morgan shared his father's feelings about Enoch, except with a fear that if Enoch left the boatyard he might also leave the town. And if he took his family elsewhere, Sharon would go too.

That was a tragedy he did not want to contemplate.

He was nineteen now and others his age were already married, some even with children. It was time for him to think of that step. Of course he had no money and no house—not a chance of acquiring one. It was not much of a prospect to offer a girl. There was very little hard money available; his father gave him a few coins to spend, but not much. He lived at home and needed little else. The boatyard was supporting all it could and there was nothing being put by, he'd heard his father say. Of course, if Enoch left he could take the man's place easily, do as much or more than Enoch ever had, and be paid the same. He dreamed of being a partner with his father.

What a dilemma. He wanted to see the last of Enoch, and yet he feared to because of Sharon.

He straightened up and stretched, looking at the sky. White clouds were scudding along far out toward the island and a stately four-masted ship glided past with all sails set and gulls following. He was building a castle of hopes on *his* notions. What if Sharon did not feel the same? They had never talked of intimate things like marriage, had barely discussed anything but trifles and pleasantries. She really knew nothing of his feelings for her, and maybe she felt nothing at all for him and was merely being civil.

He ought to remedy that at the earliest chance.

He found it at a chopping bee only a week later. A young newly married couple had put up a clapboard house north of the town and needed land cleared. Morgan and his brothers, along with dozens of others from the town, volunteered to help and rode to the site in a neighbor's wagon.

As all bees were, it was a festive gathering. More than a hundred people, including children, swarmed over the area. Men with axes made quick plans and Morgan was alloted a square of woods. It was a chill morning and he was glad to start early; going to it with a will felling trees that would be allowed to dry through the winter.

In the middle of the morning Sharon appeared, carrying a leather bucket of water and a tin dipper. He was surprised and delighted to see her. "I didn't know you'd come!"

"Father brought me." She glanced over her shoulder.

There was no one close by and the trees he'd felled hid them from view of the house and the women who were preparing food. He took the dipper gratefully, leaned close and kissed her cheek.

She laughed, and did not move away.

Since she didn't mind the kiss, he gave her another and dropped the empty dipper into the bucket. When he slid his arms about her she drew away shaking her head.

"I'm glad to bring you water, Morgan Lynn, but how much do you expect?"

"Water always makes me wild. Are you afraid?"

"No, of course not. The things you say!"

"It runs in my family. Pretty girls make all of us want to cut off our ears and throw them into the air."

She laughed again. "That's plain silly. I can't imagine your father doing that!"

"No, I guess not. Neither can I. But Brayton would."

"He certainly would not."

"Well, maybe not him either. Would you cut off your ears for me?"

"Morgan—not in a hundred years! What a thing to

say." She sucked her lower lip and looked at him from under jet lashes. "You think I'm pretty?"

"Of course you are." He moved closer. "You're the prettiest girl I've ever seen. Don't you ever look in a mirror?"

"Yes . . ."

He was being very bold, but some of his friends were of the opinion that girls liked dash in a man. He couldn't tell about Sharon, but she didn't pick up the bucket and hurry away. That was a good sign and it gave him an idea. "Who sent you here with the water?"

"No one. I thought you might be thirsty, doing all that work."

"I was. Thanks."

"You're welcome."

He glanced around. Still no one near. "Why don't we go for a walk? I need a bit of a rest."

Her eyes grew round. "But they'll miss you. And me too!"

"I doubt it. Half the town's here and no one's keeping track of us. What's your father doing?" He could guess.

Sharon hesitated. "He's drinking with some friends."

He drew her closer. Her dark eyes seemed smoky, long lashes black against her pale cheeks. A breath of perfume made his heart beat faster. Just to touch her was heady. She looked into his eyes steadily and he said as softly as he could, "Just a walk, nothing else. I want to be with you without anyone staring at us."

She half smiled and he thought she looked like a deer ready for flight. He pressed her hand, "No one will know . . ."

"Just for a while, then."

He drew her quickly into the shade of the surrounding pines. She brought the bucket and he carried the axe; if they left them and they were found by someone, that someone was sure to go in search, if only for gossip's sake.

He led her away from the sounds of axes and shouts. There was no breeze among the trees and very little sunlight pushing through the overcast. When they had walked for several minutes Sharon said, "This is far enough. We mustn't get lost."

"How could we get lost? If we walk straight ahead we'll come out on the Camden Post Road."

"You're very sure of everything, Morgan Lynn."

"No, I'm not." He faced her. "Would you rather I was wishy-washy and whining?"

Her face changed and she shook her head. He indicated the grass under a twisted oak and made his voice light again. "Here's a couch for you, milady. I'll have someone hustle tea in a moment—and maybe there's some cakes. Come on, sit down."

She sat and looked about, smoothing her dress. "I didn't see your father today."

"He stayed at home. His leg's no good for walking, you know."

"I heard about your mother and the footbridge! It's all over town. What a terrible thing! It's lucky that Goodman Tanfield was there to pull her out. Is she all right?"

"She had a bump on the head, that's all. It's gone away."

"Oh, she must have been frightened!"

"I guess it was scary, having a bridge go out from under you. We looked at the planks next day and they were all rotted underneath." He touched her hand, then grasped it and she didn't pull it back. But her fingers did not close about his. He tossed his hat to the grass. It was hard to say what he wanted to say, and he was sure that even if he got it out the words would sound awk-

35

ward. "You know I like you a lot . . ." It did sound awkward.

She didn't seem to notice. "I like you too, Morgan."

"Even in spite of your father?"

"Don't spoil it."

"What?"

"He *is* my father, and he's not as bad as you think."

He heaved a sigh. "Well, it's not your father I'm talking about. It's you."

She gazed at him, then down at her lap, and pulled her hand away. He reached for it and held it tightly, looking at the long white fingers one by one as if examining them to buy. Each nail was perfect, carefully cut, round and shining. She was a healthy girl all right. He said, "You really like me?"

"Yes, of course."

"You mean like you do any of those people?" He waved toward the throng they had left.

"Well, better than a lot of them."

He looked to see if she was funning him but her lips were grave and her eyes level and serious. She was in no hurry to commit herself, however. Maybe he shouldn't push her too much. He said, "I'm only asking because—" He halted and frowned.

"Because why?"

"Because of the time, I guess."

"What do you mean?"

"I don't see you alone very much and I'm trying to make up for it. Do you realize this is the very first time we've been where no one can stare at us, especially your father? I believe he thinks I'm going to clap you into a sack and sell you to the first boatman who offers a penny."

She laughed. "It's not that."

"He doesn't like me much, your father."

"It's his way. My father is an unsettled man, I think."

And a thirsty one, he thought. He put the hand down and picked up the other one. She watched him with a lively interest as his fingers traced the lines in her palm.

"Can you read my future?"

He nodded seriously. "Of course." He bent over the hand. "This line here indicates you're fascinated with me. See how it points in my direction?"

"You're foolish in the head. It does no such thing."

"But you *are*, aren't you?"

She sighed deeply and took the hand away. She half turned and gazed beyond him, her face suddenly older. "Father has—other plans for me."

"Other plans? What d'you mean, other plans?"

She shook her head, obviously ill at ease. "Why don't we go back?"

"What plans?" A horrible suspicion was forming in his mind. "Is he trying to arrange a marriage for you?"

She took a long breath and nodded. "I think so."

"With who?"

"I—I don't know." She looked away. "I think it might be with—a British officer."

Morgan stared at her. A British officer? There was only one within miles, Ensign David Urfe, commander of the troop quartered in the town. And Urfe was known to be a woman-chaser.

She said softly, "Father will never allow me to marry anyone in Canaan, you know. He's said so many times."

Morgan nodded dumbly; he had heard Enoch's pronouncements also. He felt deflated and beaten. Enoch was a man who could hate, and he could not have this girl without Enoch's blessing. He closed his eyes and took a deep breath. It was out in the open between them suddenly. Marriage. It had been in the back of his mind, of course, but far back, almost out of sight. Marriage was something to be talked about after other things had taken place. But Sharon was the practical sort, no fooling about that. She went directly to the nub; marriage was the only possible result of a declaration of love.

He heard himself ask, "What do you think?"

She did not answer immediately and when he looked at her she was pressing her lips together tightly. She said, "It doesn't matter what I think. You know that as well as I do."

He took her hand again. "I am—very fond of you. I guess you know that." It wasn't what he wanted to say.

"I guess I know it." She pulled away. "But it's impossible, Morgan. We shouldn't even be here like this."

"You haven't married him yet—whoever he is."

She dabbed at her eyes suddenly and turned from him. He saw with astonishment that there were tears on her cheeks. He wanted to kiss them away. Touching her shoulder, he said, "I didn't mean to—"

"It's all right." She smiled, eyes glistening. "No, I'm not married yet." She slid her small hand into his. "Help me up. We ought to go back. If my father finds—"

"Ayyyy, your father!" Morgan got to his feet and pulled her up. They stood face to face half a moment and he thought he saw—what did he see? Almost as if he'd willed it she came into his arms, and when he kissed her she kissed him back with an ardor that thrilled and surprised him. He crushed her to him, feeling the entire length of her, and had to catch his breath. His hand crept down to the small of her back. Oh, God! The feel of her! The joyous warmth of her! Her arms went about his neck and their kisses grew urgent, as if making up for years of lost opportunity, and then she was crying again.

He could not let her go, but watched the tears rush down her cheeks. He whispered, "What is it?"

Straining, he could barely hear her words, soft and hesitant. "I don't want to—to marry some—stranger."

Anger rose in him. God, what a viper was Enoch Quant! Morgan kissed her cheek and heard his voice say, "Would you marry me if I could carry you off somewhere?"

She went very still and he looked over her head to the dark leafless woods that surrounded them. He could feel her heart beat and he closed his eyes, waiting. She said, "I—I wish you could, Morgan."

He sighed. Nothing she would ever say could mean more to him, he was sure. His heart swelled with love for her. If only he could carry her off! And all it took was money, a very little money, only enough for passage. He had a few coppers in his pocket, but not sufficient to buy them a single spare meal.

Not half enough to pay a preacher.

Azariah had gone to the boatyard Saturday morning when Wager appeared at the house. Maggie opened the door at his knock and smiled, stepping back. "Come in, come in, it's warm inside."

"Yes, it's nippy." He entered the hall doffing his hat and hanging it on a peg. "I suppose the boys have gone to the bee?"

"Yes, and the girls too. Would you like some tea?"

He hesitated, then nodded. "Yes, I would. I've been walking in the cold." He glanced around. "Did Az go, too?"

"No, he went to the yard about an hour ago. He was restless this morning, he said. I think he's got Enoch on his mind."

"He's going to have to do something about that man. I don't know how he's put up with it all this long. Az is a saint."

She hung the kettle over the fire and got out the cups and a bit of the cake she'd made for Junius. In the mirror of the back window glass she pushed at her hair and smoothed her apron, conscious of the faded yellow dress and graying lace about the neck. She hadn't expected to see Wager.

"He's talking about it," she said. "I want him to borrow money and buy Enoch's share."

"Yes, he ought to." Wager stood in front of the hearth and held his hands out to the warmth. "I've urged him to go see Jeremiah Chace. He's a good Christian man and he likes Az. He's told me so." His eyes followed her. "And the best asset of all, Morgan and Junius working there. Morgan could run the yard by himself."

She measured out the tea, conscious of his gaze. "You think so?"

"Yes, why not?"

"I mean Morgan's a restive boy. I don't mean he's unstable, but he has ideas, not like Junius. I don't know where he gets it. He wants to see the world, Morgan."

Wager smiled. "Traveling is hard."

"He wouldn't care." She sat by him. "He's not like the rest of us. There's a wild streak in Morgan, mark my words. When his dander is up he'll go to any lengths. I saw it over and over again when he was a boy."

"He always seems reasonable."

"He'll do the wildest thing and think it reasonable. He's different from the others—well, Marie has a little of it too."

Wager smiled and reached to pat her hand. "Maybe there was a pirate among your ancestors, Maggie."

"That is entirely possible. My grandfather was Irish, you know. The Lord deals differently with the Irish. They're a frolicsome lot."

He watched her pour from the kettle. "Has Morgan said anything about leaving the boatyard?"

"No . . . not to me." Her brows curved in surprise. "Not to Az either or he'd have told me. Why do you ask?"

He shrugged. "Only that you said he's restless. I thought he'd settle down and marry Sharon one day. It's easy to see how he likes her."

"Sharon Quant?"

"Yes. Didn't you know?"

Maggie shook her head and stared into her cup. Sharon was a pretty girl, a slender, fragile-looking girl to be sure, but men often ogled that type, she had noticed. Morgan had never said a thing. "I don't know that I'd like it."

"Morgan marrying Sharon?"

She made a small gesture of impatience. "I wouldn't like having Enoch in the family. He's miles too close now. Do you think they're serious?"

Wager smiled. "Morgan doesn't confide in me. Or anyone else, it seems. How old is he, twenty?"

"Almost. He's nineteen." Lord! Nineteen! They grew like weeds. Only months ago he was toddling about, clutching at her skirts . . . now Wager was talking about his marrying someone. She sighed deeply and finished the tea. It made her feel so old.

Wager put his cup on the board and rose. "Well, he's certainly a good-looking lad. Takes after his mother."

"Wager! Are you complimenting me?"

"Of course." He grinned at her. "Do you get so few you don't know one when you hear it?"

She laughed. "Who compliments a housewife and mother?"

He looked at her and she felt suddenly flushed. How enormously conscious she was of their being alone in the house! It was a very rare occurrence and the outrageous thought crossed her mind that it was something meant to be.

And in the next moment Wager took her hand. He gazed steadily at her, drew it slowly up and kissed it.

Maggie closed her eyes, heart racing. She hadn't the strength to pull the hand away, nor did she want to. The room swam as if she'd had rum in her tea, and she opened her eyes to find his arms sliding about her. She murmured something—and then his lips pressed hers.

She went rigid, then fell against him, unable to do anything but return the kiss, to hold him. . . . The kiss lasted for an eternity and the rest of the world was blotted out. She heard his voice as from a great distance, saying her name. "Maggie . . . Maggie . . ." She turned her head, seeking his lips.

The pounding in her ears, like the wild surf beating against the rocks in a storm, was her own heartbeat.

Chapter Four

Marie Willa Lynn closed the door of the house behind her, glanced at the sky and pulled a thick blue shawl about her thin shoulders. Above was nothing but mist hanging just over the trees; it seemed she could reach up a slender hand and touch it. Hitching the food parcel firmly under her arm, she hurried down the street, holding up a corner of her blue and white striped skirt. She went toward the town without a backward glance, heading for her father's boatyard.

She was fifteen and strong-willed in a quiet way, a girl who dreamed of living in far places. Canaan was a town of fishermen and sailors and talk of the Orient, distant Africa, even South America was commonplace, though talk of Europe was the most common of all, in the stores or as people stood about on the streets or in the churchyard after services. But liquid-eyed females with long dark hair tied with bits of bright ribbon did not crew the ships that sailed from Canaan's wharves. It was possible for one of her sex to board only as a passenger, to pay her fare, an amount of money she could not expect to own in half a lifetime.

Even a lack of money could not stifle Marie's dreams. It was her habit to walk along the shore gazing out to the beckoning horizon, to watch the long Atlantic rollers come in, hissing and dying at her feet.

Along with her mother and sister, Becky, she often took hot food to her father and brothers, especially on cold or gray days—they would eat bread and cold meat otherwise. Her mother wrapped the parcel in brown paper and a towel or two to keep in the warmth and Marie would hurry through the town, turning west along Fort Street to the shore. The boatyard was just a short distance across the sturdy Canaan wagon bridge.

And when she had given them the parcel she was free for a short while. Her mother never begrudged the stolen moments as she daydreamed along the sand.

On the Monday after the chopping bee she took food to the yard and found her father moving restlessly outside the hut they used as an office and storeroom. He puffed his black pipe and stumped from the hut door to the narrow roadway that led to the beach. He craned his neck to see past the piles of lumber that littered the yard and greeted her almost absently when she appeared.

"Thankee, girl . . ." He took the parcel.

"What's the matter, Father?"

"Oh, there's nothing the matter." He coughed and shook his head.

It was Junius's first week. She wondered if he and Enoch were not getting on. "Is it Junius?"

He glanced at her, grunted, opened the door of the hut, and went inside with the parcel. She heard him rattle a pan. She stood on a cask, up on her toes. She could see Morgan, Enoch Quant and Junius gathered about a boat on the stocks. Enoch was probably asserting himself and pushing his authority, she thought. Jumping down, she went into the hut. It was warm inside. Her father was stoking the black iron stove and she held out her hands to it. The parcel was atop a pan on the stove. He went to the window, turned and gave her a smile.

"Get along or we'll put y' to work with a scraper."

"It's Goodman Quant, isn't it?"

"Don't you go spreadin' tales, and don't you bother your head about him. Junius is a big, strong lad well able to care for himself—and Morgan to help. Every boy's got to learn to stand on his feet."

"Yes, Father."

"Not a mother's son of 'em any good less'n he does."

She went to the door and he pointed the pipe. "Missy—I don't want you chattering to your ma either. You understand me?"

"I don't know anything to tell."

"No, of course you don't." He coughed. "That's the way it should be. You leave Enoch Quant to me." He puffed on the pipe, selected a twig and opened the door of the stove.

"Yes, Father."

"Yes, that's right, girl." He chuckled, lit the pipe and slammed the stove door shut. "Get along home."

She opened the door and looked at him. He motioned to her and said, "Enoch's tongue is a lot worse'n his bite. He's a mighty unhappy man. Junius will be fine."

"G'bye, Father."

He waved and she closed the door and trudged to the gate.

Beyond the boatyard the beach was narrow but the tide was going out. Marie hugged herself and walked slowly. The overcast had lifted and she had to squint as the yellow sun danced off the shimmering water. It was a cold day but clearing and the air was fresh and biting. As she watched the white sails of a scudding boat far out in the Sound she imagined herself on board a ship bound for—bound for Europe. She'd heard the Thames described so many times she could see it clearly in her mind's eye. London was certainly the most fascinating city in the world. A great many of the older people of

Canaan had been born in England, a smattering from Scotland or Wales. It was a far different land from this, they said, and in many ways not as good. The laws in England were far more restrictive, for instance.

But the law never touched her and Marie could shrug off those matters. Laws and taxes were something for the menfolk to worry about.

She'd never been on a real ship, one capable of crossing the great sea. She saw them often enough, however, as well as the numerous British ships of war. During the years of the War against the French they were in the Sound constantly, great ponderous-looking leviathans beating along the coast or standing out toward Block Island, invisible to the east.

Of course her father had been a crewman on various ships, and Morgan had sailed here and there, away from home for months in the summers. Everyone said Morgan could sail anything that could ship a rudder. But the way men talked of ships was sometimes incomprehensible to her. She was interested only in the fact that a ship could take her somewhere.

The wet sand curved about a small promontory, then swept back in a wide arc that was broken by outcroppings where the waves thudded and shredded themselves to white lace. Close by on the right was a low bluff thick with long green grass.

The waves rushed onto the shore making silvery arcs and she walked round them, her mind a thousand miles off—and suddenly she was startled by shouts. She whirled about in time to see a glittering wave of redcoat soldiers, screaming like maniacs, each with a long bayonetted rifle, coming straight for her!

Marie gasped and yelled, retreating into the surf in fear. The soldiers jumped the bluff and charged toward her, faces contorted. In another second they were all about her and she screamed again, expecting the thrusts of a dozen bayonets into her body.

There was a sharp whistle. Someone grabbed her and lifted her bodily and she heard their voices. Her heart pounded and she kicked out, deathly afraid for her life.

The man set her on the sand and jumped away as his companions laughed. In the next second she was facing their officer. She had seen him many times in the village and knew his name, Ensign Urfe. He smiled at her, doffed his hat, and gave a sharp command. The soldiers immediately retreated beyond the bluff, and Marie sank to her knees, eyes closed. She had never been so frightened.

Urfe said, "It's a bit of an exercise, Miss . . . Are you hurt?"

She shook her head, hand on her pounding heart. "Only half dead from fright, sir."

"I'm sorry." He got down on one knee and lifted her chin. "I've seen you before, I think. Does your father own the boatyard?"

"Yes."

"Of course. You're Miss Becky Lynn."

"No, she's my sister."

"Ahhh."

She was able to look at him. He was sunburned, not over twenty, she thought, with blue eyes and full lips, rather full cheeks and blond hair. His scarlet uniform glittered with silver and he carried a long spearlike weapon that she knew was called a spontoon. He was very handsome, with bold eyes.

He asked, "Can you stand?"

"Yes, I think so." She hoped her knees would not give way. She leaned on his arm and brushed off the sand. Her feet and the bottom of her skirt were wet, but she had been wet before.

"How did you happen to be here?"

"Walking," she said. "Is it permitted?"

He laughed, cocking his head, looking down at her. He was three or four inches taller than she, she thought, and she was slightly awed by the splendor of the scarlet coat.

He said, "You may walk anywhere you like for all of me. I was only surprised. We come here often for our exercises and I hadn't seen you before."

His accent was like a Londoner's and the way he looked into her eyes was vaguely discomfiting. He *was* bold! She had never been so close to a redcoat officer before. Maybe they were all like that. The people of the village usually avoided the soldiers, called them "red ants" to their backs, and put up with the inconveniences they caused.

"Then, sir, if you don't mind, I will continue my walk." Where did she get the nerve to say that?

He smiled. "You don't need to call me sir."

Brushing her hair from her eyes, she turned and was surprised that he followed her, the hat still in his hand. He said, "My name is David."

"That's very nice."

He said, "My middle name is Eustace, but I seldom use it."

"Well, you hardly need a middle name."

"Do you have one?"

"Yes."

"What is it?"

"My middle name?"

"Yes."

"It's Willa."

"Ummm."

They walked on. In a bit he asked, "Are you feeling better now?"

"Quite all right, sir."

"It must have been a terrible shock to see those men."

"It was terrifying!"

"They wouldn't have hurt you."

"But I didn't know that!" She looked at him in annoyance.

He smiled at her expression. "I expect they were as surprised to see you as you were to see them. I know I was. One doesn't expect a beautiful girl on a lonely beach."

She eyed him sidelong. Beautiful girl? But his handsome face was solemn. He trudged along with her, hands clasped behind his back, the plume in his hat jogging with each step. He no longer had the spontoon and she glanced back to see it stuck in the sand where they'd stopped. She could not see the soldiers, but could hear distant commands. Evidently someone else was putting them through their drill, or whatever they were about.

He said, "Willa's a nice middle name. Do you have a front one?"

"You have to have a first name in order to have a middle."

"Yes, I suppose so."

They walked a dozen steps and she said, "It's Marie."

"Ahhhh. Yes, it fits you."

She looked at him in surprise. No one had ever said *that* to her before. A name fitted her? A name was a name.

It astonished her that he was walking with her, and he was doing it by choice. And he had called her beautiful! She knew that some of the redcoat soldiers were involved with women of the village—it was common talk. Did this one have ideas that she might do the same? How her father and mother would react!

How *would* they react? She had heard her father make remarks about the British many times, but then everyone did; the redcoats were the butt of continual jokes and complaints. Even the weather was their fault, when it was bad.

Ensign Urfe kept up a chatter about this and that, about the ships they could see on the Sound and about trivial things she was sure he cared nothing for. When they reached the end of the curve she halted and he stopped beside her. The reason for her walk had long ago fled, and this new, somewhat disturbing element had taken its place. She found herself of two minds; one part wanted to chatter with him, the other half said to hurry home and forget the incident entirely.

But he was very pleasant.

The grassy bluff was low enough at this end of the beach so she could see into the meadow beyond. There was a knot of scarlet at the far side, men scattered about, some standing, others sitting; she guessed they were finished with the exercises and waiting for Urfe. She saw him glance at them, but he made no move to go.

When she turned back he was again beside her. "It's been an unexpectedly pleasant morning, Marie . . . may I call you Marie?"

She nodded, slightly confused. She was accustomed to the chatter of boys, flattery or boasts, but this man seemed very different, and his attitude toward her was not the same. Of course he was very much more sophisticated than the ordinary schoolboys of the town.

As they approached the spontoon he said, "I hope you will walk this way again, without the bayonet charge of course." He smiled and she found herself smiling in return. "Do you come here often?"

She said, "Not often but—sometimes. When I am able."

"I have lodgings in the town," he said in a casual voice, as if imparting unimportant information. "I am staying in the Hollister house. You know them, I expect?"

"Yes, but not well." The Hollisters owned a tailor shop but she had never been inside. It was mostly a place for the gentry. She saw them at church.

"Charming people," he said. "Very industrious—like your father."

They arrived at the spontoon and she halted again. He said immediately, "Thank you for the walk, Marie, I will never forget it." He bowed to her.

Never forget a short walk? She said, "Goodbye, sir," bit her lip and hurried off. Why did he confuse her so?

When she came close to the road she turned; he was still standing in the same place, hat in hand, watching her. He waved and, hesitating, she waved back and smiled.

Imagine her, walking with a British officer! What a bit of gossip that would make for busy tongues! Many of his men had seen her; probably some had recognized her. Could he manage to still all of their tongues? But maybe they cared nothing about it—why should they?

Of course she had done nothing, merely walked along the shore for half a mile and back. Should she mention it to her mother? She debated it all the way home and finally decided to say nothing. If gossip *did* reach her mother's ears, she could always say she hadn't considered it important enough and had forgotten it at once.

But she didn't forget it.

The next day, when she was sent to Goodman Porter's cobbler shop to fetch a pair of repaired boots for her father, she went out of her way to walk past the Hollister house. It was on Hart Street, surrounded by tall elms with a wood fence along one side and plantings in the rear. It was a handsome two-story building, larger than their own. Marie wondered which was his room. No smoke came from either of the chimneys, so Elora Hollister was probably at the shop with her husband.

After she picked up the boots she saw him. Ensign Urfe stepped from the ordinary as she passed on the far side of the street. She was so startled that her heart leaped on seeing him. He touched his hat and smiled. She hurried on, cheeks flaming. Why did he affect her that way? Of course he was young and handsome, and very regal in the scarlet uniform, which was beautifully tailored to show off his well-knit figure. But he was a British soldier. Her father would never approve even of her speaking to him.

But she could think . . . of going off to London with him on a great ship, seeing the sights, the theatres and restaurants, taking long drives in the country . . . Now her dreams were augmented, and the shadowy figure who had for so long inhabited those dreams had a face.

Then she saw him at church on Sunday. Another surprise; she'd never seen him there before and she heard a bit of tongue-wagging about it. "When did the redcoat get religion?" Marie felt embarrassment but of course no one could know they'd met. He did not speak to her when the services were over, merely smiled in passing, bowed politely and exchanged a few words with one or two persons as he left the grounds. She was certain he had given her a special glance. He had looked different because of the powdered wig he wore. It gave him an older appearance, she thought.

It occurred to her several times to mention the meeting to Becky, but she did not, without quite knowing why. Maybe it was because she was sure Becky would not approve any more than her mother would. So she stifled herself and said nothing to anyone.

Her mother took the food parcel to the boatyard twice in the next week, saying she needed the air, but on Wednesday Marie was given the task and she accepted eagerly. It was a drizzly day and she wrapped a cloak about her shoulders and hurried down the street, heart thumping. Of course she had no idea if Ensign Urfe and his men would be in the meadow, the chances were not good on such a day, but she was honest enough with herself to realize she was hoping.

She saw with a measure of surprise that Wager Tanfield was approaching the house as she left, but it must be that he had come to pick up something he'd forgotten. When she turned the corner she did not think of him again. Several people on Fort Street bowed to her and she waved; the drizzle let up a bit.

She delivered the parcel to the hut. There was no one inside. Standing on a box, she saw they were all clustered at the small dock, so she left the food on the pan atop the stove and went out to the beach path.

Ensign Urfe's scarlet coat was a bright spot against the grays and browns of the shore. She saw him instantly, half a mile away; he was walking, head down, apparently pacing the beach.

He was waiting for her!

She realized it instantly and wondered if he came here every day, eager to see her. Her heart began to race and she paused to compose herself, to caution herself toward calmness. She must not throw herself at him!

He came toward her, looked up, smiled and began to hurry. As he came near, both hands extended to take hers. "Marie! I was praying you'd come!"

"I—I told you. I come here often, sir."

"Will you stop calling me sir!"

She laughed. His face was so grave and troubled; then he smiled again and she allowed her fingers to curl about his. He drew her close instantly and kissed her.

"Oh—sir!" She pulled back in alarm, and as she did so thought herself a terrible ninny. What would he think of her? Lord! He'd think her a little country girl ready to flee at a word, a touch.

But he laughed and she realized in a flash he thought she was acting, being deliberately coy. Marie made herself smile, though her trip-hammer heart pounded at her temples. Of course he was unused to silly farm girls who simpered and ran off screaming for their mothers.

He kissed her again, and this time she clung to him, almost stifled by the excitement and the feeling of rushing blood. . . . She swayed as his lips left hers, tried to catch her breath, and he kissed her again.

She had to turn about, his arms still tight around her, and gasped, breathing deeply. Oh Lord! What a thing! No one had ever kissed her like that! She hadn't even dreamed of such a thing—how was she to know? She felt him nuzzle her ear and she leaned back, feeling warm and secure in his arms. Turning her head, she closed her eyes and his mouth came over hers. How incredible she felt! She turned again in his arms and slid hers about him, holding him tightly, oblivious to all else, losing herself in his heady kisses.

After a while he said, "Shall we sit here in the sand, where it's dry?"

Marie sighed deeply, lashes fluttering. Obediently she let him guide her along to the bluff and they sat in the lee of a dune with the long grasses waving above their heads. His arms slid about her again and she lay back full length with him nearly atop her. An hour before she'd known nothing of kissing and what she experienced inflamed her beyond belief. People kissed, a peck on the cheek, a quick brushing of lips, but it had never occurred to her that a man's kisses could cause such an upheaval inside her. She clung to him like a drowning person, reveling in the wonderful, giddy excitement of it, knowing in the back of her mind that she was sinning—and not caring. She did not protest when his hand untied her bodice and slipped inside to fondle a soft breast with its acorn of a nipple.

Marie had no idea how long they lay there, listening to the boom and hiss of the surf, to the high wheeling gulls—to her own pounding pulses; surely he could hear them!

But at last he said, "You must go back now. They'll miss you."

She sighed again, not wanting to stir. He was right, of course. Her mother would send Becky to look for her.

She sat up and put herself to rights, cheeks flushed. As she began to retie the bodice he took her hands away and opened it quickly, bent and kissed the bare breast, and she gasped as she felt the warmth of his tongue. She fell against him and he held her for several moments. Then he put her hands back on the bodice.

She slid them around him, hungry for more kisses.

"You are so beautiful," he whispered. "I must see you again—as soon as possible."

"I'll come here whenever I—"

"This is not a place to meet a lovely girl. Come to my lodgings on Hart Street."

"Your lodgings!" She was shocked.

"The Hollisters are never there during the day. You can slip in by the fence off Summer Street and we'll be alone and no one the wiser."

Her instant inclination was to say no. If anyone should see her go into the house, what a scandal!

He kissed her. "There are trees along Summer Street and no house overlooks the fence. You will see several boards missing. You can slip through and into the back door of the house in a twinkling." He kissed her again. "I will be there past midday, waiting for you."

It all came out so smoothly. Had he done this before—were the boards missing for a reason? No, his face was innocent of guile. "Ohhh, David—I don't know—"

His finger stopped her lips. "Please don't say you won't. Walk by the fence, just once, darling, and look at it."

She took a deep breath and nodded.

He said, "And when you do, you will know that I'm inside, waiting for you. Every day past noon."

Marie closed her eyes, feeling his arms encircle her. Was this really happening to her? Lordy! How much could happen in a single day?

She left the beach alone; he would wait, he said, and follow after a bit of time had gone by. He'd go across the meadow and through the trees. No one would ever suspect they'd seen each other. He was so careful of her reputation—she loved him so! She hurried along, across the wagon bridge, along Fort Street, and turned toward home, her heart full to overflowing, cheeks still flaming from the heart-fluttering kisses.

At Summer Street she paused, then pressed her lips together tightly and turned right to the Hollister home, walking slowly as she came in sight of the chimneys. It was as David had said. No other house on Summer Street overlooked that particular end of the street and there was the fence, with several boards missing. It would be easy to slip through in the wink of an eye and in another moment she'd be in his arms again! The thought thrilled her as she went up the steps of her home.

She felt very warm, though the day was cool and crisp and she thought her mother looked at her oddly when she went into the kitchen, but she said nothing. Marie went about her duties, her mind far away, and after a while her mother asked, "Is there anything wrong, dear?"

"No, Mother, nothing."

"You're so quiet."

"Am I?" Marie pricked her finger with a needle and sucked it. She was nervous and she saw Becky looking at her curiously.

"Not at the boatyard?"

"No, nothing, Mother, why?" She turned slightly away, pretending to gather up the hood and cloak she was mending. Did her face show something?

"You look a bit odd. Did you hear something in the town?"

"No, I'd have told you at once, Mother." She folded the cloak. "I've finished. Do you want me to card more wool?"

"I'd rather you scoured the pewter."

"Yes, Mother." Marie rose and went out of the room, sighing in relief. Her mother was so perceptive! She placed the hood on the stairs to take up later and gathered the good pewter on a tray, took it back into the kitchen and set it on the board. She began to chatter about nothing at all as she cleaned the plates, drawing Becky into the conversation, and the awkward moments passed.

But later Becky cornered her upstairs. "Maybe you can fool Mother, but something *did* happen today, didn't it? What was it?"

Marie said coolly, "I don't know what you mean."

Becky regarded her sister with a knowing look. "Where did you go today?"

"To the boatyard, of course, and straight back home."

"And who did you see on the way?"

"No one at all." Marie pretended annoyance. "I'm not a child."

"You're not the mother of five, either."

"You're thinking something where there is nothing and stop nagging at me."

Becky's face still showed suspicion. "Well, there's a look in your eye . . ."

"That's foolish."

" . . . that wasn't there this morning." Becky put her dark head on one side. "Something's happened, all right."

Marie clucked her tongue, swirled her skirts and went down the stairs with heels clattering. So it *was* showing! She'd best mind her expressions if she wanted to keep it all to herself. She was new to assignations and to guarding her words and actions . . . but she could learn.

If she wanted to see David again, she'd have to learn.

Chapter Five

Maggie sat with her husband and Wager by the fire. She poured them tea and set out a few round cakes as they discussed Enoch Quant. The first thing, Wager thought, was to talk to Enoch and make certain that he would agree to being bought out.

"But that'll warn him," Maggie said, "and his price will go up."

"No matter. He'll quarrel about any price," Azariah said.

"Thrift is a good thing," Wager replied, "but what if you get the money or a promise of it and Enoch refuses?"

Azariah shrugged. "Pride, you mean? No, if he refuses we'll give the money back and go on as we are."

"Enoch won't refuse." Wager was positive. "He desperately needs money and has no other way to get it. Not a soul in town will advance him a farthing. He's already overdrawn as far as it is possible to be and he has no credit. None."

"But what will he do if he sells his share?" Azariah asked.

Wager shook his head. "Isn't that just like you, Az. Your worst enemy, a millstone around your neck, and you worry about him!"

"Goodness! He's not my worst enemy!"

Maggie asked, "What other enemies do you have?"

Wager said, "Ask your sons."

"He's not your friend, Azariah," Maggie said gently.

"For your own sake and the sake of the rest of us something has got to be done soon about Enoch. It's long overdue. He's already quarreled with Junius every day."

"He'll quarrel at the Pearly Gates," Wager remarked, "if he gets that far. Talk to him, Az, and feel him out. I'm sure you'll find him receptive under all the bluster. But be firm."

Azariah sighed and ran a big hand through his hair. He eased his stump and looked at Maggie. "Very well, I agree it has to be done, but I think it would be better to put a handful of money on the table and tell him it represents his share."

"You want to get it over with in a hurry," Wager said. "You might put too much money on the table."

"I know what his share's worth—and so does he."

"Well, argue with him." Wager glanced at Maggie. "Az will give him more than he deserves, mark my words."

"Don't treat me like a child," Az grumped. "I'll give him his due."

Wager finished his tea and rose. "Then I'll be getting along. When will you talk to him, Az?"

"Tomorrow," Maggie said.

The corners of Azariah's mouth turned down and he looked tired. He coughed. "Tomorrow," he said.

She walked to the front of the house with Wager. It was dark in the hall as he slipped into a greatcoat. He said softly, "We've got to keep after him or he'll let it slide."

Then he moved forward and kissed her quickly. Maggie clung to him for half a moment, then let him go, heart beating fast. Would she ever see him alone for more than moments?

She opened the door and watched him down the steps to the street.

* * *

With the greatest reluctance Azariah broached the matter to Enoch Quant the following day. And as he expected, Enoch flew into a rage, shouting that Az and his entire damned family was trying to get rid of him.

"It's purely a business proposition," Azariah said with as much reasonableness in his voice as he could muster. "I'm not wanting to steal from you."

Enoch faced him in the hut, a shorter and slightly younger man, dark and scowling. He wiped his hands on his apron. What had happened that he didn't know about? Was there a fine job or two in the offing that Azariah wanted for himself? It was damned suspicious, this sudden offer to buy him out. He demanded, "Where'll you get the money? You never had no money before."

"I'll have to borrow it."

"An' use the boatyard for surety?"

"Of course. It's the only way."

Enoch moved restlessly, his mind busy. "I could do the same, you know . . ."

"Yes, you could." He could but Enoch had no sons and would have to hire help and that would lessen his profits. The fact that Morgan and Junius were paid very little because they lived at home worked to Enoch's favor though Azariah had never said a word about it. He watched Enoch, almost able to read his whirling thoughts. Enoch was upset with wondering if he was being cheated, and even if he was convinced he was not, he might still say so.

Azariah said, "I'll have to pay off the note, and if I can't I'll lose the boatyard."

Enoch smiled, as if that pleased him. He moved to the window and back. "I ain't making up my mind right off." He picked up the paper they'd scribbled figures on, looked at it and put it down. He licked his lips and went to the door, turning to rub his nose and stare at his partner. "I'll sleep on it." He went out.

Azariah sighed and coughed, stretched out his stump and winced. The figures they'd agreed upon were high in his opinion. He'd given way a bit, as Wager had predicted. Smiling ruefully, he reached for his pipe. It was worth a bit extra to be rid of Enoch, but there was no telling what the man might do . . . go for it or not. And if he agreed, then there was the matter of a loan. Money was tight, everyone said. Lord, money was always tight; had he ever seen a time when it was not? The men who used that as an excuse were the ones who would probably fail anyhow.

Enoch was of two minds about Azariah's sudden offer. He certainly coveted the money; it would pay off his debts—well, he'd pay off only part of them, of course. No sense in emptying his pockets as soon as they were filled. And he'd have enough left over to open a store, or take his family to Boston.

Boston. He thought of Boston often. There were opportunities galore in a big city, not like this little backwater village where nothing had happened in a hundred years.

Enoch stopped on the bridge and stared down at the rushing waters, watching how they flowed into the Sound. He had a friend in Boston, Captain Jennet Styles. He'd met Styles four years before when he'd gone to Riggins, a small fishing town, to examine a hulk with an eye to buying. Styles, a lieutenant then, had been there, dickering for a sloop. Enoch, with his boatbuilder's eye, had seen at once that the Britisher was being gulled into buying a wormy hull and had taken Styles aside, with the result that Styles had not purchased, and had asked Enoch to advise him instead. Which he had, and found Styles a boat at a good price.

They had talked since. Styles had advanced in rank and responsibilities, and Styles could help him a great deal, Styles had hinted. A man could prosper selling certain goods to the British army. Everything came from England, of course, but an officer in the right place could make himself a pile of money over a period of time. He'd sell the English material to the right buyers and replace it with lower-cost colonial. The difference was his profit.

Styles had hinted that he needed the right man, a man who could keep his own counsel and who had the necessary money to finance the enterprise. Enoch had hinted in turn that he had the money. And now at last it was true.

But only one thing bothered him. He knew Captain Styles to be a rake. And he knew Styles had his eye on Sharon. "She'll grow up to be a beauty, Enoch."

Could he allow Sharon to marry Styles? He'd lead her a life of misery. . . .

Enoch stared at the ships in the Sound. A British 74 glided by a mile out, topsails set, men strung out along the yards. Then a mist drifted in between and he grunted and spat. Styles wanted to go into business with him—or someone with the necessary cash.

"Leather is leather," Styles had said with a wink the last time they'd met. "The army uses leather by the ton."

It was the most attractive idea to come his way and Enoch swallowed his fears about Sharon. Nothing had happened yet. He'd write to Styles right off. The captain always needed money; the army paid damned little, he'd said many times. They'd get the business going in a hurry.

He moved off the bridge and went along Fort Street to the ordinary, plunked a coin on the board and received a pint and a shadow of a smile from Ben Robb behind the bar. He and Ben got along at arm's length, Ben being such an upright pillar of the church. Ben disliked him because he owed a considerable amount and hadn't paid a penny on it for months. The churchy ones were always the money grabbers.

Enoch took his glass and sat in a corner to think in pros and cons. His wife, Tabitha, would be against his selling, of course. Anything he wanted to do she was against. So he wouldn't consult her. He was certain she would not want to pack up and go to Boston; she liked to stay put. But progress wasn't made by being a stick-in-the-mud. One had to look to the future, and the British army was solid and responsible, and in the colonies to stay. There was trouble right along, according to the Boston newspaper, which at the same time deplored the fact that the troops were not being recalled, but were being reinforced. Smuggling was on the rise, both land and sea, and troops were necessary to enforce the law.

Leather was what Styles had in mind, and Enoch sipped, considering that he knew nothing about leather. But with money he could hire someone who did, and he'd learn quickly. He'd establish a clandestine factory and turn out the dozens of articles that Captain Styles demanded. Later they might branch out. It was sure to make him ten times the money he realized from the boatyard.

He ordered another pint.

Morgan stayed behind for a moment, to finish planing a length of planking, he said, and Azariah walked home that evening with Junius.

Junius was a much different lad from Morgan. Even at seventeen he was thoughtful and serious where Morgan laughed and was willing to hang on a corner telling stories—not that Morgan did not do his share. But Junius was not gregarious. He had taken to heart the early lessons, that work was the measure of a man, and he believed them, practiced them, almost reveled in them. Coming to the boatyard to work was growing up, in Junius's eyes. To Morgan it had been only one of many chores.

Morgan put the plane aside as soon as his father and brother left. He walked to the gate and sat under a pile of weathering timbers, hoping that Sharon would appear. She sometimes came to walk home with her father; but this night Enoch had gone to the ordinary, so that if Sharon appeared they would have a few moments alone together.

But she did not come and after a half-hour Morgan walked home alone, kicking at stones in his path.

Junius was very interested in the plan to buy Enoch Quant's share of the yard. "Where will you get the money, Father?"

"I'll get it."

"Maybe from Mr. Chace?"

Azariah looked at the young lad beside him. Junius was dark like himself, a slender boy but strong and willing. He had level brows, serious dark eyes and the good solid Lynn jaw. He had always been interested in facts, in how things worked, in tangible, visible ideas that he could handle and take apart. He was uninterested, as Morgan was, in visionary things. Probably Junius had little or no imagination, not a good thing to think about a son. Azariah sighed to himself. He must face things as they were.

Azariah said, "I intend to speak to Mr. Chace if Enoch agrees to sell."

"Do you think he will agree?"

"I believe he will. I pray he will. Wager is sure he needs the money and has no other way to get it."

"What if Mr. Chace won't lend the money?"

Azariah coughed and spat. "That is possible, of course. I'll just look elsewhere then."

Junius nodded seriously. "I think he will lend the money. We have the only boatyard in Canaan, after all. It is a good future."

Azariah put his arm about the lad's shoulders. "Let us hold that thought."

What a good future for Jeremiah Chace if the loan was not repaid. But a boy of seventeen would never consider that end of it. It was a stout risk that had cost him sleepless hours; if he lost the boatyard he'd be worse off than anyone in the town. No one wanted a one-legged man.

Azariah sent a note to Jeremiah Chace asking for a bit of time to discuss a matter close to his heart, and Chace replied that he would be glad to entertain Azariah in his home on the following evening.

It was raining when Azariah presented himself on Mr. Chace's doorstep, rapped the knocker and was admitted by the housekeeper, Widow Addie Nichols. "Come in out of the wet." She took his outer coat and shook it. "Mr. Chace's expectin' you."

Jeremiah appeared in the hall, a medium height stout man with a shaved head and round, red face. "There you are, Azariah, come in. Damned winter's on us again. Expect we'll have snow before long."

"Thank you, Mr. Chace." Azariah went into the study, warm with a raging fire. He sat as Chace pointed to a chair, and held out his hands to the glow. He watched the other pull on a fur-trimmed cap and resume his seat in an easy, wing-backed chair, legs up on a hassock.

Jeremiah was wrapped in a banyon, a flowing dark blue robe, and there were soft leather slippers on his feet, and rings on his pudgy fingers. It was a comfortable room, dark-paneled, with a kris, several black-hilted sabers and a seaman's dirk wired to one wall, and a row of ceramic and silver mugs, highly decorated with German designs and phrases; a round-bodied mandolin made of contrasting woods reclined on a sideboard and several huge whale's teeth dangled from strings over the fireplace. Chace had been long in the shipping trade. He had sailed the seven seas as a boy and young man, and made his pile as an owner.

He turned quizzical eyes on Azariah and steepled his fingers. "I expect you've come about Enoch Quant. Is that right enough?"

Azariah's face showed surprise. So Enoch had been chattering in the ordinary again, telling the world their business. Azariah knew that Jeremiah and Ben Robb were close, both elders in the church, both men of substance and property. He nodded and Jeremiah smiled.

"I wonder you've put up with him this long, Azariah."

"I couldn't do otherwise."

"I expect not. Well, I hear your son, Junius, is working there with you. Junius is a good lad, I'm told, a hard worker. Is that so?"

"Like Morgan," Azariah said quickly.

"Oh, yes, but Morgan's got a bit of a way with him. They're not the same and everyone knows it if you don't."

Azariah coughed and sighed deeply, looking into the flames. "I know it, sir. But Morgan doesn't shirk his duty, not for a minute."

Jeremiah waved a pudgy hand. "Yes, stand up for your sons, Azariah. You're a good and truthful man. God's teeth, I wouldn't have seen you else." He reached out to his side and pulled in a bottle and two glasses.

They clinked pleasantly as he set them on a table stool and pulled the cork.

"I thought you might come to me, Azariah. You want to buy Enoch out." He poured from the bottle and winked. "Is that right enough?" He handed his guest a glass of amber brandy.

"Yes, sir, it's right enough. That's what I'm asking."

Jeremiah looked at him keenly and lifted his glass. "Well, it's one thing to ask, and it's another to grant." He smiled and clinked glasses with Azariah. "Here's to a bit of damnation to the redcoats." He drank the brandy and smacked his lips.

Azariah sipped, watching the stout man. It was one thing to grant? Did that mean no? But then why had Jeremiah seen him at all? Jeremiah Chace had a reputation as an amiable, fair man who remembered his lowly beginnings—something others of the gentry did not. He said, "I have only the boatyard to put up as surety, sir."

His host showed a row of teeth. "That's not quite right, Azariah."

"No? Why not? I've nothing else, Mr. Chace."

"Oh yes, indeed you have!"

Azariah was confused. He coughed and shook his head, staring at the apple-cheeked man. Jeremiah's bushy white brows looked more pronounced in the firelight and his bright blue eyes sparkled.

Jeremiah said, "You have Morgan."

"Yes . . ." What in the world did the man mean?

"You want to borrow money. I want something from Morgan."

"Ahhhh." Azariah nearly spilled the brandy.

"I need a master for the schooner you're building for me, Azariah. And Morgan is the man I want. Can we strike a bargain?"

Azariah sat stunned. It was the last thing he'd expected! He seemed to be thinking in a fog, thoughts tumbling about, making little sense. Morgan, master of the schooner? Of course he meant smuggling!

"Drink your brandy, sir," Jeremiah urged. "Good for the blood."

Azariah drank it off and Jeremiah took the glass to pour into it again. "Well, what do you say?"

"I—I hardly know." He coughed and felt for his pipe.

"Take your time. The schooner isn't finished yet."

Azariah stared at the other. "How do you mean, sir—about Morgan?"

"I want to bring goods from the southern islands. I tell you this in confidence, Azariah. I intend to run back and forth, through the British blockade, and I need a man who's not only fearless but smart, who knows ships and tides and the winds and who'll look out for the price of a cargo."

"But—Morgan's only a boy!"

"He's no boy, Azariah. Look at him. God's ass, do I know him better than you?"

"Well . . . he's competent enough with a sailing craft, but so are others."

Jeremiah leaned close and touched his own nose with a thick finger. "Ahhhh, yes, that's so. There *are* others. Plenty of others who can reef and steer and buy a keg of nails and all the rest. But I don't want the others. I want the man with the pedigree, the man I can trust. I also want the man who's got enough guile to slip through where the others you spoke of will fail."

Azariah sipped the brandy in silence, feeling stunned. Did Jeremiah know Morgan better than he did? True, he was apt to think of Morgan as only a boy. . . . And what Jeremiah wanted was a man who

69

could live with danger. Smuggling was not a trade for the squeamish or for cowards. Lord! What would Maggie think?

He gazed at Jeremiah and saw twinkling eyes. His glass was filled again and Azariah sighed. "It's a bargain I didn't figure on, sir."

"I can see that. But there's time to sleep on it. When d'you think the schooner will be finished . . . a matter of weeks?"

"A month maybe." Azariah put the glass down. "A little slower in this cold weather."

"Yes, of course. But bad weather's good for what I've got in mind, and safer, too, for the crew. It's damned hard to see a small craft in a stormy sea. The sooner the better, Azariah. And if you come to a decision—the decision *I* want, mind—I'll give you the money when *you* want."

Azariah rose and nodded. "I'll let you know, sir."

He went out into the hall, shrugged into his greatcoat, said a few words to Widow Nichols and went out into the rain. He was nearly home before he realized he hadn't bargained at all with Jeremiah. He'd accepted it, Morgan or nothing. Maybe Jeremiah would have loaned the money without Morgan in the deal.

But the closer he got to his own hearth the more he was positive Jeremiah would stand firm on that demand. He did want Morgan. And in a way it was a high compliment; he'd spoken of pedigree, and of trust. And a little of wildness.

He knew, as he entered the house and slapped his hat against his leg that Morgan would go for it like a shot. Like a shot from a thirty-two pounder!

But what would Maggie say?

Chapter Six

Marie did her chores and sat at the board between Morgan and Becky with a trencher before her, listening with half an ear to the conversation, but thinking of David.

The stubby homemade white candles in the wall sconces across the room burned with a pure, steady flame, each shaped like an orange-colored leaf, long drawn out . . . they seemed to be burning inside her. She could feel the warmth spreading throughout her and she had to pull her eyes away from the hypnotic glow. She forced herself to concentrate on what her father was saying, but after a few seconds the words began to blur into meaningless sounds and she was back on the beach in David's arms, feeling the rough cloth of his uniform coat against her cheek.

The meal finished, she scrubbed the board, conscious of her mother's eyes, mopped it dry and brought wood for the fire without being asked. Then she found a place in the corner of the room and took up a handful of broom corn and began to scrape the seeds out. With the seeds removed she would wrap the corn about a handle and tie it securely. Brooms did not last long and it was a good idea to make as many as possible at a time. Her father had bought a bundle of corn from someone along the waterfront and brought it home only last week.

What would David's room be like? Different from

her brothers', no doubt. She stopped scraping and looked at the heavy wooden comb—she *had* made up her mind to go there! Absently she picked seeds from between the comb teeth and dropped them into the wooden tub with the other refuse. She had known all along, hadn't she? But not admitted it to herself.

Her mother asked, "Is the corn infested, Marie?"

She jerked her head up. "What? No, no it isn't." She began to scrape furiously, biting her lower lip. How transparent she must be!

Becky said in a sly voice, "You should have seen how she looked at Goodman Tanfield."

Marie gave her sister an annoyed glance, but felt quietly assured. Let them think that. Her mother was smiling . . . and then it was forgotten.

She put the corn away for tying on the morrow, carried the tub of seeds to the back door and slipped upstairs with a taper. It was cold in the little room and she pulled a shawl across her shoulders and sat by the window looking out into the dark. Becky was seeing a young man now and again, but only to talk to, Becky said, and Marie wondered if they had been as close as she and David on the beach. Probably not or Becky would have told her. They had always confided in each other. Would it be different now that the confiding was much more important? Did she want to reveal to Becky how she felt?

No, it was something else. She wanted to keep her secret even from Becky because David was a British officer. She knew exactly what Becky would say, what anyone would say, because everyone was grumbling about the British for one reason or another. The redcoats considered themselves superior to native Americans in every particular—and showed it.

Except David. She knew he did not.

When Becky came upstairs, Marie was getting into

bed. She pulled the blankets up and lay still, eyes closed, pretending to be asleep so Becky would not engage her in trivial whispering. And long after the candle was out she lay with her thoughts, seeing his face, feeling his arms. . . . What would it be like to be Marie Urfe? She would move up in station and they would have to call her Mrs. Urfe!

It was with a great effort that she made herself busy in the morning as midday approached. It had rained off and on, and she watched her mother prepare a parcel of hot food, then give it to Becky to deliver. It was a wrench to see Becky hurry out, but it was best, she thought, not to insist on going herself because then they would know. They would know there was a reason, and Becky would guess, if her mother did not, that she was seeing someone.

She stayed in the house the entire day, never once venturing outside, but David was never far from her thoughts. What did he do on days of inclement weather? Did he exercise his men in the rain, or was there a place indoors? She dared not ask anyone; girls were not supposed to wonder about military things. Did he sit in the ordinary, or did he remain in his room at home, idling the time away till she came?

How could she go there? She'd have to steal a bit of time after taking food to the boatyard, but if she were seen in the town—Lord, the footbridge was out!— someone might mention it to her mother or Becky, and questions would be raised. Why did she take so long? Why did she not come straight home?

There were no convenient answers to such questions. Of course it was all because she had to see him without others knowing. It did add a bit of spice to the adventure that put color in her cheeks. Did anyone notice that?

When she could find the moments she made quilting

designs and cut them out of heavy paper, and wondered as she did so if it might be possible to trade designs with another girl of her acquaintance in the town, as a way to gain an hour or two away from her mother's eye. Time was everything, and she had so little to herself.

She was mending shirts the next day when her mother prepared and wrapped the food parcel. "It's raining again, Marie, dear. Take your cloak and heavy shoes."

Marie controlled her expression, but her heart was pounding as she changed into the thick leather shoes that would keep out the wet, and fastened a hooded cloak over her shoulders. She drew on mittens and hurried out along the muddy road clutching the parcel. It was cold and drizzly as she passed Summer Street and glanced toward the fence where the boards hung loose. It was nearly midday; would David be waiting, or had he forgotten her?

Her father was not in the hut, but Junius saw her and came in, rubbing his raw hands, holding them out to the stove. "Bless you, little sister—do you have to go already?"

"There're things to do," she said over her shoulder and slammed the door as she left.

It rained hard for several minutes as she crossed the wagon bridge and hurried along Fort Street. Pulling the hood down she bent her shoulders under the downpour, thinking how welcome it was. It might keep prying eyes indoors. She went up High Street to Summer, avoiding the main part of town. Summer Street was a quagmire and she had to walk in the weeds at the side; she crossed it, glancing about under the dripping trees, and ducked through the fence. She ran along it to the house, heart thumping, nearly biting her lip through. What if one of the Hollisters was home! What excuse could she give?

The rear door of the house opened suddenly, slamming back, and she nearly screamed. But it was David, grinning, coming to meet her. "You did come after all!"

She fell against him, cheeks flaming, holding her pounding chest to keep her heart in. He pulled her inside and shut the door quickly. He murmured that all was well, she was safe in his arms, they were alone. Pushing the hood back, he kissed her hard, held her tightly and she gasped for breath.

He said, "You've no idea how much I wanted to see you!" He stripped the sopping cloak from her and hung it by the back door. "I've been watching the fence for days and I was sure you'd decided never to see me again."

"It isn't easy to make time, and I mustn't stay long." Did she sound like a ninny? David looked very different without his scarlet uniform coat with the glittering decorations. He wore only a ruffled white shirt and white breeches, and she thought he appeared younger.

"Just seeing you is enough," he said and drew her close again.

There was a small fire on the kitchen hearth and the room smelled of food and smoke. It was a larger kitchen then her own, painted a yellowish color that she thought slightly unpleasant. Pots and pans hung on one wall along with wooden implements, and a trencher was sitting on the trestle board, half filled with soup, a spoon still in it. He had probably been eating when he heard her in the yard. His arms enfolded her and his kisses took her breath away, but before she could recover he was hurrying her up the steps to the second floor and her heavy brogans clattered on the bare boards, making her very conscious of them. He was wearing soft pumps, like slippers, but then he'd been inside, out of the rain.

He led her into a bedchamber at the rear of the house. Through one of the small panes she could see the tops of trees and the dull glitter of a glass window half hidden by branches on the next street. He drew the curtains quickly and the room became dim, a man's room with his uniform coats on pegs, a short musket standing in a corner, boots against the wall and a sword and sash by the bed. There was a wash basin, a lamp and a green trunk with his name lettered on it in script. Another pair of boots was half under the bed and he kicked them back with a twitch of his toe.

She had an impression of green and white wallpaper, then he was holding her again, murmuring love words that seemed to resound and echo in her brain. She was a dove, he whispered, a little kitten, a precious rose of rare beauty and she was his forever. Marie had never heard such phrases before. Her lashes fluttered and an intense excitement filled her chest, crying for release. She stood almost on tiptoe, quivering, holding him—and then he suddenly picked her up and laid her on the bed.

In an instant he was beside her before she could object, arms about her, kissing her hotly. The room closed in and she gasped, her heart bursting. She plucked at his arms, her thoughts running riot. The pounding in her chest was a physical hammering. She had to get free, for a moment at least! It was all too sudden, too close! She was trembling and afraid—but wanting him too.

She wrestled free, and soft hands pulled her back. He kissed her cheek gently and one hand smoothed her hair. His voice was soothing, and the fear began to recede.

Eyelids fluttering, she heard him whisper that he was

sorry, he had not been able to resist her charms, that he loved her deeply and would never in the world harm a hair of her head.

The doubts fled and she turned her head, seeking his mouth. Her arms reached for him and she closed her eyes; how could she be afraid? She gave herself over to his soft caresses; he touched her gently, lips less demanding and she relaxed in the precious warmth of his embrace. How wonderful he was! How understanding. . . .

The heady kisses sent increasing, insistent flames through her body and she could not protest when deft fingers untied her bodice and gently pulled the chemise aside. Murmuring love words, he bared red-nippled breasts and his breath was hot on them. She breathed deeply and fast, writhing as if in pain, and lush images flooded her mind, driving out all else.

Marie hardly realized that he had slid her skirt and petticoats up, kissing her the while. A warm and gentle hand caressed her naked thighs and she moaned as it reached upward. A great sea of desire surged and roared through her head, and her body twisted. . . .

Suddenly she felt him atop her and her arms held him in a fierce embrace. She cried out in bewilderment when he brutally entered her. The rushing sea crashed about her and the stinging pain made her writhe—she felt his body driving and straining. The bed squeaked and protested; he was panting, thrusting hard, and she heard herself moan aloud . . . and then the sea receded.

David rolled off, gasping for breath, and lay beside her without a word. Marie was still, feeling an ache in her loins as she stared at the pale ceiling, frightened and alone. Where were his kisses now?

Then she heard him curse.

He was sitting up and she looked down at the blood.

She was bloody, and the bed was soaked with it! She stared at his contorted face—how different he looked all at once! He was angry and she lay back again, afraid, hands to her face as the tears came, all the beautiful images gone. He'd taken her and now all was over—

He cursed again and got up to bring the basin and water. "Damn! I should have known—you're a damned virgin! Here, lay still or you'll stain everything."

Márie felt drained and helpless, unable to cope with such opposing emotions; then he picked her off the bed and gave her a cloth. "Get yourself dry." She turned away, not wanting to see the anger, ashamed that she'd come, confused by his changing attitudes. She wanted to run down the steps, out the back into the street and keep running. First, sweet love words—and now this!

But he pulled the sheets off the bed and put them into something outside the room, saying he'd take care of them later, and after a bit forced away his dark mood. He came across the room to embrace her. "I was forgetting," he said, "Forgive me, it's all my fault." He laughed shortly. "You've made a pile of work f'me, you have."

"I—I'm sorry."

"Of course you are." He kissed her. "But that's behind us now, isn't it? Y'better fix your hair, it's late."

She thought of time for the first moment since she'd entered the room. Lordy! It must be hours gone! He held a square of mirror for her while she clawed at the tangled locks. She'd never hear the last of this day!

His arms held her very tightly and he whispered, asking her forgiveness again. He hadn't meant a thing he'd said. She was his dearest rose and the light he worshipped . . . and gradually she softened; it *was* all due to his surprise. Of course it was, and that was all of it, his curses were forgotten. His love for her was diminished not one whit.

It was late, he said once more. She must go so that no one would suspicion, so that she could come again. He slapped her bottom as she hurried down the steps, and held her tightly again at the back door, kissing her breathless.

"You've got to come again, my darling, you must!"

"Yes—yes—" She wanted to, now that everything was all right again.

"Promise?"

She would promise anything. She pulled the cloak about her, yanked at the hood and ran down the back steps into the puddled yard, hearing his goodbyes ringing in her ears. She had a last glimpse of him at the open door, standing nonchalantly, smiling with a hand raised, then she stepped through to the street.

It was still raining lightly and a wind came off the ocean to whip the tree branches, but she felt none of the chill. Her nipples were still hard as buttons and it seemed she yet trembled in delicious trepidation as his hands roved up her thighs. Lord! What a wild and wicked thing she'd done! What would she say when she got home? That she'd dallied in the town? Would the lie sound plausible? It was the only thing she could think of; she'd say she dawdled from window to window, never realizing the hours were slipping past. And if she had to, she'd take her medicine for it.

As she came nearer the house the enormity of what she'd done seemed to strike into her vitals. Anyone who looked at her would see it instantly! They'd turn her out, scream at her and the town would shout her through the streets. . . .

When she went up the steps to the door, she leaned against it out of the rain for the moment, staring back toward Summer Street, feeling the fear return. It would gain her nothing that though she'd participated she'd had no real enjoyment of the fornication. Only his kisses and his touch, only a passion and a willingness that had played her false. It had been like a whirlwind enveloping her, clouding her senses, negating every lesson she'd learned.

But David had known exactly what to do—he must have done it before. But still he loved her, he'd told her so, and he'd shown how he loved her. His anger had been only a momentary thing, as when someone dropped a china cup on the floor and saw it smashed. It had shocked her, but it had passed and the loving hands returned. How could she blame him for the single lapse? She should have told him at once that she'd never been with a man before.

Taking deep breaths, she got herself under control, opened the door and went inside.

Her mother was not in the house. Becky came from the kitchen to stare at her. "Where have you been? I went to the boatyard to look—"

Marie hung the soggy cloak by the warm hearth and spread its folds. Luck was with her this day! Her mother out. She smiled at Becky. "Where's Mother?"

"Gone into town, to Goodman Burley's store, I think. Where were you?"

"Nowhere." Marie went to the stairs. "How long has mother been gone?"

Becky smiled with half her face. "Long enough. So you *have* been meeting someone. Who is he?"

"I've only been window looking. Nothing else."

"And will you swear that on the holy book?"

Marie shrugged and climbed the stairs. "Will you hold the book?"

She changed the heavy shoes. Probably the foot of David's bed was muddy too; the thought almost made her smile. She imagined him busy washing and hanging the sheets to dry in front of a roaring fire, before the Hollisters returned.

Nearly two hours had gone by. Lord, she was lucky her mother had been away—and Becky would not tell on her. A hand to her breast, she sat for a moment by the window feeling the reaction; she was tired, and trembling. Her legs felt weak as if she'd been running hard. It was raining outside, the stark tree limbs were black and the puddles were lengthening, brown water gurgling off the roof. Was she a woman now? Did the fact that she'd been taken by a man make her a woman?

And now David expected her to come to the house again. It was clear from his words. But now there was a breath of doubt inside her. Did he love her as he said? If so, why had he been so angry?

She felt a trembling confusion. It had all happened too quickly, in a rush that she'd been helpless to do anything about. As she tried to think back on it, everything seemed to blend—great happiness on seeing him, heady kisses and embraces, and suddenly he was atop her and there was pain—then anger.

It was the anger that troubled her the most. Did he really love her?

Did she really love him?

Chapter Seven

Maggie was appalled that Jeremiah Chace would propose such a human bargain. Her brown eyes flashed fire as she pounded the table-board when Azariah explained what they'd talked about. Morgan was not a bit of property to be bought or sold! And he was certainly not fodder for some damned British cannon on the high seas!

Azariah coughed and his big fists opened and closed as he rode over her objections. "He may never even see a British ship."

"That's ridiculous, Az! They're like the leaves on the trees. Of course he'll see them."

"It's a large ocean, Maggie."

"You talk as if you're willing to let him go!"

Azariah had a spate of coughing, then shook his head. "He's almost a man—look at the facts, Maggie! You can't keep him hanging onto your skirts forever."

She turned away, glaring, wondering if he was right. Was it because Morgan was her firstborn? Maybe even her favorite? He *was* doing a man's work now in the boatyard. But when she thought of him on the deck of a schooner, chased by a British warship with all guns run out, it was something else. How terrible it would be if Morgan sailed off on the schooner and never came back! Or what might be worse, came back with a leg gone, like his father.

She sucked in her breath, teeth gritting. The schooner was like a toy, easily torn into nothingness if one cannon ball smashed into her. A little wreckage would float for a time on the waves, but cargo and all would go down . . . and she would never know where.

Kneeling, she put more wood on the fire, then rose, forcing the thoughts from her mind. Not one thing was to be gained by seeing Morgan drowned or cut to pieces by British grapeshot.

Azariah changed the subject, talking about the gossip of the ordinary; people were optimistic about the new king, George, the third of that name, who was expected to be more understanding of the needs of the colonies. He was expected to withdraw most of the troops, for instance, and ease the restrictions on manufactured goods, which would make smuggling less profitable.

It was true that Connecticut had a king's charter and practically managed her own affairs by means of the legislative assembly, but the king's ministers could step in whenever they wished.

She listened to him with one ear, but it was impossible to banish all thoughts of Morgan and the schooner. Not that she loved him any more than the others, but none of them were about to risk their lives. Then, of course, there was something about Morgan; he had the qualities she'd seen once in Azariah, a long time ago— and even more. He had a strength that Az lacked, though God only knew what Az might have done had he not lost the leg. But he *had* let it defeat him.

She could not get it out of her mind that Morgan might come home with only one leg and she closed her eyes, squeezing them together to shut out the pain. No, God could not let that happen! Of course it was possible for Morgan to be seriously hurt at the boatyard by falling timbers or any of a hundred other accidents. But none like the guns of a British broadside deliberately firing at him.

She cared nothing for the law side of it; no one did because the king's law was stupid and resented by all. It was only the chance of harm or death. Even if Morgan escaped the guns, he might be caught. And the redcoats were fully capable of hauling him off to some dank prison on their rain-shrouded isle thousands of miles away. Everyone knew the stories of men confined in prison hulks or prison yards, held for petty reasons but broken in minds and bodies, dying from lack of food.

Lord! Let it not be Morgan!

She had such hopes for Morgan. She knew he had ideas of his own about building ships or sailing them; he had many times expressed to her his dreams, knowing his father would not be receptive. Morgan had private plans to expand the boatyard to build larger craft. Azariah was slow to accept such ideas partly because of costs, and partly because of Enoch Quant. Az was mostly content to let things slide. Morgan was not.

But Morgan would not force issues with his father. He would deal with Enoch in a hurry, but she knew he respected Azariah's wishes.

Was Azariah right, that she was hanging on to Morgan? She wasn't conscious of it, and yet it might be so.

Inevitably the conversation came round again to the issue at hand and she would not let herself come to a decision. She prevailed on Azariah too, to wait, to say nothing to Morgan. Of course she knew what Morgan's reaction would be! He would probably work night and day on the schooner to get her ready.

The next evening Wager Tanfield came to the house, and when they were alone, was drawn into the discussion. She was resentful when he sided with Azariah. "If you deny him this, Maggie, he may never forgive you."

"Then don't tell him!"

"He'll find out," Wager promised. "Too many know of it already, Ben Robb for one. I know that Jeremiah's asked those who know about it to keep the secret, but it'll get out. I expect that even Enoch will know sooner or later."

Azariah coughed. "I pray that Enoch will be the last to find out."

She said hotly, "Mr. Chace had no right to—"

"He's a businessman, Maggie. He doesn't want Morgan dead any more than you do."

She knew it was hopeless. They were like a couple of preachers citing Scripture, happy in their righteousness. Abruptly she left them by the kitchen hearth and went upstairs to be alone, but wishing at the same time she could talk to Wager. Would he have an influence on Morgan? She sighed deeply. Probably not, in this regard. She knew in her heart that Morgan wished for a happy chance to pluck him out of the boatyard; if not this opportunity, then some other. She could not hold him, no matter what.

They were right that Morgan was a man. She sat by the window, not seeing the shadowy trees outside; he was a man and he had the right to make his own decisions. She stared at the hands in her lap, grudgingly admitting that Wager's argument was sound, though she was not at all sure that she would ever see Jeremiah Chace again without resenting him.

Yes, Morgan was capable of making his own decisions, as she was of making hers. Morgan's life was just beginning, and in many ways, so was her own . . . though he could probably plot his course better than she. The pitfalls around her and Wager were as numerous as the dead leaves in autumn.

Well, where Morgan was concerned she would have to make the best of it. She got up and faced the mirror, dabbing at the motherly tears, willed them to stop and went downstairs again. Wager smiled at her as if he knew what she was thinking. Perhaps he did.

She put the kettle on, as if nothing had happened, and listened to them talk. Wager was showing Azariah some drawings he'd made for a firm in Newport, a fine sloop for a gentleman of means. When the discussion was finished he rolled them up and Az turned his attention to Brayton to explain some of the intricacies of algebra, and she touched Wager's hand. His fingers closed over hers tightly.

She made the tea, feeling her face flushed, but they would think it from the heat of the fire. She handed the cups around. Wager showed her some sketches he'd made of boats and gulls.

When she went to the door with him later he asked, "Do you know the Widow Riley? She lives on High Street."

"Yes, of course. The deaf woman."

Wager smiled. "Exactly. The deaf woman. Do you imagine she'd like company now and then?"

She stared at him in the gloom, suddenly realizing what he meant. The widow was deaf and couldn't hear a thing. . . . He glanced toward the kitchen, kissed her quickly and went out, leaving her gazing at the dark slab of the door.

Wager was suggesting they meet there!

Slowly she returned to the kitchen and sat by the hearth, thinking of the hut by the creek. Azariah coughed, cleared his throat and closed the book he'd been reading with Brayton, telling the boy to go off to bed.

When Brayton had gone he asked if she wished to discuss Jeremiah's offer again.

She said, "I thought you'd settled it. You men settle everything so easily and logically."

"Don't be a shrew, Maggie. It *is* logical, or most of it is."

"So you want him to go?"

"Of course not." Az sucked on his pipe, then tapped it out on the hearth. "But if I were his age I'd want to go." He met her eyes. "You want the truth, I expect."

She sighed and nodded, looking at her idle hands. Morgan had won, and never even known he'd been in a battle. "Go see Mr. Chace then, and do what you have to do."

"It's the only way."

She nodded, thinking that she had also won something for herself. She had decided, almost without realizing it, to embark on a journey with Wager; something she *had* to do for herself. She would hold back no longer.

Azariah said, "I'd like to see Enoch—"

Maggie rose and slammed the kettle against the black iron pot hook. "Damn Enoch Quant!" She glared at Azariah, who stared at her with round eyes.

Azariah was in bed asleep when she crept in beside him. She lay for an hour staring into the dark, listening to the house settle and creak. The Widow Riley was old, infirm and deaf; she lived in the same house she'd been married in fifty years before. Most of the rooms must be closed off because the old woman would hardly be able to keep them up. Tomorrow, Maggie thought, she would go and see. The house was nearby, only a few moments' walk.

What would it be like to meet Wager completely alone?

Azariah brought up the subject of Jeremiah Chace's schooner as he and Morgan walked to the boatyard next morning. He explained how he'd gone to see Mr. Chace and he glanced at Morgan as he related Jeremiah's terms. When he realized them, Morgan gave out a whoop.

"Sail the schooner for him! I'd sail it across a desert! You told him yes, of course?"

"I discussed it first a long time with your mother." Morgan sobered. "And what did she say?"

"I'm telling you. It's settled that you're to go if that's your wish." Azariah was grumpy. "And you can thank Wager for his help in the matter."

"I will." He eyed his father. "What is it?"

"It's a dangerous thing Jeremiah's asking. If you meet a fickle wind they'll have you, and the redcoats know how to hate."

Morgan was silent for several moments. "But you'll be rid of Enoch and have the boatyard. That's a good omen, isn't it?"

Azariah coughed and grunted. "I dunno how far you can stretch an omen like that, but let's hope there's play in it. I think it's a damned high price and so does your mother—but I wouldn't tell her that." He glanced at the sky. "You ought to have the schooner launched about the time the first snow falls. What d'you think?"

"Just about," Morgan said.

He spent the day in suppressed excitement, working over the schooner lovingly. He reexamined her with a new and more critical eye; it was all different now that he was to be her master; her lines had to be perfect. He forgot to come to the hut at midday and Junius had to go for him before the food Marie brought was cold.

And it was a good day for another reason. Enoch Quant had not come to work. Late in the afternoon Sharon arrived with a note saying Enoch was sick; Sharon thought it was from something he'd eaten.

Azariah thanked her gravely for the news and asked if she would mind walking down to the stocks to inform Morgan. She said she would be happy to.

Morgan was astonished to see her and glanced around instantly. "Did you come with your father?"

"No, he's home in bed."

"Ahhhh, too bad." Morgan smiled and drew her into the lee of the schooner where prying eyes could not easily see them. He slid his arms about her. "You're the second most beautiful thing I've seen today."

"What?" She let him kiss her.

"All right—you're the first." He slapped the side of the schooner. "And this is the second. I'm to be her skipper!"

"Morgan Lynn, what are you talking about?"

"You haven't heard the news?"

"Would I ask if I had?"

"Well, of course it's a secret—but you won't tell your father, will you?"

She shook her head. Morgan explained quickly and was surprised at the changing expressions on Sharon's lovely face. Her eyes grew troubled. "So that's why Father has been talking of Boston!"

"Boston!" He hadn't considered that Enoch might move away—not on this amazing day. "What about Boston?"

"I don't know. I've heard them talking, but they don't tell me anything, of course."

"Maybe he's just going there—business."

"He has no business that I know of."

He lifted her chin and kissed her. "I'm going to marry you, Sharon, and don't ever forget it. One voyage and I'll have enough for—"

"That'll take months!"

He held her very close, kissed her cheek and gazed over her shoulder. She was perfectly right, but maybe Jeremiah Chace would advance him a bit of money. It was worth the asking.

As he, Junius and his father walked home that night, Morgan stopped them on the dark street and faced

Azariah. "There's something I've been thinking about . . ."

Azariah chewed his pipestem. "What is it?"

"You told me that Mr. Chace would have the money for you whenever you agreed to the deal. Is that right?"

"That's what he said."

Morgan glanced at his brother and took a breath. "If you give Enoch Quant his money he'll leave—"

"A blessed thing," Azariah said. "The crux of it all."

"Except for one thing. He'll leave and take Sharon with him. He's talking about going to Boston."

"Ummmm," Azariah said. "You've talked to Sharon?"

"Yes."

"And what is it you've been thinking about?"

"Will you delay giving Enoch his money till the schooner is finished?"

"What a mazy brain you have," Junius said.

Azariah tapped the pipestem against his teeth. "You want to marry Sharon?"

"Yes, of course."

"All right then. But you'll have to put up with Enoch for another month."

Junius groaned.

Chapter Eight

Brayton Eric Lynn, a slim and wiry boy of fifteen, Marie's twin, had come to the end of the school term the summer before and had prevailed upon his mother and Azariah to allow him to take a job with Eli Burley, the storekeeper. It was part of the agreement that he would continue his studies at home, and he was perfectly willing. Brayton was a studious lad and enjoyed mathematics, his father's interest also.

But he had an urge to get on with his life. The common school taught him nothing of business and dealings with his fellows and he was seldom allowed to listen when his elders talked of such matters. It seemed to him he must do as he'd heard all his life, start at the bottom and work his way to the top.

Eli Burley was a kindly man, a widower with no children, who took a fancy to the young Lynn boy, and when Brayton suggested he help during the summer, Eli agreed. The summer job continued into the fall.

The store was large, by Canaan's standards, an entire building with store, storerooms and shed on the ground floor and Eli's quarters in the rooms above. Eli had inherited the building and business from his father, had in fact been born in those rooms. He was a man with a large stomach, white hair that fluffed over his ears and sharp gray eyes behind the usually grimy glasses he always wore. He was slow-moving, loved to chatter and spread gossip among the town ladies, and began to leave more and more of the ordinary and heavier chores to Brayton.

If boxes or sacks had to be moved it was Brayton who tackled the loads. It was he who received the goods in the alley behind the store and helped out behind the counter. In two months Brayton was perfectly at home filling orders, and regular customers began to find him a bit more accurate in that respect, if not quite so generous with a cheese knife.

In the afternoons, when customers were fewer, Eli began to take an hour off now and then to nap. "I've been standing on this floor f'forty years," he said to Brayton. "There's times my back gets to acting up."

"Go ahead, sir," Brayton said.

"I'll just lie down for a bit. If Goodwife Dagget comes in, watch that she doesn't slip a finger under the scale."

"I will, sir."

By the time fall came around, Eli Burley was taking regular naps in the afternoons, and sometimes they lasted till nearly dark. The absences gave Brayton a chance to study the store and to revise the layout to make things easier for himself. The items most in demand were brought closer to the counter with the cash box, and those seldom called for were relegated to the top shelves. He also studied Eli's account books, discovering that a number of people were sadly in arrears. When he spoke of this to his employer, Eli sighed and shook his head, saying that some were unable to pay up and he figured he was stuck.

But Brayton was sure those families were not going without food. They were buying it elsewhere. With Eli's blessing he went out to collect and managed something on each bill. He collected nearly all of it, over a period of time.

Eli was delighted and gave him a raise of one shilling a week.

Eli was also surprised and happy to find, when he totted up the accounts at year's half, that despite the usual costs plus what he paid to Brayton, including the raise, his business had brought in a third more than the half before. It was the first time in decades that that had happened. Could it be due to the lad's help? Eli was generous enough to think that it might.

And he was getting in his regular naps to boot.

He began to look with particular favor on young Brayton Lynn.

Becky Elise, who turned sixteen on the twelfth of May, had rounded out in the past four months. She was a slightly taller girl than her sister Marie, with dark reddish hair, a shade darker than her mother's, but with her mother's graceful carriage. She had the dark hazel eyes of all the Lynns but was possessed of an impish smile none of them could match. It would, her father often said, get her into trouble one day, unless she married early and was kept properly at home.

Many brash boys of the village had walked with her when she would allow it, had promised her moments she would not quickly forget and shown exceeding interest in her future, but though she was pleasant, she only listened.

She encouraged one or two with looks and smiles, but when they became serious Becky did not. She had not seen in them anything out of the ordinary.

It stopped raining the day after Marie's curious absence; no matter how she nagged, Marie would tell her nothing, and that day Becky had been allowed to walk into the town to purchase yarn and thread. On the way she paused in front of Porter's cobbler shop where there were a number of framed portraits in the window. A small card informed her that they were the work of Orlow Gordon, and that similar likenesses could be had for a nominal sum.

She recognized none of the men depicted. The portraits were of hard-eyed merchants, with expressions carved in iron, and all were surrounded by a kind of snowy haze. She could see Orlow at work inside the shop, hammering on a boot sole; she knew him from church meetings, a mild-mannered young man with flaming red hair and pale eyes. She had not known he had artistic ambitions. Apparently he wished to augment his slender earnings as Goodman Porter's assistant.

He looked up, as if he had seen her shadow, saw her at the window and smiled. She smiled back and, on an impulse, opened the door, which had a tinkling bell, and entered.

Orlow rose at once, wiping his hands on an apron, and came forward. "Well, this is an honor, Becky Lynn, or do we have boots being repaired for your father?"

"No . . ." She shook her head. The shop smelled strongly of leather and oil. Goodman Porter was not at his usual place. It was a smallish room with shelves filled with boots and shoes, black and brown, with several benches and a door to the back, standing part way open. She could see the end of a bunk bed and the edge of a table.

She said, "I saw your pictures."

"Oh, yes . . ." He glanced at them and she thought he seemed a bit embarrassed. "They're not very good, are they? Goodman Porter said I might put them there, but no one's said a word until you."

She said with the sly smile, "Could you do one of me?"

"Oh—" He seemed startled at the idea. "Well, you'd have to sit, of course, sit very still and not move at all—and I don't know if I could."

"Why not?"

"Well, I don't know if I could do you well enough. I've never tried to do a—"

"To do a what?"

"A pretty girl." He flushed, not meeting her eyes.

She put her head on one side and regarded him with an amused smile. Before she could reply she heard the back door squeak, open and close. In a moment a tall, very grimy young man stood in the doorway pulling off a cap. His dark hair was tousled and he gazed at her in surprise.

Orlow said, "Louis! What're you doing here?"

Louis was perhaps twenty-two, face shiny with perspiration, and Becky's heart beat faster. This was a man very different from Orlow; his gaze was direct and interested without being insolent and when he smiled at her she could not help smiling back. She had never seen him in the village before.

Orlow said, "This is Becky Lynn, Louis. Her father runs the boatyard."

Louis bowed and his white teeth flashed. "How nice to meet you. Your father is named Azariah?"

"Yes." He had a French accent, and underneath the grime he was very good looking. His clothes were old and patched; his hair was too long, falling over his ears and she wondered all at once if he had come from Canada. Maybe he was a fugitive from the war.

Orlow said, "You shouldn't have come into town in daylight. What if someone saw you?"

"This charming young lady sees me."

"She'll say nothing to the British—" Orlow stepped to the window and peered out. "There might have been soldiers about!"

"I looked first." Louis glanced down at himself. "Pardon my miserable appearance, mademoiselle, but I am working as a woodcutter."

Orlow said, "He sells cut wood to Mr. Carnon. Louis, you must—"

"I am out of sight," Louis protested.

Becky said, "You're from Canada!"

Louis smiled and shrugged. "My country has lost that empire, lovely lady. Yes, I am hunted by the redcoats."

"She won't tell them," Orlow said again.

"Thank you. They would put me on one of those prison ships, take it out to sea and sink it."

"Louis is hoping to get passage to France," Orlow said. "It might be easier here than in a city. There is only a small detachment of troops here and their officer is a jackass—pardon me, Becky."

She gazed at Louis in near fascination, never having seen a fugitive before, and he retreated a step under her scrutiny, obviously perturbed by his grimy appearance. She said, "Orlow is right. Anyone in the town will know you are a stranger. Where do you stay?"

"In my house," Orlow said. "He comes in at night to bring the wood to Mr. Carnon."

"The horse is lame," Louis indicated the back. "I had to come in. I do not want him hurt."

Orlow glanced along the street again. "You take too many chances. You should have waited."

Louis smiled ruefully and shrugged again. "Then I will go back to the woods until dark—if you will see to the horse." He pulled the wool cap onto his head and bowed to her. "It was an honor, Becky Lynn. I no longer see beautiful girls. Today was good for my soul." He smiled and went into the back room and in a moment she heard the rear door squeak.

Orlow said, "I wish he could get a ship—"

"How can he with that accent!"

"Oh, I will buy his ticket, of course. It is only necessary to find a friendly captain. His English is excellent, but the accent would give him away in a second. He was a major in the French army and just now the British will jail any Frenchman and worry about the right of it later. Any Frenchman, I mean, who has no papers and cannot prove who he is."

"Why did he not stay in Canada?"

"I don't know, but he is eager to get to France." Orlow peered at the street. "Will you excuse me, Becky? I must take the horse to the smith before Goodman Porter returns."

"Of course." She went out to the street, the matter of the portrait forgotten by both of them. Orlow locked the door behind her and put a card in the window. She walked on into the town to make her purchases.

Louis had called her beautiful.

It was all she could think of, and even when she entered the store her thoughts were far off. What did he look like with all the dirt washed away? She stared at her brother, Brayton, when he came to wait on her. "What d'you want?"

"What?"

She bit her lip hard. "I almost forgot what I came for. . . ."

That same night, after the evening meal when the kitchen was cleaned and she went outside to the privy with a candle, Louis was there.

He loomed up in the dark, white teeth smiling, hair combed. She stifled a yell at his shadow. "It's Louis," he said quickly.

"You frightened me!"

"I am sorry, mademoiselle. Please forgive me."

He had changed his clothes and there was no smell

of grime on him. She was astonished when he took her hand. He said, "I had to see you again." He kissed her fingers.

"Louis, you shouldn't be here!" She glanced toward the house. The back door was closed and it was misty in the yard. She blew out the candle.

"I have always gone where I should not." He came very close to her. "I wanted to tell you something."

"What?"

"When I saw you today in the cobbler shop—you made my poor heart thump." He slapped his chest several times. "There is something about you, Becky Lynn—"

She stared at him, scarce believing she was talking to him. "How did you find this house?"

"Orlow told me, of course. He also told me not to come here. You will not give me away?"

She was silent, not knowing what to say to him. How bold he was! Were all Frenchmen like him? Then how could they lose to the British?

He said, "I am making you worried." He looked at the house. "Then I will go away. Do you want me to go away?"

"Yes—well, no—but yes, you must go! If my father saw you here!"

"I am told your father is a good and kind man."

"Yes he is. But—"

He kissed her fingers again. "I will see you soon, Becky Lynn, I promise. Look for me."

"Where?"

He smiled. "Look for me." Then he turned and was gone in the dark.

The experience was so surprising and unexpected she stood almost dazed as he disappeared. He must have waited for hours, watching the house! When she went inside again her mother said, "Is something wrong?"

"What?"

"You look as if you'd seen a ghost."

"I do?" Becky touched her face. "I—I had a fright, but it was only a cat." She put the candle on the counter, astonished that her mind had worked so quickly and produced the imaginary cat. No one questioned her further.

When she got into bed sleep would not come. Her thoughts were all of Louis—she did not even know his last name! It was foolish of her to dream of a Frenchman, a fugitive from the redcoats. She ought to be thinking instead of somone with a real future.

Louis had said there was something about her, and she felt the same mysterious attraction. She never had felt that before. It was subtle and indefinable, but it was there; almost from the moment he'd come into the room she'd felt *something*.

And in the gloom of the yard under a misting overcast his presence had made her heart race, and not from his sudden appearance or from fear. Because of *him*.

She pressed her lips on her fingers, on the same place his lips had touched. She would look for him! Lordy, she would look everywhere, every second.

Chapter Nine

Maggie waited for a day when the mists and rain let up before she went calling. The Widow Irene Riley lived in a decaying house on High Street, and Maggie had not been inside for many years, not since old Goodman Riley's funeral, a thing she was not proud of. She should have looked in long ago. Riley had been a sailor in his youth and later an employee of one of the warehouse firms near South Beach Street, and Azariah had known him well.

When she went to the front door no one answered the knock, so she picked her way around to the back, through a yard thick with weeds and tangled vines. After much waving at the windows she attracted the old woman's attention and the door was opened. Widow Riley leaned on a cane, beckoned to her, smiling broadly, obviously delighted to have someone call. Maggie stepped inside the smoky kitchen and was appalled at the condition of the house. It was difficult to keep the expression off her face.

The widow was completely deaf and could not read or write. But conversation was possible because she could read lips to an extent, the only way she'd gotten along for years. She found a pair of grimy spectacles, put them on and peered at Maggie, saying she would put on a kettle for tea, and yes, she felt very well. Her speech was slurred and her clothes were soiled and smelled a bit.

The main trouble she had, she said, was that she was forgetful. Too often she misplaced the specs and could not find them for days.

Maggie insisted she sit, and made the tea herself. She discovered that the old woman lived in two rooms, the kitchen and what had been a study. The rest of the house was unused, dusty and uncared for. Much of the furniture was covered with rotting cotton sheeting and the stairs creaked alarmingly when she hurried up; the upper floor was the same, dusty and empty.

Conversation was not extensive, but Maggie learned that there was no key to the house. It had been lost years ago, and next time she came, Widow Riley said, she must simply walk in and announce herself. The chimney was sooted up and there was much danger of fire because of it. The roof leaked also and the siding, especially on the north side of the house, was falling into ruin. Widow Riley did not even know about it. She stayed in the kitchen by the fire day after day, fumbling with her knitting and dreaming.

Soon after, when Maggie saw Wager and told him what she'd seen, he was shocked. He would speak to a group of men from the village, he said, and organize them to repair the pressing damage to the house. The chimney could not be ignored; if the house caught fire it might take others on the street.

Azariah was also surprised to hear that the house was in such bad condition. He had been passing it for years, he said, and had not noticed. He was curious why she had happened to call and Maggie said she'd thought about the old woman and it was a spur of the moment decision. She looked over Azariah's shoulder as she said it and saw Wager smile.

Later she thought to herself that she was learning to dissemble.

Wager was as good as his word and in several days

101

the chimney was swept and the siding replaced by volunteers led by him. Maggie and a few of the neighbor women cleaned the first floor of the house, scrubbing and polishing, to the widow's astonishment. Other men cut and piled a huge amount of wood under the back sheds and filled the kindling box to overflowing.

When the others had finished and gone, Maggie climbed to the second floor and cleaned one of the bedchambers. The room had little furniture, a bed and washstand, but the bed was sturdy though the pad had rotted through long since. It could easily be replaced. And since the widow could no longer climb the stairs anything they put in the room would be safe from prying eyes.

The Riley house was not ideal as a meeting place, but was probably the best the town could offer. It was very nearly impossible for two people who were not married to each other to be together undisturbed or undiscovered for any length of time. The house had several things to recommend it, being very close by, and there was no chance of the widow overhearing them. Maggie would make a practice, she said, of calling on the old woman frequently so that if others noticed her entering the house it would cause no comment.

Wager was able to come to the house from Dover Court, the next street to the north. It was possible to walk along the fences unseen.

Nearly a week passed before she and Wager had a moment alone in her kitchen to whisper together. "Come to the widow's house tomorrow," he asked, "in early afternoon?"

She nodded, feeling the flush of excitement burn her cheeks. Tomorrow!

She sent Becky to the boatyard with hot food the next day and walked immediately to the widow's house, let herself in and sat with the old woman for half an hour with tea. When Wager appeared it was necessary to distract the widow so that he could slip through the kitchen when her back was turned, an easy thing to do.

Maggie excused herself then as soon as possible, left the widow sitting by the fire and went quickly upstairs.

It was the first time they had been alone since the little hut, the day she'd fallen into the creek, and suddenly her boldness gave way to fear as she faced him, wondering whether he felt the same now. But he took her into his arms immediately.

"It's been forever! I couldn't have stood it another day!"

Seeing and holding him was hugely different from the shadowy dreams and daily wool-gathering, the glances and secret finger-touches. It was a heart-hammering thing and for long moments she stood with him, her thoughts like a crazy-quilt pattern. She received his kisses with increased desire, telling herself at the same time that she must be sensible—but knowing in her heart that sanity had long since fled. She was here in this house with Wager because she wanted to be.

He had brought a new pad for the bed and sat her down. "The deaf cannot hear, of course," he said, "but they can feel vibrations."

"I promise not to pound my shoe on the floor."

He laughed, sat beside her and took up her hand. "I've been wondering what it would be like, being alone with you."

"And I the same."

"I feel a bit awkward—I mean, this is new to me."

She leaned to him and kissed his cheek. "There's a bridge to cross, and when we're over it everything will be better." She laughed with him. "And a bridge brought us together, didn't it!"

"I bless that bridge every second of my life." He laid her back and leaned on an elbow beside her, looking down. His finger traced the outline of her cheekbone and he bent and kissed her lightly. "But it didn't start with the footbridge, not with me. I think I've been in love with you for years."

"And never said a word?"

"Never dared to say one. Never dared to touch you." He kissed her again. "But I wanted to."

She lifted her hands up and pulled him down. "I want you to."

He slid both arms about her and they lay together very closely. He'd been in love with her for years? Then it was not a sudden whim on his part; the knowledge made her feel more at ease, though it was difficult to examine her own past feelings. Certainly she had been drawn to Wager, but of course had not once allowed herself to think about love.

And it was equally difficult to think ahead, and it might be better not to try. Let the future take care of itself and live only for today, for the moment. It was certainly more comforting.

The room was dim; it had only two small windows and one was partly boarded up. The ceiling was dark, of rough, unplaned wood where they had repaired the roof and not bothered to finish the inside room, since it was unused. The walls had been papered many years ago and it was curling and peeling in the corners.

She rolled onto her back as Wager began to undress her, kissing her neck and breasts. Then he slid out of his coat and pushed it onto the floor, sat up and removed his shoes.

"There is never enough time," he said softly. "When must you go?"

"I'd rather not think about going."

"You're a remarkable woman, Maggie. I know I'm not good enough for you, but I'm happy to be here."

She smiled, putting her arms about him. "Let's make a pact between us."

"A pact?"

"Yes. For peace of mind we never touch each other except when we're here in this room."

"That might be hard to keep."

"But it'll be easier if we agree. Then when you're in my kitchen we can be strangers."

"Perhaps you're right. Very well, a pact." He kissed her lingeringly, holding her close.

It was all different and yet the same; she was able to put Azariah out of her mind completely. He belonged to the other house, to another life. This was more fleeting, with no future, but she must not think ahead. She allowed Wager to remove her skirt and petticoats, then she closed her eyes and gave herself over to his kisses and his love. She could hear the wind in the trees outside the house; now and then a branch scraped along the boards, and once a gust of wind sent rain spattering against the panes, but they were far-off things. She was conscious only of closeness as they moved together. Love seemed to fill her being and the sweet urgency that came at last to flood her with contentment was his also. They lay in each other's arms for a very long time . . . until at last he stirred, whispering that it must be late.

With great reluctance she allowed him to help her dress again, wishing for time to stop. And when she was dressed and off the bed she clung to him. "I don't want to let you go."

"One of us must be strong—I think it should be you."

"Would you stay if I asked?"

"Probably, so please don't ask."

Maggie sighed. "I'll go down to the kitchen first. I don't feel so strong."

Widow Riley was dozing in her chair by the fire, which was a bed of glowing coals. Maggie beckoned to Wager and he hurried down, kissed her lightly and went out the back door.

She let herself out the front. Don't think, she told herself, especially of tomorrow; what was important was *now*. Yesterday was past and tomorrow not here yet. It seemed to go against the grain of every proverb and rule she'd been taught, but she was in love and rules didn't matter. They were made by men, though men pretended they were direct from the Almighty.

She went across Dover Court to Pearl Street. Above all, she must not be sorry. From now on she was two people, Azariah's wife and Wager's lover. What fey tricks fate played, and why had it singled her out? Perhaps because she was receptive; she hadn't been conscious of desire outside her marriage but maybe it had been there lying just beneath the surface, waiting to roil her heart. And it had. Blessed fate!

Enoch Quant sat in the ordinary with a pint before him and a scowl on his dark face. "There'll be an end of it, you mark my words," he said to Ben Robb and a group of fishermen who regarded him from beneath drawn-down brows. He tapped his finger on the bar. "I gi' them two, maybe three years, and there'll be an end."

"End of what?" Ben asked.

"What'd I say? An end o' shipbuildin'. Right here in Connecticut. King's law, that's what it'll be."

A sailor asked, "So that's why you're gettin' out, Enoch?"

"'Course it is." Enoch raised his glass. "I'm a good subject of th' king, ain't I? Him bein' new on the job in a manner of speakin'." Enoch laughed at his joke.

"They say he'll be a good king," someone said.

Ben Robb leaned on the bar and nodded to them. "It tires a man sometimes, being a good subject, but the king's the king, I say. Does Azariah think the same's you?"

Enoch shrugged. "I guess not. Me'n Az never thought the same on anything. We don't even spit in the same wind. Az lissens to 'is wife. Maggie's got the britches."

"Damn good-lookin' woman," Cephas Foot said. He was a fisherman on shore because of the fog, a husky, dark man with hulking shoulders. He fixed Enoch with a squinted eye drawn into a corner. "But you dead wrong about ships, Enoch. They's no law against fishin'."

Enoch grunted. "Maybe not." He drank the rest of the pint and shoved the glass across the bar, saw Ben Robb's look and fished out a coin. "Azariah's goin' to pay me, he says, but I ain't seen a shilling."

"Az does what he says," Ben remarked.

"Ay, when it suits him. When it suits 'im. Take it or leave it, he says to me about the boatyard."

"That's hard to believe, Enoch. Not Az."

"Well, in effect he did. Maybe not in them words, but it was take it or leave it all right. We don't need you no more, shove off."

Ben Robb looked at Cephas, who raised his shoulders an inch. Ben wiped the bar and shook his head, winking. Enoch used his mouth more than most and no man knew which way his acid would flow.

Enoch said, "He got two sons, y'know, so it's three against one. If I don't take the money they'll squeeze me out right enough." He looked from one to the other of them and tipped up the pint.

Cephas asked, "What you going to do then?"

"Do when?"

"When you get out of the boatyard."

"Oh, I 'spect I'll buy a fishin' boat and go out alongside you."

Cephas blew out his breath and snorted. "The hell you say! You'd drown yourself the first day!"

"Not me!"

Ben Robb asked, "You ever do any fishing, Enoch?"

"Naw. Maybe I'll buy me a tavern like this one."

Ben chuckled and filled his pipe. He regarded Enoch narrowly, wondering why the man was so evasive. Enoch had always been a hard nut to crack. Maybe because there was no meat inside.

Enoch finished the pint and peered through a window. It was dark. Rain dribbled down the panes and a horn was blowing its mournful tune over near the warehouses. He pushed away from the bar. "I'll say g'night . . ."

He walked unsteadily to the door, pulled his coat closer about him and went out.

Cephas said, "I don't think Azariah done it like he says. But if I was Az I'd have pushed him out a damn long time ago."

"Anybody but Az would have."

Chapter Ten

When Marie went to meet David the second time it was easier. She came from the boatyard, hurrying as fast as she dared lest she cause comment, turned into Summer Street and ducked along the fence. David was at the door, grinning at her, slapping her bottom as he kissed her.

He hustled her up the stairs to his room and immediately pushed her onto the bed, jumping beside her. Marie sat up instantly. "Wait a bit!" Where were the kisses now? The soft words?

David pulled her down, arms about her. He whispered urgently, "We haven't the time for foolery, have we?" His hands were at her bodice.

She didn't think it was foolery and she found a stubborn resentment welling up inside her. Was that all he wanted—to get atop her? She pulled his fingers away and saw the eager expression on his face change to petulance. He said, "I thought you wanted to see me . . ."

He was pouting exactly as she'd seen her sister and brothers do when they were small and denied something they wanted. She said, "I'm not a doxie!" She had overheard the term and knew it meant a loose woman. His eyes widened; then he was all apologies and kisses. He had only rushed her because of the limited time they had together.

She sighed, curled into his arms as her heart pounded, and kissed him back with ardor. He lay beside her, kissing her cheeks, her lips and her chin, rubbing noses, then kissing her neck as she giggled. He lightly bit her breasts through the cloth and his hands roved her body. She writhed, clutching him close and rolled onto her back. How she loved him!

He slipped atop her pulling her skirts up, and her heart began to race. The gentleness left his fingers and he became urgent suddenly and when he entered her, thrusting hard, she moaned. Her knees came up and the pain was gone as she clung to him as if she were drowning—and was all at once astonished at the moaning ecstasy that flooded her as he moved gently . . . then more quickly. Nothing had prepared her for the exquisite sensation, and she trembled in his arms, seeking his kisses, panting, gasping. His thrusts were hard and he panted in her ear and the bed creaked alarmingly.

Marie ran her legs over his and locked her heels around them, holding him when he would have moved away. He chuckled and writhed against her as she made little noises in her throat and pulled his head down to kiss her.

Rubbing her nose with his, he grinned. "So it's different today, is it?"

She nodded, seeking his mouth. Everything was different today, and always would be. She would look back on these moments as the real beginning of her life, the flowering of her body.

When he pushed at her she let him go. He rolled and slid off the bed, saying he had to go into the town on army business. He looked down at her with a smile, then sat and untied her bodice, opening it and baring her breasts. Marie caught her breath as he kissed them, one after the other, taking the nipple and half the breast into his mouth. She twisted, then pulled at him, wanting him again.

"You're more than I hoped for," he said.

She smiled, gazing at his lips.

"Come again tomorrow."

"You know my time isn't my own. I will if Mother lets me."

"Well, you can try." His hand roved over her shoulders and down across her breasts. "I have some news for you."

"What?"

"I'm going to resign my commission and go back to London."

Her eyes rounded. He was going back to—

He said, "I've just had a letter from my father. He wants me to come and join his firm. So I'm going to leave the army—" He bent and kissed her.

She stared at him in dismay.

He paused and smiled. "But I want to take you with me."

She took a long breath of relief. "Go to London!"

"Of course. We can be married in—anywhere, Boston maybe. It wouldn't do to perform the ceremony here, would it? Then we'll take ship and—"

"David! Go off to London. What would I do there?"

"Be a beautiful lady, of course." He squeezed her breasts. "Come, get up and get dressed. I must go into town."

"Can't we talk about—"

"There's an inspection to prepare for, and I must put in my papers for release." He smiled and lifted her up. "You must come again tomorrow."

"If I can." She wriggled back into his arms, but he slid off the bed.

"Tomorrow."

"Can we talk then?" She fastened the bodice.

"Yes, of course."

"I'll try to come."

"Very well. I'll be waiting in hopes." He embraced

her. "My little flower, my dearest darling . . ." He pulled her erect and smoothed her clothes as she fluffed her hair and retied the ribbon. He led her down the stairs and kissed her warmly at the back door, whispering goodbyes.

Marie walked home feeling a glow about her. David had promised they'd be married and go to London! It was a thing to savor and comprehend a little at a time. Such a long journey was a tremendous undertaking— and to be married! Lord! Of course the marriage would be more acceptable when he was no longer in the army; her father might not object at all then, especially when he saw how much they loved each other. Of course it was a question of time. David had seemed to want to go immediately, had mentioned Boston. Well, it would work itself out. It had to.

When she reached home she sat on the bench by the front door to calm herself and get her composure back. Her hands still trembled, and her mother and Becky were both so discerning that they would surely notice her excitement. She must keep it hidden for the time being, deep inside.

Of course she would not be the first girl to marry a Britisher, but surely the first in Canaan. She could expect a wave of gossip and double-meaning talk, even though David was no longer an officer. But when they went across the ocean it would be left behind forever. She tried to imagine how they would live, their house and the newness . . . the parties and teas . . .

She looked at the sky as the rain began to come down hard. Droplets made circles in the brown pools of water in the street. It would probably be a month or two before the wedding could take place, and in that time she would have to cut and sew a dress and plan the arrangements . . .

With an effort she forced the exciting thoughts from

her mind, told her throbbing heart to be quiet, and went inside. When she saw David next she would have to discuss with him how they should tell her family. It must be soon. It was going to be impossible for her to control her raging emotions very much longer.

Even as she entered the kitchen, Becky eyed her.

The next day was unexpectedly warm and no one went to the boatyard with food. The day after, Brayton appeared near midday to change his breeches and stockings, which were soaked because he had unloaded water-soaked vegetable sacks from a wagon. He stayed to have a bite to eat, then took a parcel to the boatyard on his way back to the store.

It was three days before Marie was able to hurry down Summer Street to the broken fence and slip inside. But the back door of the house was latched, and David did not meet her. Though she rapped and rattled the door, no one appeared.

She stamped her foot in annoyance; something had kept him from the house. She sighed and turned away. Probably she should expect it would happen from time to time; he would never do it deliberately.

She walked home deep in thought, slightly surprised at the intensity of her disappointment. How quickly he had come to be the most important, and certainly the most exciting, thing in her life. It was a cold day but not raining so he was probably out drilling his men in the meadow, making up for the days of downpour. The thought was comforting. She would see him tomorrow, if her mother allowed.

Becky was the only one home when she arrived, busy at the hearth with a stew in a large pot. She was muttering under her breath as she tried to adjust an obstinate pot hook. She paid no attention as Marie took up a hand loom and straightened a handful of hemp and coarse flax to weave into a grain bag. The bags were used in the spring to pack away blankets, clothes and other cloths in a cedar chest.

When Becky had the fire going to her satisfaction, Marie asked, "Where's Mother?"

"Gone to visit the Widow Riley, I expect. You're back soon."

Marie shrugged. "I didn't feel like walking on the beach."

"Is it raining out?" Becky went to the window.

"A little."

Becky turned about and gazed at her. "Will you watch the stew for me?"

"Yes, why?"

"I want to go out for a minute, before Mother returns." Becky hurried to the front room and pulled a cloak from the hall rack. Without another word she opened the front door and disappeared.

Marie stared in surprise. Such a thing had never happened before. Where was Becky going in such a hurry, in the rain? She rose and opened the door and looked toward the town, but no Becky. Then she saw her.

Becky was running in the opposite direction!

Standing on the porch, Marie put her hands on her hips, watching her sister. Only a short way north was William Lane, the north end of town, and beyond that was nothing but woods and fields. Becky's action was so unexpected!

The cold began to bite at her and she moved inside. Shaking her head in bewilderment, she went into the kitchen, lifted the pot lid and stirred the stew absently, her thoughts returning to David. He had been at the house every other day that she knew about, but he had said something about an inspection. Perhaps another officer was coming from Boston or somewhere to make an inspection. That was very likely, and his time might not be his own.

She sat and took up the loom, fingers flying, thinking about the wedding. Marie Urfe . . . that would be her name. It didn't quite have the same lilting sound as her own, but that was nothing. He was going to work in his father's firm? She hadn't asked what kind of firm. She didn't even know if David was rich or poor, but of course if he was an officer he must have money or position; an officer had to have one or the other.

She really knew very little about him. But she had plenty of time to learn, a lifetime in fact.

Remembering the stew, she got up and stirred it again.

An hour passed until the door opened and Becky scurried in, hung up the sopping cloak and came breathless to the kitchen. "Is Mother still away?"

Marie nodded. "Now who's meeting someone?"

"Well, goodness! I'm almost seventeen, you know." Becky looked down. "I'd better change my shoes."

"What's his name?"

Becky strode to the stairs. "Louis Boyer." She hurried up and Marie heard her clattering about. She'd never heard the name Boyer. It could be no one who lived in Canaan. She went to the stairs and called.

"Where did you meet him? Is he a seaman?"

"No. He's a Frenchman." Becky came downstairs. "But don't you tell anyone. It's a secret."

"Why?"

"Because the red ants will get after him. I told you, he's a Frenchman from Canada. He works at cutting wood." She stirred the stew and built up the fire. "He's trying to get a ship back to France. Orlow Gordon is helping him. Lordy, Marie, he's so handsome!"

"But, a Frenchman! Does he speak English?"

"Yes, of course." She began to describe Louis, telling of his compliments and the way his eyes looked at her. In the middle of it the front door opened and Maggie entered, pulling off a soaking coat.

Becky whispered, "Remember, not a word!"

That night Marie lay in bed unable to sleep, thinking of David. She was not too young for marriage; other girls were wedded at fifteen, but her parents might well protest her going off to London. Of course she had to go somewhere—wherever her husband lived. Would they seriously object, even forbid her to marry him?

If they did, could she run off with him? So much depended upon him, and she'd discussed almost nothing with him. He'd merely said he was leaving the army and would marry her.

It was a great deal, but not enough. Not nearly enough for dreaming.

A new storm came in the night and by morning it was pouring rain, so that no one left the house except Brayton, who ran most of the way to the store. Azariah, Morgan and Junius remained, grumbling and pacing the rooms like so many caged tigers; Morgan stood at the windows glaring at the weather as if it were something personal, inflicted just on him.

Marie worked at her usual tasks, at the loom and at sewing, unable to dredge up an excuse to get out. What would David think when she stayed away day after day?

She listened to the men talk, mostly about boats and ships and the British blockade and what ideal weather it was for running past out to the open sea. Jeremiah Chace's schooner was nearing completion, Morgan said, and the hardest work was done. He and Junius had long ago put the first streak around the hull and the other planking had been fitted and the tree-nails trimmed. Junius had been caulking and scraping for a week. The better she was scraped the faster she'd go through the water.

Morgan had decided to paint her black, maybe with a brown stripe and a bit of yellow between the wales, but dark was the ticket, to be as nearly invisible at night as could be.

The Boston papers, Azariah said, were talking of men using copper to sheath the bottoms of ships to discourage worms, but it was terribly expensive and scarce. Tallow, resin and brimstone would have to do for the schooner.

Jeremiah had decided to call her after his wife, Annora, and had hired men to carve the stern counter, putting in a few scrolls as well. Listening, Marie decided it was a pretty name, and hoped it would be lucky for her brother.

The weather kept them inside for nearly four days and caused much flooding in the streets and a few leaks in the roof. Marie begged to be allowed to carry food to the boatyard the first day it let up, saying she needed the exercise, and her mother agreed. Becky was sent to Eli Burley's store and Maggie remarked that she would visit the Widow Riley early in the afternoon to see how she'd fared through the storm.

Marie hurried through the town to the yard and did not stay a moment. The rain might break upon them again at any time. She ran back across the bridge and along Fort Street. Her heart was pounding when she turned into Summer Street and slipped through the fence.

But the house was still locked and no one answered her rapping.

She sat on the porch and cried in frustration. Where was David? Why had he not managed to send her a note if he was unable to meet her? She sat for half an hour, hoping against hope that he would appear, but he did not. Then she rose and picked her way into the soggy yard to look up at his windows. They were small, blank apertures without curtains or drapes and looked very lonely. She bit her lip and stared at them, wondering why the curtains had been taken down. Perhaps to be washed.

Her heart heavy, she returned home, changed her wet shoes and sat in the kitchen with the loom, staring into the fire. Her mother was still out and Becky was upstairs; should she confide in Becky, ask her opinion? After all, Becky was nearly two years older.

It was terribly disappointing not to see David, and even more disconcerting, because of his declarations of love, that he had not written to her. A note could be passed; it would be difficult for her, but should be easy for him. Why had he not done it?

Becky noticed her mood as soon as she came into the kitchen. "What is it—has something happened?"

"No, nothing." Marie busied herself with the loom. It would be wise to chatter of other things, she thought. "Have you seen Louis again?"

"No—I went by the cobbler shop but he wasn't there, of course. Orlow says he stays in the woods."

"I saw several ships anchored offshore."

"Yes, I saw them too but Orlow says they're bound for the Orient. He wants Louis to go there and get another ship, but Louis will not." She shook her head with a grim expression. "I think Louis is a daredevil. He thumbs his nose at the soldiers."

"He sounds very exciting."

Becky smiled. "More exciting than anyone else in this dull little village."

Smiling inwardly, Marie said nothing. After a bit she put away the loom, got out the iron and affixed it to a hook and tong, then laid out the ironing on the table-board. She was finishing the work when her mother returned, flushed and smiling from the cold street.

"It feels like snow."

"Come and sit by the fire," Becky said. "I'll put the kettle on. I'd like a bit of tea myself. How is the widow?"

Maggie shrugged. "Her joints are stiffening, I think, but it's the chill. When it's too cold she doesn't go out to the shed to fill the woodbox. Did you spool the thread, Marie?"

"Not yet, Mother."

"Well, it can wait. What shall we have for supper?"

Marie had to force herself out of a feeling of listlessness, to join in the conversation, to carry on with her normal tasks, and it was trying, but easier when the men returned after dark.

Morgan was full of talk about the schooner. The carved counter was ready for installation, the two masts had been delivered that day, early in the morning, in fact. And each bore a broad arrow that had to be planed off quickly before Enoch saw it. The arrow was the customary mark of the British navy, placed on trees to be reserved for their hired crews. The navy required the best, of course, and Morgan was delighted to steal a march on the king.

Azariah chuckled as well. "We burned the shavings in the stove. A tree is only a tree and now no king's inspector can say aught."

"But it's counter to the law," Maggie said. "You could be fined or imprisoned!"

"Where's the evidence?" Morgan asked with an innocent look. "You may search the ship, my lord, but there's not a broad arrow in the yard." He held out his wrists. "Else take me away."

Becky giggled at his play-acting and Maggie said,

"What about Enoch? He might inform on you just for meanness."

Azariah nodded. "We took care that it didn't happen. Junius kept him busy with an argument while the planing was done. You've no fools for sons, Maggie dear."

Junius said, "Speaking of the soldiers, there's a new officer in town. Did you hear?"

Marie stared at her brother, feeling suddenly icy. She heard her mother ask, "What d'you mean? What about Ensign what's-his-name?"

"Ensign Urfe? He's been transferred," Junius said, to Marie's horror. "I heard it from Goodman Robb's hired boy. The new one is called Illingsworth, he said."

Marie leaned against the doorway feeling ill. The unexpected words struck into her like spears piercing her body. David transferred! Where had he gone? Would she see him again? Her world had suddenly collapsed. She slid onto a chair and bent her head over a skein of yarn, praying no one would notice her. She knew she was pale and she twisted the yarn, gritting her teeth against the terrible faintness that seemed about to overwhelm her.

Chapter Eleven

Becky discovered, not entirely to her surprise, that Louis figured in her thoughts most of the time. She had gone walking in the woods with him once since he'd come to her home at night and they'd talked and finally held hands for a short time, and on her leaving Louis had kissed her. It was little more than a peck on the cheek, but she'd thought about it for days.

He affected her differently from the other young men of the town, and she thought it was not only because he was from a different culture, but he had a different outlook, one not so provincial. He talked of France and Europe as if they were just over the horizon and he treated her as if she were very important, a woman and not a girl. And he listened when she talked. Her father and brothers did not always do that.

The day the storm finally retreated he was in her yard again at dark, astonishing her as he had the last time, grinning at her startled expression. "But I had to come, *chérie*. I had not seen you for an eternity!"

She led him away from the path into the deep shadow of the house, and at once his arms were about her. Becky did not hesitate an instant, returning his kisses with the same fervor. She would think tomorrow; she would worry tomorrow, if it came to that.

His kisses made her knees weak and she pushed against his chest at last to gain a respite from the whirling emotions that filled her mind. She should not be feeling this way about a man who was about to take ship for far places. He laid his cheek on hers and she felt the strength of his arms, the pulse throbbing at his temple, and the warmth of him.

He said, "I don't want to leave this place—the promised land."

"You mean Canaan?"

He kissed her softly. "No, I mean you. I don't want to leave you."

"But if you stay here . . ."

His mouth slid over hers to stop the words. In a moment he whispered, "Do you want me to go, *chérie*?"

She shook her head. It was the truth, foolish and impractical as it was; she felt a closeness with him, something that no one else had aroused in her. And she had known him such a short time!

He said, "I don't think I can go without you. My heart would not permit it."

"But Louis—the danger!"

"There is only one solution."

"What do you mean?"

"You must come with me."

She pushed back and stared at him in astonishment. "Go with you?"

"Why not?" He pulled her into his arms and kissed her. "It is not so—"

The back door of the house creaked open and her mother's voice called, "Becky—are you all right?"

Louis dropped his arms instantly and she stepped quickly to the path. "Yes, Mother."

"What are you doing?"

"Just—looking at the sky."

There was a pause, then her mother said, "Don't take a chill."

"Yes, Mother."

The door closed and she ran back to Louis. "I must go in."

"Yes." His arms closed about her. He kissed her, then let her go. "Think about it, *chérie*." He faded into the dark.

Becky dreamed of it every moment afterward. In bed she stared into the gloom, hearing Marie toss and turn, and thoughts of Louis filled her—go off on a ship with him! Was it possible?

Of course it was possible; it could be done, but could she do it? Louis thought she could, but then Louis was a daring, laughing man, probably afraid of nothing on earth, willing to tempt the gods, eager to face whatever came. And wanting her.

It was all so sudden she could hardly believe her feelings. But when she was with him it all changed in a twinkling; then everything was easy. The mountains leveled and the ocean seemed a pond. But away from him doubts piled up to the sky. Did she love him? Did he love her? He had said so many other things but not those words. . . .

She slept finally, and when morning came into the room, pale and cold, she sat up conscious of nothing but the memory of Louis's lips on hers and his arms about her, and she felt lonely.

Marie pushed out of bed, her face strained, deep blemishes under her eyes as if she hadn't slept well. When Becky mentioned it, Marie shrugged and turned away, mumbling that she'd had bad dreams.

The day passed, an ordinary, easily forgotten day, but at night Louis was in the yard again, waiting for her. Becky went out quietly, closing the rear door of the house with care so that no one would notice her absence and she might steal an extra moment with him.

Her joy at seeing him was exquisite; she rushed into his arms eager for his kisses, but when he asked she had no answer for him.

"Give me time to think," she said.

"I understand."

"Are the soldiers hunting you?"

He laughed. "They cannot find me."

"You are so positive."

"I know the soldiers. They are lazy idlers and do nothing if they are not pushed into it. All soldiers are the same, *chérie*. They will catch me only if someone informs."

"How many know you are in Canaan?"

"Very few."

"Enough."

"You, most of all."

Sighing, she nestled close. "I must go inside—"

"I will come again tomorrow." He kissed her lovingly. *"Au revoir, chérie."* In a moment he was gone.

When she returned to the kitchen Wager Tanfield was there, talking with Azariah. He smiled at her as she went past and she heard him ask why Marie seemed so downcast. Her mother replied that Marie was often a moody child. Azariah said there was nothing wrong with Marie. They were all being foolish.

But that night when they went to bed, Becky lay still, unable to fall asleep as she thought about Louis—and from across the room she heard odd sounds. Was Marie crying?

As silently as she could, she slipped out of bed and padded to Marie's bedside. Marie *was* crying. Becky sat on the edge of the bed. "What is it?"

Marie looked around at her. "Nothing."

"You're crying because of nothing?"

"I'm not crying."

Putting out her hand, she touched Marie's face.

Tears. "No, of course not. A little rain came in the window."

Marie turned onto her stomach and pulled the blankets over her head.

Gently Becky said, "Everyone's noticing that you're acting strange. Even Goodman Tanfield spoke of it this evening. What's happened?"

It took a dozen minutes before Marie would talk, and then the words spilled out in a rush. Her liaison with Ensign Urfe and her crushed dreams . . . his promises and the sudden transfer without a note to her, not a word!

Becky hugged her sister, murmuring phrases she hoped would be comforting. Little Marie had suffered her first broken heart but it would probably not be the last. Every girl languished through such experiences; they were usually not fatal, and though David Urfe was obviously a heartless creature she would get over him and all would be well.

Marie did not think so, but she got to sleep at last, and in the morning looked less tired.

The weather took a turn for the better. The skies cleared as a stiff breeze blew away the mists and it was hardly cold enough for her breath to turn to steam as Becky walked along Main Street toward the sparkling ocean.

At South Beach Street, near the wharves, she halted to stare out toward distant Long Island. A British frigate with all sails set was standing toward Block Island to the east, and several merchant ships were anchored offshore as several smaller craft moved among them. It was the most peaceful scene in the world, she thought, the kind of day to go on board one of those ships with Louis. . . .

She would have to leave the family behind. What would she say to them? What excuse could she have for running off with a man not her husband? And a Frenchman at that! What a scandal!

Would Louis marry her? If his words were not twisted as David Urfe's had been to Marie, he would. But it could not take place in Canaan. Not while the British sought him, and her family would not stand for a secret marriage.

There were so many problems, and all because she wanted to conform to the wishes of her parents and the demands of custom. If she simply ran off—

But to run off would hurt her family deeply, even if she were of marriageable age and considered a woman. Their neighbors would look askance at the Lynns in church or on the streets because they had a daughter who cared so little for the conventions, who actually dared to run away with a Frenchman she barely knew.

Put that way it was impossible.

But with Louis's arms about her it *was* possible. Could they understand that? She had a feeling her mother would.

Maggie noticed that Marie seemed upset at times but she did not suspect the implications, perhaps because her own life was full to bursting. She had the household to manage as always, and she had her other life. She met Wager twice a week, occasionally three times. The Widow Riley was never so well attended.

When she questioned Becky about Marie, Becky had avoided mentioning her sister's unhappy affair. She said to her mother, "I think she's just mooning. You know how she is—probably in some fancy."

Becky had been sworn to silence, a situation she did not approve of, but she was sure Marie would weather the storm that engulfed her. With her lofty, near-two year's seniority, Becky confidently believed nothing was seriously wrong that time would not heal. Marie would meet someone else and forget David Urfe.

Except that Marie did not.

As the rains came oftener no more trips were made to the boatyard; the men heated up their own meat on the days they were able to work, and Marie stayed indoors most of the time. She took up several knitting projects, Christmas presents for her father and brothers. That allowed her to sit by herself a great deal. She did what was asked of her with no complaints and thus Maggie had no reason to worry, though she often gazed thoughtfully at her daughter, wondering how to get closer to her.

The menfolk were less understanding, or less willing to put up with Marie's moods, and there were times when she ran out of the kitchen and up the stairs to burst into tears on her bed. Their rude teasing was more than she could bear, especially when it came close to hitting home as they speculated loudly that she'd been kissing some boy in the churchyard.

Maggie did her best to curtail the chatter. "Leave the girl alone. Let her get over it, whatever it is."

Azariah agreed, saying young girls got peculiar ideas in their silly heads and it was best to ignore them.

Morgan took small part in the usual banter, thinking to himself that little Marie seemed to have the same sort of look in her eyes that Sharon had in the times they managed to be alone. But it was obviously foolish to think that Marie was seeing someone because she was seldom out of the house. Their father was probably right.

Compared to Marie, Becky seemed complacent and utterly normal, easy to talk to and outgoing. Maggie had no inkling that Marie's apparent inner turmoil drew attention to her, and away from Becky.

However, Becky was well aware of it and took full advantage of it. When Maggie was off visiting the widow, Becky made hurried trips to the nearby woods to meet Louis. He had set up a tent shelter in a hollow; it was dry, not particularly warm, but she could be with him. On the days when the weather was bad it was frustrating. Days full of annoyances. Why had she not met Louis in the summer?

As Christmas approached Becky began to be aware that her sister was increasingly agitated and disturbed. She often cried at night when she thought Becky was asleep, and finally Becky could stand it no longer.

She got out of bed very late and went to Marie. "What in the world is it? Has David returned?"

Marie shook her head.

"Then what?"

"I—I can't tell you."

"Of course you can! We've always shared our secrets."

Marie's eyes grew huge in the gloom of the room. She blurted, "Becky—I think I'm pregnant!"

Becky felt as if she'd been struck a blow. She stared at her sister, unable to speak. Pregnant!

"I've missed my time—two weeks ago." Tears flooded her cheeks. "What can I do?"

Becky felt tears coming to her own eyes. She hugged Marie. Her brain seemed turned to jelly. What was there to do? Oh Lord—pregnant!

After a bit Marie said, "I've thought of going after him—I'm sure I could find him—"

"No, that isn't right." Becky tried to dry her eyes.

"And then we could be married. David wants to marry me—it's just that he was transferred."

"Maybe there's some other reason. Maybe you're not—"

"I know I am." Marie sighed deeply and rubbed her stomach. "I just know I am." The tears came again. "I want to find David."

Becky's mind was clearing; the terrible implications hung over them like a sword, but there had to be something they could do—there *had* to be! "You'll have to tell Mother," she said.

"Oh, Lordy, I can't!"

"You have to, Marie. She'll know what to do. How can you go on this way? She already knows there's something wrong."

"I think I'd die!"

Becky hugged her tightly. "She'll understand. I know she'll understand, and—"

"She'll tell Father."

Becky got up and pulled a blanket off the bed, draping it around her. She sat with her feet tucked up. "You told me, didn't you?"

"Yes, but—"

"Mother isn't your enemy, for goodness sake!" She cupped a hand about Marie's frightened face and brushed the dark hair back. "She'll know what to do and all the worry will be gone."

"Not all." Marie sighed as if her heart would break. "There's still the baby."

"That's a long time away. We can make up a story—" She had no idea what kind of story but she had to comfort Marie as best she could. "Promise me."

"Promise what?"

"That you'll tell Mother tomorrow."

Marie closed her eyes and hung her head. Becky slid an arm about the thin shoulders, holding her close. Marie was so defenseless, and the enormity of the crime that had been perpetrated upon her was so great—and worse, she had to bear it all. David was off somewhere, scot free. They sat on the bed, heads together for a long time, neither speaking. Marie's shoulders moved as she sobbed, but at last she gave a long sigh and looked up, tears glistening in her eyes. She nodded. "Yes."

"All right. Now go to sleep. It'll work out. You'll see." She kissed Marie's cheek again and slid off the bed, praying she'd done the right thing. She got into her own bed and stared into the gloom, thinking about Louis. How easy it would be for him to do the same to her, but it was impossible to believe he was capable of it. And yet Marie must have had similar thoughts about David. Men *did* have things their way. . . .

Of course so far she'd never allowed Louis to possess her completely, though God knew he'd wanted to, and she'd wanted him. Marie had been foolish in that respect, but she'd loved David, and trusted him.

Did she love Louis any less because she would not let him?

Becky sighed and turned uncomfortably. Louis had not pressed her, or begged her or pouted; he was as aware of the consequences as she. His only request was that she come with him to Europe. And she still had not made up her mind. It was such a great step!

She lay awake for more than an hour and got up twice to listen to Marie's breathing. Apparently her little sister was asleep, exhausted by the ordeal but relieved that she had told someone.

In the morning they breakfasted together and when the wooden bowls and spoons were washed and put away Marie seemed on the verge of speaking several times, but each time she hesitated, even when Becky motioned urgently. Then Maggie drew on a cloak and went out quickly, saying she wished to go to Eli Burley's store and back before it rained again.

When the door closed behind her, Marie sat with a deep sigh. "It's so hard to start. I don't know where to begin."

"Begin anywhere—just start talking."

"It's easy for you!"

Becky went to her, hugged her and said in a soft voice, "I don't mean to gnaw on you about it. I'm sorry."

Marie leaned against her. "I know he's somewhere thinking about me, Becky. It's the army that did it, not him. The army transferred him in a hurry so he couldn't write."

"That must be it."

"I know he'll write soon and tell me where he is."

"Of course he will."

Marie was silent for a moment. "Are you still seeing Louis?"

"Yes."

"Do you love him?"

Becky took a breath. "I think so—he wants me to go to France with him."

"To France!"

"I think he'd stay here if he could, but the redcoats would never permit it. There's too much strong feeling with the war just over and all. Anyway, he says he must get to France."

"Why? I suppose his family is there."

"More than that. He won't tell me why, but I know there's something else."

"That's very mysterious."

"Yes, it is. But he won't say a word about it except that he must go." She shrugged. "Something to do with the army maybe. Men can be odd—look at Morgan, how he's crazy to go to sea on the schooner."

Marie got up and moved to the rear window to look out. "It's raining again." She hugged herself. "And it's cold in here, too."

Becky went to the hearth; it wasn't cold in her opinion, probably just Marie's state of mind. But she put more wood on the fire, then filled a kettle and slid it onto the hook for tea.

The water had begun to boil when Maggie entered, doffing her wet cloak and hood. She had a clothful of vegetables, which she put into bins, and smiled when Becky offered her tea. She sat and stretched out her feet to the warmth.

Marie said, "Mother . . ."

Maggie turned, brows lifting.

"Mother, I have to tell you something."

Chapter Twelve

Maggie was shocked at Marie's hesitantly told story, but did her best to control her features. She saw immediately that Becky already knew the details and she realized at once why Marie had been acting as she had. The child was nearly beside herself with worry and guilt, an incredibly heavy load for a girl of fifteen to bear.

Becky's advice had obviously been the reason Marie had come to her, and she felt very proud that her daughters trusted her. The solution was something else again. To Maggie, David was gone and a solution was all that remained. Marie must somehow be extricated from the predicament and the easiest course was a medical one, some method that would get Marie to abort. But there was only one doctor in Canaan, Isaac Lunt, a middle-aged quack, and worse, a pillar in the church. She could envision him, red-faced and outraged at Marie's confession that she was going to have a baby without the benefit of marriage.

When she offered the suggestion Marie astonished her again, shaking her head. "I want the baby, Mother."

"Lordy! Marie!" Becky said. "You never said a word about that before!"

Marie faced them. "He's coming back. He promised me. And if he can't, I'll go to him."

Maggie put her arms about her daughter and said softly, "You have to face the chance he won't."

"But he will! He's going to resign from the army and come back for me. I know he will."

"He's run off—" Becky began and bit her lip as Maggie glared.

"All right, darling," Maggie said. "We'll all pray that he comes back."

Marie closed her eyes, her head on her mother's shoulder, feeling Maggie's arms tight about her. Thank goodness Becky had been right and her fears were all unjustified. Her mother *did* understand. There had been no storm and no shouting, and now the story was out, her foolishness and headstrong behavior—to say nothing of the moments of wild exhilaration with David. Her mother must realize there had been those.

The tea that Becky made had been forgotten, and now Maggie put the kettle back on the hook, her face mirroring troubled thoughts. A child out of wedlock! And Marie herself was but a child. When and if people heard, the entire town would be horrified. Yet there was a feeling deep within her that Marie had the right to choose. It was not a feeling, she realized, that would be shared by very many, perhaps not even Azariah, though she was sure he would defend his daughter. He would have to be told.

When she mentioned it to Marie the girl nodded. She had thought that far ahead, thank the Lord.

Becky poured the tea and they sipped it together sitting by the fire, a sad little group, Maggie thought, and quite different than before; they were the same people but she knew their relationship had changed subtly.

Marie was ill at ease, feeling that her mother had never looked at her in quite the same fashion, but it was not a look of judgment, rather one of compassion, and she began to feel very close to her. She began to have faith that a way would be found to have the baby and yet preserve them all. Her mother could move mountains if she wished; a way would be found. It *had* to be found.

Maggie said at last, "I will tell your father tonight, after you've all gone to bed. He may be difficult about it." She smiled at Marie. "If he is upset later make no reply. He'll be unhappy and frustrated . . ."

"What about the boys?" Becky asked.

"There's no need for them to know just yet. In a few months there'll be no hiding it, but for now—"

"Maybe she could go away, to Boston or—" Becky shrugged.

"I'll wait till David comes," Marie said firmly.

Maggie nodded, with a warning glance to Becky. "Let's see what your father says. He's a sensible man and when he gets over the initial shock we'll come to a decision."

The atmosphere of the house had changed, though they did their best to pretend nothing was amiss. Even Azariah noticed it, looking from one to the other over supper. "You're all acting as if someone's died. What's happened?"

Maggie said, "We've been discussing Christmas, that's all. It does add to the work."

Becky attempted to change the subject. "How is the schooner progressing?"

"Too slowly," Morgan said, making a face. "Mr. Chace was in the yard yesterday promising two six-pounders, but the Lord only knows where he'll get them."

Junius said, "He hinted at friends in Massachusetts."

"Pop guns," Azariah stated, turning down the corners of his mouth. "What good are six-pounders when the British have twenty-four?"

"It's speed—" Morgan began.

"Stop talking of guns," Maggie said petulantly.

"They're better than nothing," Morgan went on. "But I'd rather have swivel guns. Of course *they're* impossible to get." Suddenly his attention was drawn to his sister. "Have you been crying, Marie?"

"She does look peaked," Junius said, concerned.

Marie shook her head.

"She got a dash of pepper in her eyes," Becky said quickly. "Poor thing."

Morgan had not been sleeping well for weeks; the schooner was nearly completed and the nearer the time came the more his dreams were jumbled. He constantly saw himself clinging to a line as the slender craft heeled to a brisk wind, showing her heels to a British frigate. . . .

He slept in the same room with Junius and Brayton. When they were small their father had built four bunks against the walls, very much like those aboard some ships, and they were still using them. When he awakened again soon after getting to sleep, he slid out of the bed and pulled on breeches and shirt. There was no sense tossing and turning for an hour or more. He would go down to the warm kitchen, sit by the banked fire and further his plans for baffling the British. He had an idea that he could temporarily and at will change the schooner's outlines to make recognition difficult. If she looked different each time she was seen by the British it ought to confuse them.

When he started down the narrow steps he heard voices from the kitchen. His bare feet made no sound, and halfway down he paused, hearing an angry outburst from his father. Azariah growled that Urfe ought to be horsewhipped!

Urfe? Morgan frowned. Ensign Urfe was the only man of that name he'd ever heard of, and the ensign had been recently transferred. His mother's voice was low and insistent and Morgan could not make out her words. Why were they talking about Urfe? Curiosity got the better of him and he continued down the stairs to the bottom and stood close to the open kitchen door.

He was shocked to hear that Urfe had gotten his sister Marie pregnant and then gone off without a word to her!

His father paced the kitchen, stump rapping the wood floor, more angry than Morgan had ever heard him, and his words alone would have curled Urfe's spine and soul could he have heard them.

Morgan padded back upstairs, his thoughts whirling. Marie violated! Had Urfe raped her? His parents had not said so, but how else? Surely Marie would never voluntarily submit to him, a British soldier! Now it was suddenly clear why Marie had been withdrawn and upset these past weeks, and no wonder. The shame of being raped! God! He felt guilty all at once that they'd teased and made fun of her. He looked at the door of her room, wanting to go in and apologize. But he could not do that, of course. He was not supposed to know.

Pulling off his clothes, he slid into the bunk bed to stare into the dark. What would his father do? But what *could* he do? It would be Marie's word against Urfe's if it came to that. And Urfe would have the advantage, naturally. The more he thought about it the more his anger grew. Urfe had taken his pleasures and cast her aside to bear the guilt and shame.

It took hours to fall into a troubled sleep, and in the morning his anger was greater. He did his best to conceal it; after all, he'd been eavesdropping. He pretended a general irritability, but everyone else seemed to be preoccupied as well and no one noticed his gruffness.

By midday it began to snow, a feathery drifting that came down so lightly it took hours before it began to whiten secluded nooks. In the middle of the afternoon

Morgan made an excuse to walk into the town. The off-duty redcoat soldiers customarily hung about one particular grog shop just off South Beach Street. They were not welcome in Ben Robb's inn.

He asked the first soldier he came to about Ensign Urfe. "Has he been transferred?"

"That 'e has, but what do you care?"

"He owes me two pounds."

The soldier laughed. "Then you'll 'ave to go to Belford to collect, laddie."

"Belford!" It was a town nearly fifty miles west, almost to the New York line.

"Aye, Belford." The soldier yawned in his face. "Y'ought to know better than to loan anythin' to an orficer." He turned away.

Morgan went back to the boatyard in deep thought. Belford. He'd never been there but he knew a few who had; it was on the post road. Ensign Urfe was probably stationed in an army installation of some kind. It shouldn't be hard to locate an officer.

His father looked at him oddly when he returned to the yard but said nothing. There was plenty to do below decks on the schooner and he spent the rest of the day at various tasks, his mind far off. Could he bring Urfe back to Canaan and force a marriage? Probably not. He didn't want to, and he had no idea if Marie wanted him. The only thing to do with scum like Urfe was to grind him under his heel. Punish him severely and make sure he knew why. Whipping came to mind.

Morgan was under no illusions; he knew that if he openly harmed a British soldier, officer or not, he'd be arrested and charged and it would be years before he saw the light of day again. What he had to do must be done in secret.

And the first thing was to acquire a horse. It was not difficult. Luther Parkman, a carpenter who worked frequently in the boatyard, owned a fine sorrel mare. Morgan came to a quick agreement with him, after swearing him to secrecy, and Luther promised to have the mare ready that evening after dark.

The hardest thing was to get his hands on a pistol. Ben Robb owned several but was reluctant to loan one, and finally Morgan went to Jeremiah Chace. Mr. Chace had four pistols and when Morgan declared he had none and needed to practice against the chance of using one on the schooner, Chace quickly produced a sturdy horse pistol made by Sayers of London, complete with patches, powder flask and cast balls.

He hid the cloth-wrapped pistol and flask under the front steps of the house when he returned home after dark, late for supper. "I was talking and lost track of time," he told his mother.

"Well, sit down," Maggie said. "There's warm spoon meat and carrots and onions. Becky, put the kettle on again."

"Yes, Mother."

"Junius tells me you've got the rigging up, Morgan."

"Yes, wormed, parcelled and served."

"When will you launch her?"

Morgan shrugged. "Soon. Maybe a week." He glanced at his father, who nodded. The six-pounders Mr. Chace had delivered were waiting under canvas, hidden from prying eyes, including Enoch's, until the last minute. They'd sway them up onto the deck from the wharf at night. No coasting vessel would need guns and the schooner *Annora* was to masquerade as a coaster. Jeremiah Chace would see to those details.

Once launched and out to sea past the blockading squadrons the *Annora* would begin a career of mystery, based on speed and the dark of night. She would never appear in an American port again in daylight and never become acquainted with British customs officers. If they heard of her it would be only hearsay, a glimpse by some topman—it was to be hoped.

Morgan thought of these things as he ate, then sat staring into the fire. In all probability he would not be with the *Annora* on those voyages. Not if he punished Ensign Urfe and was seen doing it.

But that was for the near future. In the upstairs bedroom, alone, he arranged his only heavy coat, hanging it on a hook with a sheath knife looped on a belt underneath. In the pocket of the coat he shoved a wool cap that would be more snug and warmer than his usual tri-cornered hat.

In the kitchen he watched to see where his mother placed the last of the meat they'd had for supper. A little packet would be good to have thirty miles or so along the road.

But at last everyone went to bed. Marie went first, then Becky, and when he climbed the stairs he heard them talking in their room. Marie had gained a bit of color in her cheeks in the previous day or two. What a burden she'd been bearing! And her real hurdles were yet to come.

He smiled grimly. And so were Ensign Urfe's.

In bed with the candle snuffed he closed his eyes to wait. Junius and Brayton whispered for several moments, then both became still. He heard the house creak now and again as the warmth left it; somewhere outside, far off, a dog howled and another took up the gossip. When they stopped it was very still except for the distant sound of a horn, which meant that fog was stealing in from the sea.

He was patient for what he thought was an hour; it was probably two hours before midnight. He slid from the bunk in his stocking feet, drew on his breeches and shirt, buckled the belt about his lean hips and put on the coat. He went softly downstairs carrying his boots. Wrapping the meat and a chunk of bread by the light of a stub of candle, he thrust it into a pocket, pulled on the wool cap and laced up his boots by the front door.

He deliberated about leaving a note but decided against it. If all went well he'd be back in two days and they'd know from the manner of his going that he was on a definite errand. He was sure his mother would guess it. He blew out the candle.

Outside in the cold he shoved the patch box with a half dozen lead balls and the powder flask into his coat pockets, put the pistol in his belt and hurried along the street toward Luther Parkman's home. He met no one at all and every house was dark. Near the shops he saw old Charlie Larson, the lamplighter, placing his ladder against a pole, swearing softly to himself.

Luther's mare was where he'd said it would be, saddled and tied to the fence at the rear of the house, shying away as Morgan approached with soothing words. He mounted the horse, turned toward Fort Street, which ran directly into the post road, and forced himself to walk the animal across the bridge before he let her run.

Maggie woke early and lay awake for a few moments listening to Azariah's steady breathing, feeling vaguely uneasy. She put it down to her continuing concern about Marie, slid out of bed and dressed quickly in the cold.

She uncovered the coals in the kitchen and got a fire going again and as it crackled, gaining strength, she went to the back door and gazed out at the sky. It was overcast but not raining or snowing; the puddles in the yard looked frozen but the ground was dry. She went into the parlor and looked at the brass and mother-of-pearl clock Azariah had brought from England many years ago. It was just past six in the morning. Let them sleep another few minutes.

In the warming kitchen she mixed a thick cornmeal and milk porridge and poured it into a large pewter bowl to heat. She built up the fire and went back to the stairs; the chill was out of the air now and the house was creaking. She rapped on the stair rail with a wooden cup and went back to put the kettle on.

In several minutes Brayton came downstairs buttoning his shirt. "Why'd Morgan get up so early?"

"What? Morgan isn't up."

"Well, he isn't in bed." Brayton warmed his hands at the fire. "His coat's gone, too."

Maggie stared at her son. Morgan not in his bed? She hurried up the stairs and into the boy's room. Junius, half in his breeches, cleared his throat and said good morning. She barely nodded to him. Morgan's bed did not look slept in, and yet she'd seen him go upstairs last night.

She asked, "Did Morgan say anything to you?"

Junius frowned at the empty bed. "Where's Morgan?"

"You don't know?"

"No, of course not."

His coat was missing, as Brayton had said, and so were his boots. She heard Azariah getting up and ran into his room, closing the door behind her. "Morgan isn't in the house, Az. Did he say anything to you?"

"Say what? He isn't in the house?" He was astounded.

"Is there any reason to go to the boatyard so early?"

Azariah sat blinking on the edge of the bed. He shook his head. "I can't think of any. He's damned eager to get that schooner rigged, but—"

142

"I doubt if he slept in his bed last night." She sat beside him. "You don't suppose—"

"Suppose what?"

"That he's gone after that ensign, do you?"

Azariah stared at her. "Lord God, Maggie!" He grabbed his wooden stump and began to buckle it on. "It'd be the kind of wild thing he might do!"

She jumped up and went to the door. "That's what I was thinking." She opened the door, then shut it again. "How would he know where to go?"

"Oh, that shouldn't be hard to find out. Matter of fact, Morgan walked into town yesterday . . ." His eyes were round as he stared at her. "I wondered about that."

"Then he could have asked the soldiers."

"Yes." He nodded.

She came back to him. "But if he went after Urfe, how did he find out about Marie? Did you tell him?"

"No, certainly not!" He glanced at the door. "Maybe she did."

"I doubt it." Maggie sat on the bed again. "We've got to tell them something . . ."

"No, we don't." He patted her hand. "We can say we don't know what Morgan's up to, and it's the truth! Let them think it's something about the schooner."

She said with asperity, "What I'm worried about is what's happened to *him*! If he's gone after that man how did he do it? Do you think he stole a horse?"

Azariah shook his head helplessly. "Dammit, we don't know he went after Urfe. It might be something else—like Sharon. Maybe they ran off!"

Maggie said, "He went after Urfe. I know it. I *know* it."

"Well, *I* know one thing: Morgan can take care of himself. And better'n most. He's strong and quick and

143

he's smart too." He scratched his head. "Did you look around for a note?"

"There isn't one." She brooded. "He's not so smart if he went after that ensign. He'll be surrounded by soldiers! They might kill Morgan!"

"You're just worrying yourself, and you don't know what's happened. He may come walking in the door any minute."

Maggie dabbed at the starting tears and rose. "I suppose so. But it's the not knowing that's hard." She sighed and opened the door. Becky and Marie were on the stairs. She beckoned to Marie and went into the girl's room.

Marie had said nothing at all to Morgan and was startled to learn he had gone. Maggie said, "Then it's something about the schooner, I suppose . . ." She dredged up a smile. "Come on, let's get breakfast."

The sorrel mare was a willing horse, eager to run, and Morgan made very good time, though he knew it would take him until well into the next day to reach Belford. He walked the horse through each village along the way, not wishing to alarm light sleepers; because of galloping hoofs someone was liable to imagine an Indian raid.

Between villages the road was well marked, having seen much traffic during the summer. It was a post road and had been for nearly a hundred years. There were even a few milestones still leaning among the weeds. He sang to keep himself awake, and talked aloud of Sharon. Now and then he got down and walked alongside the horse to breathe her.

Exactly what he would do to punish Ensign Urfe was not clear in his mind, but it would be drastic. He wished he had one of the long leather whips some of the wagoneers carried. Then he'd cut the shirt off the man and mark his back so he'd never forget the occasion as long as he lived.

How he would get Urfe out of an army post or a military station was something he'd have to consider when he arrived and studied the situation. He had no idea what the army had built in Belford or why Urfe was there, but there had to be a way to reach him. There had to be.

By dawn he was well along the road and had met no one. He'd noticed several places where wagons were camped for the night and by daylight he noticed people were beginning to be up and about, making fires and preparing breakfasts. It reminded him that he was hungry. He opened the food he'd brought along and chewed the meat and bread, wishing for a bit of tea to wash it down.

He began to meet other travelers, men on horseback, a few wagons draped in canvas.

Several hours after dawn he stopped in a small village and went into the tavern to order tea with a drop of rum. "How far is Belford?"

The man behind the counter was stout with close-set eyes and a large nose. "How are you travelin'?"

"Horseback."

"Then it's maybe two hours. You got any news?"

"No . . ." He drank the tea and went on. By now the family had discovered he wasn't there and he started to feel guilty that he hadn't taken the time to write a note. They'd all be worried about him. He wasn't supposed to know about Marie, so what would they think? That he'd run off to sea? No, not with the schooner so near completion.

They'd guess where he'd gone. The closer he got to Belford the more certain he was that they'd know.

Belford was a two-penny town, only a cluster of shacks and stores and shops, then more shacks and a straggle of houses behind the stores. But on the slope of a hill north of the town was the army establishment, five long barracks with smoke rising from each one and a half dozen other buildings surrounding a flagpole.

Morgan's heart sank. How to pick out Ensign Urfe from all that? It was far more than he'd imagined. He knew it wouldn't do for a colonial to go into the camp inquiring for an officer; they'd probably throw him out, no matter what story he told. He looked down at his rough clothes. He'd never be able to claim a relationship, even friendship with Urfe. No one would believe him.

He sat the horse at the edge of the hamlet and watched a company of redcoats drilling in a field. Looking down the road he could see a half dozen red uniforms along the street; that meant the men got time off just as they did in Canaan. That might be the best way to confront Urfe. Watch for him to come into the village.

Morgan took off the wool cap and scratched his head. Of course it would mean he might have to stay nearby much longer than he'd intended, but no other idea presented itself to him. He looked at the sky, overcast but not threatening rain; he would sleep in the woods to save tavern rent.

Nudging the mare, he rode into the hamlet and halted in front of the ordinary with its sign of a bull surrounded by thistles. Two soldiers were sitting on the bench by the windows, smoking clay pipes. They stared at him as he dismounted and went up the steps.

One said, "Where you come from, Jocko?"

"Haynes," Morgan said promptly, naming the first town he could think of.

"Where's that?"

Morgan pointed vaguely toward the east. "That way . . ." He went past them into the tavern.

The innkeeper was surprised to see him; he lifted gray, bushy brows. "You travelin' this time o' year?"

"Come from Haynes," Morgan said again. "On my way t'New York Town. Hope t'get there before snow."

"You'd best hurry then. It's colder'n a bear's ass."

Morgan ordered a pint and looked around him. The room was even more plain than the tavern in Canaan, more undecorated in every way, except for the several regimental flags and coats of arms painted directly on the walls. It was obviously a gathering place for common British soldiers. The benches and tables, all bulky, heavy furniture, were scarred and unpainted and had doubtless seen many brawls and looked forward to more.

There was no one else in the room. It smelled of ale and urine and was barely heated. Morgan asked casually, "Where do the officers drink?"

The innkeeper's mouth turned down. He was a big man with black hair turning gray, a heavy paunch that stretched his brown apron tight, and sloping shoulders. He was probably an ex-redcoat himself, Morgan thought. Probably a noncommissioned officer who'd saved his pay and bought himself an inn in an army town. He squinted looking into the light.

"Cross the street there, sign with the cross."

The innkeeper busied himself restocking kegs; the liquid smelled like cider and now and again he paused to sip a bit and smack his lips. Morgan finished the pint, decided not to order another, and went to the window. Across the rutted street was a smaller, long, low building with a white sign on a sturdy pole in front, a red Maltese cross. It swung on chains and he could hear it squeak in the breeze.

That was where he might find Urfe.

As he stared at it, a pretty young red-headed girl appeared at the door and tossed a bucket of gray water into the drive that led to the rear of the tavern.

The innkeeper came from the back, breathing hard. "You got a mighty long ride ahead of you, friend." He wiped his hands on the apron. "Y'ought to go by boat."

"Well, yes, but I can't afford the fare," Morgan said. Most people traveled by ship or boat because of the miserable roads, and his excuse was weak but the innkeeper only shrugged.

He went out to the mare and rode back the way he'd come, eyeing the redcoat camp. He'd have to find a spot where he could keep the gate in view, to see when the soldiers were allowed to go into the town.

And then he'd have to find a way to keep watch on the tavern with the sign of the Maltese cross.

Chapter Thirteen

The morning dragged by and Morgan did not return. Maggie saw Azariah and Junius off to the boatyard, and Brayton to the store, and all promised to send her word at once if they learned anything at all.

After the kitchen chores were completed Becky looked out at the sky. The day was not warm, but not icy cold either, and she begged to be allowed to go into town to see if she could discover anything.

Marie wanted to go also, so both girls hurried off and Maggie sat by the fire, imagining every sort of danger—till she told herself she was being foolish. Az was quite right; Morgan was not a simpleton and was a match for most grown men, a thought that brought her back to danger again. She rose and set herself tasks to keep her mind from racing. Somehow Morgan had found out about Marie and had gone after Ensign Urfe. It was the only thing that made sense.

But Morgan was incapable of murder. If he had gone after Urfe it must be to punish him. The thought reassured her. Morgan would find Urfe, punish him somehow, perhaps by a beating, and come home. It was unthinkable that he would kill the man!

But the more she thought about it the more uneasy she became. Was Morgan angry enough to attack Urfe in the midst of his soldiers? He would probably not get away alive.

Morgan was not stupid. Only—what if Urfe recognized him? Beating or no, Urfe would set soldiers on his trail and they would never stop till they had him in charge—or till he was dead.

Lord! Morgan had embarked on a course that could only lead to disaster! No matter what he did the law would be on him. Maggie paced the kitchen, feeling cold inside. Why hadn't he said something to them, taken them into his confidence? She sighed, knowing the answer. He'd been afraid of what they'd say. Morgan was headstrong, no doubt of it; he hadn't allowed anyone to get in his way. And he was willing to take the consequences.

She sighed deeply again, biting her lip. Even as a child Morgan had been willing to take what was coming to him when he'd disobeyed. How many times had she seen him grit his teeth and utter not a single sound when Azariah had taken a strap to him? Morgan had a sense of what was right and he was capable of standing up for it whatever happened. Whatever!

But now she prayed that he changed his mind and returned without seeing Urfe. He could not change what had been done; he would only add to the misery. But of course it was not likely Morgan would reverse his decision; if he were angry enough to pursue the Britisher he would not hesitate to carry out his plan.

The girls returned at length without a snip of gossip concerning Morgan. His absence had apparently been noted by no one in the town.

Maggie wanted nothing to eat at midday. She forced down a bit of bread and warmed-over fish from the Saturday dinner, but was too edgy to sit for long. The day was fair. Becky said she should go out and take a walk; it was no good pacing the floor.

Maggie shook her head, wanting to be home should Azariah send her news, but when the clock hands at length admitted that an hour had passed she drew on a cloak and let herself out. Almost without conscious thought she went to the Widow Riley's house.

The widow was asleep when she arrived, dozing in her easy chair by the coals of the fire. Since the chimney had been repaired and cleaned it took much less wood to heat the room and keep it warm. The widow's periods of dozing now stretched to hours.

To her delight Wager appeared shortly after she arrived and they embraced in the upstairs room. He said, "I was at the boatyard this morning. So Morgan's gone! Where in the world to?"

She sat on the bed. "I'm not sure . . ." Obviously Az had told him very little.

He sat by her, one hand on hers. "I've never seen Az so upset. But he would tell me nothing. Did Morgan leave in a hurry?"

She nodded, facing him, knowing her expression was troubled. But she had to trust him—how could she not? Clasping his hands, she took a long breath. "We think Morgan may have gone after that ensign—"

"Urfe? The one who was transferred?"

"Yes."

Wager was startled. "But what connection can there have been between them?"

Maggie closed her eyes and leaned against him, feeling his arm slide about her shoulders. "It was not between him and Urfe—but Marie."

He breathed, "Marie?"

"They had a secret affair, and now Marie's pregnant."

Wager gasped. He pulled her around and stared into her eyes. "Marie is pregnant? My God! I can hardly believe it!"

"It's true. And now Urfe's gone, without a word to her."

He drew her into his arms again. After a moment he

said, "And Morgan found out about it. Lord God, it'd be like him to go after Urfe . . ."

She closed her eyes, able to hear his heart beating. His coat was rough against her cheek and smelled vaguely of salt water.

He asked, "How did Morgan know?"

"He found out somehow. Az said he talked to some of the soldiers in town, so he knows where Urfe went."

"I see." He kissed her cheek almost absently. "Poor Marie. . . . What can be done?"

"She wants to have the baby."

"What?"

"She thinks Urfe will come back for her."

"But how can she?"

Maggie sighed deeply, feeling tears misting her eyes. "She loves him. She believes in him."

He took a long breath and pressed his lips together. "The fact that he left without any word to her makes no difference?"

"No. She's made excuses for him—that he had no time."

"She wants to believe it, then."

"Yes."

Wager held her tightly. "And Morgan—he said nothing to you, just disappeared?"

She nodded.

"Then there's nothing to do but wait till he returns. Do you suppose he wants to bring Urfe back?"

"I don't know. What do you think?"

"I doubt it. It probably wouldn't be possible."

She nodded again. "I think Morgan will punish him—somehow."

Wager sighed. "Punish him . . ." He held her closer, then lifted her head and kissed her. "Morgan's a sharp lad."

"Yes, so Az says! He's so smart he's putting his neck

152

in a noose!" She faced him, eyes blazing. "I know you're trying to ease my feelings, but—"

"Maggie! Let's not talk of nooses just yet. Morgan isn't foolish enough to walk into a British camp and haul Urfe out by the hair!"

She made a little gesture of defeat and put her head on his shoulder again. "No, of course he isn't. But I'm worried sick and there isn't a thing in the world I can do about it but wait."

"And waiting is difficult. But you mustn't let yourself think the worst. Don't dwell on it, anyhow. Do you know where Urfe went?"

"No."

"Then I'll try to find out. And if I learn anything I'll come to the house at once. Have you thought about Marie—I mean, having the baby?"

She shook her head. "Thank goodness that's months away yet."

"Yes, the immediate thing is Morgan, and he may return at any time." He kissed her. "I think you'd better go home in case he does." He rose and pulled her to her feet. "Try not to look on the dark side. I realize it's easy to say, but you mustn't worry yourself into bed."

She slid both arms about him and pressed her cheek to his. "You're a very understanding man, Wager. No wonder I love you."

"And I you."

He held her tightly for another moment, kissed her and let her go. She went down the stairs dabbing at her eyes, looked into the kitchen and beckoned him.

Morgan rode past the post gate, around the next turn of road and into the woods. Off the road the ground was muddy and the going slow; he made a wide circle to come out opposite the gate, dismounted and tied the mare in a patch of grass, then took up a position in a clump of trees where he could see without being seen.

Hours passed, and several times he nodded off to sleep, to wake annoyed with himself. It was the most tedious wait he'd ever experienced. The time crawled by and nothing at all occurred except for the occasional appearance of a rider or a wagon on the road and the changing of the guard at the gate. He ate the remainder of the food he'd brought and his stomach growled more and more as the afternoon waned.

As dark approached a number of soldiers straggled from the barracks, through the gate, and headed for the town. The men walked, a half dozen officers rode, but Morgan could not tell if Ensign Urfe were among them. He wished he had a spy glass.

But it was obvious he would have to go into the village again. Mounting the mare, he rode slowly through the woods paralleling the road and turned when he reckoned himself opposite the town. He came to a field that someone had cleared; tree stumps were everywhere and there was a strong smell of smoke and ashes. He got down, tied the horse and walked to the road. He was at the far end of the town opposite a sprawling house with a blacksmith's sign. To his right, five buildings away, was the sign of the Maltese cross. There were a few wagons along the street, a number of horses tied to hitchracks and a group of soldiers arguing in the center of the road.

He went back to the field and approached the cross. It had a low fence and a roofed area where several horses were picketed. Beyond that and close behind the tavern was a large stable. There were lanterns lighted inside and one over the wide door. He could see a stableboy just inside drinking milk from a jug. Someone called from the tavern and the boy put down the jug and ran toward the street.

Morgan followed, keeping in the deep shadows. Two

officers had arrived, silver insignia glittering in the lamplight as they dismounted and turned the horses over to the stableboy. Morgan thought one looked like Urfe. They strode into the building and the boy ran the horses to the stable and disappeared.

Morgan hurried around to the front of the building and looked in through a diamond-paned window, grimy and barely transparent. He was able to see the bar, tables and chairs, five officers and two girls. Obviously it was not a busy night. He could hear a muffled chatter of voices, most of it drowned out by the shouting in the road behind him. The soldiers had stopped their clamor when the officers had gone by but then resumed it. Morgan silently urged them on; their sounds would cover his.

He was standing in weeds and visible from the street if anyone should happen by and look his way, but no help for it. Slipping off the wool cap he rubbed an area of the window clean. The room suddenly jumped into a sharper focus.

To his right, at the end table by the hearth, sat Ensign Urfe, talking and laughing with the same redheaded girl who had thrown the water into the road earlier.

Morgan glared at him. How to get him out of the room alone?

He walked back to the drive, past the door of the tavern, and halted by the stable. The boy was sitting on a keg eating a chicken leg. He looked up as Morgan entered the stable.

"Who're you?"

Morgan countered, "You know Ensign Urfe?"

"The new one—blond?"

"Yes." Morgan dug out a shilling. "This's yours if you take a note to him."

"I can't write no note."

"You can't read or write?"

The boy shrugged. "What's the use of it?"

"I'll write the note and you take it to him. Is there any paper in here?"

The boy grinned; he was round faced and slack jawed, dressed in near rags. He got to his feet and ran to the back of the stable, reappearing in half a minute with the stub of a pencil and a scrap of paper.

Morgan used a planed board as a desk and printed the letters:

Ensign Urfe: I will be in the stable in five minutes.

> Marie

He folded the bit of paper and gave it and the shilling to the boy. "Don't tell him where you got this."

"He'll ask."

"Then say you don't know."

The boy frowned. "I got to know—he'll beat me."

"All right. Tell him it was delivered to you by a stranger. You don't know me, do you?"

"No . . ."

"Then it's the truth." He pushed the boy through the door. Urfe should be consumed by curiosity on receiving such a note. His blood racing, Morgan watched the stableboy hurry to the door of the tavern.

He paced up and down the stable, then went outside and stood in the shadow of the open door. Urfe might not come alone, and he'd need a handy retreat.

He slid the horse pistol from his belt and pulled back the cock and frizzen to feel into the pan with a finger. It was primed. He let the frizzen down to cover the pan and chewed his lower lip. Where the hell was Urfe? He shoved the cocked pistol into his belt and rubbed his hands together, warming them for the moments to come. He'd send the stableboy away and beat Urfe within an inch of his life. He might even break one of his arms, as he'd seen a sailor do once in a fight by the waterfront.

Ensign Urfe came to the stable in a rush, pushing the frightened boy ahead of him. Urfe was very angry, snarling threats. He stopped in the doorway, slapping his calf with a leather crop. "Where is she?"

The boy said, "I don't know, sir."

Morgan looked along the drive. No one had followed Urfe. He stepped into the light.

Urfe heard him, whirled, and astonishment rounded his eyes. "Morgan! You sent that note?"

Without waiting for an answer, he jumped Morgan and slashed with the crop. The first blow sliced across Morgan's cheek and the attack made him retreat a step and throw up his arm. He kicked out, connected, and Urfe swore and rushed him, slashing again and again with the crop. Morgan twisted away, stumbled, went down on one shoulder and rolled. Urfe's boot drove into his side, causing a sharp pain to sear his vitals. In the next instant Urfe jumped on him with bootheels seeking his face.

Morgan heaved and kicked but the other was a madman, bent on crushing him. Morgan managed to get the pistol out. He pointed and pulled the trigger as Urfe screamed. Powder smoke swirled and the shot sounded like a clap of thunder. The horses moved restlessly inside the stable.

Urfe staggered back, bent double; he swore again and fell to his knees, staring at Morgan, holding his middle with both hands. He slowly fell onto his side and his hat danced away. His eyes glared into the dirt.

The stableboy said breathlessly, "Jesus Lord! You've killed him!"

Morgan crawled to the body, turned Urfe over and

felt for a pulse, knowing he'd find none. The pistol ball had gone in dead center. Urfe was no more. He gazed down, anger draining away, and sighed from the bottom of his soul. "Sleep tonight, little sister," he muttered.

He made no move as the stableboy circled him, then ran toward the tavern, shouting.

He hadn't meant to kill the man, but no one would believe it. Getting up, he took a long breath, put the pistol into his belt and turned away. He broke into a run, heading for the field where the mare was tethered. The boy would have a crowd of redcoat soldiers in the stable yard in minutes.

And worse, the boy had heard Urfe say: "Morgan!"

It had not gone as he'd planned. Glancing over his shoulder he saw men with lanterns moving into the drive. How quickly would they get a pursuit started? He untied the horse, mounted and walked her toward the woods, knowing he was invisible; his clothes and the mare's color were advantages. Let them scatter and look for tracks.

Of course they might question the innkeepr in the common tavern. He'd tell them a stranger had passed, heading for New York, and probably strangers on the road were few and far between this time of year. He'd asked about officers too. . . .

Damn! Now that it was over, he had regrets. He hadn't wanted to kill Urfe, just punish him severely. But he hadn't counted on Urfe's recognizing him so quickly. The ensign had probably taken the trouble to find out who Marie's father and brothers were.

He had a sinking feeling, as if he were only beginning to realize the rapist was dead. He knew it, but now he *felt* it like a great weight pushing him down, a weight as heavy as the entire British army. The stableboy would tell them the name he'd overheard—and of course they'd have the note he'd written. Why had he signed it "Marie"? What a fool thing! It should be a simple matter for them to backtrack to the town Urfe had just left and find out who Marie and Morgan were. Both Lynns.

Morgan looked back. In his mind it was a certainty. With one of their own dead, an officer at that, the British would never rest till they had him, and for sure they'd call it murder. They would see to it that the stableboy told the magistrate the right story.

He knew he was very nearly hanged. Morgan put a hand to his throat. He could almost feel the rough texture of the rope.

But the damned redcoats couldn't hang him until they caught him! And he'd make that as difficult for them as he could. The mare was a willing animal and he let her run when he reached the road and headed east.

He met no one at all, and didn't expect to. Most travelers pulled off the road for the nights because the roads were so miserable. Probably no one in the colonies, he'd heard men say, knew what a good road was. Frequently he had to rein in and walk the mare. Now and then the road narrowed to a deer track and it would be easy to wander off into the woods, then have to find the path again.

He stopped after an hour, jumped down and put an ear to the ground listening for a pursuit, but heard none. Moving on, he wondered if he should return to Canaan. He might well bring down a hornet's nest on his family. By this time the redcoats had shaken all the details out of the stableboy, and even if he could not hear a pursuit, they'd be along. If nothing else, the British were thorough, and it was that thoroughness he feared. They were capable of rounding up his family for questioning. They could be arrested and locked up!

On the other hand, if he did not lead the soldiers to

Canaan his family might remain safe, even if the British knew who he was. They respected the law.

Now he was glad he hadn't written his family a note. None of them knew where he'd gone and could honestly state as much. They didn't know where or know why. Even if they guessed it, they couldn't be compelled to say so.

But he had to return the mare and the pistol. If he did not it would lie on his conscience like a coating of lead. He could return the mare at night, leave her where he'd found her, with the pistol and a note that it belonged to Jeremiah Chace. He could depend on Luther Parkman to return it and keep his mouth shut.

That was the solution. Return to Canaan at night and leave it that same night. God! If only Urfe hadn't spoken his name! Now everything was gone up in smoke . . . the schooner and his dreams. And Sharon too.

Would he ever see her again?

Chapter Fourteen

When Louis saw Becky next, he brought her a flower from the woods. It was a tiny yellow blossom with a dark center and a stem only inches long; it had no smell, but it was the only flower anyone had ever given her and she hugged him and tears came to her eyes.

His lips close to her ear, he said, "Come to France with me, *chérie*. I do not think I can go without you."

"How can I go?"

"Just by doing it." He tilted up her face. "Do you know I love you very much? Do you know I must be with you?"

"But—my family!"

"*Chérie*. You have a mother?"

"Yes, of course."

"Is she with her parents now?"

"No, of course not."

"You mean she left them for a husband?" His voice went up in pretended surprise.

Becky clung to him, her forehead brushing his chin. He was right, of course, people went their separate ways, sooner or later; they lived their own lives, loved their own loves. . . .

He pressed his lips to her cheek, looked into her dark eyes for a moment and smiled. "I will come again, *chérie*. Look for me."

He released her and turned away. In a moment he

was gone and she leaned against the building, eyes closed, lonely, hugging herself.

In her bedroom she took out the flower and gazed at it by the light of a softly glowing candle. The flower was love, the expression of love and it would last but a very short time. But when it was gone Louis would give her another, and another. He would give her love; he made her feel wanted and needed and she was torn with wanting to go with him, and staying. If she went she would have him, and if she stayed she would have nothing but the memory of his arms and his kisses—and memories were not life. They were only reflections in the mind that faded with the years. Louis would give her life because she felt as he did, that she could not live without him, and when he asked her next, she would say yes.

Enoch Quant sat in the ordinary, a pint at his elbow, feeling a little tipsy from too many pints. He listened to the chatter about him. Fishermen discussed catches and prices, warehousemen growled of their problems and the short tempers of foremen, a few talked of the blockade, and Owen Porter said it was a damned black shame that Louis Boyer was unable to get a ship to carry him back to France.

Enoch looked around. "Boyer—a Frenchman?"

"He's a good man, French or not."

"A Frenchman here in Canaan?"

Porter asked, "Why not?"

"A damned Catholic!"

Porter sneered. "Since when was you a religious zealot, Enoch? What do you care for any church? Have you dropped a penny in the box for two score years?"

"Well, maybe not the church. But a Frenchman! We fought those bastards not very long ago."

"*You* fought them?" Porter laughed.

Even Ben Robb smiled. The fishermen hooted. Everyone knew how Enoch Quant fought the Frenchies with his adze in the boatyard . . . safe, yet complaining that his feet were not meant for marching. Enoch had not marched one single rod to gain the hard-won victory at Quebec, but when it came to talk—

Enoch said, "Where is this Frenchman? How does he live?"

"By cutting wood," someone said.

"I've seen him at night, hauling it to town," Cephas Foot told them. "The lobsters are asleep then with their bellies full."

Enoch listened and remembered the name. Louis Boyer. It annoyed him that a Frenchman should live in the village, go about freely, if at night, and even make a living under the noses of the British. It offended him. Let the rest make their jokes about his war service, but he knew deep down that he had contributed. He'd built ships, hadn't he? Someone had to do it; it was damned important work and he'd done it expertly and willingly. Of course he'd been well paid, but that was only his due.

It was pitch dark and misty when Enoch left the tavern. His home was on Fort Street on the eastern edge of the town and when he reached it only one window showed a light. Tabitha was sitting in the kitchen that smelled of meat and smoke, long-faced as usual, waiting up for him. Her brown, mousy hair was drawn back from her forehead and she looked him over with tired eyes.

"There you are . . ."

"What's that mean, there you are?" He mocked her, pitching his voice higher. He tossed his hat to the table and sat down facing the fire to hold out his hands.

"D'you want some tea?"

He shook his head. "Nothing." He stared into the flames, thinking about the mysterious Frenchman. Was there a reward posted for him?

She asked, "What you glowering about?"

He glanced at her sidelong. "Questions! Lord, questions! You ask the questions, woman."

"What d'you expect? I'm in this house day after day, never hear no talk—"

He snorted. "*You* never hear no talk? You talk t' your washtub." He turned to face her. "You ever hear anything about a Frenchman?"

"What?"

"A Frenchman, livin' in Canaan?"

"No, of course not. How could a Frenchman live in a little town like this and not be known?"

Enoch nodded. She'd have heard something. He peered at her, wondering if she were lying. But then, she'd have no reason. Maybe the men in the ordinary were joshing him. But not likely; they'd been serious enough, especially Owen Porter. The gossip simply had not come Tabitha's way, but now he'd put the idea in her head she'd ask about it. He knew her.

He lay in bed beside her later, mulling about a reward. It might not be much, a few pounds probably, maybe ten, but money was money and the law was the law. It was his duty to tell the proper authorities about a fugitive Frenchman, wasn't it? Of course it was; he was a good subject of the king.

Maybe the reward would be as much as fifteen pounds.

Captain Charles Hewes-Bradford was put in charge of the investigation concerning Ensign David Urfe's murder. Hewes-Bradford was a tall, gray man, clean-shaven and distant. He had purchased his commission only a year past, thinking it would be an interesting change from his clubs and associates, and he'd have much to tell when he resigned it. He thought of his sojourn in America as a vacation in uniform. He looked magnificent, the ladies all said, in his beautifully tailored uniform. It was scarlet with a gold gorget and epaulettes, the coat faced with white and buttonholes edged with lace. The crimson sash about his waist had been given him by one of the ladies of the royal court.

The ensign's murder was a damned nuisance and he was annoyed to be assigned to it, especially when he'd planned to do a bit of shooting.

With his staff, Lieutenant Evelyn Turney and Sergeant William Freconay, he rode to the inn with the sign of the Maltese cross and sat in a corner sipping wine as he interviewed the persons who had been in attendance that particular evening.

There had been several officers present but they had little to say, not having been involved. They recalled that the ensign in question had become angry and had stalked out, shoving the stableboy before him, and shortly after they'd heard a shot. But none of them knew what it was about.

Sergeant Freconay brought in the stableboy, saying he'd witnessed the shooting, and Hewes-Bradford gave the lad a minute.

"Tell me what you saw."

The boy, whose name was Bert, repeated in a halting voice the same story he'd told everyone who'd asked. That Ensign Urfe had become enraged when he read the note—

"Where is the note?" demanded Freconay.

The boy shrugged. "I dunno, sir. It got lost."

"Lost?"

"There was so many trampin' about, sir. Maybe a hunnerd!"

Hewes-Bradford directed Lieutenant Turney to have

the grounds and the stable searched and Turney hurried out. He turned to the boy. "Did this colonial shoot the ensign?"

"Oh, yes, sir. There was a fight—"

Hewes-Bradford snapped his fingers. "Who owned the pistol?"

"The stranger, sir."

"Ahhh. So he brought it with him, obviously intending to use it."

"It was under his coat, sir," the boy said.

"And you saw this murder with your own eyes?"

"Oh, yes, sir."

"Anything else?"

The boy stared at the wall. "No, sir."

Hewes-Bradford dabbed at his nose with a lacy handkerchief. "Then run along, boy." He glanced at Turney, who stood by the door. "What luck?"

"None yet, sir."

"It seems we will do without it."

"Sir, the note may be valuable."

Hewes-Bradford made a face. "Then find it if you can. You will write out the report. I will expect it in the morning."

"Yes, sir." Lieutenant Turney came forward. "Unfortunately, sir, the stableboy cannot read and has no idea of the contents of the note."

"As I said, we will do without it. The ensign is dead, is he not? Are we to allow colonial ruffians to murder us? Certainly not. Note or no, the felon must be tracked down and hanged. It is a matter of prestige. I think you see that?"

"Yes, sir," said the lieutenant.

Colonel Franklin saw it as well. He read the brief report submitted by Hewes-Bradford and nodded his powdered head, took off his glasses and smiled. "Excellent, Charles. Now tell me, what do you think really happened?"

"I imagine the ensign was involved with a colonial girl, sir. He had a disgusting reputation. Probably her young man came, found Urfe and shot him."

"Yes, I imagine you're right. I've sent patrols along the roads. It'll make our presence felt for a time, do what we can do."

"You think he'll get past us, sir?"

The colonel shrugged. "They're better than we are in the woods, aren't they? Thank you, Charles."

Hewes-Bradford saluted and went out.

Morgan rode into the woods as it began to get light. He was exceedingly careful about his tracks, dismounting and brushing them out with a handful of branches. When he was satisfied that no British patrol would notice, he set off through the trees to find a place to sleep. After an hour he found a hollow where there was grass, picketed the mare and curled up near her.

He slept for five hours and woke ravenous. The sky was gray but high, a glowing bit of sunlight flooded the land under the cloud cover, and it did not smell like rain. He fingered the pistol, thinking he could probably shoot a rabbit and broil the meat, but would the shot attract attention? No telling. The redcoats must be out in force by now, patrolling the roads if nothing else. He hoped they were short of men.

Mounting the mare, he set off eastward through the woods, crossing meadows, listening. . . .

It was a fascinating game and he found himself enjoying it. It was something like what he'd imagined the days to come would be like, when he sailed the schooner and outwitted British men-of-war. It was a game, but there were real dangers, and the first came an hour before midday. As he approached a grove of ancient trees he heard voices and halted instantly, a hand on the mare's muzzle. The sounds seemed to come from beyond the grove and he turned the mare, dismounted and led her into a gully.

He rubbed her forehead and watched a troop of ten mounted redcoats pass within forty feet. To his critical eye they looked tired. They had probably been up half the night and were lolling in their saddles, some half asleep.

When they passed, Morgan climbed out of the gully and walked to the spot he'd seen them and found a well-used path. It confirmed his opinion that the British would stay on the roads; they weren't much for prowling the forests. He went back, mounted the mare again and continued east. He walked the horse for the most part, crossing a number of low hills, stopping now and again to listen. How good a description had the stableboy given them?

In the middle of the afternoon he veered toward the post road, tied the mare and went on foot to the road to watch. After an hour a troop of mounted soldiers came along, eighteen men and an officer. The officer looked bored and Morgan had an almost irrepressible urge to fire the pistol into the sky and throw them into confusion.

He was able to get himself in hand and return to the mare unseen.

His hunger nearly got the better of him as dusk began to fall. He came to a village and since there seemed to be no soldiers about, he rode around to the rear of the tavern and went inside, after peeking through the windows. The innkeeper was a stout man with protruding eyes and a red face.

He looked at Morgan suspiciously. "You got money, lad?"

Morgan showed a handful of coins. His clothes, not the most fashionable at the best of times, were dirty and wrinkled from sleeping on the wet ground. He had a stubble of beard and probably looked like a footpad. He explained to the man that he'd been left behind by a wagoneer to wait for a bag of tools, which were now tied to his horse outside. He was trying to catch up.

The innkeeper made a face, satisfied. He suggested a cut of beef and half a loaf of bread and Morgan quickly assented. The inn was plain and smelled of cooked food; it had sturdy chairs and stools, the tables were heavy planks and the floor was layered with brown sawdust. He could hear voices in the taproom, and when he went to the door was startled to see five redcoat soldiers sitting around a table. Two stared at him.

Morgan turned about as the conversation suddenly diminished. He hurried into the kitchen, a long narrow room with a huge fireplace at the end. He explained, "I'd like to take the food with me. It'll save time."

"Suit yourself."

Morgan waited, shifting from foot to foot. If the soldiers asked if he were a stranger . . .

A cook wrapped the beef in brown paper, gave him half a loaf for his pocket and the innkeeper received his shillings. As he went out the door one of the soldiers called to him.

Morgan kept going. He slammed the door behind him, ran around the tavern, jumped on the mare and dug in his heels. It was full dark with a thick overcast that smelled clammy. He headed into the woods and as soon as the lights of the tavern had disappeared turned east again, walking the mare. The outcry behind him dimmed. With any luck they wouldn't know where he'd gone.

He chewed the bread and opened one end of the paper. The smell of the warm meat was almost overpowering. He had to force himself to take small bites and chew them well.

The soldiers at the inn must be without horses since he'd seen none. Maybe they were stationed along the road to question travelers. Morgan headed back to the road and halted to listen when he reached it. Nothing. He nudged the mare and went east, chomping the bread and meat.

Twice on the road in the dark he halted and turned the horse into the trees after hearing strange sounds. The first time a wagon creaked by. At the second a startled deer fled from him.

He reached Canaan long after midnight.

On familiar ground again he went by backroads and paths to Luther Parkman's house, tied the mare where Luther would find her at once and, since he had no means of writing a note, took the pistol with him. He consoled himself that Jeremiah Chace could afford its loss.

It occurred to him that he might try to remain in the town, since he knew every inch of it, but it would be difficult for his family. He would be unable to work in the boatyard, and if he could not work on the schooner he preferred to be some other place.

He went to the waterfront and sat beside a wharf, staring out to sea. If the schooner were only a bit farther along he might hide till she was ready, but he knew in his heart that it was too chancy. The best thing to do was leave—until the British no longer looked for him. In a year or so he could return home with a changed name and an older face. He'd write the family as soon as possible and let them know he was alive and well.

But for the moment, he must get away.

He got up and started east along the beach, heading for Isak Tilley's shop. Isak was a ship's chandler and knew nearly everything that occurred along the waterfront. He was also a good friend who could be depended upon, come what may. Isak had worked with Azariah for years, and Morgan had known him all his life. The shop was on South Beach Street facing the town. Behind it was a fenced yard containing anchors, blocks, timbers, capstans, hogsheads and kegs. Isak lived above his store with his wife, Annie.

When he reached the store Morgan climbed the fence and curled up by Isak's back door to wait for dawn. A light coming on in the house at an odd time might be noted.

He spent the next hours waking and dozing, but was asleep when Isak opened the rear door. He woke and grinned at Isak's startled face. "Morgan! What you doing here?"

"Waiting for you."

"Well, come inside out of the cold." Isak was a skinny, gray-haired man with a long nose and bright round eyes. He was dressed in black breeches, white shirt and gray apron and had a habit of pulling at an earlobe. "You got to have something this time o'morning?"

"I didn't come to buy, Isak. I have to get out of town."

Isak halted and turned. "What—out of town? What for?"

"I mean, out of the country."

Isak stared at him. "What you done, Morgan? Out of the country!"

In quick sentences Morgan explained his predicament and Isak's brows rose. He told Isak everything, but left out Marie, saying that he and Urfe had quarreled. Isak looked doubtful, but asked few questions. His manner said that he thought there was more to the story but it was obvious Morgan was dead serious.

Isak pulled his ear and frowned. "Then what you want is a ship, that it?"

"I do. Deep sea or a coaster south."

"I can get you on a ship. D'you care where she's bound?"

"I can't afford that luxury." Morgan pulled the pistol from his belt and put it on the nearest table. "This belongs to Jeremiah Chace. Maybe you'll get it back to him with my thanks."

Isak nodded. "I see Jeremiah near every day. That the gun you shot 'im with?"

"That's it. Please tell my father you saw me too and that I'm fine. Tell him I didn't dare bring the soldiers down on them—that's the first place they'll go. They might be watching the house this very minute."

Isak nodded. His wife called down the stairs to him, "Who's there, Isak?"

"Be up in a minute!" Isak yelled back. He drew Morgan into the store, away from the stairs. "Happens Noah Harryman came in a day'r two ago with a cargo of ginseng roots. That's his sloop out there." He lifted his chin toward the ocean.

Morgan was surprised. "Bound for China?"

"You said you didn't care."

"Well, China . . ." Morgan shrugged. "The redcoats'll never look there, will they?"

"Not till whales grow feet. The lobsters think Noah's bound for Spain." He winked. "So he'll get blowed down to the Canaries and go on from there. You got any baggage?"

"What you see." Morgan was not surprised at the subterfuge. American vessels weren't allowed to trade with China; that was the exclusive province of the "Honorable John Company," the British East India Company. But the trade was very lucrative and Chinese

172

merchants were eager to get ginseng. American skippers chanced it, and many became rich.

Isak asked, "Are you hungry? You look starved."

"I am."

"Then come on upstairs. Annie's making breakfast."

After making sure there was no one around, Isak left his wife in charge of the store and took Morgan down to the near wharf, where he kept a boat. It was a gray, misty day with a brisk, cold wind blowing and Morgan was glad to take the oars, driving the boat through the lacy whitecaps to the sloop.

She was named the *Pelican* and was larger than he'd thought; about eighty tons, Isak said. She rocked at anchor, her single stout mast making lazy circles in the mist. Two men leaned on the bulwarks and watched them approach. One hailed Isak. "What you doin' out in the wet, you ol' stringbean?"

Isak yelled, "I come t'ast you not to put t'sea in that old tub. You'll all drown." He nudged Morgan. "The shipworms must he holdin' hands to keep her afloat."

The men laughed and Morgan grabbed a thrown line and pulled in the oars on the sloop's port side. He tied on and waited for Isak to go up the side.

A voice said, "Hell, this old tub'll outsail anything you ever seen. Who you got here?"

Morgan scrambled up and dropped lightly onto the deck. He faced a brown-bearded man with a square, tanned jaw and arms like a wrestler's. The second man had gone aft where two others were sitting on the deck.

Isak said, "This here's Capt'n Noah Harryman, Morgan. We's cousins . . . in a manner o' speaking." He looked at Harryman. "This's Morgan Lynn. I reckon you know his father."

They shook hands; Harryman's grip was like steel.

He said, "Course I know Azariah. You look a bit like him too."

Isak said, "Morgan's got to get out of the country for a spell, Noah. I told him you'd take him along."

"What kind of trouble you in, boy?"

"Redcoat trouble, sir. I got in a fight with an officer and he turned up dead."

Harryman whistled. "Up in Maine that's what we call travelin' trouble, sure'n the Lord made tears. What can you do?"

"Anything you put me to, sir."

Harryman nodded. "That's a good answer. You'n me's going to get along." He turned and yelled, "Orris!"

A man came toward them from the bow. Harryman said, "Orris will take you forward, Morgan. That all you got, what you're standin' in?"

"That's all, sir."

"Then you c'n draw from the slop chest." He motioned and Morgan hurried to join Orris.

Isak watched him go. "He's a good lad, Noah. See he gets back safe and oblige me 'n Azariah. When you slidin' out?"

"With the tide. Maybe another hour." He put out his hand. "See you in a year, Isak."

Enoch Quant picked his time carefully, the early afternoon, when people were busy at their daily tasks, to approach Ensign Illingsworth as he studied his men at drill in the meadow. Enoch came to the edge of the trees and waited. Illingsworth looked around, hearing dead leaves crackle. He looked Enoch over and let him stand.

"I want t'talk to you, sir."

Illingsworth was a tall, lanky, flaxen-haired youth

with a prominent nose and squinting eyes. He examined Enoch again, taking his time. "For what reason?"

Enoch glanced around nervously and hunched his shoulders. "I have certain information."

"Very well." Illingsworth glanced beyond Enoch as if expecting to see other eyes. "What is it?"

"Is there a reward for fugitive Frenchmen, sir?"

Illingsworth shrugged. "I have no idea. You mean just *any* Frenchmen?"

"A French officer, sir."

The ensign was astonished. "A French officer living in Canaan?"

"I have good reason to think it, sir."

"Incredible. What's he doing here?"

"Wanting to get on a ship, so they say."

"Who says?"

Enoch became hesitant. "My—er—my—I mean—"

"Very well. D'you know this man's name?"

"Louis Boyer, sir."

"Boyer! And where is he?"

Enoch shook his head. "I've heard he works as a woodcutter. Maybe he lives in the woods."

"Ahhh. And what is your name?"

"Enoch Quant. I own the boatyard."

"Is that so?" Illingsworth eyed him. "I was told it was owned by someone named Lynn."

"We own it together," Enoch said gruffly.

"I see. Well, Quant, I will act on your information. If the man is a fugitive and wanted, and if there is a reward, you shall have it. Is that sufficient?"

Enoch turned, his eyes sweeping the forest. "But don't hand it to me in the street, sir."

Illingsworth smiled. "I understand. I will be discreet."

"Thankee, sir." Enoch hurried off.

Ensign Illingsworth stared after him, hands clasped behind his back. He was new to North America and only twenty-two, son of a wealthy tradesman who had made his fortune in the mines.

When the drill was finished and his various administrative duties completed, Illingsworth returned to his room in the Hollister home—he had taken over Ensign Urfe's recent quarters—to write letters. One was addressed to his superior at Belford, relating the information given him by a man named Quant, boatbuilder.

The letter went out by the morning post.

Chapter Fifteen

Maggie's relief was enormous when she heard that Morgan was safe. Azariah sent Junius to her with the message that Isak Tilley had seen Morgan and put him on a ship bound for the Orient because of what Morgan had done.

She and the two girls sat open-mouthed as Junius related what Isak had said. Morgan had tracked down Ensign Urfe and in a quarrel had shot him dead! He hadn't intended to kill the man, Isak said, it had just happened, but the British would hang him if they caught him.

Hearing of Urfe's death, Marie burst out crying.

She rushed upstairs, screaming that it could not be so, and was inconsolable. Maggie hurried upstairs into her room and sat on the bed, at a loss to treat this new outburst. Nothing she said made any apparent change in Marie. She listened to the sobbing, unable to halt the tears; Becky stood in the doorway, and they looked at each other.

When Maggie went downstairs she and Becky sat in the kitchen gazing at the dancing flames in the fireplace. Becky asked, "Why is she taking on so?"

"Because she loved him."

"Even after what he did?"

"Even after that. That's why she wants the baby. It's part of him, and now I think she'll want it more than ever."

Becky picked up her knitting and sighed. "Poor little Marie . . ."

"She's angry, too."

"What?"

Maggie lowered her voice. "Her brother killed him, after all . . . it's a terrible hurdle to get over . . . if she gets over it."

Becky stared, her face showing the dismay. "But Morgan didn't mean to—"

"Morgan went after him and as a result Urfe is dead." Maggie felt herself curling inside as she said the words; her stomach twisted and her throat felt tight. What Morgan had done was horrible—but she knew he hadn't intended it. Lord! Why had he insinuated himself into the matter? Of course, he hadn't known how he'd hurt Marie. . . .

Becky said, "But *how* can she have the baby?"

Maggie shook her head, lines growing in her forehead. It was stony ground they'd have to cross one day, not too many months in the future. She said, "There's time to think and plan for it."

After a bit she went back upstairs and sat by Marie on the bed. "You'll ruin your eyes, child."

Marie turned, hair tousled, face red and an accusing look twisting her lips. "Morgan killed him deliberately—and he had no right!"

"No, of course he didn't! It was an accident!"

"Yes, he did! He went there to kill David."

Maggie put out her hand. "He's your brother! He'd do nothing to harm you—how can you think such a thing? He went to find—"

"Mother—he went to kill David! I know it, and I'll never forgive him! He had no right."

Tears came to her eyes and Maggie bent her head. "Marie—Marie—"

Marie's voice was harsh. "David was transferred,

that's all. He was going to resign from the army and go to London to work for his father. In a month he'd have been back for me—without his uniform."

There was a silence, then Maggie said, "I wish you could sleep, child. Can I bring you something hot?"

Marie turned away and put her head on the pillow. "He would have come for me."

"Of course," Maggie said, pulling the blanket over Marie's back. "Are you hungry?"

Marie shook her head. "I don't want anything."

Maggie bit her lip hard, gazing at her youngest. Wasn't Marie believing what she desperately wanted to believe? *Had* to believe? She sat silently, hands in her lap, and after a while Marie said, "Leave me alone, Mother . . ."

Maggie rose and went downstairs feeling wrung out. She must gather her thoughts and prepare to meet this new challenge. Mostly she must be understanding toward Marie. The girl was undergoing the most difficult thing anyone could face, and no wonder she clung to the idea that David was coming back for her. Because if she did not, she was lost.

And at the same time Maggie was positive Urfe would never have gone off without a word unless he had intended to leave Marie behind. The briefest note would have been enough for the time being. Only a line. One single word of love.

The day turned warm and for a time the sun came through the clouds. Becky scrubbed clothes in a washtub on the back porch and hung them out to dry on a rope line strung between the house and the privies. In the early afternoon Marie came downstairs and silently took up the loom. She sat in a corner of the warm kitchen that smelled of cooking and busied herself, her eyes red.

Becky came inside and began to peel potatoes. After an hour Maggie said, "The boys will have to be told about Morgan."

"And tell them about me," Marie said softly.

"They don't need to know about that yet."

Marie gave her a look, a flick of an eye. "They'll wonder why—why Morgan did—what he did."

Maggie sighed and nodded. Marie was right; the boys would wonder, and they might ask questions of others and that would draw attention to the family. It would be best to tell them and control the situation at once. Marie was thinking clearly enough on that score.

When Azariah and the boys returned that evening, Maggie took Az aside and he agreed. It was the better choice of a poor situation, and he thought the boys were mature enough to adjust to it.

They were astonished to learn what had happened, staring from their father to Marie in the telling, and when the story was finished Marie went immediately up to her room and got into bed, exhausted. She fell asleep with the candle-lantern still glowing on the chair beside the bed. Maggie saw the flicker of it on the wall and went upstairs to pinch it out.

She placed the lantern on the floor and sat on the chair for a long time, listening to Marie's deep breathing, wondering what she could do to ease the hurt in the girl. It was a horrid thing for her to hate her brother.

Morgan was lucky, in a way. He'd gone after Urfe in a burst of anger and got it over with, and been willing to take the consequences. And not everyone could do that, surely not herself. There were too many others to think of first.

Maggie was not a deeply religious person. She feared God and she went to church regularly because it had to be, but in the gloom of the little bedchamber she bowed her head and prayed that Marie would come through the ordeal unscathed and with a measure of happiness. Marie was not a sinner; she had loved David too deeply and had given too much, but it had been more because of innocence than lust—though she was sure such a thing could not be said about him.

And obviously Morgan hadn't thought so either.

The next day she saw Wager again in Widow Riley's upstairs room. He was there when she arrived, lying full length on the bed, eyes closed; he had not heard her on the stairs.

She paused in the doorway to smile at him. He was every bit as handsome as he'd been ten years before, brown hair curling over his forehead. She scratched on the door jamb and his eyes opened. He smiled and sat up, swinging his feet to the floor.

"I was thinking about you . . ."

Sitting beside him, she kissed him quickly. "You're very bold to come in this way. Did the widow see you?"

"Yes, I brought her a present. She thinks I went out the front door. You look marvelous."

"What kind of present?"

"Just a bowl of walnuts. I bought several bags from Brayton yesterday." He lay back and gazed at her. "I must admit I'm hungry for you. I think I miss you more and more. I want to talk to you every day." He took her hand, noting the tiredness for the first time. "What is it—are you all right?"

"I suppose it's Marie."

"How is she?"

Maggie shook her head and her face grew solemn. "Not well at all." She told him about Isak Tilley and Morgan's going. "Now she knows that Morgan killed Urfe. It's upset her terribly."

"Ummm, I can see that it would. Morgan's headed for the Orient? Then he'll be gone for a while."

"Maybe a year, Az says."

He smiled. "But then the British won't get him. That's the good part of *that*."

"Yes . . ." Her arms reached for him and their embrace sent fire seeping into her insides. She lay beside him and sighed contentedly. It was cold in the room but she scarcely noticed. Under the shawl she wore an ordinary cotton dress of light blue with a low neckline and he slid his hand inside it as she snuggled to him. He whispered, "Is my hand too cold?" She shook her head and moved her cheek against his.

She pushed the dress off her shoulders and turned onto her back as Wager kissed her neck. The troubles of the past days drifted away, and as his lips reached her breasts she breathed out and writhed. The blood pounded at her temples and the room seemed to swim in a silvery haze; she pulled at him, wanting him, feeling the flush of desire spreading through her body like dancing flames. Her skirts came up and she moaned as he joined with her, rocking his body with hers, then thrusting, lips seeking her mouth. Sensation flooded her and time dropped away. They moved and stopped, and moved again . . . and nothing else mattered. . . .

She came back to earth as Wager whispered, "What a beautiful woman you are, Maggie Barth."

Her hands came up and caressed him, lips pressed to his cheek. "I'm not, but I love to hear you say it."

"You were in a fantasy world."

"Was I? How could you tell?"

"Only a guess. What were you dreaming about?"

She smiled. "All my best dreams are of you." She held him tightly when he would have rolled away. "Don't talk, let's just lie still. I want to feel you close . . ."

He slid both arms about her and their breaths mingled. It was a wondrous moment of peace and blessed fulfillment and she basked in it, soothed by his touch and the intimate warmth of his body . . . but it had to end. The chill of the room began to intervene and at last Wager moved away and sat up, saying that next time he came he'd bring blankets for the bed.

As they dressed he asked, "Tell me how you feel about us."

She gazed at him in surprise.

"I mean," he said, "do you think about things like guilt?"

Maggie took a deep breath then nodded. "Yes, now and then. I try not to bring it here, but it comes with me occasionally whether I want it or not. Do you feel it too?"

He moved closer. "Of course. Morality has been preached to us all our lives, and we're breaking those laws."

Sighing, she closed her eyes and clung to him, warm in his embrace. They *were* mature people, aware of the risks they took but needing each other, and not just for the fleeting sexual satisfaction they received. She knew she drew life from him, strength she no longer had from Azariah. Each day that passed seemed to bind them more tightly together, she thought, and the stolen moments in the little room were her most precious possessions, forming the memories that she would have to content herself with until their next meeting, because each time they parted was a wrench, a sadness that it could not continue. But each parting was the beginning of the next joyous encounter; she must look at it that way.

He embraced her downstairs near the kitchen door, smiling with a rueful reluctance that he must leave. The widow's back was turned when he went out and she watched him through the rear window as he disappeared along the fence toward Dover Court. Already she was looking forward to his arms and the dreams between times.

With him gone, the real world returned and Maggie hurried home, the shadow of guilt reminding her that she'd sought pleasure with Wager while her daughter was suffering. But Wager helped her to remain strong, to be able to overcome her problems; without him she would be only a body beset with chores and tasks, growing weary and uncertain . . . one day to sit by a fire as Widow Riley did, waiting for release.

When she arrived she found Marie in a black mood that she could not be jollied out of, even by Becky. And as the days passed she did not throw it off.

There were times when she smiled, seeming to forget, but the mood crept in again no matter what was said to her; and she cried at night, Becky told her mother, like a pitiful, whipped child.

During the days, Marie went about her tasks as she always had, with her mind seemingly far away. She seldom spoke unless spoken to, and usually had to be jolted into answering. When the weather permitted, Becky took her walking, sometimes to South Beach Street and back, she reported, but Marie only stared at the ocean, saying nothing.

Then one morning Marie announced that she'd received a note from David. He was coming for her soon.

"A note!" Becky said. "Where is it?"

Marie only shook her head. She smiled and took up the loom.

During those weeks, Becky saw Louis often. Now and then she hurried off to the woods north of William Lane and spent a few moments with him, and nearly every night he came to the house after dark. But when the snow began to fall, piling up in deep drifts, coating the world with white, it became more difficult.

She told him about Marie, shading the story to make her sister ill rather than pregnant, and said it was impossible for her to go away at present. She was needed at home.

Louis said, "*I* need you too."

"We must wait a little longer. If you love me you will wait . . . Besides, there is no ship to take us away." She'd heard Junius say it only yesterday.

"There will be soon." He kissed her longingly. "I must not stay here in Canaan too much longer, *chérie*, or I will be caught."

"You never said that before!" She stared at him in the gloom. "Have you seen something?"

"There is a change. I think the British know I am here—at least I have seen their patrols in the woods where none have ever been before. It is possible someone has informed."

It was another worry to add to her list. If Louis were taken it would bring down her world as Marie's tragedy had done for her. It was easier for the British to track him, now that the snow showed footprints so obviously, he said, and he had taken to sleeping all the time in Orlow Gordon's house. It was safer, and warmer, but it put Orlow in jeopardy.

She knew he had no wish to pile those troubles on her shoulders, but it was plain that if she would immediately run off with him they would be relieved.

What should she do?

She began to see, as winter closed them in, that she had only one course of action. She knew deep down that if she did not go with Louis she would live out her years in regret. She would become bitter and faded and never really know love again, and she began to experience something of what Marie was feeling.

When she saw Louis again, she clung to him and whispered that she would go with him, but that she had to tell her mother first, and he agreed.

With that in mind, they made their plans.

Chapter Sixteen

Christmas came, a strained and not too joyous occasion this year. Maggie led in the singing of carols, half-hearted by all, she thought, and presents were exchanged.

A Christmas dinner was eaten: Indian pudding, and bacon and veal with vegetables. Azariah had bought a bottle of rum and Maggie served it in pewter goblets. But the holiday was gone almost before she realized it.

Her thoughts were divided between Marie and Wager, each of them different as the cardinal points of the compass. In between she ran the household.

Marie seemed not to change from day to day. She lived in a kind of half-world of her own making, doing her chores and the necessary housework, but not fully entering into the life of the family. When pressed, she said she was waiting.

The physical evidence of Marie's ordeal slowly began to make itself apparent, adding to her distress. Marie could no longer attend church and various neighbors began to inquire about her. Was she ill? Had she gone away?

It took all of Maggie's fortitude to smile and bear up and she leaned heavily on Wager; if it had not been for him, she often thought, she might retreat.

It was with genuine astonishment that Maggie one afternoon found herself engaged in a conversation with Becky that began with innocuous questions.

"Where did you and Father get married?"

"Here in Canaan, child. I thought you knew that."

"I suppose I did. But you've been out of Canaan?"

"Yes, certainly. Once I went to Boston, and once to Gordonville in Vermont. Why do you ask such questions?"

Becky, sitting with a loom in her hands, shrugged lightly. "I know that Father has sailed all over the world . . ."

"Yes, he was a sailor once."

"I—would like to travel too."

Maggie smiled. "Perhaps you will, one day."

Becky was silent a full minute. "May I ask you something very serious, Mother?"

Maggie eyed her daughter. Becky's face was devoid of expression except that her eyes seemed very bright. "What is it?"

"Do—do you love Father?"

Maggie straightened and her eyes rounded in astonishment. Had Becky stumbled onto something? Her heart seemed to skip a beat and she put a hand to her throat. "Of course I love your father! What an odd thing to ask. Are you quite all right, Becky dear?"

"Of course I am, Mother. But what if Father asked you to sell the house and pack everything into a wagon and move away—to some other town. What then?"

"I would go with him! It is my duty as a wife to go where my husband goes. Becky—what is behind these curious questions?"

Becky hesitated. She studied the loom as Maggie waited, moving a chair to sit opposite. She began to suspect that Becky was leading up to something very important to her.

Very softly Becky said, "I have to tell you something, Mother—and I don't know how to begin—"

Maggie took a quick breath of apprehension. So

close on the heels of Marie's troubles! She felt her teeth grit, fearing another like admission. Her face must have betrayed her sudden fear because Becky shook her head.

"Please don't think I've done anything—"

Maggie let her breath out and closed her eyes. "Thank the Lord!"

"But, Mother, I want to—" Becky stopped and put the loom down, twining her fingers together. She bent her head and her jaws worked.

Maggie urged, "You want to—what?"

Becky almost blurted the words. "I want to go away with—someone." She risked a glance at her mother, then back to her hands in her lap.

Maggie stared, as if at a stranger. "You want to go away with—who?"

"Someone you don't know. A man named Louis Boyer."

Maggie leaned back feeling faint. So much all at once! A hundred thoughts rushed through her head. Becky had obviously been seeing this man—whoever he was—in secret! She'd had no inkling of it! Becky had become involved in a love affair with—a man named Boyer. Not an English name! How in the world did her daughters become involved with foreigners? Marie with an Englishman and now Becky with—who? How much else went on under her nose?

Becky waited patiently. She said, almost under her breath, "We want to be married, Mother."

"But—but we don't even know him!" Maggie felt herself churning inside; she did her best to put on a calm face. She would hear this through. Perhaps it was not what she feared.

"I met him," Becky said slowly, "several months ago. He came from Canada where he was a French soldier."

"A Frenchman . . ."

"Yes."

"Have—have you been intimate with him?"

"No, Mother."

Maggie glanced toward the stairs. Marie was in her room, knitting a blanket for the coming baby. She stood and poked at the fire to cover her trembling hands. A Frenchman!

Becky said, "Louis cannot stay here in Canaan, of course. The red ants would jail him if they caught him. He wants to go to France as soon as possible, and take me with him."

"And marry you—when?"

"As soon as we can, Mother. He is a good and honest man and we want your blessing."

Maggie turned. "This is utterly ridiculous! I have never heard such nonsense!"

"Mother!"

"A young girl proposes to run off with a stranger, a man of another country—and a man wanted by the authorities! How does that sound to you, Becky Elise? If you were me, how would you feel?"

Becky flushed. "I thought you'd be more—"

"Hush, girl! The thing is completely out of the question. Of course you cannot go! Your father would be enraged even to hear of it! The town would probably drive us out. You would shame me and your father!"

Becky rose, eyes glinting. She said in an even voice, "I do not intend to give him up."

"But you certainly will! It cannot be permitted. Your father is a sick man. How much misery do you think he can abide?" She broke a stick in half. "First Marie and now you!"

"I'm not a child, Mother. I will be seventeen in May."

"You are a dreamer! To run off to France with a man you barely know! What can you be thinking of?"

She felt a twinge of guilt as she said the words. But this was not the time to think of her own involvement.

Becky said, "He loves me—and I love him. As dearly as you love Father."

"You don't know what you're saying."

"I think I do."

Maggie paced the floor, pausing to gaze earnestly at her daughter. Becky was standing her ground, not giving an inch. She moved closer, frowning. "You're not to see this man again. Do you understand?"

Becky took a deep breath and Maggie could see her jaw muscles tense; she shook her head. "I cannot do that, Mother."

"You're determined to do as you say?"

"Yes, I mean exactly that."

"Your father may change your mind."

Becky shrugged. "If he beats me it will do no good."

Maggie turned away, tears beginning to gather at the corners of her eyes. She had always known the day would come when she'd lose her girls; it seemed to be coming much too fast. Becky was right. She would be fully grown by summer, and older than Maggie had been when she'd married Azariah.

Becky came up behind her. "I don't want to go away like this, Mother."

"When do you plan to go?"

"I don't know. As soon as Louis can get passage on a ship."

Maggie walked to the front door and back; she felt her anger dissipating, its place taken by resignation. There was probably nothing she could do to stop Becky if the girl had made up her mind, and any definite move in that direction would probably strengthen Becky's resolve and drive a terrible wedge between them. That would be the worst thing of all.

She halted in front of Becky and her hands cupped

Becky's face. "Nothing will ever again be as important to you as this decision, and I want you to make the right one."

"I've thought about it and thought about it. It *is* the right one for me, Mother."

"If you have any doubts at all . . ."

"I have none, Mother."

Maggie drew her close. She took Becky's hand and pressed it to her lips and Becky was suddenly crying, her shoulders moving. Maggie held her tightly, then released her, tears glistening in her own eyes.

"What in the world are we crying for? It's not as if you're off somewhere in a coffin!"

Becky smiled through the sobs. "No, it isn't . . . but I'm . . . I'm so happy you understand, Mother."

"I'm trying to understand."

"I—I want you—to meet Louis."

"Yes, I certainly do want to meet him! Is he much older than you?"

"Only a few years." She dabbed at her eyes. "Shall I bring him here tonight?"

"No, no—it might be better if I saw him first. Your father's health may not permit him this second shock without a good deal of preparation. Let me first break the news to him. Can Louis come here during the day?"

"I will ask him."

Maggie nodded, kissed Becky and stepped back, still holding her hands. What an incredible situation! In all her days she'd never envisioned such a remarkable occurrence! Her daughter taking up with a fugitive Frenchman! It was almost more than could be believed.

She turned from Becky to stare into the fire. How was she going to find the words to tell Azariah?

* * *

Sharon Quant was shocked by the news that Morgan had gone away without a single goodbye—not so much as a word on paper, not even a hint!

Her father came home from the boatyard to say that a funny thing had happened, that Morgan Lynn was gone and nobody knew where. Shocked, Sharon sat still, eyes round as shillings, staring at him, thoughts whirling. Her parents knew nothing of her feelings for Morgan and she was not included in their discussion. She was suddenly left behind, wondering. . .

"Morgan gone?" her mother asked. "Where'd he go?"

Enoch said in annoyance, "I told you! Nobody knows where."

"But someone has to know. What about Azariah?"

"Az don't know nothing."

"Ahh, maybe he just ain't telling you. What did Junius say?"

"He don't know either."

Tabitha shook her mousy head. "It's a mighty funny thing if no one knows, Enoch. Did he do something?"

"How d'I know? He just up and left in the middle of the night."

"How did he go?"

Enoch's voice rose. "I already tole you, Jesus Lord! How d'I know?"

"Don't swear in front of the girl."

"Well, he up and left, that's all."

That night Sharon cried into her pillow. But the next morning she found an excuse to walk into town and hurried to the Lynn home. Maggie answered the knocker and smiled to see her.

"Sharon! What a pleasant surprise. Come in, come in, I've got the kettle on." She pulled the slim girl inside and shut the door. Sharon had come about Morgan, she knew.

Marie sat near the hearth, knitting. She looked up as Sharon entered. She looked very pale, Sharon thought, though she hadn't seen Marie for months.

"Sit by the fire," Maggie said, and pulled out a chair. "How's your mother?"

"She's fine. . . . But she doesn't know I'm here."

"Oh?" Maggie said. "Then I expect you've heard about Morgan? He's gone off for a time."

"My father brought the news home last night. Where did he go?"

Maggie poked at the fire. "We're not sure," she said carefully. "He took a ship and we think it's bound for the Orient."

"China! Then he'll be gone at least a year!" Sharon was astounded. A year! She stared from Maggie to the silent Marie. "Why did he do such a thing?"

"Because—" Marie began.

Maggie cut her off. "Morgan got into trouble with a British soldier."

"A soldier!"

"Yes. They fought and, rather than go before a magistrate, Morgan went aboard the ship. That's almost all we know."

Sharon digested it. It was a very thin story, she thought, not nearly all of it. But Maggie Lynn did not seem disposed to elaborate. Morgan had fought with a soldier?

She asked, "What did they fight about?"

Maggie did not answer quickly. "Men quarrel about things, you know . . ."

"Yes."

"The soldier might have provoked him."

Sharon nodded. The crux of it was what they'd fought about; that seemed clear. But it was also clear that Maggie was not going to reveal more. If indeed she knew more. She sipped the tea Maggie gave her and watched Marie's flying fingers. Marie seemed to be knitting a tiny sweater, something for a baby. Probably one of their neighbors was about to give birth.

A year! Morgan would be gone a year!

Sharon finished the tea, and they chatted for a time. She could hear the sounds of coughing from upstairs; her father had mentioned several times that Azariah was ill or had stayed home. She wondered if he were in bed.

When she left the house she felt slightly easier in her mind; at least she knew some of the facts, and even if Morgan was escaping from the law he was safe for the time being. That was the most important thing. But a year! It was forever. Would she know him when she saw him again?

Did Morgan really love her? And if he did why did he go without a word? Maybe there hadn't been time. . . . If he'd been in a terrible rush with soldiers close on his tail—there had to be a reason. Morgan *did* love her; he'd said he wanted to marry her, after all. That was not something said lightly.

Several days later her father brought home a Boston newspaper, and when she had a chance to read it, Sharon noticed an item that a British officer, Ensign David Urfe—who had once been stationed in Canaan—had been killed in Belford during an altercation with an unknown man. She knew that Belford was a town to the west, near the New York line, not so far off.

Had Morgan been the "unknown man"?

Morgan might have quarreled with Urfe when the man had been in Canaan. Would he journey to Belford to continue it?

Maggie Lynn had made it sound as if the quarrel with the soldier had taken place in Canaan, but maybe she didn't know, or maybe she had deliberately insinuated that it had. Sharon read the item over again. If this had been the quarrel Maggie mentioned, what kind of provocation would send Morgan fifty miles to continue it?

The curious thing to her was that Morgan was not the quarrelsome kind. He might be a daredevil or a little wild, as some people said, but not one to pick fights. She thought it very odd that he would pick a fight with a British officer, of all people. But maybe Urfe had started the quarrel. Morgan was not one to back away, but why Urfe would do it she could not imagine. The more she thought about it the more curious it seemed. Morgan never talked with the soldiers at any time, for any reason; she'd heard him say as much.

But the worst was that he was gone. She had not seen him every day, of course, but she'd known he was nearby. She *could* have seen him if she'd wanted. Now he was gone and she felt lonely. Her thoughts kept returning to the moments they'd spent alone in the woods the day of the chopping bee. How foolish she'd been not to stay longer with him, not to have been a little more intimate with him. She'd wanted to, but she'd stopped him at every turn.

In bed at night the memory of his brief kisses burned her heart and she cried, with no one to hear.

Chapter Seventeen

Junius Barth Lynn was a steady, serious boy, not given to pranks and not one to exhibit a lively imagination. He did better in the boatyard than Morgan because he did not go from one thing to another but finished what he started. Even Enoch Quant let him be after the first few weeks, and anyway, Junius did not react as Morgan had. Enoch had always been able to get a rise, one way or another, from Morgan—but a few times he realized that Morgan had been pushed to the brink of violence, and he had backed off. This did not happen with Junius.

Morgan's going, Junius thought, had left a somewhat bitter taste in his father's mouth because now there was little chance of buying out Enoch. Azariah had not been back to see Mr. Chace because he feared there was no point to it. Jeremiah had wanted Morgan to sail the schooner, and now Morgan could not. Ergo, Jeremiah would not advance the money.

Junius did not necessarily agree with his father, but he felt it was not his place to argue or to see Jeremiah alone. He did discuss the matter on their walks to and from the yard.

"Perhaps Mr. Chace will still lend the money."

Azariah thought there was no chance of it.

"But it *is* a business proposition, Father. There's the interest to be gained."

Azariah coughed and said he was sure Jeremiah

cared little for such a small proposition. He dealt in cargoes and in enterprises that turned over far more quickly.

So the matter was not pursued, though now and then Enoch mentioned it. He had other plans in mind, he said, and hinted that he might come down a bit in the agreed-upon price.

However, it happened that on one of his infrequent trips to the boatyard to inspect the schooner's progress, Jeremiah Chace himself brought up the subject again.

They were standing inside the hut with the stove cherry red to defeat the icy weather outside. Jeremiah said, "A damned shame Morgan's gone off like that, Azariah. Will he be back, d'you think?"

"Not for a twelvemonth, Mr. Chace, not likely."

"God's ass, that's damned bad."

Junius spoke up, braving his father's eye. "But we'd still like to buy out Goodman Quant, sir."

"Ahhh, you would?"

"Junius!" Azariah said sharply. "Mr. Chace's stated his terms."

"Don't be hard on the boy, Azariah. It's a fair question, ain't it? It's business."

Azariah's face changed. "You'd consider it?"

"I said, it's business. And solid, not the kind that rides on the bowsprit of a damned boat under British guns. Let's talk about it, Azariah."

Azariah smiled. "Indeed I will, Mr. Chace. Indeed I will."

And after Jeremiah had gone Az clapped Junius on the back. "I never thought he'd want a part of it, boy. Maybe I'm getting on and crotchety."

Junius said, "It might be a good idea, Father, to settle the price now with Enoch before Mr. Chace talks too much in the ordinary."

Azariah smiled. "That's right. I'll speak to him before he leaves the yard tonight."

Junius was a serious-minded lad, but not a monk. On Sundays he had often walked about the village with Olive Yurman, daughter of a neighbor; she and her family lived on the same street and he had known Olive all his life.

At sixteen she had developed into a beauty; her face was oval, with liquid brown eyes, and her body was showing excellent signs of womanhood. She was frequently in the Lynn house on one pretext or another and as they both grew into their mid-teens they touched, met as if by accident, and even held hands in the near dark of the street.

Little of this escaped their elders and it was generally accepted that one day Junius and Olive would marry, and because of that a good many small indiscretions were overlooked, such as their kissing when they thought themselves unobserved, of Junius's arm about her waist when it should have been at his side. Maggie took care to invite Olive to small gatherings, birthdays or holidays when sweet cakes were made and the tea was spiced with cinnamon.

Now and then, they were left by themselves, usually by happy chance, sitting in a parlor or kitchen, and had actually an opportunity for conversation. On one such, soon after Morgan's disappearance, they sat in the Lynn kitchen, with the smell of baked bread in the air, in the middle of a Sunday afternoon, and found themselves alone.

Junius said, "I had a dream not long ago that we had our own house . . ."

"That we were married?"

"Yes." He glanced around, then touched her hand. "But had no children yet."

"Tell me about the house."

"It was much like this one, only smaller." He felt her fingers curl around his. "I've been saving toward a house, you know. I've twelve pounds put by—"

"Twelve! How wonderful! And I've been sewing. My hope chest is nearly full, though I don't see much money."

"Things are going to be hard," he said seriously, "with the blockade tightening. But we'll manage."

"I know we will."

He felt a tiny pull on his hand, and leaned toward her. She moved her chair and their lips met, just a breath of a kiss at first, then more urgent. His heart began to race and he half turned to her; his arms went out, embracing her. He was surprised at her surging response—and then they heard footsteps on the stairs. He could see the disappointment on her face as they quickly moved apart. There was plenty inside him!

Maggie came into the room and immediately went out again and up the stairs without a word. They heard a door close.

Junius stood and pulled Olive up, holding her tightly. It was the very first time he'd held her completely in his arms and the excitement of it made his blood pound. He felt a giddy sensation that was difficult to control. Her body was warm and eager, her arms held him every bit as compellingly as he held her. Her kisses were even more urgent than before. In a moment they were breathless; she was flushed and he perspired as his temples throbbed—the things that flashed through his mind!

When he released her she came into his arms again, seeking his mouth, and it astounded him that she was as eager as he! But he had to sit down, embarrassed by what was happening to him, and Olive seemed to realize it, smiling as she stood over him, holding his head against her breasts. He felt their firm roundness and warmth and closed his eyes, wonder if he would ever forget this incredible moment. With both hands he reached up and pressed her breasts together and heard her murmur his name. Then she sat by him, gently pulled his head around and kissed him softly until Junius could hardly breathe.

He was still flushed when Maggie came slowly down the stairs again, making noise with her heels. She went first into the parlor to look at the clock, then entered the kitchen and went directly to the fireplace and knelt to poke the logs.

Junius realized, as his head cleared, that his mother had more than an inkling of what had happened in the kitchen, and when his eyes met hers, he thought she smiled.

That winter Azariah's cough became steadily worse and he began to cough up a blood-flecked phlegm that he hid from Maggie when he could. Dr. Lunt, a nervous, irritating man, came to the house and examined Azariah, diagnosing the trouble as an aggravated cold and prescribing meat broths, a mixture of brandy, egg and milk and plenty of rest.

Junius and Enoch ran the boatyard and got along at arm's length. The schooner *Annora* was completed and launched and Jeremiah Chace appointed a man from Maine to sail her. A number of fishing boats were hauled into the yard for repairs and Luther Parkman and several others worked steadily when the weather permitted.

In February, when Azariah was able to be up and around a bit, he and Junius went to call on Mr. Chace once more. Jeremiah received them in the same warm study, smelling of spice, sat them down with brandy glasses in their hands, and a paper was drawn up after a discussion between them. There was no need for a lawyer, they agreed, since they were all men of good will with no evil intentions one against the other.

A copy of the paper was made for Azariah, the two were carefully compared, and Jeremiah immediately paid over the money. The sole stipulation Jeremiah made was that Junius must remain at the yard. If Junius left, as Morgan had, the money was at once due and payable. Ordinary sickness was excluded.

When the papers were signed and hands shaken, Jeremiah poured out more brandy. Afterwards Junius walked home with his father, slightly surprised that it had all been so easy.

"Business is done on faith," Azariah said. "If it weren't for faith everything would be at a standstill."

"Then Mr. Chace has faith in us."

"In *you*," his father said. "He knows that what work I do at the yard could be put into a soup bowl. It's you he expects to profit by." He glanced at his son. "D'you have any doubts?"

Junius shook his head.

When he thought about it later, he considered that he had given the right answer; he had no doubts about himself, about his work at the boatyard, or about his future. It seemed to him that his life was falling neatly into place, a very satisfactory feeling. It was exactly what he wanted.

And when he told Olive, she was delighted also. It was precisely what she wanted too.

Enoch Quant had the doubts. He was very pleased to receive the money in cash, and quickly signed the paper relinquishing all rights in the boatyard forever. But afterward his usual perverse self began to make itself felt.

Sitting in the ordinary, he listened to the fishermen's talk and he wondered. . . . He had been listening to the same chatter for years, of catches or of British ships, and of the high cost of repairing and maintaining boats. Now that he was no longer part of the boatyard such talk seemed pointed at him. Had he sold a sure-certain income for a pittance?

The money had diminished a bit when he'd paid over what he owed Ben Robb, and there would be no more settling accounts with Azariah at the end of the month. When Cephas Foot asked him how it felt to be unemployed, he said he would enjoy it.

Then he said, "I didn't have no choice, you know. I had to get out."

Cephas cocked his head. "You was forced out, Enoch?"

"Them Lynns, they're like mice, always scurryin'."

Cephas winked at the others. "I thought you was a cat, Enoch."

"Hell, you know Azariah never did pull his share—with that peg-leg and all. Now he's laid up three days out of four—"

"I thought them Lynn boys took up that slack."

Enoch drained his pint of brown ale. That was true, of course; maybe it was a mistake to say that about Az. He had too many friends. He shoved the mug across the bar to Ben. "Them boys're fair workers, but they got to be told ever'thing."

"Not Morgan," said a fisherman.

"Not Junius either," said Cephas. "What boys're you talking about?"

Enoch glared at them. "I been at that boatyard for years. Don't you figger I can see with m'own eyes? You come in maybe once in a month but you knows ever'thing."

"Enoch is right," Cephas said in a dry voice. "He built that schooner for Jeremiah all by his own hands, ever' plank and spar. That right, Enoch?"

Enoch slammed down the mug. He glared round at his tormentors and stalked from the tavern in anger, muttering to himself as he heard the laughter behind him. He'd fix them all if he could. . . .

When he arrived home Tabitha was grumpy about his taking the money. "Now what we going do when it's gone?"

"Like I told you, we're going to Boston. I'm sick of this town anyways."

"What about the house?"

"I'll sell it. Put it up for sale tomorrow."

"It's a terrible time o' year to be travelin'."

Enoch blew out his breath. "Don't nothing please you? What you want, woman? You know what you want?"

Tabitha glared at him. "I want something put by, and maybe a smile now'n then! But that's too much to ask with you, Enoch Quant. What you expect t'do in Boston you can't do here?"

"I've told you a hundred times! I'm gonna do a lot of business, that's what. Where's some paper? I want to write to Cap'n Styles."

Chapter Eighteen

Louis Boyer lived in the single basement room of Orlow Gordon's small house and came and went by means of a shed door that connected to an unused stable. In this manner he was able to avoid the streets and to approach and leave the house through the fields, not far from the woods.

Out of consideration for Orlow, he never approached the house or left it directly but always moved along the fence lines, despite the snow; then, upon reaching the end of Dover Court, made for the creek. With the advent of deep snow he had been forced to give up hauling wood into town; he returned the horse and rig to Marcus Carnon and spent his days closer to a fire. He had come to Connecticut with a considerable amount of money, but it was steadily dwindling, though he spent as little as possible. A goodly amount had to be saved for the ship fares for himself and Becky.

To his joy, Becky had agreed to go with him and now nothing remained but to find a captain willing to chance a British search. That task was up to Orlow. Since the patrols, it would be completely impossible for Louis even to enter the town during the day, let alone pay someone to row him out to an anchored ship.

Somehow the British were aware he was in the area. Louis was positive because of the increased patrols and from the gossip Orlow picked up. The soldiers had probably been warned to say nothing, but in the manner of soldiers everywhere they gossiped among themselves and were overheard.

Then Orlow came home one night to say that it was common talk that a Frenchman had been seen—a French soldier—and a reward of twenty pounds had been posted for his capture.

But on subsequent days Orlow reported that the soldiers were half-hearted about the patrols, believing that it was foolish to assume a French officer would remain for long in a little village like Canaan. It was a definite factor in allowing Louis to remain at large.

Orlow too was fortunate that no one noticed his increasing interest in ships. He made an attempt to cover this by sketching them, and even made a painting of a ship for Goodman Porter's window. He borrowed Isak Tilley's dinghy and rowed out to each merchant ship that dropped anchor at Canaan, but was unsuccessful until the brig *Fortune* appeared.

Fortune's master was Captain Gabriel Holguin, a veteran seaman who had begun his career fifty years before as cabin boy, a man who held a fierce dislike for the British navy and its high-handed ways. He sat Orlow down in his cabin, a square-paneled cubicle painted buff and black, with whale's teeth and brass mounted muskets adorning the bulkheads, and served up a bottle of Jamaica rum.

"My bo's'n tells me you want passage to France, that right, sir?"

"Not exactly, Captain," Orlow said. "It's not for me but a friend and his wife."

"Ahhh—issat so? A wife!"

"Is that possible?"

"Oh yes, certainly, if she can stand the voyage. There ain't any children, I hope."

"No, sir."

"Where in France, the channel or the Med?"

"The Mediterranean would be best."

Holguin nodded approvingly. "I go from here to th' Azores and on to Marseilles. Your friends are in luck."

"There is one thing more—"

"What's that?"

"My friend is a Frenchman, a recent officer from Canada, and the British would like to get their hands on him."

Holguin was silent for a few ticks of the clock, then he smiled. "They would, eh? What the devil is a Frenchman doing in Connecticut? Never heard such a damned thing."

"Trying to get a ship."

"Well, he's found one. Is she French too?"

"No, sir, born here in Canaan. The redcoats will search your ship, won't they?"

Holguin grinned, wrinkling his weathered face. "If I don't know my ship better'n some fat-ass, flat-footed lobsterback, then they can hang me from m'own yardarm. I could hide half the town and they'd never find 'em. I'll have m'cargo on the wharf this time day after tomorrow. You have your friends come aboard at night before then."

"Tomorrow night, then."

"Good. I'll hang a lantern on the seaboard side after dark. You got the money?"

Orlow dug into his pocket.

Becky was more excited by Orlow's news than anything she'd ever experienced. She was actually going to Europe! With the man she loved! It took hours before she could settle down enough to think of planning.

It would be necessary for the family's sake, her mother said, that her disappearance seem proper and plausible. They would announce that letters had been exchanged between Becky and certain cousins living west of New York town, and that she would soon be going there for an extended visit. Of course there would be talk about her departure in the middle of winter, but there was no help for that.

Orlow Gordon was brought into the discussion and he suggested that she go aboard the brig openly; he would request Captain Holguin to post a change of plans, that he would put in at New York for a particular cargo. The chance that someone from Canaan would find out that the ship had never gone near New York was so slight as to be not worth considering.

On the day that Becky and her mother planned to confront Azariah with the fact of her going, Azariah stumped home on Junius's arm in a state of near-collapse. He spent an hour in front of the kitchen fire recovering from the tiring walk, coughing terribly, then, with Junius and Brayton helping, went upstairs to bed. It was no time to shock him with Becky's plans.

But the boys were told: "Your sister is going away for a time—"

Junius said, "Going away! Going where?" He stared at Becky.

"To France."

Brayton said, "So it's true about the Frenchman!"

Maggie was surprised. "How do you know about him?"

"It's all over town the red ants are looking for him. Who else would Becky be going away with?"

Maggie was startled by Brayton's calmness. Junius, however, was not so blasé. "When will you be married?"

"When we arrive in France," Becky said. "Unless the ship captain can marry us."

"It isn't proper," Junius said stubbornly, and he continued his unbending attitude though Maggie explained that circumstances could not be altered. If Louis were brought into the open, the British would have him.

Becky said with some sarcasm, "It's my soul, brother dear, not yours. And it's not the worst thing you'll hear in your life, I'm sure."

"I worry about your soul as much as my own!"

"That's enough about souls," Maggie said. "This must go no farther. Junius, do you promise?"

"Yes, of course."

"Brayton?"

"Yes, but what about the Frenchman? Where is he?"

"His name is Louis Boyer," Becky said. "You'll see him soon enough."

Becky managed to meet with Louis to prepare him for the encounter. "They know I intend to go, but I'm not sure they all approve."

"And your father?"

"He is ill and doesn't know. Mother will tell him after we've gone, when he's able to bear it."

Louis clucked his tongue. "I wish it were not so. Is the illness very serious?"

"I fear it is." She made a face and shook her head. How many times had it occurred to her that she might not see him again.

That night Louis came to the house for the first time. He wore patched but clean breeches and coat and Maggie could see that he had taken great pains with his appearance; she also saw that he was apprehensive and more than a little nervous, which she grudgingly admitted to herself was to the good. If he had been a rogue like David Urfe he would probably be very self-assured.

Becky was edgy as well and the meeting was strained; both boys sat silent staring at Louis, the first

Frenchman either had ever seen. Maggie found herself forcing the conversation, doing her best, despite her reservations, to put Louis at ease. It was not good manners to be silent and she was glad when Brayton asked him about soldiering.

Louis said, "I fought for my country as any man would, but that is all in the past and I am not a soldier now."

"You speak English very well," Junius said in a grudging tone. Becky thought he seemed determined not to like Louis.

"I went to Canada as a boy and was brought up in both languages, though I fear my accent is very pronounced."

"He speaks perfectly," Becky said.

He smiled at her and Maggie looked down at her hands in her lap. It was difficult to maintain a feeling of reserve. Louis was plainly a man of considerable charm, without thrusting it upon others. He seemed to her a man of inner strength, the same as Azariah and her son Morgan—and Wager too. Louis was a pleasant-looking man, almost as handsome as Wager, and a good deal broader. It was a strange feeling, and not an easy one, gazing at the man who would take her daughter away, perhaps for years.

The small talk flowed around Maggie and she half listened. There were so many questions she wanted to ask, but she must have faith in Becky. The fact that they had resisted intimate embraces was in itself reassuring. Louis apparently had more strength of character than the ensign beloved by Marie.

Maggie could not help noticing how Marie stared at their guest and she wondered what thoughts were spinning in Marie's head. Did she compare David Urfe to this Frenchman? Did she see in Becky and Louis what might have been for her and David?

Becky served tea and cakes while Louis told them about France and the place where he and Becky would live, for a short time at least. He intimated that when his business in France was finished he wanted to return to the colonies and be accepted. The recent war would soon be forgotten, he thought, and people would be busy with the business of living, a far more important thing than fighting. Even the British would have to admit that.

Marie excused herself when she finished the tea and went up to bed; Brayton went soon after, saying he had to rise early and get to the store because Eli Burley had lately suffered a number of sciatic attacks that made it difficult for the old man to get up and down stairs.

Maggie felt her early resentment falling away; it was so easy to allow herself the commonly held opinions of foreigners, but gazing at Louis and hearing him speak, he did not seem at all "different." He had an accent, but other than that he might have been one of her own sons.

And it was obvious in his every glance how he loved Becky. Maggie felt a twinge, seeing the looks, thinking that Wager looked at her in exactly the same way when they were alone.

Then, as it grew late and rain pelted the rear windows, Louis rose, saying he must go along or Orlow would worry, thinking he'd been taken by a patrol. Then Maggie asked the question she'd been dreading. "When will you go?"

"Orlow has talked to a captain," Louis said. "He will take us. Becky will go aboard tomorrow afternoon and I will row out to the ship with Orlow after dark. The ship will sail on the morning tide."

Junius asked, "What about the British?"

"Captain Holguin has prepared a hiding place for

me. The redcoats will search the ship, of course." Louis smiled and shrugged. "My fate is in his hands."

Becky said quickly, "Captain Holguin despises the British."

Maggie rose with them and took both their hands. Then Becky was in her arms, with tears streaming down her cheeks. She felt Louis's arms about them both, but no one said anything.

With Maggie's help, Becky that night reviewed what she would take, not a great choice, for she must travel lightly. She had only a single canvas bag for clothes and a homemade knapsack for small articles; the knapsack had a shoulder strap and several buckles.

When Becky went to bed at last, Maggie paced the kitchen, beset with doubts and forebodings. Becky was sixteen, but still a child. Would another mother allow her daughter to go away in this fashion? Probably not. It caused her fresh doubts. What would Azariah say when she told him?

When she got to sleep, Maggie dreamed of great waves and a roaring wind and woke in a sweat to lie quietly as she could beside Azariah, listening to his steady breathing. It was a good night for him; the cough did not wake him as it often did and she prayed it would continue.

She dreaded the day she'd tell him about Louis. She had seen him angry only a few times but this might well be one. She felt his strength should be saved to combat his sickness rather than to rail at Becky, or at her. How would she go about it? He was sure to ask where Becky was.

She sensed that Azariah's health was a fragile thing, not the cold the doctor diagnosed. She had far more experience of Azariah's moods and feelings than he. Azariah was seriously ill; she knew it in her bones.

She would do what she had to do. She would break it to him very gently when he was able to understand it.

She worried for sleepless hours about her decision, fell at last into a troubled dozing and was glad when dawn lightened the room. She got up when Azariah began coughing and swearing between coughs; she dressed, saying she would make him some hot tea and bring it up. The tea seemed to soothe his throat.

Becky came into the kitchen as her mother was building up the fire. She had been unable to sleep longer, she said.

"How is Father?"

"He complains of being tired."

"Let me take the tea to him this morning."

Maggie hugged her daughter. "Of course. He will remember that one day."

The parting was very difficult for Maggie. She longed to talk to Wager about it, but that was impossible. He came to the house that morning, but there was no way to see him alone. Both Brayton and Junius stayed home—Brayton came back from the store—and after a bit Wager left, after kissing Becky's cheek and wishing her Godspeed.

Though she tried not to, Maggie cried while saying goodbye to Becky. But it was only goodbye for a short while, Becky promised, because she and Louis would soon return. Brayton and Junius carried her two bags and Maggie stood by the door feeling forlorn, tears in her eyes, watching them go. But Marie was dry-eyed and very solemn, as if she were twice her age.

"She will be back, Mother."

The rain turned into a light drizzle, misting the trees, drifting into Maggie's face to mingle with her tears; it was the kind of day to see a daughter off, she thought.

When the three were out of sight, Maggie reluctantly

closed the door and slowly climbed the stairs to sit with Azariah. His sprawling bulk sagged in the bed under an ocean of blankets, and his face was gray as beach sand. His eyes were closed when she entered and they opened only momentarily to watch her sit. She took up her knitting bag with numb fingers, thinking how her family was all at once splintering like a tree branch hit by a great axe. Nothing was the same as it had been only a week ago.

She did not realize she was sitting stiffly without moving, when Azariah turned his head to stare at her. "What's the matter?"

Starting, she took up the skeins of yards, sorting them out. "I—I was thinking of Morgan."

Azariah started to cough, his face red, and Maggie bit her lip, feeling pity for him. He had always been a strong man; how he must hate this terrible affliction, and having to stay in bed. Color slowly drained from his face again as the coughing petered out and he lay back, breathing as if he had run a great distance. She pressed a hand to his forehead. It felt feverish.

"Can you eat something?"

He shook his head weakly. "I don't want anything."

"You've had very little breakfast."

"I don't want anything." He turned away from her in a sudden spate of coughing.

Maggie put the bag aside, rose and went downstairs and looked at Marie. She was barely showing, but a thick cloak would cover her belly. "Will you go for the doctor, child?"

Marie stood at once. "Yes, Mother." She started from the kitchen and turned. "Is he worse?"

Maggie nodded silently and poked at the fire. Was it cold in the room, or was it she? What was she fearing for Azariah? As Marie pulled the cloak about her thin form, Maggie filled the kettle and hung it on the crane, then shoved sticks into the coals. She heard Marie go out the front door.

Did Azariah have consumption? She had begun to suspect it. What was happening to her family? Had God turned His face away from them? It was as if Morgan's departure had loosed a fateful flood and Marie's ordeal had afflicted them with a plague.

No, she must not think that way. It would all turn out for the best. Except perhaps for Azariah; did anyone recover from consumption? She feared for him. How she feared for him!

The mists cleared as they reached the wharf, a good omen, Brayton said, for the beginning of a voyage. Junius walked to Isak Tilley's store and returned rowing the dinghy, which he tied, and Brayton handed down the bags.

Becky gazed with fascinated eyes at the tall, two-masted ship that would be her home for the next month or so. It was a stark picture, gray masts and spars rising against a cold sky with gulls swooping low near her stern. She climbed down into the boat and sat in the sternsheets with Brayton's arm about her waist and Junius pulling expertly at the oars.

When they came near she saw the brig was a storm-battered hulk with bluff bows and eight or ten ports along the side. Junius craned his neck to look at her and said, "She won't be fast, but she'll get you there." It was reassuring.

Junius shipped the oars and tied on, hollering to several men on the deck that a female was coming aboard. After a bit they dropped a canvas rig and Becky managed to get into it with Brayton's help, sitting with her feet toward the side of the ship to ward it off, and they pulled her up.

Captain Holguin was there to greet her, a spare, red-faced man with cocked hat and long black coat. "Welcome, Miz Boyer—easy there, lads. Set her down like a feather—"

Becky was startled to be called Mrs. Boyer, but she did not protest. She thanked the sailors who had pulled her up. They grinned and hauled up her bags. Brayton and Junius scrambled up the side, clinging to lines, and Brayton embraced her.

"Maybe you won't get seasick. But if you get it remember to take white of an egg, and eat as much as you can."

She thanked him and Junius put his arms about her. "Goodbye, and don't forget us."

"How could I do that!"

The two had a present for her, a pair of fur-lined gloves, which Brayton pulled from a pocket. "They ought to come in handy."

Becky kissed them both. "Thank you . . . thank you!" She introduced them to Captain Holguin. "My brothers, Captain, come to see me off."

He lifted his hat to them and went aft shouting to someone as Brayton and Junius went over the side into the boat. Junius yelled up at her to write them when she arrived and she called back that she would. Then Junius rowed away with Brayton waving from the stern seat. She leaned on the bulwark and watched them till they disappeared round the wharf.

At her shoulder Captain Holguin said, "If you'll follow me, Miz Boyer, I'll show you t'your cabin."

It was on a lower deck, a deck that smelled of tar and other undefinable odors, a tiny, rectangular room with two bunks built into the wall, a round stool with a rope that kept it tethered to the opposite wall, a built-in washstand with a pitcher and bowl half enclosed by a coaming, a candle-lantern hanging from the ceiling, a few pegs on the wall near the door, and nothing else. Becky stood in the center of the cabin feeling closed-in and stifled. The lantern smelled horribly; was she expected to live in this cupboard for weeks?

Some of what she felt must have showed on her face, for Captain Holguin, in the open door, smiled and said, "Besides me own, lass, it's the largest cabin on board."

She nodded. Her bags were on the floor already. "Thank you, Captain."

"I expect Mr. Boyer t'night. By this time tomorra we'll be long gone from these parts." Holguin touched his hat brim. "Make yourself free of the ship, ma'am, and lock yourself in when you're inside." He indicated the iron latch. "You're the only female on the ship."

That was not good news. She sat on the lower bunk when he'd gone, got up to latch the door and sat again in near-gloom. The lantern barely dispersed the shadows. There was no port for air, only a number of round holes augered along the top of the door. But it was a beginning, and Louis would come to her in a few hours. Then everything would be all right again.

She looked at the top bunk. Of course he was expected to sleep there. She felt a sharp jab of reality; they were man and wife to everyone on board. Her new life was really starting.

The excitement of the coming voyage would not let her remain long in the tiny cabin. She drew on her new gloves and went on deck to gaze at the shore. The deck was littered with kegs and bales, piles of rope and odd-shaped implements; men swore and sweated, ignoring her as they worked to get the cargo into the holds. She walked forward and stood by the cathead gazing at the little town, able to make out the boatyard off to the left. How long would it be until she saw this sight again? How she would miss her family. . . .

Louis came aboard after dark. She was in the cramped little cabin, curled on the bunk, when there was a rap on the door. She sat up. "Who's there?"

"It's me," Louis said. "May I come in?"

With a glad cry she rushed to open the door and fall into his arms. He jumped inside, latched the door and held her tightly. He smelled of salt water and cold and his coat was damp. She said, "I thought you'd never get here!"

"It took longer than I expected. There were soldiers on the wharf, so we had to launch the boat through the surf." He pulled off the coat, hung it on a peg and embraced her again. "I can only stay a short time, *chérie*."

"What! Why?"

"Because the soldiers on the wharf were getting into a boat. Captain Holguin thinks they may come here any moment to search us."

Fear turned her icy. "Lord! What if they find you?"

"They will not. Trust the captain to find a good place." He kissed her. "And you must not give me away with that long face."

She clung to him. "Louis—what would I do without you!"

"Those are not proper thoughts. We will never be apart again. Only this little time, to fool the redcoats. They will come and poke about the ship, then go away, and we will have each other. I promise."

It was all she could do to let him go, then latch the door again. With him gone it seemed even more gloomy in the cabin. Sighing deeply, she curled up on the bunk and drew blankets over her to wait out the hours. She longed to be able to spend one day after the next with Louis and never have to worry about his going away. So far it had been one parting after another, with hurried meetings in between and nothing satisfactory. But their time was coming. She cast her thoughts ahead to it.

She was awakened by the tramping of boots overhead. Opening her eyes, she could make out a pale wisp of light stealing in through the air holes in the door—it must be morning. She had slept through the night. Where was Louis?

Hard heels came along the passageway outside the cabin door and suddenly there was a loud rapping and a voice growled, "Open the door—open up!"

Becky slid off the bunk, pulled a shawl about her and unfastened the latch with trembling fingers. The door was yanked open and she stared at a hard-faced man in a red coat. He was backed by a half dozen of His Majesty's soldiers with muskets and bayonets. The man pushed into the cabin, shoving her aside. He poked a hand into each bunk, grunted, glared at her and tapped the top bunk. "Who sleeps there?"

"N-no-no one," she managed to say, half frightened to death.

His brows rose. "You're travelin' alone?"

"I'm g-going to meet my husband."

He grunted again, frowned at her with narrowed eyes, went out and slammed the door. Becky took a long breath, hugged the shawl close and sat on the bunk, still trembling. What would she do if they found Louis?

The search took more than an hour and she came out when she heard them assembling on deck. As the last of the soliders went over the side into the boats Captain Holguin shouted orders; the brig's anchor came up, dripping mud, and the topsails were let go. Becky stood at the rail amidships and the wind blew the hair into her face. The sails filled and the ship's motion changed. They were suddenly gliding through the green water and her heart beat faster. The houses along the far shore merged and blurred and then slowly began to fall away astern.

All the sails were set and drawing, and suddenly Louis was there, catching her up, kissing her in front of grinning seamen.

They were off! The journey had actually begun.

Chapter Nineteen

Maggie felt a very great sense of loss, seeing Becky go. It was too soon after Morgan's disappearance. She found herself sitting before the fire, staring into the flames, with her hands in her lap. The house was different, the same house and furniture, but different and lacking.

She had long ago tried to prepare herself for the time when her children would grow up and move away to their own households, but what had happened with Morgan and Becky had been too sudden.

It was Morgan who worried her. There were too few details. Even when she'd gone to Isak Tilley's shop and talked with him, it was not enough. And another curious thing: the British authorities had not come to question her. It was as if they had no idea who had killed Ensign Urfe. Tilley had told her that Morgan was positive they were pursuing *him*, that they knew his name and exactly who he was.

Apparently Morgan had been wrong. She was happy they did not know, but it left so many questions unanswered.

She had given up discussing it with Azariah. His attention wandered after a short time; his thoughts were so often turned inward; he worried so continually about his illness. It never got any better. There were days when the cough seemed to leave him for a time, when he was able to walk to the boatyard, but he was always tired when he returned, ready to get into bed again.

Marie was filling out as the weeks passed. Her condition would be apparent to any woman, almost at a glance. Maggie knew it was time something be planned. She discussed it with the boys one evening when Azariah was asleep. If Marie stayed in Canaan to have the baby the fact would cause a sensation, if the news got out. It would also cause trouble. Dr. Lunt could be depended upon to spread the evil word and the locusts would come seeking her. . . .

Junius was willing to go with her to another town, he said, if they could get someone to run the boatyard. But where would they get the necessary money? Maggie pooled their resources, a mere twenty-three pounds, not nearly enough. There were a few things they might sell, she thought, but even so there would not be enough.

Brayton said the only way was to borrow the money, if they could concoct a story to tell a lender. He was sure Eli Burley, his employer, would lend them the money, but he would surely want to know the why of it. He would ask embarrassing questions when he discovered Junius and Marie had gone away, and he would find out. There was no way to hide it.

After the boys had gone to bed, Maggie sat alone in the kitchen. There seemed to be no answer but scandal. Their name would be dirtied in the town; Marie would never be allowed to rear her child in Canaan.

The next afternoon she went to see Widow Riley, and while she sat in the kitchen that smelled of vegetables cooking, Wager appeared. Maggie distracted the old woman, and when she met Wager upstairs a bit later she was astonished to find herself crying. They sat on the bed together and he held her tightly as the tears gushed. She could do nothing to stop them. It was as if the troubles of the last few days were all bound up together, more than she could contain.

Wager was patient, waiting it out. "Is it Becky?" he

asked at length. He knew she'd gone away with Louis on the ship.

Maggie lay back, dabbing at her eyes with the hem of her skirt, feeling wan. "It's Becky—and Marie—" She clutched at him as he lay beside her and moved into the shelter of his arms. "Sometimes I feel at the end of my tether." She made a little gesture of resignation. "What will I do about Marie?"

"She must go away, is that it?"

"Yes." She turned her head to him, wanting his kiss. His lips brushed hers and he stroked her hair.

"I've been thinking about that, and I have an idea that may work."

"What is it?" She grasped his coat as if fearing he might move away.

"I have a sister in Massachusetts, not far off really. What if we sent her there?"

"A sister!"

"She lives in a town called Westfield with her husband and two sons. We're on good terms."

"Would they take her in?"

"If I went along and asked them."

"Wager! Would you do that?"

He said simply, "Maggie, I'd do anything for you. Anything you asked."

She closed her eyes and snuggled closer, tightening her grasp. She felt protected and secure, at peace for the first time in days. He kissed her cheek and she smiled, stirring like a child in half-sleep. His lips nuzzled her ear. "When do you want her to go?"

"Soon . . ." She looked at him. "Do you think it will cost very much?"

"No, not very. The main thing is the story."

"Yes."

"We'll have to tell some lies. We'll have to say that

Marie is married, for one thing. No one in these colonies would have a thing to do with her if she is not."

Maggie nodded and closed her eyes again. "We will do what we have to. I'll have a very serious talk with Marie."

"Good. That's the first step." He kissed her eyelids. "It must be a plausible lie. We might say that she ran off with someone, got married in a strange town, and then he was killed somehow—perhaps by robbers along a road."

"But why can't she go back to her family then?"

"Because they loathed the man and will *not* have his child in their house." He kissed the end of her nose. "Will that suffice?"

"I—I believe it would." Maggie turned onto her back and smiled up at him. "What a devious mind you have, darling."

"It's good to see you smile."

"It's only because of you. You're very good for me, Wager."

"How is Azariah?"

She sighed. "Not well at all. Come to see him soon."

"I will."

She looked at him. "You were about to say something?"

"Yes. I'd like to be good to you in another way."

She drew him down and kissed him. "I believe that would be better than medicine." She began to undress.

Afterward Maggie closed her eyes and it seemed that cool air wafted through the room, soothing her eyelids, passing soft hands along her throat, and she felt that all her worries were far off in some hidden place. Morgan was safe and would come back soon, and Becky would appear with a new grandchild. . . . All the fears and torments were banished as Wager slid his hand over hers, turned her head and lay his cheek against hers. She sighed contentedly. "It makes all the waiting worthwhile."

"What d'you mean?"

She said softly, "I think of you when I'm away from this room."

"Yes, and I you."

"—and the waiting is very pleasant."

"The waiting?"

"Anticipating, perhaps. I sometimes think I'd be lost without it, without something to look forward to—with you. I need something to remember, to hold when we're apart."

"You're a precious body, Maggie. How was I ever lucky enough to have you?"

She kissed his cheek fondly. "None of this is real, you know. We're dreaming, you and I, and one day we'll awake to wonder where it went."

"Well, I don't intend to wake up."

She sighed again. "Well, I'm afraid it's time now. Marie will be fretting. Will you write to your sister soon?"

"I'll do it immediately, to go out by the next post."

Wager's suggestion made her feel very much easier in her mind. Maggie went about her tasks sure that a solution was in the making. Wager would take Marie there, a distance of about fifty miles. The baby was not due till July, and if they could wait till early spring . . .

Louis had almost no baggage at all, a small cloth sack with a razor and soap, tobacco and pipes and a few underclothes. He had less than thirty pounds in his pockets after the fares were paid, and the clothes he stood in. The two of them would indeed be starting out with nothing.

The first moments of their meeting were intense.

Becky felt her heart full to bursting with the excitement of the voyage and Louis. When they fell onto the bunk she opened her arms to him. He began to undress her, then paused. "*Chérie* . . ."

"What?" She bit his ear.

"The captain cannot marry us—we will have to make the journey as we are."

"I know. He thinks we are already married."

"Yes. Orlow told him that. He was afraid the captain would not take us unless we were."

She kissed him. "Then we are married and will have to make the best of it."

He laughed and slipped the dress from her shoulders. "We will be married as soon as we reach France. You will have time to become used to your new name."

"I've already thought of it a thousand times." She removed her smallclothes and pulled the blanket up about her neck. What a wild, crazy excitement to be completely naked with him! He pushed out of his clothes and slid in beside her and the first embrace, skin to skin, was like a sudden drenching shock that took her breath away. She had dreamed of it but the reality was so much more compelling!

She gave herself up to his caresses, squirming and shuddering as his hands moved over her velvet skin as no others had ever done. His kisses became urgent and her heart pounded and she gasped to get her breath. He seemed to know exactly when she was ready and gently slid atop her. Becky was trembling and afraid, but wanting him, and when he entered her she thought she would swoon with the intense sensation. There was a little pain mingled with the riotous desire that flooded her, but she ignored it. The blood throbbed at her temples and she barely heard his whispered, "Shall I stop . . . ?"

She held him in a drowning grasp. "No—no—no—" Lord! No! She would die if he stopped! She rubbed his bare back and pushed upward, all inhibitions flown. Her slim legs encircled his and their breaths mingled—and then she moaned aloud and her back arched as she cried out, lost in the engulfing ecstasy that invaded her body, permeating every inch of her being. It left her trembling and weak. Louis kissed her neck and cheek, still moving sinuously with her.

She felt herself drifting into a fog that had no end; the world was gone and only she and Louis remained. She'd never expected such vivid feelings and exquisite agony, and when the sudden convulsive ecstasy came again she moaned, twisting and shuddering, feeling Louis driving into her . . . and then slowly the sensation withdrew, leaving her longing for its return and yet satisfied that it had happened. Louis was beside her, breathing deeply, arms about her protectively, and she felt she had never loved him so much.

The next days were all of a kind; they walked on deck when it was fair, when the decks were level as a roadway, and stayed below when they slanted steeply and the wind howled through the rigging like bands of evil spirits. The sea was constantly changing, sometimes blue and deep green and sometimes gray. And when the driving winds swooped down they hurled enormous billows of rushing water aboard and whitecaps were everywhere about the ship and stinging sheets of spray were flung like bullets into their faces. Then Captain Holguin ordered lines strung along the decks as safety measures. But when the wind shrieked, Louis kept her below decks, saying he would not take a chance of losing her to the angry gods.

They spent hours on end in the tiny stuffy cabin, and

the bunks were the only places where rest was possible. She lay naked with Louis, sleeping and talking and now and again making love, and the days slipped by.

Often she did not know when day took the place of night. Storms darkened the skies and the ship's timbers creaked alarmingly as the brig plunged and rolled and the wind screamed. Louis held her tightly, promising that the ship would master the sea, that soon there would be tranquil skies. And then she would pull him atop her and lose herself in the wild excesses of love.

He told her often that he was the envy of every man on the ship, and she flushed with the realization of what he meant. But of course they were married, so far as anyone knew, and their intimate moments were their own.

Louis was right. The skies did clear as they neared the Azores Islands. They sailed into a round harbor where small, white, red-tile-roofed houses decorated the dark hills. The islands were volcanic, Louis said, and belonged to Portugal. They had long been subject to earthquakes. Many of the people were involved in the slave trade.

She went ashore with him and a dozen or more of the crew, dined in a strange-smelling, flower-bedecked restaurant, drank wine that made her head reel, and returned to the ship before sunset.

The *Fortune* took on water and a few supplies, hauled up the anchor the afternoon of the next day, and glided from the harbor under topsails, pointing her jib eastward toward the great rock, Gibraltar, a British fortress.

Captain Holguin maneuvered to gain the straits after dark, not wishing to call at Gibraltar. They sailed into the Mediterranean under a crescent moon that was only partly obscured by fleecy clouds. After the stormy Atlantic, the Mediterranean seemed calm as a lake.

Since she and Louis were the only passengers on board the brig, they were frequently invited to Holguin's quarters for wine, conversation or cards, which Louis played very well. Becky had been reared to think of cards as undesirable if not evil, and it was not easy for her to overcome her early training. But under Louis's urging she quickly became proficient. She told herself that, after all, a bit of gambling could not hold a candle to her more important sins, such as sleeping with Louis daily.

But she did not allow the idea of sin to dwell in her mind. The love she bore for Louis was greater, and dearer to her.

The journey was nearing its end, and Louis's interest seemed to increase. His restlessness was obvious. During the day he was constantly in the ratlines or even high above in the crosstrees with a glass, eager for a sight of land. They would leave the ship at Marseilles, he told her, and proceed inland for several days to the town of Mirande where he had relatives who would care for them.

Becky was apprehensive about the end of the journey, not knowing what to expect. Louis was positive things were about to change for the better and he could hardly wait; she wished she could feel as he did.

He hinted often that a new life awaited them, but it was impossible to pin him down. He would only smile and kiss her, saying that she must wait a bit longer. The mystery soon palled, however, and she stopped asking him. It was his only failing, she thought, teasing her in that manner.

But Marseilles could not be put off. They approached it very late in the afternoon in a rainstorm. A pilot came out to meet them and guide them in—Louis told her about it because she stayed in the cabin, out of the stinging wet. It was pitch dark when she heard the anchor let go and soon Louis rapped at the door, excited and eager to get ashore, though it would be necessary to wait for morning. That night he made love to her with more than his usual fervor, saying that to be back in France gave him new life.

Chapter Twenty

Enoch Quant arranged with Goodman Julius Grinton to sell his house and property, packed up the family valuables (not a great amount), and bought passage on the schooner *Elmira Dove* for New York.

The money was paid over in Ben Robb's ordinary, and in honor of his going Enoch bought a round for the house, the first time in the memory of anyone there that such a thing had happened. Cephas Foot said to his cronies, behind his hand, that it would probably be talked about in Canaan for years.

Buying the drinks was an occasion for Enoch to make a speech, which he did, though it was brief. He was leaving Canaan, he said, waving his glass at the audience of five, having been finally edged out of the boatyard by the Lynns. But he bore them no ill. He paused to sip from the pint and the others exchanged glances.

"It ain't Azariah's fault," he told them, "it's them cubs, Morgan and Junius." He wiped his grizzled chin with a forearm and the flat planes of his dark face gleamed in the firelight.

"Morgan's gone," someone said, and Enoch turned toward the voice, eyes narrowing.

"Thass right, Morgan's gone." Enoch made a wry face as if smelling something poisonous. "But where's 'e gone? To raid the British, I expect. Heard 'im talk of it many's the time."

"Words, Enoch," Ben Robb said from behind the bar. "You don't know none of that for fact. Not for fact."

"Where is 'e then?" Enoch retorted. "Az ain't talking and Junius neither. I say he's out raidin' commerce and selling it in the Indies like a pirate." He grinned round at them. "There was another pirate named Morgan, if I recollect . . ."

"Names don't mean nothing," Cephas said.

A sudden hot anger swept Enoch. "You all standin' up for the Lynns! I did my bit same's they. I ain't runnin' off!"

"You're going to Boston."

"But I told you. I told ever'body. I ain't going in secret! Morgan, he just up and left at night. That ain't Enoch's way. I work same's you and you, and you. My money's just as good's yours. And I don't force nobody out when they help build up a business—"

"You got paid," Ben Robb said.

"For the show of it!" Enoch slammed the glass down. "Next year that boatyard'll be worth twice more, maybe three. You think them cubs'll send old Enoch 'is money? No—he's out in the damned cold!"

Ben picked his teeth with his little finger. "Somebody hold a pistol t'your head to sign that paper, Enoch?"

"You're all against me," Enoch said heavily. His teeth clicked and he pressed his thin lips together tightly as he glared at them. "You're all against me." He shoved both hands into his pockets and stalked to the door in dead silence. Turning, he gave them all a glance, sorry now he'd bought the drinks, opened the door and went out.

Ben Robb sighed, picked up the bar cloth and wiped away an imaginary spot.

Cephas said, "That man's a fool."

* * *

Wager spread the blankets on the bed; they were dark red wool bought at the fair in Hartford, he said, and stored in a closet for a half dozen years. Maggie slid under them, half naked and gritting her teeth against the cold. There were goose bumps under his hands as he pulled her close. He moved atop her at once as they embraced, allowing the warmth of their bodies to surround them.

"Lord, you feel good," she said, rubbing her hands briskly up and down his back. "It's been so long . . ." She kissed his neck. "I feel selfish, having you all to myself."

Wager smiled. "I'll never be able to think of you as selfish or frivolous."

"Frivolous!" She looked at him out of the corner of her eye. "Is there a woman in all the colony who could be called frivolous?"

He laughed. "I suppose not, but there're some who want to be admired and mooned over, asking favors and giving nothing in return."

"How do you know these things?"

He bit her ear lightly. "I hear about them in the ordinary, of course. The talk there is plainer than in church."

"Talk about women?"

"Yes, a good bit."

She moved languidly, opening her knees as the warmth began to make the bed cozy. They lay quiet for a long time. It was peaceful and she felt content, her eyelids beginning to grow heavy. She stirred when Wager's hand slipped down between them and her hips seemed to arch of their own accord; she moaned as he slowly came into her, his lips pressed to her cheek. She heard him whisper, "I love you, Maggie Barth . . ." And she smiled into the dark and tightened her arms about him. The warm, exquisite sensation of his moving loins caused her mouth to open, gulping in cold air as she matched her movements to his, her eyes heavy-lidded. How she needed him! It had been too long, with Azariah lying sick and the added work since Becky had gone. It had been a week at least.

She gave herself up to the rhythm of love, seeking release, her heart full. The creaking protests of the bed were a delicious counterpoint, but they faded out of consciousness as she moaned and twisted all at once. Her knees came up and Wager surged and she cried out in involuntary exhilaration that was quickly replaced by a sensuous flood of fulfillment.

She could not have said how long they lay together. She wanted time to banish itself, not to remind her of the duties awaiting. She might have slept, but Wager stirred and over her soft moans of protest, moved aside, then rubbed her damp skin with a cloth, around her breasts and down between her thighs as she twisted and pulled at him. She wanted more but he whispered that he must go even if she did not, and lifted the blankets to slide out.

In that second the front door of the house opened and a woman's voice called, "Irene—Irene, it's me—"

Maggie was awake instantly. She sat up, staring in consternation at Wager. "Who is it?"

He shook his head, a finger against his lips. She watched him pull on his breeches and tiptoe to the door, shirt in hand. He looked down the stairs and back to her. "Rowena Nicholson," he said in a hushed whisper.

Rowena was a neighbor living only three houses away. Maggie bit her tongue and folded back the blankets to slip out. The bed squeaked and Wager moved his hand to her urgently, shaking his head. She stayed still, half naked, breasts exposed to the chill. Could Rowena hear those slight noises?

Wager approached, pulling on his shirt. "She's in the kitchen." He helped her off the bed and handed her clothes. "Damme, what's she doing here?"

Maggie said softly, "She helped us clean the house." Apparently Rowena dropped in on Widow Riley from time to time; they were about of an age. She dressed quickly, her mind busy with the scandal should Rowena take it into her head to climb the stairs. What a sensation it would cause!

"How long'll she stay?" Wager growled from the door.

Maggie moved to stand beside him, head cocked. She could hear Rowena shouting at the old woman in the kitchen, trying to carry on a conversation; she ought to tire of that soon. It occurred to Maggie to run down the stairs and pretend she'd just entered the house; it would prevent Rowena from exploring, in case she took the notion. But as the idea slid into her mind Rowena came from the kitchen, yelling that she'd only stopped in for a moment.

"Thank the Lord," Wager breathed, his eye to a crack. He pulled back suddenly and stared at Maggie. His lips formed the words, "She's looking up here . . ."

But the front door slammed in another minute and when Wager looked again she was gone.

"Let's hurry," Maggie said. She folded the blankets on the bed and put them neatly in the center of it as Wager opened the door.

As she hurried toward home she began to tremble in reaction. What if Rowena had climbed the stairs! Did the woman suspect what was going on? Lord, let it not be so! What would she do if she could not see Wager? She could not even comprehend how empty her life would be without him. He was her every reason for existing. . . .

She heard Azariah coughing as she went into the

house. In the kitchen Marie said, "He's been coughing like that all morning. Isn't there anything you can do?"

Maggie shook her head, making a face. She dropped her cloak over a chair. "Did you take him tea?"

"Yes, a while ago."

"I wish summer could come." Maggie went up the stairs and stood in the doorway, looking at Az. What could she say to him that would be comforting? She went in and sat on the bed, took his hand and squeezed it. He looked at her dully, then closed his eyes.

"I'm done for, Maggie."

"Don't talk like that! You're going to get better. It's not long till summer. Then we'll have you out in the hot sun."

"No, it's consumption, isn't it?"

"Az, dear, we don't know that it is!"

"I wish Morgan would come home. Funny how I think of him so much. And where's Becky? When I asked Marie a while ago she didn't answer." He stopped to cough, turning his head away, leaning half out of the bed.

Maggie said, "Becky's doing a job of work in town. Do you want more tea? I'll fix it with lemon."

"Yes, give me some." He lay on the pillow when the coughing spate was over, white as the sheet, breathing fast.

Maggie went down the stairs conscious of the lie. She must tell him soon about Becky or his wondering would make it worse. She put the kettle on and Marie said, "Someone came to the door a while ago, Mother."

"Who was it?"

Marie shook her head, a hand on her rounding belly. "I didn't go to see."

Maggie stared at the girl, then went to the back window. It was a problem she hadn't foreseen; of course Marie couldn't open the door and show the town her condition, and with Becky gone—She sighed deeply and looked at the sky, dull and overcast with the wind bending the small branches of the trees almost double.

When Marie went off to have her baby . . .

She stepped back into the kitchen, poured the boiling water into a cup, squeezed a bit of lemon into it and stirred, watching it turn amber. She ought to tell Azariah today—now. It was foolish and hard on her to go on telling lies. And sooner or later he would get it out of Marie.

She took the tea upstairs and sat by the bed as he sipped it. "Az—there is something I must tell you. . . ."

Marseilles was one of the great ports of the world, dating back farther than Roman times, Louis said. He was excited as a boy to be back on his native soil— even though he'd spent years in Canada. His roots, he told her, went deep.

They said their goodbyes to Captain Holguin before noon and went over the side into a small boat manned by a red-shirted and deeply tanned boatman who put them ashore on a rickety fishermen's wharf where gulls screamed and wheeled, fighting over every scrap in the morning sun.

To Becky, everything but the boats was strange. They walked along a cobblestoned street into the city and she saw with round eyes the oddly dressed fishwives with huge baskets of smelly fish on their heads and heard their shrill voices as they hawked their wares. It had never occurred to her to wonder how it would feel to be in a completely foreign land, listening to the so-different cadences of a foreign tongue on every side. She clung to Louis's arm as they walked, afraid to lose him. She stared at fishermen and boatmen; they were bare-headed and wearing odd hanging caps with baggy, loose trousers, some rolled to the knees. They mingled with dock workers and peddlers who shouted, displaying goods from their packs, many calling to her and Louis to come and look. In the doorways of the shops were merchants and tradesmen, better dressed than the others; they smoked their pipes and discussed the passersby. An occasional horseman came by and several heavy wagons lumbered past, horses plodding with heads down and drivers flicking long whips and calling to those on foot to beware, stand aside! *"Gare!"* There were brown-robed priests who stared at her, she thought, as if divining the sinful facts of her life. There were sailors from the square-rigged ships in the harbor and a few brazen-eyed girls who gazed at Louis, then at her. Becky glanced back to see them talking together and she wondered if it were obvious to everyone that she and Louis were not married. Several gendarmes stared at her too; they were dressed in blue uniforms with short swords and gaitered legs, hands clasped behind them as they strolled in pairs.

Louis asked directions several times, telling her he was bound for a certain section of the city. He had been here many times as a child, before going to Canada, but now everything was changed. They would find a hotel, he said, in which to spend the night, then go on to Mirande in the morning if all went well. She wondered what he meant by that.

He found an unprepossessing hotel, not overly clean, she thought, off a crowded street. She was tired to death and had an impression of brown walls and narrow dim hallways, and an old woman in black who scowled at them. Louis did not volunteer information and when they arrived she was too tired to badger him, glad to stop walking and drop across a bed.

But she was astonished when Louis announced that he was going out and would return shortly.

"But where?"

He only smiled. "Rest, *chérie*. I will not be long and you are perfectly safe here." He cautioned her to lock the door behind him and was gone.

Tears of frustration welled up in her eyes. Louis had always been vague, but she had put together ideas of what their life would be like, and none of this reality matched her dreams. She went to a window, pushed aside the sleazy curtains and looked down at the street. It was very quiet, rutted, with broken cobblestones and piles of trash and buildings across from her that looked ancient. It smelled too of a hundred ancient odors and she turned away, feeling wretched. The cheap room was plain and barren. Once-white walls were faded in places to yellow-brown, seamed with cracks and pitted with holes that showed the dusty wood underneath. The bed was creaky, complaining when she sat on it, and there was no chair, only a short wooden bench painted dark red, the color of the only cabinet in the room, and of the door.

She gritted her teeth; she must not allow herself to sink into self-pity. Louis would be back soon, probably with a surprise for her, and all would be well again. He would never leave her for very long in a strange city.

But he did not return for more than an hour, and she thought he had a look of satisfaction, as if he had accomplished something important. He also brought food, rolls that were still warm, and cooked beef, along with a bottle of red wine. They spread the feast on the bed and ate it as he told her he had, quite by accident, run into a friend from the past and they had talked. When she would have asked questions he gave her no chance, chattering about the village of Mirande where his cousins lived, and then undressing her.

Louis was expert by this time at removing her clothes

and she forgot her concerns and frustrations and lost herself in his arms.

The next morning, when he disappeared again, she thought of the "friend" he'd met by accident. What was the mission that had brought him to France—and why did he not tell her about it?

Louis left the hotel and went directly to the Rue d' Aris, to the bakery shop of his old shipmate, Victor Buchon, who was astonished to see him.

Victor was a squat, powerfully built man with black hair, a round face and almost no neck. He had small black eyes beneath jutting brows and smiled a good deal. He wore a gray apron over shirt and brown breeches and looked tired.

"Louis—is it really you!?"

"It is, *mon ami*. I have just come from America. It is good to see you. Is your father still alive?"

Victor shrugged and shook his head sadly. "Alas, no, not for a year."

"I am sorry to hear it." Louis glanced around the shop. "Then you are the proprietor?" It was a spacious room with glass cases and a marvelous smell of baking bread. The walls held a few crudely painted landscapes and the floor was tiled. A woman watched them from a doorway to the rear.

"*Oui*, I am the boss—except for Aimee, my wife." Victor indicated the woman with a nod of his head. She disappeared behind a curtain. "Are you married, Louis?"

Louis nodded. "My wife is at the hotel."

"I have waited for you to come, but I had begun to think you were dead in the war."

"I was lucky. Where are the others? Do you see them?"

Victor lifted his heavy shoulders and dropped them. "There are no others." He smiled crookedly. "Just you and me."

"Ahhh, that is too bad. *Qu'est-ce que se passe?*"

"One thing and another, disease and jail—" His eyes flicked to the curtain and back. "They were not saints."

"None of us were." Louis nodded sadly. "So now it is you and me."

"Have you got the details, Louis?"

"But of course. I would not have come otherwise. There would have been no reason." Louis took a square of paper from an inside pocket. It was worn and dog-eared, folded several times. Victor looked at it hungrily, licking his lips. He watched Louis put it back and his eyes were very bright.

Victor said, "When can we go for it, then?"

"It is a question of money. We need money for passage or for a boat—as well as to live."

Victor made a gesture of annoyance. "Money! *Mon Dieu!* It is always money. I have no money. What about you?"

"It took every sou to get here. Is there no way we can raise enough?" Louis glanced at the shop.

Victor noted the look. "I only just get by, and Aimee is a leech with the smallest coins. But you have relatives?"

"*Oui*, I have cousins at Mirande. I have not seen them for five years or more, but maybe they will loan me the money—if I promise them a share."

Victor shrugged again. "Then promise. There will be enough. Go there at once, Louis."

Louis nodded. He walked toward the door, seeing the curtain move. "I will come back when I have the money."

"*Pour combien de temps partirez vous?*"

241

"Not long, I hope."

Victor smiled and clapped his back. "Do not lose that paper. Maybe I should make a copy?"

"I will not lose it. It has been with me through many years and I think I could write it from memory." He patted the pocket. "*Au revoir,* Victor. It is good to see you again."

"*Au revoir,* Louis. My prayers go with you."

Victor watched Louis stride away along the street, then turned to confront Aimee, who was staring at him. She said, in a voice loaded with suspicion, "What are you planning, husband?"

She was short and dark with large sunken eyes that burned as with a yellow flame. Her mouth was wide and gold circlets hung from her heavy earlobes. Victor smiled and patted her rump.

"I am planning nothing. You are overworking your brain, my dove. Louis is only an old friend." He shrugged. "We plan only a glass of wine together."

Aimee's petulant mouth turned down and her brooding eyes followed him. She had married Victor expecting a life of ease, or at least more ease than she'd had, but it had not turned out that way and the reality had sharpened her tongue. She was aware that long in the past Victor had kept company with a gang of men who were not above criminal acts to gain money and she feared that one day he would take up with them again because the bakery was barely making ends meet.

However, the man who had come to see Victor and whom he called an old friend did not seem the same type as the others; it mollified her somewhat. Perhaps he was telling the truth.

She did not notice then, several hours later, when he sent their oldest boy on an errand without mentioning it to her. The lad returned in half an hour and Victor met him in the alleyway behind the shop. The boy said, "Henri will be there as you asked, Papa."

Victor grinned. "Good. Say nothing of this to your mother."

He met Henri just before dark in a small cafe only five minutes' walk from the bakery. Henri was sitting alone at a table in the rear of the dimly lighted room, a drink before him. He was a short man, no taller than Victor but thin, with a lined face and unblinking eyes. He was dressed as a workman and dark hair curled out from under his cap. When he smiled to greet Victor the missing teeth in the front of his mouth were very obvious.

"What is so important, Victor? You want someone dead?"

Victor sat down, glancing around nervously. "You joke in the wrong places, my friend." There was no one within earshot but he lowered his voice. "I have seen Louis."

Henri stared at him for half a moment. "Louis? You mean Louis Boyer?"

"*Oui*. Louis Boyer." Victor grinned. "That straightens your spine, does it not? He came to my shop today—out of nowhere! He says he just arrived from America."

"*Le bon Dieu!* Louis—after all these years!" Henri leaned toward him. "Does he have the map?"

"*Oui*. I saw it."

"What did you tell him?"

"I said that I was the only one left of the survivors and—"

Henri cut him off. "But there are four of us!" He scowled.

Victor touched the other's arm. "It was necessary to think very fast. It will be easier to get the paper if he thinks there is no one but me, will it not? We will surprise him, take the map and go our way. With it we do not need Louis. He was not really one of us anyway."

Henri smiled broadly. "You are right as usual, Victor. You have done well. Where is he now?"

"In a hotel. But tomorrow he goes to Mirande to see his relatives, hoping to raise money."

"Ahhhh, and we will let him get the money—"

Victor nodded. "Then we will take the money and the map—so!" He snapped his fingers.

Henri snapped his fingers and laughed. "So!" he said.

Chapter Twenty-One

Maggie leaned over a box of apples, picking them up one by one, putting some aside, when she saw the wagon through the door of Eli Burley's store. It was a drayman's wagon with boxes piled in the back, heading toward the beach. Tabitha and Sharon Quant sat on the seat by the driver and Enoch walked behind, scowling at all who stopped to stare.

Maggie stepped to the door as they passed and Brayton came up behind her. "Was that Goodman Quant?"

"Yes."

"I heard they were taking ship today for Boston." Brayton stepped outside and watched the wagon disappear toward South Beach Street.

She said, "He's going without a word to anyone?"

"Well, Enoch had no friends here, Mother. Have you heard what he's saying about Father?"

"No, and I don't want to know."

"He says he was pushed out of the boatyard."

Maggie looked at her son with annoyance and went back to the apples. That would be very like Enoch, and he overpaid, too. Probably the town was well rid of him. She put aside a dozen apples, asked Brayton to bring them home with him later, and walked toward the shore.

Brayton was right; Enoch and his family were taking a ship, a three-masted schooner anchored off the end of the main pier. Maggie stood by the warehouses and pulled the shawl tight about her shoulders, feeling the sharp bite of the sea breeze. She was glad to see the last of Enoch; she barely knew Tabitha. She saw Sharon glance her way, then look steadily ahead, and she knew Sharon had recognized her. Maggie raised her hand and Sharon responded with a wave. She must be very sorry to leave the town.

Turning, Maggie walked back up Main Street. The snow had been cleared off the walks and most of the street and lay piled in dirty, streaked heaps beneath the trees. Soon it would be gone, washed away by the spring rains. And then it would be time for Marie to go.

She paused and looked back at the sea, thinking of Morgan. What wouldn't she give to know where he was. . . .

Enoch counted out the passage money to Captain Frank York of the schooner *Sceptre*, and hired Luther Parkman's wagon to haul their belongings packed in boxes to the pier. Luther's son, Harve, loaded the boxes and drove the wagon.

It was a cold day; the ocean was gray, flecked with whitecaps and a stiff, icy wind swept over the surface hurling spray before it. With Enoch's help the boxes were lowered into a wide, flat-bottomed boat and lashed down under canvas by two burly boatmen. Tabitha and Sharon climbed cautiously down the wooden rungs of the short ladder to the boat and they pushed off with Enoch standing by the boxes, staring back at the town. He was damned glad to be leaving, and no one had come down to the wharf to see them off.

The schooner rocked at anchor, a battered, once-white craft with only four or five feet of freeboard. She looked frail, but Captain York had said she was fast. They would be in Boston before they knew it.

The accommodations were simple and cramped.

Sharon was put into a cabin that barely contained her. Enoch and Tabitha shared another with two bunks, one atop the other. Tabitha complained on seeing it but there was no other, York said, take it or leave it. And since the boxes were aboard and stored away, and Captain York was eager to make sail, they took it. Tabitha cried softly. She hadn't wanted to leave Canaan.

Sharon said nothing at all but when Enoch looked at her he knew what she was thinking. He went up on deck to get away from them.

It was a brief journey but a hard one. The gods of the sea were feuding; the winds blew angry gusts and the green water came aboard almost at will, it seemed to Enoch, and swept everything before it not lashed down. Tabitha was sick most of the way, moaning and crying that she was sorry she'd ever married him, though Sharon did her best to comfort her mother.

The harbor was dangerous with ice but the winds abated and Captain York dropped the hook amid a cluster of other schooners and smaller craft and sent his cargoes ashore.

Tabitha dried her eyes, put on a brave front and was rowed ashore with Sharon and Enoch were she sat on the pier, head in her hands, while Enoch settled with the boatmen. Enoch bought a *Newsletter*, read the ads and selected a rooming house. He hired a wagon to carry the family and boxes and they rode to Haven Street, a muddy quagmire. The boxes were unloaded and carried upstairs to their rented rooms, two small bedchambers and a sitting room heated by an iron stove.

Sharon stared through a grimy window pane at the strange town, feeling more lonely than at any time in her life.

The next morning Enoch set out to see Captain Styles.

It had rained during the night and the streets were flowing with muddy brown water, swirling round the poplar and locust trees, carrying off the last of the snow. By asking directions he quickly found British troop headquarters, an out-of-date private house, a rectangular brick building lacking frills of any kind, though it had a stoop before the front door, which faced the street.

Four redcoated soldiers were grouped on the walk in front of the building and one of them stopped him as he was mounting the steps. " 'ere, you—what you want?"

Enoch said, "I'm looking for Captain Styles."

"Oh—you know 'im, do you?"

"Yes, I do."

"You got any papers?"

"No, I just came to town. Is he inside?"

The man looked at the others, who shrugged. No one knew. Reluctantly the first man rubbed his broad chin and pointed to the stoop seat, telling Enoch to sit. He went to the door and disappeared inside. In several moments he was back beckoning to Enoch.

"Go down the hall. Can you read?"

"A little."

"Cap'n Styles's name is on the door." The man rejoined his companions, losing interest in Enoch.

Enoch went inside and found himself in a narrow hallway lighted by widely spaced lanterns hung from the ceiling. There was no runner on the floor and the walls were painted brown; it was like walking into a cave. There were a number of doors opening off the hall, all closed, all bearing printed signs. Captain Styles's was the third. The door was standing open and as he approached, Styles came to the door and greeted him.

"Enoch Quant! I never thought I'd see you in Boston."

"I wrote, sir, you remember . . ."

"Yes, but I thought you might have changed your mind. Come in."

Enoch closed the door behind him. Styles was resplendent in a perfectly tailored uniform with gold regimentals; he wore a powdered wig and his long pink face was newly shaved. He was not an ugly man but not handsome either, having a too-long nose, large expressive eyes and a wide mouth over a bluish lantern jaw. He indicated a chair and sat behind his neat, carved desk.

Enoch was impressed with the room. It was obviously half of a larger room that had been partitioned, and had a fireplace of white bricks and a yellow tile hearth with brass andirons, a decorative carpet covering most of the pegged floor, maps and flags on the walls as well as complicated-looking charts, and a row of chairs by a long table that was piled with books and papers. The walls were papered with silver stripes and there were framed pictures of hunting scenes here and there. A fire warmed the room and Enoch looked at it longingly, wanting to hold his hands out to it.

Styles wrote something on a bit of paper and passed it across the desk. "This is where I live. I'd rather you didn't come here again, Enoch. Did you bring your family?"

"Yes, sir. I come about the leather business we talked—"

"I know. I'll assign a man to help you get started with it. His name is Sergeant Gideon Dyer and you can trust him completely. Will you come to my quarters tonight?"

"Yes, sir." Enoch could sense he was being dismissed. He rose, put the paper in his pocket and went to the door, turning as he opened it. Styles gave him a parting smile and Enoch went into the hallway feeling like a bit of dung from the street.

Two British officers came into the hall, gave him a look and ignored him as they went past, reeking of perfume, talking of racing horses.

The guards on the street pointedly ignored him when he emerged and he walked away, growling under his breath. Did they have to treat him with such contempt? How else could he have found Styles except by going to headquarters? The man was unreasonable, and damned snotty into the bargain. Of course Styles was concerned because of his position, dealing with a lowly colonial in business. If it were known that he were in trade it would ruin him socially.

Well, he would have to swallow the insults to get the money Styles's position and influence would bring him—much as he hated it.

Tabitha was sewing when he returned to the rooming house. She looked up hopefully. "Did you see the captain?"

" 'Course I saw him."

She waited for a moment. "Well, what did he say?"

"He was damned glad t' see me. "We'll do business all right, and plenty of it. He's got a man t'help me get it started—"

"What man?"

"Somebody named Dyer. Don't know who 'e is. I'll meet him tonight, probably, at Styles's house. Where's Sharon?"

Tabitha sighed. "There's a girls' school not far from here. She went there to see if they had an opening."

"A girls' school! What's anyone want to teach girls for?"

Tabitha firmed her lips. "Girls can learn to read and write, same's boys. And Sharon is good with children, you know."

"Damned nuisance, school. Never did me no good."

Tabitha opened her mouth to reply, decided to reconsider and kept her peace. To her knowledge Enoch had spent less than two continuous weeks in school; he could write his own name and cipher but little else. Sharon had spent several years in the local school in Canaan and read books with ease. Enoch probably resented it.

When darkness fell, Enoch drew on a heavy coat and gloves and walked to the address given him by Captain Styles. It was a good distance away on a street with many large red brick houses. Styles obviously lived well. Enoch found the house, went round to the back and rapped on the rear door. It was opened by a black servant dressed in a magenta jacket and black breeches. The man was expecting him and showed Enoch inside at once.

"You sit by the fire and I tell the cap'n you here," he said. Enoch was glad to warm his hands and feet.

Styles kept him waiting another twenty minutes. Then the servant answered a bell and reappeared to beckon Enoch. They walked up to the second floor where a door stood ajar. The servant pointed silently and Enoch nodded.

It was an elegant room with ivory wallpaper and thin blue draperies on the windows; the furniture was covered with a shiny material that Enoch thought must be satin; it was figured and the wood was polished and there were satin pillows everywhere. With Styles in the room was a big, hard-bitten man with sparse brown hair and small, rather protuberant eyes. He was dressed in a dark blue suit of workingman's cut and eyed Enoch curiously as he entered.

Styles had doffed his uniform and sat in an easy chair with a pillow behind him; he wore a black velvet suit with a white ruffled shirt and slippers on his feet. He did not rise but nodded toward the big man.

"This is Sergeant Dyer, Enoch. He'll answer your questions, as soon as you shut the door."

Enoch hurriedly closed it.

Styles said, "This is Enoch Quant from Connecticut."

"Glad t'meet you, Enoch," Dyer said in a harsh voice. "We'll get on."

"Yes, sir," Enoch agreed.

Styles said, "The sergeant and I have served together for five years. Sit down, Enoch, and we'll discuss our project." Styles picked up a glass from a small table at his elbow. He sipped and looked Enoch over as he sat gingerly on the edge of a chair. "You look cold, sir. Dyer get our guest a taste of rum."

Enoch saw that Styles was drinking flip, a mixture of rum, beer and a sweet syrup heated by stirring with a red-hot loggerhead. Dyer, however, merely poured a dollop of rum into a tumbler and handed it to him. Dyer then stood behind Enoch's chair.

Styles said, "This is what I propose, Enoch. You will put yourself into the leather trade—in secret. Sergeant Dyer will show you the building he's picked out, and give you a list of what's necessary to be manufactured, along with the proper specifications. How much money do you have?"

"About two hundred pounds, sir."

"Hmmm. Well, that should be sufficient for the moment. I'd rather you had more . . ."

"I'll have more, sir, when I sell my house in Canaan."

"I see." Styles sipped his drink and glanced at Dyer. Enoch craned his neck to look at the big sergeant but Dyer merely stared at him with no expression.

Enoch asked, "Where do I buy the leather, sir?"

"The sergeant will show you. All that sort of thing is routine, which you will soon learn for yourself. The most important factor, however, must never be forgotten."

Enoch raised his brows.

"Secrecy," Styles said. "My name must never be mentioned by you to anyone. No one. Do you understand that?"

"Yes, sir. No one."

"Good. If it comes to that, I will deny it, of course."

"What do I charge for the goods, sir?"

Styles seemed annoyed. "All that is routine. Sergeant Dyer will give you a list and show you how to make the charges. They will pass through my hands for approval. This fact is the key to our profits." He gazed at Enoch steadily. "You will pay me two-thirds of those profits. Is that also understood?"

Enoch was astounded. He rose from the chair. "Two thirds!"

"My dear fellow, none of this would be possible but for my position."

Dyer pushed him down in the chair again. Enoch hardly noticed. "But, sir—how can I live on such a small—"

"It is your affair how you live, Enoch. I have stated my terms. I will provide you with expert and experienced help." He nodded toward Dyer, "and my protection. In return I expect cooperation and secrecy. And I assure you that if a single word of this venture reaches me from outside sources I will immediately close down your factory and deny any allegations. I will run you out of the city and deny we ever met. I have the power to do as I say."

Enoch was helpless in the face of the threat. He knew that Styles meant every word and could carry out the threat, which would put him into the street poorer than the lowliest indentured servant. He had no choice. He nodded dumbly, wondering how much they would allow him. What would one-third be? Had he exchanged one back-breaking job for another that paid even less?

Styles managed a tight smile. "Very well, then, we are in trade, Enoch." He lifted his glass. "Here's to a profitable and long lasting association."

Enoch looked at the rum in the tumbler and sipped it, letting it slide down his throat warmly. This was nothing of what he'd expected, or been led to believe when he'd last talked with Styles. Things changed, and not for the better, for him. He was to put up the money and Styles would reap the profits, and there was nothing in the world he could do about it—not even protest.

When he got up and went to the door he saw the first indication that Sergeant Dyer was something other than a block of stone. His lips moved slowly to accomplish a near smile.

Enoch thought about that smile all the way home. It reminded him of the smile of a snake as it approached its prey.

Sharon was miserable, although she did her best to conceal it from her mother. She knew Tabitha had nothing to do with their situation and was powerless to change it, and it was useless to discuss anything with her father.

But it was not so much the conditions of her life and the place where she lived—it was Morgan. If only she knew what had happened to him! If he were safe. Since talking to Maggie Lynn, she was dead sure that Morgan had gone after and had killed the ensign, and been pursued by British soldiers. How could there be any other explanation for his taking a ship bound for the Orient? He had given up the thing that meant more to him than anything else in the world—Jeremiah Chace's schooner.

The Orient! As she said the word over and over to

herself it seemed farther and farther away. A year's journey under the best of circumstances.

She longed to see him, and thoughts of their tryst at the chopping bee were constantly in her mind. It was her best memory of him, and she still smiled to herself at the foolish things he'd said to make her laugh.

Would he return at the end of a year? How long were British memories? Probably a year was not so long a time in the eyes of the law; they would take him if they could, and then he would be thrown into one of their innumerable jails or prison hulks, from whence few emerged whole. It made her shudder. Morgan was so vital and alive. . . .

She went willingly to the girls' school, the possibility of work being a welcome change to take her mind off the present.

It was a small establishment on a side street, a brown frame building, stark and undecorated, with an unobtrusive sign: *Miss Preston's Seminary for Young Ladies.*

Sharon knocked at the side door and after a moment was admitted by a matronly woman dressed in a dark blue uniform who asked if she wished to become a student.

"I came about the advertisment," Sharon said, showing the torn bit of newspaper, and the woman nodded as if remembering, asking her to come along. She was taken to a small, square office where Miss Preston presided. Miss Preston was a heavy, brown-faced woman of slightly more than middle age, with deep-set eyes, jowls and a double chin. She wore a dress of the same blue cloth and her breasts rested on the desk top as she regarded Sharon with what might be called suspicion.

"Why did you come here for work, young lady?"

"Because I need the money," Sharon said honestly.

"And do you have any qualifications?"

"I have had three years of schooling, ma'am, can read and write and cipher—and I like children."

Miss Preston nodded. "Are you married?"

"No, I am not."

"Is marriage a possibility for you?"

Sharon had the instant impression that Miss Preston disliked the idea of such unions. She said, "No," very distinctly.

"You have no young man courting you?"

"None at all."

"A pretty girl like you?"

"No, ma'am. None."

Miss Preston smiled and her face changed, softening. "Very well. I will give you an opportunity to show me what you can do. Miss Janet will take you to the children's room."

Miss Janet was the woman in blue who had admitted Sharon; she was thick-waisted and probably nearsighted, from the way she squinted. The children, she explained, came from nearby homes and required someone to look after them afternoons till dusk when their parents would fetch them. There were fourteen children ranging in ages from six to nine, she said, and it would be necessary for Sharon to keep them occupied and out of trouble. How she did this, Miss Janet implied, was up to her.

Although this was a school for girls, Miss Janet went on, Miss Preston had for several years taken in male children under the age of ten for afternoon supervision and to help in making ends meet.

The children's room was a large rectangular area with a few high windows and a single door, painted in a light brown color with dark blue trim. There were benches, painted black, four tables, painted the same brown as the walls, and a number of sturdy black chairs. It was not a pretty room, Sharon thought, and she wondered as she gazed at it, and at the unsmiling children who sat on the benches staring at them, if flowers would relieve the starkness. If she had carte blanche, she would see.

With the manner of an army sergeant Miss Janet bade the children rise, then introduced Miss Sharon as their overseer. She did not use the word teacher, and Sharon thought she saw speculative looks in the eyes of the several boys. Possibly they were considering how much leeway they would be able to pry from this rather fragile-looking young woman.

When Miss Janet left the room Sharon quickly instituted one of the games she recalled from her own school in Canaan, and kept the children busy for an hour, tiring many of them out. These she allowed to rest on the benches, which gave her another idea. When the last game was over she insisted they all lie down and rest, and several of the younger ones went off to sleep at once.

However, one of the older boys, a stocky blond named Dennis, insisted on playing ball instead, obviously testing her. When he woke the sleeping ones, Sharon firmed her lips, took the ball away from him and ordered him to lie down as well. When he refused, his lower lip jutting out, she realized her job was on the block.

She asked him once more and when he frowned and shook his head, her fist struck him in the middle of the chest and he sprawled backward on the floor, legs spread, a look of incredulity on his round face. Sharon gritted her teeth, instantly sorry, wanting to run from the room. He had hit his head hard but he refused to cry. When he sat up, Sharon was standing over him, her fist ready again. He got up slowly, keeping his distance from her and meekly lay down as she had ordered.

She had passed her first test, she thought—though her knuckles hurt.

The remainder of the day was easy, and that night at home she soaked her hand in hot, salty water. It might be better if she acquired a wooden paddle for use when needed. Just the sight of it might be enough.

She dreamed of Morgan that night, stocky and smiling at her, and when she attempted to hit him in the chest with her fist, he kissed her.

Chapter Twenty-Two

There was a public coach that ran from Marseilles into the interior, not too many miles from Mirande, but it cost too much, Louis said. Instead he found them a place in a farmer's near-empty wagon. The farmer was returning home after having sold his chickens and hogs, and was happy to receive a few coins to allow them space in the straw.

The wagon, drawn by two venerable horses, moved at a snail's pace along a track that could be called a road only by the most flattering. They spent the first night in the woods and the second in a little village, where Louis managed to get them quarters in an inn. There Becky was able to bathe. Never before in her life had she endured such privation; her parents were poor, but so far her life with Louis had been abject poverty, though he insisted it would soon change for the better.

She wanted to believe him. His cousins would receive them with open arms, he said. She would see. . . .

The third night they spent in a farmer's shed, sleeping on straw, and departed in the morning before they were discovered. Louis stole half a loaf of bread and a pot of meat which, he said, they needed more than the farmer.

Louis's attitude, despite the poverty, was good, she thought. He was cheerful and sure of the future, though he did not enlighten her about what she had come to think of as the mystery. There was something he was not telling her; it was an almost tangible something, hanging in the air.

And there was one other matter—their marriage. Louis had not mentioned it since they'd landed and when she brought it up he only shook his head, saying it was not yet time.

"Why is it not time?"

"Because one must post banns—it cannot be done overnight."

"But people marry in France!"

"Of course. Wait until we get to Mirande, *chérie*. Then all will be different, I promise you. I will go and see the priest and we will make arrangements."

"Priest? I am a Protestant."

He sighed, gazing at her. "Yes, I have thought of that. You must change your religion."

"*I?* I do not wish to change. *You* may change."

"But, *chérie,* that is impossible. This is France, a Catholic country. How could I change?"

She was silent, biting her tongue. Louis was not quite so understanding as he had been. Or was religion something very important to him? Surely he had not decided he wanted no part of marriage! She dared not ask him, unwilling to risk the answer.

He changed the subject abruptly, telling her about his cousins. They were his uncle's children, Etienne, Jules and Jules's wife, Clotilde. "They are farmers and raise sheep and cattle and were very prosperous when I saw them last."

He and Etienne had been very close when they were young, Louis said, but he had not seen him for many years.

"Do they know we are coming?"

Louis smiled. "No, but they will be glad. You will see."

Becky nodded, wondering to herself how glad her

mother would be to have two near-strangers suddenly appear and ask to be taken in. When she thought about it that way she began to have real misgivings. Louis was so optimistic and sure of himself.

When they parted from the farmer and his wagon, Louis pointed to an ill-marked track that led to the right, saying they must go that way, and if they hurried they would arrive before dark.

They arrived an hour before dusk, as a light drizzle began to fall. The weather had been fitful since they'd left Marseilles, but now it seemed to have made up its mind to douse them. Louis rushed her through the tiny village of Mirande. She saw only the fronts of shops. A very few people stared at them; then they were half running along a muddy road lined with tall trees.

"The farm is not far," Louis said encouragingly. "Soon you will be eating soup before a roaring fire."

Becky made no reply. She was cold and miserable, her shoes wet and full of mud, her hair stringy and probably filthy. Much as she loved Louis she would give a year of life to be back home in Canaan, in the comfortable house, with or without him. Many times she'd heard her father say he'd had his fill of something or other. Well, she'd had her fill of France, Becky thought.

She stopped short of thinking she'd had her fill of Louis. Perhaps he was right, that things would change soon. They could hardly get any worse. She must give him the benefit of the doubt, mustn't she?

When a group of houses came in sight Louis hurried her faster, then paused as if in indecision. She asked, "What's the matter?"

"I think this is it—yes, it must be, though I remember it as larger. And those trees have grown so much they change the look—" He took her hand and they walked up a rutted, muddy lane as the rain came down in torrents. He looked as bedraggled as she, hair streaming into his eyes, clothes sodden. He peered about as they walked. "There was a house there—but it has been torn down—" He pointed to the left, "And there was a stone fence there . . ."

Becky followed him, trying to pick a path between the puddles. If this was not the farm what would they do? Her heart sank. They would have to return to the village and ask for charity.

Louis stopped in front of the largest house, what would have been little more than half a house in Canaan and poor by most standards. He glanced at her, then rapped on the door. Becky closed her eyes, huddled at his back—let it be the right house!

Louis rapped again, harder, and the door opened a crack. A man's face peeked out, one suspicious eye staring at them. Louis asked, "Is that you, Etienne?"

The door opened wider and she saw a man about the same height as Louis but thinner, with a hawk-like face, high cheekbones and black hair. "Who asks for Etienne?"

Louis took a step into the light from the open door. "Etienne! Do you not know me? Where are your eyes?"

"*Bon Dieu!*" The man's face seemed to lengthen and his eyes were startled. "Louis! Louis, is it you?"

"Of course it is me. I have come with my wife—"

Becky was surprised at the word. Two others came to the door, another man, smaller and heavier than Etienne, and a stout woman. Both glared at them as Etienne said, "Come in, Louis, come in!" He took Louis by the hand. *"Comment allez-vous?"*

"I am well, thank you," Louis said. He pulled her inside and shut the door.

She was in a small, smelly room heavy with smoke

from the fire and from pipes. The fireplace took up one end of the room and there was a board table and two benches, two small sack-covered windows and several candles guttering on the table. It was the sparest room for living she'd ever seen and in Canaan would hardly be considered a shed.

Becky could understand little of the conversation. She knew only a handful of French words, and wife was one of them, but it was easy to read expressions. Etienne was genuinely glad to see Louis but the other two were sullen and unresponsive, both staring at her as if she were something Louis had found in the road.

After a bit the woman went into an ell, which Becky saw was the kitchen, and returned with two wooden bowls; she gave one to her and one to Louis, with spoons. It was potato soup. She ate it hungrily, edging toward the fire. Etienne brought coarse bread and a bottle of red wine and seemed to be asking innumerable questions, which Louis answered between bites. She caught some of the words. America—ship—soldiers.

Louis kept an eye on her and now and then spoke in English, saying his cousins *were* glad to see them, and everything would be all right; he wanted to cheer her up, of course. The chatter continued for an hour, then Etienne rose and Louis got to his feet and helped her up. Becky swayed with tiredness. Even her bones seemed exhausted. Louis said that Etienne would show them to their room; he said good night to Jules and Clotilde, and Becky smiled and bowed, then followed Louis outside. It was still raining.

Etienne took them to the next building, a square stone hut with a board floor that creaked as they walked on it. The room smelled of dust and of animals and was cold and dreary inside. But there was a fireplace with stacked-up wood. Etienne had brought a coal in a tin cup and soon had a roaring fire going. He took a candle from a pocket, lighted it and stuck it onto a small clay plate.

The hut had two stools, a bed against one wall and a table. A family had been living in the hut, Louis told her, relaying the information from Etienne, but they had gone away weeks ago. The hut also had a back door and outside it a hand pump for water. When Etienne left, Louis filled a bucket and hung it over the flames to heat.

She faced him. "They don't want us here, do they?"

He sighed and made a face. "It is only Jules and Clotilde. They say times are hard. But Etienne is happy to see us."

Becky sat on the hearth and stared into the fire dully. "What are we to do, Louis? When can we go back home?"

"Home—to America?" He was astonished. "We have only just arrived!"

She looked at him and back to the fire. "Why did you come to France, Louis? What is all the mystery?"

He hesitated. "You are tired, *chérie*. Let me help you undress and bathe. In the morning—"

"I want to know now."

Louis sat by her and began to unfasten her dress. "It is not your affair."

She whirled, pulling away from him, her face angry. "You insisted—begged—that I come here with you, and you promised we'd be married! Now you say this is not my affair! What will you say tomorrow? I want to go home, Louis. I am tired of this—this hand to mouth existence! It is not what you promised me!"

"*Chérie* . . . after you sleep you will feel better."

"I will not! You took me from a comfortable home and brought me here where everyone speaks a strange language and I have one filthy dress to my name—"

"*Chérie,* please!"

"—and one pair of muddy shoes—"

"You will have more, I promise!"

"What good are your promises, Louis Boyer? I have listened to all of them I want!

"*Chérie,* you are tired and feeling sorry for yourself—"

She spat at him. "I am feeling *angry*! I am only sorry I listened so long! I want to go home. Do I make myself clear? I want to leave this place. They do not want us here. They did not expect us and they resent us. They are not the kind of people you said they were! When did you last tell me the truth, Louis?"

"Please, *chérie*. We are both tired and irritable. Let us talk of this in the morning."

"No! We must talk *now*. Tell me what the mystery is. I have come this far with you. I deserve to know."

Louis sighed deeply and shook his head. "You are a stubborn woman, Becky Lynn."

"I am angry and I am determined. Tell me!"

Louis stared at her, his mouth a firm line. "I have not told you for several reasons and—"

"I do not want to know your reasons." Becky glared at him. "I want to know what the mystery is. You are treating me like a child."

He was silent for a moment. "Very well." He sighed again as if it were painful to relate the story. He glanced toward the door and lowered his voice. "I was a partner with a ship's captain before the war. I had money left me by my father. The ship was a privateer sailing against the British and the Dutch."

"You were a pirate!"

He looked pained. "We did not call it that. Their ships sailed against us too. Nevertheless, we took a number of prizes and a great amount of booty."

"Ah. Where is it?"

"It is still in the ship."

"What do you mean, still in the ship?"

"The ship is sunk. We were attacked by two British warships and forced to run for our lives after an exchange of broadsides. We were holed below the waterline. That means—"

"I know what it means."

"Umm. Well, our ship was finished. But then it was night and we were faster than the warships. We ran into a cove on the North African shore and the ship went down that night in thirty feet of water. She is still there."

"I begin to see. Then the man you met in Marseilles—"

"Was one of the survivors. He and I are the only ones left."

Becky frowned. "But if he has been living in Marseilles all these years why did he not dive for the booty long ago?"

Louis smiled. "Because he did not know where to look."

"You said—"

"I was the only one of the crew surviving who could read and write, and what was more important, navigate. I had ascertained the latitude and longitude of the cove." He patted his pocket. "I still have it safe. The coastline of North Africa is thousands of miles long. It would take a lifetime to investigate it all, and even then the ship might not be discovered because she is a quarter of a mile offshore. It is necessary for one to know the exact spot."

Becky stared into the flames. So this was the mystery, a great booty taken at gunpoint, but now protected by the sea. She said, "On the shore of Africa?"

"Yes, across the Mediterranean, which is not a large sea."

"But it is offshore and thirty feet down? And encased in a wreck? That may not be easy." She poked at the fire with a stick. "I have heard my father and brothers speak of such things."

"No, it will not be easy, but it has to be done. There is a fortune waiting."

She noted that Louis again glanced toward the door. It *was* a dangerous secret; she now understood his reticence. "Let me see the paper."

He showed it to her, a nondescript scrap folded and ragged. She carefully unfolded it and spread it on her knee. It was a map, a single line showing the coast, with a crude hatching marking the locations of several hills. The compass bearings were drawn in from two of these hills and the longitude and latitude neatly lettered. She stared at the X offshore. With this bit of paper any sailor who could navigate could easily find the spot. What was beneath the waves? A great booty, Louis had said.

She gazed at him, seeing the planes of his face stand out sharply as the firelight flickered. "Does the man in Marseilles know you have this paper?"

"I showed it to him." Louis shifted uncomfortably. "It was his right to know. He is a survivor, after all."

"And did you let him make a copy?"

He shook his head. "This is the only one."

"Do you trust him?"

"Yes, of course I trust him."

She refolded the map. Louis trusted him, but not enough to allow a copy to be made. Louis was a good and honest man, but he'd had some feeling about the other man, apparently, even if he didn't realize it consciously. "Does he know where you've gone?"

"You mean, does he know we're here in Mirande?" Louis took a breath. "Yes, I told him that . . ." He glanced at the door nervously. "But we need each other. As you say, it will not be easy to dive to the wreck. Victor will not double-cross me."

Becky stared at the bit of folded paper in her hand. Louis could be killed for this; if the man, Victor, had it he might easily hire men to do his bidding and not have to share with Louis.

Some of what she was thinking showed on her face and Louis said, "Is there a place you can keep it safe?"

Becky nodded. She could sew it into her cloak. She rose and brought the cloak to the fire, took a knife and began to make a slit in the neck band.

Watching her fingers, Louis filled his pipe and lit it with a twig from the hearth. "If we'd had the money we'd have gone directly to the cove," he said. "That was why we came here. I hoped to borrow from Etienne and Jules."

"Victor has none?"

"He says he has not."

"Then what will we do now?"

He took a long breath. "I do not know. Etienne suggests I stay and help them work the farm. But I am not a farmer, and it will not help us to get the necessary money. We must have a boat, provisions and other supplies, enough for a month or more. I do not know how long it will take to raise the treasure."

"Can you find the treasure?"

"Yes, it is in heavy boxes."

"Boxes?"

"Everything is locked in iron boxes or chests. Also, I will have to learn how to dive."

She glanced at him in alarm. "You!"

He shrugged. "It is a question of money again."

He was right, of course. Money was the key to everything. But in all probability the fortune was safe enough where it was. It would take a miracle or extraordinary luck on someone's part to stumble upon it; in fact, it might moulder there for all eternity, gradually settling into the mud.

She threaded a needle and sewed up the slit very carefully, tied off the thread and tested it. She could barely feel the folded paper inside, and only because she knew it was there. She dropped the cloak over the end of the bed.

"Louis, do you have other relatives?"

"To get money from?" He gave her a half smile. "No one."

"Then we will have to earn it. What can you do?"

"I was a soldier, and I can sail a ship."

"And you know piracy."

He lifted his brows. "I was a privateer. I can use a sword and firearms. I'm afraid my skills are limited."

"You were a woodcutter when I met you."

"Anyone can cut wood. I could probaby beg on the streets too, and it might make more money than woodcutting."

She went to him. "Louis, my darling, you can learn anything. You have only to try. If you can sail a ship does it have to be a warship?"

"No, certainly not." He scratched his chin, looking at her. "I wonder if there is a shortage of ship's officers."

"Let us go back to Marseilles and find out."

"A very good idea!" He caught her about the waist and pulled her onto his lap. "But first, to bed. I haven't put you into a decent bed for days."

She kissed him lightly. "The water is hot and I want a bath. Then you may do as you please."

"As I please?"

"First lock the door." She rose and began to undress.

The door had a wooden bar which made an effective lock. He poured the water into a basin, then took off his own boots and clothes, hanging them near the hearth. Sitting on the stool, he watched Becky as she hung her clothes up and turned, an alabaster goddess in the golden candlelight. With a square of cloth, he began to wash her with water from the basin. She let her hair down so that it flowed over her shoulders.

"You are so beautiful . . ." he said. He moved the cloth down her back as she wriggled, looking at him with roguish dark eyes.

Her feet were muddy and he washed them one by one as she pirouetted, holding onto his shoulder. He washed her legs and her belly, then her breasts, and as he dried them he was unable to contain himself longer. Picking her up, he dropped her onto the bed and fell beside her, burying his head between her neck and shoulder as she squealed.

"Hurry . . ." she breathed in his ear, and he slid atop her.

Chapter Twenty-Three

The morning dawned bright and rainless, with clouds boiling overhead, white and fluffy as if newly laundered. After a breakfast of ground meal and milk Louis walked out to the field with Etienne, to talk over old times, he said. Becky heated water and washed out his shirts and her only other dress and hung them on a line. Winter, she thought, looking at the sky, was slowly giving way to spring.

She sat on the front steps of the stone hut and stared at the distant blue hills and the trees across the road, thinking of home. How was little Marie? She should be well rounded by this time. Only a few months till the child was due. . . .

Her thoughts were interrupted by sight of four men on horses. They came along the muddy road, walking the animals. They rode in a straggling single file, looking for all the world like so many bandits, each of them staring at the farm as they passed as if it contained something of great value—or a plague.

She had seen others pass by but none had stared as these men were doing. If they saw her they gave no sign but their eyes took in every detail. It caused her a strange feeling of unease.

When Louis returned in the middle of the afternoon she told him what she'd seen. He looked startled. "There were four men?"

"Yes. On horses."

"Can you describe them?"

"Well, on horseback I can't say how tall they were. They dressed like workmen and the one in front was heavy-set with black hair."

He stared at her thoughtfully and she could see the idea she'd put into his head the day before churning about. He was wondering how far he could trust Victor.

She asked, "How many survivors were there in all?"

"Seven, not including me."

"Is it likely that all but you and Victor are gone?"

He sat by the hearth and slowly worked at the bowl of his pipe with a knife blade. "Victor said they were either dead, scattered or in jail and I have no reason to disbelieve him."

"What kind of men were they?"

He gazed at her curiously. "They were all from the lower deck . . ."

"Ah. You were the only officer?"

"I was not, strictly speaking, an officer. I was part owner."

Becky nodded. "But not one of them."

"No." He frowned at her, realizing what she was saying. He and Victor, and the others, were of different castes. There was a gulf between them, of speech, of education and wealth. They might easily consider him fair game in the deadly business of recovering treasure. He filled the pipe and lighted it, puffing absently. Yes, he had been a fool to tell Victor where he could be found. Victor might have lied to him—maybe there *were* other survivors! Victor might bring them here to Mirande, discover for himself that Etienne and Jules were penniless, and try for the map.

That meant they would have to kill him—and probably Becky as well.

When he turned about on the stool, Becky was staring at him. She said softly, "We must leave here tonight, Louis. It is no longer safe."

* * *

It took Becky only a moment to pack the canvas bag. She had packed and repacked it so many times. Louis managed a packet of food from Etienne, telling him privately at the same time that they must leave, which astounded Etienne.

"But why do you not leave in the daylight?"

"Because some men are after me."

"Mon Dieu! How is that possible? Who knows you are in France?"

"I met someone in Marseilles. It is a long story, Etienne, and I do not wish to involve you. If they come here and you know nothing you cannot be harmed."

Etienne's eyes grew round with astonishment. "It is that serious?"

"Oui, it is."

"Then where will you go?"

"Back to America. *Adieu,* Etienne. One day I will be back."

"Wait—you must take a horse. We have a dozen or more eating us poor."

"I cannot pay . . ."

Etienne looked offended. "I do not want money. Come." He walked into a pasture, put a rope about the neck of a chestnut horse and brought it to the near fence. "I cannot give you a saddle but I will put a blanket on the horse's back later. Then I will tell Jules the animal strayed."

"You are a true friend, Etienne." They embraced.

"I pray *le bon Dieu* keeps you safe."

When Louis went to the horse an hour after dark there was a gray blanket on its back. He led the animal to the stone hut where Becky waited. Jumping onto the horse's back, he pulled her up behind him and they rode out to the road.

Becky said, "I wish it was raining."

"Raining!" He turned to look at her.

"If those men are your enemies they will probably be watching the farm."

He laughed. "Then hang on. We'll show them our heels!" Louis kicked the chestnut's side and the horse broke into a gallop. Becky's arms slid around him, the canvas bag flopped against her back, and they pounded along the muddy road at headlong speed. At least, she thought, they were leaving the farm better off than they'd arrived. Now they had a horse.

Of course, they also had brigands after them. . . .

The brigands did not make an appearance for an hour. Becky was hopeful they had gotten away unseen, but it was not to be. On a long, straight stretch of road she looked back to see them in the moonlight, only flitting shadows, but very real. Louis swore aloud when she told him.

Louis had no weapon but a clasp knife; their only chance was speed or evasion, and Louis left the road at the first opportunity. When the road curved to the right, he went left, down a slope and into a sparse wooded area with thick grass underfoot. He was forced to walk the horse because of the brushy tangles. In half a mile he halted and they listened for the pursuit, hearing none.

"We've lost them," Louis said, looking at her over his shoulder. "But I think we're lost ourselves. Can you tell direction by the stars?"

Becky craned her neck. "There are no stars." She pointed ahead of them. "I think that way is south."

"Shall we head for Marseilles?"

"That is the place they'll look for us. It might be better to go to another port."

"Yes, you are right. We will go to Argenton. It should be easy to get a ship from there."

"If we had money . . ."

Louis nudged the horse and they continued. "We have a little money, and I can help work the ship. We will manage, *chérie*."

They rode steadily for an hour as she reflected on Louis's unfailing optimism, which was part of his charm. He refused to see the negative side. They found themselves in a wide meadow where the mist hung low, where occasional trees loomed up like monsters as they passed. There was a house at the end of the meadow, unlighted and silent, and several cows hung their heads over a rail fence and stared at them.

They came upon a road suddenly, unable to tell if it was the same road and if it was, if the four men had come along it. But it was the easiest track and Louis followed it while Becky continued to look over her shoulder. It was possible that the men had given up the chase, she thought; there was so much country in which to hide.

But there was also a fortune at stake, more money than all of them put together could ever earn. They would probably not give up at the first reverse.

When it began to get light Louis turned off the road and headed for a wood, saying they were too conspicuous. If they were seen in daylight it would be easy for four men to round them up. In the trees he slid down and lifted her off the horse. It was cold and she wished for a fire, but that was impossible. Louis brought out the food sack and they ate bread and cold meat. Argenton was some distance from Marseilles, he said, toward Spain. They should reach it in a week if they were not driven in the wrong direction.

Becky's spirits dropped. A week! Could she survive for that long? Already she was cold and they had no prospects for a house to sleep in; she looked round her at the damp grass and at the mists trailing through the tops of the nearby trees. Would she ever be warm again for two days at a time? Louis sensed her mood and embraced her with words of encouragement. She clung to him, closing her eyes wearily. Lord! She was tired!

Louis said, "I will make us a shelter so we can rest here for a while. You watch the road, yes?"

She nodded and took up a position behind a copse where she had a view of the road as it curved away from them down the slope. The mists curled and churned and after a bit the weak sun was blotted out and a light drizzle began, forming beads of moisture in her hair. She drew the cloak closer and waited patiently. An hour passed, and as she was about to rise to see what Louis had accomplished, there was movement on the road, far to her left. A man came along on a plodding horse, followed by three others; all looked tired and unhappy. Becky sat very still, hardly daring to breathe. Obviously the four had missed them, gone far ahead and were now returning to pick up the trail. She held her breath as they passed the spot where she and Louis had turned off the road. But the men continued moving away till they were out of sight.

She rose and hurried into the wood. Louis had built a lean-to with his clasp knife and was weaving the final branches into it to make it rain-tight. He smiled when she told him the four had gone by.

"They will never find us now," he said. "Come, you must sleep while I stand guard."

"But you need sleep also."

"Do as I say. Am I not the captain here?"

"But—"

He turned her about, hands on her shoulders. "I was the soldier, not you. Sleep. I will wake you in two hours."

He had made a bed of fine branches and leaves, covered with a blanket, and she had barely put her head down when she was asleep. When she woke, she knew instantly it was hours later. Louis was sleeping beside her and it was raining hard. She slid her arms about him and watched the rain form tiny rivulets that rushed off to join others. An occasional drop worked its way through the roof branches, but not enough to be concerned about. She had been wet so often in the last month. . . .

When he woke finally he said he'd watched the road until it hypnotized him; the men did not return and finally, when it had started to rain, he'd curled up with her. They ate more bread and meat from the sack and toward dark the rain let up. In Louis's opinion the pursuers had gone back, discouraged. Their prey could have gone in a dozen directions and four men could never possibly search them all.

He said, "Someday they will tell their grandchildren how close they came to a fortune."

"Let's hope that's true."

"Of course it is true. Come. It will be dark in another few moments. Let's be on our way."

He had an infectious enthusiasm that would not be denied. They climbed on the chestnut, walked the animal out to the road and went south.

Long after dark they came to a crossroads and a sign. The sign was nearly impossible to read but Louis swore it pointed to Argenton, off to the right, so they took that road. Riding behind him, Becky lay her head against his back and dozed as the miles fell away.

She woke, stiff and uncomfortable, when the horse halted. It was not raining and she could hear a dog barking somewhere off to the right, sounding flat and distant. Louis said softly, "Are you awake?"

"Yes . . . what is it?"

"An inn." He pointed.

She barely made it out, a large dark shape without lights, standing just off the road. She looked at the murky sky. "Is it near morning?"

"It must be. And no sign of them." He glanced back. "We are safe now, *chérie*." He nudged the chestnut and they moved closer. There was a large stable behind the inn and Louis got down in front of it and went inside. He was back in a moment. "The stableboy is asleep in a stall."

She protested when he would have helped her off the horse. "We cannot stay here, Louis!"

"Why not? You are tired and need a bath—"

"But we have no money!"

"We have enough." He pulled her down and kissed her. "I want to see you smile again." He pushed up the corners of her mouth. "You look like the ogre who frightens little children."

It made her suddenly conscious of her miserable appearance. She must look a fright! As she combed at her tangled hair, Louis put the horse in a stall. How good a bath would feel! She went without a word when he led her around to the front of the inn. It was a gray-brown building that looked like a fort with its iron bars on lower windows. They would be two travelers on their way to Toulouse, Louis said. He would do the talking and she must only shake her head if anyone spoke to her.

Dawn was rapidly approaching and she could see that the inn was really not a fort but a weatherbeaten building of wood and stone, probably very old, with a sign that depicted a rooster in the act of crowing. The front entrance was heavy with carved wood and the door studded with huge nails or bolts. It looked to her like the door of a castle. There were two small windows and through them she could see a man in a leather apron lighting lanterns. He came to the door at Louis's knock. He was stout and unshaven with tattered clothes under the apron and was not surprised to see them. Louis talked briefly with him, passed over a few coins and smiled at her.

He spoke to her in French, pulled her along to a stairway and when they went up it whispered that he'd rented a room and when there was water heated she could go into the *salle de bain* for her bath.

The room was small and nearly square with rough wood walls, a bed and chair, washbasin and lantern. There was no floor covering and no pictures. The two uncovered windows faced a forest of very old trees, the branches of the nearest scraped the side of the building. The room was unheated and dark but Becky removed her shoes and fell onto the bed. Louis immediately lay beside her and they curled together with the blankets over them and slept.

When she woke it was still daylight and there were sounds from the inn, distant voices, a far off clatter of metal as if pots were being rattled, footsteps in the hallway and from somewhere the sound of a child crying. Becky lay quietly staring at the dark ceiling, thinking of home. Then Louis woke and stretched, moved, reached for her. She felt his hand slide down her thigh, then up under her skirts. She turned toward him, whispering, "Please, darling, you'll wrinkle my clothes."

He laughed and pushed up the skirts, rolling her onto her back. She clung to him, eager for his kisses though his face was stubbled with beard.

There was a rumble from outside the room and she looked to the window to see the lightning flash, then a gust of wind hurled raindrops against the panes. Louis moved atop her and she sucked in her breath as she felt him enter and push upward. . . . Her legs slid around him and the bed squeaked; he looked down at her. "Ahhh, now you're smiling . . ."

"Of course I am. It's been so long!"

"Several days, my dove." He kissed her cheek and she gave herself over to the sensuous movement, hearing the rain beat against the side of the house and drum on the windows; it drowned out the sounds of the squeaking bed. Her mind felt open and aware and the delicious rhythm filled her being, overflowing with love of Louis. All the troubles and harshness of the past month were forgotten as her arms held him tightly. She felt the wild, exhilarating thrusts send her headlong into ecstasy, and as it welled up she moaned. The thunder rumbled and crashed, shaking the inn as if to tear it to splinters. She cried out in blessed agony as the rain slashed, then gradually eased. The angry muttering of the thunder diminished as the storm rolled over them and she turned her head, seeking Louis's kisses.

She held him from getting up, needing the close warmth of his body, wanting the crush of his arms. He caressed her, running a finger across her eyelids, kissing her nose. "It is time, *chérie*, we must go."

Becky groaned, thinking of the jolting horse and the muddy roads; how marvelous it would be to remain in bed. "You promised me a bath."

He chuckled. "I am sure there is hot water enough by this time. I will shave and we will both have baths." He sat up and looked down at her. "In a few days we will be on a ship again."

"I am sorry you were not able to go after the treasure."

"It will not stray, *chérie*."

"What will you do when we get to America?"

He made a face and rubbed his jaw. "There are Frenchmen in New York colony. Perhaps money can be raised for an expedition. I will form a company and sell shares."

"Then the secret will be out."

He frowned. "A way can be found—we must give it thought."

"If the British learn their ships caused the sinking, they may claim the wreck."

Louis smiled. "No one will tell the British anything." He pulled her off the bed. "But we do not have to make those decisions this minute. Come, on your feet—"

"I would rather lie in bed for the rest of the day." She dropped back onto the bed and pulled the blanket over her.

Louis reached to grab it and stopped short, cocking his head. There were sounds in the hallway. Footsteps seemed to stop before their door and he shot her a warning glance, then motioned.

Becky slid out of bed as he pulled on his boots.

Victor Buchon was irritable. His usual smile was gone and in its place a scowl. Somehow Louis and the girl had given them the slip. How Louis found out he and the others were in Mirande was annoying and not a little astounding. But he had, and they had escaped from the farm.

And managed somehow to evade them on the road. They had searched the damned road and all the side roads and found nothing. They had even crept up on a shack and burst inside positive they had Louis at last—and found only a shepherd and his wife in bed, startled and indignant.

Henri and the others, Gerard and Colin, were sure that Louis would head for Marseilles. Had he not taken the road south? But Victor thought Louis would stay far from Marseilles now that he knew Victor had lied to him.

So, when they came to the crossroads, Victor insisted they go west toward Argenton. They could find no horse's tracks that led that way, Gerard said.

"But it has been raining! The water has washed out all the tracks, imbecile!"

Henri growled, "Why would he go that way, to Argenton? It is shorter to Marseilles."

"What does he care for shortness? He will go where he thinks we will not follow.

"Louis is clever," Gerard admitted.

"He is not too clever," Victor said. "You will see." He got them started along the road though Henri protested that if *he* were running from someone he would go directly to Marseilles.

"Of course," Victor agreed. "And you would find nothing there."

"That is foolish. There are a thousand places to hide!"

"Nevertheless, Louis will go to Argenton. If we do not catch him first."

But even Victor's confidence began to erode when they galloped for miles and met no one, saw nothing to interest them. They came to another road leading south and Henri insisted Louis would have turned into it. The argument started over again, but at last Victor pushed them onward. He had a feeling about Argenton.

When they came to the inn, Victor's face wreathed in smiles. "He is here. I can smell him!"

"You smell the girl," Colin said.

Victor shrugged and sought out the innkeeper to ask about two people, a man and a girl, who had come that way the night before. "They are dear friends and we were separated."

He was delighted to learn such a couple was indeed in the tavern. The room was pointed out to him.

In the hallway out of sight of curious eyes, they examined their pistols and Victor sent Colin outside to stand guard by the stable where Louis's chestnut horse occupied a stall.

He whispered, "We will break open the door and shoot Louis instantly. Do you understand?"

"Why must we shoot him?"

"Because, inbecile, it is much easier to search a body than a live man. Is it not so?"

Gerard shrugged. "What about the girl?"

"Are you made of argument? Who cares about the girl?"

Henri said, "After it is over we could take her—"

Victor was exasperated. "We will shoot Louis, take the map and go instantly! The innkeeper will send for the police. Do you want to spend your life in jail?"

Henri did not. "How do we break down the door?"

"With our shoulders, of course." Victor led them down the hall, pistol in hand, and put his ear to the door. "I hear sounds," he whispered. "Hurry—"

Louis hissed, "It is Victor and the others! We must go out through the window."

Becky grabbed up her cloak and the canvas bag, and was startled when Louis threw a chair through the window. He snatched the blanket off the bed, folded it over the sill and climbed out quickly.

"Come—climb over me. Hold my feet and drop to the ground."

"But we are on the second floor!"

"*Mon Dieu!* I know that! The ground is soft—hurry!"

Biting her lip, Becky did as he said, holding onto his clothes. She tossed the cloak and bag down; the bag plopped on the wet ground. With Louis urging her to make haste, she climbed down holding onto his body—his legs—and let go. As she fell, landing on soft grass, she heard the crash of the door in the room they'd just left.

Louis fell beside her. Instantly he was up, pulling,

half-lifting, hurrying her away toward the stable. It was dark under the huge trees; there was a shout from the window, then a pistol shot. The bullet smashed into a shed on her right and she heard Louis growl, "*Les vauriens!*"

He had hold of her arm, hurrying her so fast she had no time to think, heart in her mouth. The pistol shot meant the pursuers were desperate! She saw the shadow that detached itself from the stable and gasped. Louis said, "Colin!" He hurled himself at the man. Becky heard herself scream. She saw the smoke and flash of the pistol. Then Louis had bowled the man over. They were on the ground and the pistol skittered away. She ran and picked it up.

Louis fought savagely with the man he'd called Colin. They grunted and cursed, rolling in the wet grass. Grabbing the pistol by the butt, Becky moved closer. When Colin's body was jerked atop Louis, she struck out with all her strength. The pistol barrel connected and Colin collapsed.

Louis pushed him off, stared at her for a second, then grinned and got to his feet. He rushed into the stable and came out with two horses, the chestnut and a gray. "Come—" She ran to him and he tossed her up on one and flung himself on the other. In the next second they were pounding from the yard, turning into the road. She heard shouts behind them but they were soon drowned out by the drumming hoofs.

Wrapping the cloak about her she yelled at Louis. "Are you hurt?"

"No," he shouted back.

In the first mile they came to a village astride the road and Louis slowed to a walk. It was full dark and lights glowed from many of the windows. A few people stared at them curiously as they passed. At the far edge of town was another crossroads with ancient, leaning signs. Louis signalled her to follow and turned to the left. He trotted the horse only a short way, moved off the road into a brushy area and halted. When she came up he said, "Maybe they will think we have gone that way. Come on."

He saw the pistol she still carried and held out his hand for it. "You were in time, *chérie*." He smiled.

"Did I kill him?"

He looked at the barrel of the pistol and she saw the dark smear of blood. He shrugged and shoved the gun into his belt. "Even if you did not he will not be on our trail." He led back to the road and they continued west.

She asked, "Who was he?"

"One of the crew of the ship. A man called Colin Patoche."

"Then Victor lied to you."

"*Oui*, so he did."

The reaction was setting in and Becky felt herself trembling. She held onto the horse's mane with both hands as icy shivers ran up her spine. Louis had been very close to death at Colin's hands; the pistol shot must have missed him by a hair's breadth. And they were still not out of danger. The pursuers would kill them on sight, or kill Louis and work their will with her . . . she shuddered. They might do unspeakable things if they searched and did not find the paper. It would be well not to think of that.

The rain came again toward dawn, light and drizzly but cold. When they went up a rise of ground Louis halted and they gazed behind them at the long, straight road that disappeared into mist. Then Louis swore.

"They are coming." He pointed and Becky saw horsemen in the distance and her heart fell. Would they get away alive?

Chapter Twenty-Four

Junius was nearing eighteen, becoming a man. His days were spent dealing with grown men who wanted no childishness, who demanded answers. The boatyard prospered because of his industry and diligence. With his father at home a great deal of the time, he was in charge. From a slender dark-eyed boy he became a hard-muscled man who had learned every aspect of the work.

As the weather moderated he went out on the Sound with various boats and occasionally with Wager Tanfield as they discussed lines and sailing points. Wager's interest was in improving the speed and handling qualities of the boats and ships he designed. His reputation was growing by word of mouth. Satisfied owners told their friends and men came from as far off as Maine or Virginia to consult with him about a fast schooner, a sloop or a brig. And when he could, Wager recommended the Canaan boatyard to his clients.

The schooner *Annora*, built for Jeremiah Chace, was mentioned several times by newspapers as having outrun British patrol craft; she was gaining a measure of notoriety, and everyone knew where she'd been built. Of course Jeremiah swore to the authorities that the schooner was no longer his to command.

Junius also spent hours sitting by his father's bed discussing the work. It was a pretense they both enjoyed. Now and then when Azariah came down to the kitchen Wager would enter into the talk and the three would sit, cups of tea at their elbows, and chatter about the trade, with Wager adding bits of gossip he learned on his various trips. It did Azariah a world of good.

Maggie sometimes sat and knitted, listening to the talk; she loved to be with Wager even though others were present. But more often she went upstairs to tend Marie. Marie was definitely showing, six months along, and declared she could feel movement. To Maggie's expert eyes she looked in perfect health though she was thin, but she had always been thin.

When they were alone Marie sometimes talked about David as if he were close by. She seemed to refuse to believe he was dead and Maggie never remonstrated with her. What good would it do?

Marie had knitted a shelf full of tiny clothes, booties and blankets and had made a list of names, which she declared several times she must talk over with David.

Junius stopped to see Olive on his way home, something he often did. Her father worked as a wagon driver for one of the warehouses on South Beach Street and frequently did not come home till very late. When Junius entered, Olive came from the kitchen and her mother said, "Will you have a cup, Junius?"

"Thank you." He sat in the parlor with Olive. She was wearing a blue checked dress with a round neckline that dipped low enough to show an exciting cleft, which increased his blood circulation. As she leaned toward him it opened so that he caught his breath, remembering the kisses she'd given him in their kitchen.

They sat for several moments as he tried to think of something that would interest her, and could not. She touched his hand and said, "Tell me about the new schooner. Is it to be larger than you thought?"

"Two masts," he said. The schooner was to be built for Mr. Drew Renfield and would be a slightly larger craft than the *Annora*. "I hope when Wager draws the plans we can talk Mr. Renfield into making her a little larger. It'll cost very little more."

She squeezed his hand. "Ohhh, I hope so." She drew away as her mother came from the kitchen with two cups of tea.

"How's your father, Junius?"

"Not much better, I'm afraid, ma'am."

"He isn't well enough to come to church?"

"No, he barely gets about nowadays."

"Have you heard from Becky?"

"No, ma'am. But we ought to get a letter any time."

Goodwife Yurman placed the cups on a wooden stool. "The young ones are lax nowadays." She went back to the kitchen.

Junius took the moment when her back was turned to plant a kiss on Olive's lips. Olive squeezed his hand again. Then they both sipped the tea very properly.

The next afternoon Wager called at the house, talked for an hour with Azariah in the bedroom, then came downstairs and sat with Maggie and Marie in the warm kitchen.

Marie ought to go to a doctor, Maggie thought, but not to Dr. Lunt. Wager agreed as Marie sat quietly with her loom and said nothing at all. There was a doctor in Payton, Wager said, only a three- or four-hour drive to the north, who had an excellent reputation.

He also had received a letter from his sister and she was quite willing to take Marie into her home. "So it's all arranged."

"You're a good friend, Wager," Maggie said. Marie looked at him and barely smiled. But as Wager and her mother discussed when she would go to the sister's home her busy fingers stopped and she listened intently.

* * *

Sharon Quant went doggedly about the business of managing the children in Miss Preston's school. During her first week she begged for several tins of paint and three ragged brushes, and supervised the repainting of the black chairs. The new paint was a pleasant shade of yellow and the children entered into the game with enthusiasm, each doing his bit of work till it was all completed.

Several times each day Miss Preston entered the room and stood watching, arms akimbo, saying nothing. At the end of the painting session Sharon was invited to enter Miss Preston's office again and went with some little apprehension.

But Miss Preston was smiling and Sharon sat down, taking heart. "The room does look brighter," she ventured.

Miss Preston said, "Yes, I think it does. The chairs were painted black because the paint was given us and that is not always the best reason, I expect. But you've done well, Sharon. I am very pleased."

"Thank you, Miss Preston."

"The children like you and that is important. I also see that you're having no trouble with Dennis."

"We had our differences at first," Sharon said slowly, "but now he sees that he must obey."

"I daresay," Miss Preston said with a half smile and Sharon wondered how much she knew of the incident with the boy. But nothing further was said about it and Miss Preston began a new tack. "I think it's time we got better acquainted."

She began by askng if Sharon minded questions about her family, and Sharon did not. However, she had no real idea of her father's business and could only say that he had recently been a boat builder.

During this discussion Miss Janet entered and sat demurely by the door, listening. Miss Preston's questions were not searching and after a bit Sharon was able to relax, though when the talk turned to the future she was less at ease. She had no plans, she said, and was very happy at the school. And since the talk had gone well, Sharon risked saying she wished she could make a bit more money.

"Do you think you might teach?"

"I would love to," Sharon said. "I'm good at arithmetic . . ."

"I'll keep it in mind," Miss Preston said, with a glance at Miss Janet. "We're one happy family here, you know. Are you content living at home?"

"Yes. Mother gets lonely. She's made no new friends in the city."

"I expect that'll change. Perhaps one day soon you'll consider taking a room here at the school. We have several, of course."

Sharon had never thought about where Miss Preston lived and was surprised to hear it. Miss Preston went on a bit about her garden, which Sharon had not seen, and suggested that Sharon might have one of her own. Then she wished Sharon a good evening and rose from behind the desk.

Sharon walked home thinking she'd finally been accepted as a full-fledged member of the school; that she now had steady employment and would one day become a teacher. It made her feel very good indeed. Now if only Morgan would return.

The following days passed tranquilly; she had no further trouble with the children and felt at ease with Miss Preston and with Janet, who frequently came to eat a bite of lunch with her in the garden outside the children's room.

At home, her father talked of nothing but his business interests which, she gathered, were much concerned with the redcoat army, though he cautioned her to say nothing outside the house.

Then one Sunday her father insisted she accompany him on a walk. She had planned to read, but he ordered her to get dressed, and when she appeared, soberly attired in one of her two ordinary dresses, he impatiently told her to put on her Sunday best.

"But why, Father? Are we going to church?"

"We are going for a walk, young lady. Do as I tell you!" He grumbled as she returned to her room, and when she finally reappeared, looked her over critically as if it were a matter of great importance. Sharon gazed at her mother in astonished curiosity, but Tabitha only turned her face away, her expression unreadable.

There was a small park three squares away and Enoch headed for it immediately. Sharon had almost to run to keep up. She had no breath left for questions.

At the entrance to the park Enoch stopped, looked her over again, then put her hand firmly on his arm and they entered, walking slowly as Enoch's head swiveled from side to side.

Sharon asked, "Who are we meeting, Father?" But he only grunted.

It was a chill day and there were only a handful of people in the park, most passing through, and only a few children shouted and chased each other through the leafless trees.

One of those who walked slowly along a central path was a tall, thin man in a dark velvet suit with dragoon boots, a doublet of figured yellow and lace ruffles on his shirt front and at his wrists. He wore a black cocked hat and a sword buckled under his coat. Sharon thought he stared at her as they approached.

She was not surprised when her father stopped short and doffed his hat. "Hello, Captain Styles," he said. "I didn't expect to see you here."

It sounded as false as anything she'd ever heard, and the captain gave her father a look almost of disgust. But he lifted his hat to them. "Hello, Enoch. Is this your daughter?"

"Yes, she is. This's Sharon, Captain." He turned to her. "This's Captain Styles of the British army."

"I'm honored, Miss Quant," Styles said with a slight bow.

Sharon managed a smile, though she felt icy inside. It was all perfectly clear to her in an instant. Her father was showing her off to a prospective husband! And her mother had known it.

She felt wretched, like a slave on the auction block, and underneath it a fine edge of anger. Styles was examining her every bit like someone looking to purchase and it was all she could do to remain with her chin up, gazing past him.

Her father had no thought for her feelings, but Styles seemed to sense her anger and after a few stilted sentences gave her a toothy smile, lifted his hat and walked rapidly away.

Enoch gazed after him, face screwed up as if in thought, his dark features lined. He watched Styles out of the park, then took her arm briskly. "A'right, lass. We'll go home now."

"Father—"

He glanced at her. "None o' your whimpering. Cap'n Styles is a good catch f'you. He's rich and he got position too."

"So you *are* thinking of marrying me to him!"

"It's past thinkin'. You're his." He paused. "If he'll have you."

Chapter Twenty-Five

Becky rode astride the gray and hung on for dear life. The saddle was too large for her and her feet did not quite touch the stirrups; there had been no time to adjust them. She followed Louis, both horses galloping toward a wood. Far behind she could make out the shapes of their pursuers.

She was afraid—a dry bitter taste in her mouth—as much for Louis as for herself. They would certainly kill him. She had no illusions now. Victor and his men seemed relentless; they had not been fooled by the last subterfuge and would be on the lookout for more. She glanced at the sky, overcast but permitting a diffused light. Lord! If it were only night again.

There was nowhere to hide. On each side the fields stretched away, weedy and flat, but ahead was the wood. It seemed to come toward them with frustrating slowness.

The road, barely a cart track, ran directly into the trees, and when the branches closed above her head at last, Becky took a deep breath, conscious that she'd been breathing in gasps. Louis glanced back at her and smiled. He shouted, "We'll lose them now!"

She wondered how. Their muddy tracks in the road could be followed by a blind child. If they branched off from the road the tracks would be plain as a signboard.

But the road was not straight; it followed the path of least resistance, curving around clumps of giant trees or folds in the ground, and in half a mile they came to a narrow wooden bridge. As they galloped over it with a thunder of hooves, Louis yelled and reined in on the far side. Becky slowed and turned the gray in a circle as she saw him jump down and run back.

The bridge provided a passage over a deep gorge that had been carved out by flood water; it was primitive, made of cut poles with the bark still on, spiked and roped together. The roadway was composed of round poles of nearly equal diameters with dirt hard-packed over them. She watched as Louis dug into the dirt with a sharp stick, tugged at one and with great difficulty pulled it up. The dirt spilled away and he upended the pole into the gorge with a yell of triumph.

He looked at her, "They won't get across this!" He dug at the next pole and it came up easier. The heavy poles were not spiked down, probably because of a scarcity of metal, but stayed in place because of the packed dirt and because few people used the bridge.

In ten minutes he had opened a yawning hole ten feet wide. A man might easily make his way across using either side, but no horse could cross until the poles were replaced.

Becky called out when she saw their pursuers on the far side of the bridge. Louis ran to his horse and they rode off as someone fired a pistol. The ball went wide and in the next moment they were out of range and Louis was laughing, saying it would take them hours to get across.

They paused in the next village long enough for Louis to spend the last of their money on food, and they ate it as they continued. The skies churned and boiled but the storm passed them by. When she asked him, Louis said that Argenton was a seaport town on the river Savane, which meant plain. They would come to the river soon, he thought, and follow it to the sea.

Louis was correct. They came to the river within hours, a sluggish, muddy stream about a hundred yards wide but narrowing in places to half that. They saw no bridge. The road curved to follow the stream south and in another hour they came to a fishing village that sprawled along the bank. It comprised a few dozen shacks and houses and a church with a high spire.

Louis still had the captured pistol and exchanged it for a night's lodging at a small inn, including a supper of boiled mutton. The inn was dark as a cave and had a shabby taproom that smelled of ale and urine and cooked cabbage. The main room had heavy tables and benches resting on packed earth and in midday the room was lighted by several candle-lanterns that hung from the ceiling and provided their own smells. They ate the mutton from wooden bowls and sopped up the juices with chunks of coarse bread while the skinny, gnome-like landlord watched and picked his teeth with a straw.

Becky was tired to death, barely able to chew the tough meat. The pounding from the hard saddle and the everlasting worry about a bullet in the back had drained her. She was happy to climb the rickety stairs to the second level. Their room was a cell with a rope bed only inches off the dusty floor, boasting a straw mattress that was lumpy as a plowed field. But Louis was able to get them a pail of hot water and she stripped to the skin and bathed, though the room was cold.

The bath revived her somewhat, and Louis's embraces in bed were reassuring. They would go to the coast, he promised, find a ship—and, what was more to the point, find the means of passage. One way or another they would reach New York town in the colonies, and the next time they came to France it would be with enough money to do the job properly. There were millions in gold at the bottom of the cove, he whispered, and it would belong to them alone.

Millions!

No wonder Victor and his friends had pursued them with such diligence!

His hands soothed her, seeming to banish the tiredness. They lay in complete darkness. The single window gave no light, and the noises of the taproom came to them as a far-off babble. He kissed her tenderly. "I know it has been hard for you, *chérie*. It did not happen as I expected."

"You did not know they would turn on you. It was not your fault."

"I should have thought of it. There is so much at stake."

"Do not blame yourself, darling."

"It is my fault that I put you in so much danger." He sighed deeply and held her close. "But I think the danger is past now. In the morning we will go on to Argenton and our luck will change."

"Of course it will."

She turned onto her back and he leaned over her, kissing her lips; his hand moved slowly from one breast to the other. He said, "*Chérie*, I want very much to marry you—perhaps in Argenton it will be possible."

"Lordy, yes—"

"It cannot be done quickly in France . . ."

She sought his mouth, then said softly, "I cannot go home unmarried."

His voice was surprised. "You cannot?"

"No." She nestled closer. "I'm afraid—"

"Of what?"

"I mean—I think I'm—"

Louis sucked in his breath in sudden excitement. "You're pregnant!"

"I think so. Are you disappointed?"

He kissed her joyfully. "I'm delighted, *chérie*! We're to have a child! I love you! I love you! It is the most wonderful thing in the world!"

"Then we must find a way to marry."

"Of course we will! I will find a priest in Argenton who will hurry it along. It has been done before, I am certain, and it can be done again. I will explain the circumstances—"

She pulled him down, kissing him wildly; his arms slid about her and one questing hand moved along the soft flesh of her inner thighs. From downstairs came the sounds of someone singing a sad love song she'd heard before . . . where had it been? Then she rolled atop him, smiling into the dark, joining with him, sighing in deep pleasure as their bodies moved sensuously. . . .

Though their sojourn in France had been hard, she felt a change; they were going home and Louis loved her. He was happy about the coming child and he would find a priest and cut away all the stifling customs that stood between them and marriage. He was right, they'd had no time to post banns—but he loved her and that was all that really mattered. He was her strength and her peace . . . and her love.

She woke once in the night to find herself on her side, with Louis close behind her, his arms about her. Lifting her head, she listened to the dark and heard nothing. The little town was asleep, not even rain disturbed the silences, yet she felt a vague uneasiness she could not put a name to. Louis stirred and she lay back, gazing into the gloom wondering if Victor and his men had caught up to them. Perhaps they were even now in the stable. . . .

But she must not frighten herself. It was probably impossible. Louis had explained how terribly difficult it would be for them to climb down into the deep gorge and haul up the poles without ropes. It might take days.

When she woke in the morning she was alone. Louis had dressed and gone and for a moment she felt a stinging fear, then told herself she was being foolish. He had gone out and would be back shortly. She must not be so jumpy. If Victor had come to the inn there would be gunfire and noise, and she had heard none.

But Louis did not return till she was up, washed and dressed, impatient as a child. She opened the door at his rap and the sound of his voice. He laughed when she fell into his arms.

"What is it, *chérie*? You wish to make love again?"

"I was worried!"

He sat her down on the edge of the bed. "I have sold the horses." He showed her the money. "It is not far to Argenton. I have also rented a boat, which we will leave with a certain person, and we will go as soon as we have breakfast. Does that please you?"

She hugged him. She would never have thought of selling the two animals. "It sounds wonderful!"

"Then put on that old cloak and let us go."

Louis was in a fine, jovial mood, laughing and bantering with the innkeeper's wife, a large fat woman with a red face and stringy gray hair. He easily persuaded her to prepare them a packet of food, which she wrapped in paper and tied with string. They ate fried meat and bread with a bit of red wine and Louis counted out coins gravely.

When they went out to the street Louis halted suddenly and pushed her back into the inn. "Victor!" he said, and swore.

Becky caught a glimpse of horsemen at the end of the street and felt icy all at once. Would Victor follow them to the ends of the earth?

Louis called to the woman, saying his wife's brother was in the street with friends that he and his wife were eloping, and was there a back door? There was.

Through the kitchen. The woman hurried them into a snaky alleyway, pointing the way to the river bank. She would tell the brother-in-law nothing, she promised.

Louis translated as they ran through narrow dirt streets. He was positive the woman would tell all she knew for a few coins.

They came to the river suddenly. Gray-brown houses gave way to a brown riverbank and weathered piers, a cluster of boats and a few fishermen examining nets. One man beckoned to Louis; he was short and dark with broken teeth. His clothes were dirty and wrinkled and a pipe jutted from one corner of his mouth. He had untied a boat and was holding it close by means of a long stick. Louis said something to him as Becky climbed down several rungs of a ladder and dropped into the boat. Louis followed and pushed off in the next second. He fitted oars into wooden holes, grinned at her and pulled strongly, sending the boat gliding over the oily waters.

Catching her breath, Becky looked back. The horsemen were nowhere to be seen; the fishermen gazed at them curiously and the boat owner stood, hands on hips, as he watched them, probably wondering what the rush was all about. She bit her cheek as the river bank receded; the current swept them downstream as Louis pulled on the oars, and she felt cold.

But they had gotten away.

She was beginning to think they had given Victor the slip when she saw them, tiny figures on horseback, galloping to the pier. But Louis laughed when she pointed them out. "They will never catch us now."

But he frowned when he saw them gallop along the bank.

Becky asked, "What if they catch up?" The river narrowed ahead of them, making a wide turn to the right. Were they out of pistol range?

"No matter," Louis said positively. "We'll have the river between us. When we reach Argenton we'll disappear into the town before they can cross the bridge."

So there was a bridge at Argenton! Of course there would be; it was a busy seaport after all, and there was undoubtedly a road along the coast.

She jumped at the sound of the shot but Louis laughed. No one could fire accurately from horseback, he said. Victor was only wasting ammunition. Several more shots were fired but only once did she see a splash, a long way behind them. If they continued to fire that way, Louis told her, they would attract soldiers or gendarmes.

But privately she thought Victor must be raging. How infuriating to see his prey in the distance and not be able to close with them. And despite Louis's argument there was always the chance of a lucky hit . . . lucky for the pursuers.

The river narrowed as it made a wide, gentle curve, and moved swiftly in the main channel. Becky watched the horsemen approach, her heart in her throat. They seemed to come so fast! And the boat moved so slowly.

They fired again and again, the sounds like distant pops, not at all dangerous. But she screamed when a ball smashed into the stern, cutting a deep groove only inches behind her. The bullet remained embedded in the wood and when she touched it, it was hot. Another ball cracked overhead and she ducked, wincing at the vicious sound.

Louis pulled hard at the oars, keeping the boat far over to the opposite bank, and he made her lie down to present the smallest target possible. They would also blend in with the foliage of the bank, he said, and anyway they were at the far edge of pistol range; as soon as the river widened they would be completely out of danger.

As they came out of the curve the river widened and, Louis said, looked shallow. Its color changed to a light brownish-green and there were several islands ahead, small bush- and tree-covered sand spits hardly a man's height above water.

Becky sat up, wondering if the river were shallow enough for horsemen to come splashing into it. And as she turned her face toward the shore, she saw the twin blossoms of gray gunsmoke as the horsemen fired. One of the bullets cracked overhead.

The other struck Louis in the foot.

The pistol ball smashed through the side of the boat and Louis yelled, dropping the oars to grab his foot. Becky screamed and lunged toward him. The boot was bloody and Louis was obviously in pain, but he tugged out his clasp knife and gave it to her, grunting through clenched teeth for her to cut away the boot.

How she got it off she could not later have said. She nearly bit through her lower lip, doing her best to ignore the blood till the boot was over the side. The shot had struck just below the ankle, and bits of bone were everywhere. She saw instantly that he would have to get medical care at once. Ripping her petticoat, she bound up the wound. Louis showed her how to make a constricting bandage that would shut off the flow of blood. She thought it a miracle that he did not faint or collapse.

Another half-dozen shots were fired at them as she tended Louis, but she hardly noticed any of them even though several kicked up the water close by. She helped Louis to lie in the bottom of the boat, then she grabbed the oars, sat amidships and began to row. It was not the first time she had done that.

There were more shots but she forced herself to ignore them and attend to the business at hand. She must get Louis to a doctor or he would certainly lose the foot, and maybe part of his leg.

She eased the boat farther to the left, into the main current, as they passed the string of islands. Victor and his men could not see them with the islands in between, and they went more swiftly. Perspiration poured off her and she longed to stop and comfort him, but she dared not. She thought he lost consciousness several times as she rowed and she prayed he would stay that way. Unconscious, he would not suffer the pain so much.

Looking over her shoulder, she could see the tall spire of a church. They were nearing Argenton! The river widened into a delta and there were more long, snaky islands, grassy and clumpy with brush. The pursuers were far off to the left, almost out of sight, and Becky took heart. They would certainly arrive at Argenton well ahead of Victor.

She found it difficult to stay in the main channel. Other streams went veering off to the left, but she began to meet other boats, under sail or being rowed, and a few flatboats with canvas-covered cargoes. She followed one that headed for the town, which she could see clearly now. Houses and ramshackle buildings appeared along the banks, some built on stilts over the water. A few piers jutted out, with small boats clustered around them like beetles. Then she saw the distant bridge. It was a long, low stone affair arching over the river, looking as if it had been there for a century.

A strong breeze was blowing off the sea, bringing with it vagrant gusts of rain that she welcomed, turning her face up. It was cold and refreshing . . . but it awakened Louis. He groaned, pale as weathered canvas, his face twisted with pain, and she cried aloud to see his misery.

The long barge moved slowly away as she dropped the oars to tend him. When she looked again the boat was drifting to shore, and in another moment grounded on sand. Becky scrambled out and pulled it farther onto the shingle; she stood on a shelf of sand only a hand's reach away from a low bank where a curving road followed the river. Across the road were battered sheds, and beyond the near rooftops the tall church spire.

Louis mumbled, "W-where are we?"

She climbed back into the boat. "At Argenton." He looked so pale she could not keep the expression of pity off her face and it tore her heart to see his wan smile. She said, "We've got to get you to a doctor. Can you sit up?"

Grunting, he pushed himself to a sitting position and climbed to the stern seat, dripping sweat. She helped hold the wounded foot and he slowly clambered from the boat and lay full length on the wet sand, tears in his eyes from the pain and effort. He lay only inches from the road but she knew she would never be able to lift him up the bank. He was too big and heavy; she would have to leave him and go for help.

Kneeling beside him, she kissed his cheek. "Tell me how to ask for—" Her eyes caught a movement. A man walked beside a horse and cart, moving into the town. He looked to be a farmer, middle-aged and gray, but strong. Becky rose and ran toward him, calling that her husband was wounded and would he help?

The man stared at her in astonishment, and as he came opposite the boat, halted the cart, unable to understand her. She took his sleeve and pulled. He came to the edge of the road and saw Louis. *"Qu'est-ce que c'est ici?"*

"He must have a doctor!" Becky said in great agitation. "Doctor—doctor—"

"Oui, le docteur," he said, nodding. He jumped down and looked at the bloody bandage around the foot. Louis opened his eyes and focused on him.

"I was shot by bandits," Louis said haltingly in French. His eyes rolled up.

Becky cried and patted his cheeks. The farmer pushed her away, got down on one knee and worked his arms under Louis. He picked Louis up as if he were a child and hurried off to the cart with Becky running after to guard the foot. The farmer laid him in a bed of straw and they bundled more straw about the foot. Louis came to, spoke to the man, then the farmer clucked at the horse and they moved along the road.

Louis said, "He is taking us to a doctor. It is not far."

"Thank the Lord," Becky said fervently. "It must hurt terribly—"

He made a face. "Like the very devil! It is on fire." He lay back and closed his eyes.

He held the sides of the cart with both hands and she put one hand over his as she walked beside him. He said, "I am sorry about all this, *chérie*. I should never have brought you here. I should have come back for you. I was selfish—"

"No, no, no, Louis, please, you mustn't think like that. You will be better in no time."

He said very softly, "They will take my foot off. It cannot be made whole again."

She began to cry, dropping her head down so that he could not see the tears filling her eyes. She stumbled as the cart turned; she heard voices and rubbed her eyes. They were in a very narrow street lined with small, huddled dwellings hardly more than shacks where people stared at them from doorways and chattered to each other.

The street widened suddenly and she saw women gathered about a stone well. All fell silent as they saw Louis. Several crossed themselves at the sight of the bloody bandage. Becky caught a glimpse of fields to the right beyond the houses; then they turned again into a narrow street lined with the backs of houses and a stone fence.

Immediately she heard hoofbeats and an involuntary cry escaped her lips. Turning, she saw them, three riders led by Victor, who grinned in triumph!

In a moment they crossed the square by the well and Becky screamed as she saw Victor's pistol. Victor reined in by the cart. The farmer stood by in amazement and Louis raised himself on an elbow, his face twisted in agony.

Becky ran at Victor, screaming. She heard the thunder of the shot, saw the smoke spurt from the pistol muzzle—and the world turned hazy. Colors smeared across her consciousness, and she fell to the roadway.

Chapter Twenty-Six

Louis was dead. Someone slapped her awake and instantly she began to sob. In that instant she saw him lying in the mud of the street, face mottled with dirt and white as paper. They had pulled him off the cart, which was nowhere to be seen, and his clothes were half cut away. They had searched him and Victor was angry.

Becky could not understand his words but his rage was obvious. He shook a fist at her, shouting one word over and over again. *"La Carte!"* It slowly penetrated her brain. *Carte* meant map. He wanted the map he'd seen in Louis's possession. She shook her head, pretending not to understand.

She cried out as one of them slapped her hard. She fell back, frightened of the knife she saw. One, a big skinny man with gaping teeth, advanced on her with a shimmering blade. She sobbed, "I don't know about a map—"

He grabbed her at the neck and the knife flashed. Becky cringed, thinking he would plunge it into her body. But instead he slashed her clothes, yanking her dress at the neck, baring her to the waist. She shouted and kicked as three of the men held her and tore her clothes off. Then Victor pummeled her about the head and she fell into unconsciousness again.

When she woke, head aching and eyes burning, they were mounting the horses and Victor yelled at her.

They rode off as she heard a distant whistle. Becky sat up, chilled; she was naked, stripped to the skin.

Her clothes lay around her and she snatched up the cloak and examined its neck. They had not found the map!

Voices intruded and she turned, holding the cloak before her. A group of women approached, one with a blanket, which she put around Becky. Another bent over Louis's body, said something to the others and they all crossed themselves. Becky began to sob as she saw the woman close Louis's eyes.

Suddenly the gendarmes arrived, four men on horseback, with dark blue uniforms and short carbines, asking questions. Two of them went after Victor and his men. One man, who spoke halting English asked her name. She told him that Louis was her husband, and they were heading for the town from Mirande. She did not know why the strange men had attacked them. She wondered, from his expression, if he believed the story. He talked with his companion for a moment, and then the other man rode off.

Becky was able to clothe herself; the dress was ripped to the waist but the cloak covered her and she gave the blanket back.

The policeman was back in half an hour with a wagon. They put the body into it, helped her onto the wagon seat and went into the town to the police station.

The man who spoke English took her across the street to a hotel. She was given a cell-like room on the second floor, and told not to leave until an officer called on her. The room was painted a dull yellow with one window, grimy on the outside, a small bed, a chair and a candle. It was, she thought, like being in prison.

When the officer arrived he had a woman with him, with a covered tray of food. She put the tray on the bed and went out. The officer made a polite little bow and introduced himself.

"I am Lieutenant Roland Bricard, mademoiselle. Please allow me to present my condolences on the unfortunate death of M'sieur Boyer."

"I was his wife, sir."

"Ahhh . . . is that so? It was a tragic affair and we all regret it deeply."

"Thank you." She gazed at him in surprise. His English was better than her own. He was a tall, very dark and good-looking man with high cheekbones and a long black moustache that he occasionally pulled. Asking her permission, he sat and removed his uniform cap.

"May I ask, Madame Boyer, where were you coming from?"

"From Mirande, where my husband has relatives."

"I see. And you were going . . . ?"

"We intended to take ship for America."

He nodded, fished in a pocket and withdrew a handful of money. "This was found on your husband's body. It now belongs to you." He rose, put it on the bed by the tray and resumed his chair. "Can you imagine any reason why you should have been attacked?"

Becky shook her head. "We had nothing." She looked at the money. "Except that . . ."

"No jewels?"

"No."

"Can you tell me why they searched your husband and yourself?"

"No, I cannot. I do not know why they didn't take the money."

He tugged at the moustache. "They did not take it because they were looking for something much more valuable."

Becky shook her head helplessly. "We have nothing valuable, Lieutenant."

"Is it possible your husband owned something which you do not know about?"

She hesitated. "I suppose it is possible . . ." She took a breath. "But if so, where is it?"

He fingered the moustache. "What are your plans now, madame? Do you still wish to go to America?"

"Yes. My family is there." She looked at her hands. "When will—will Louis be buried?"

He rose. "In a day or two. I will see that you attend the funeral. We deeply regret this murder, madame. It is the first time in many years that brigands have actually come into the city." He paced to the door and back. "My superiors are very angry and parties of men are searching for them now. If there is anything you can tell us, we would be grateful." He looked at her inquiringly.

Becky chewed her lip. She could not tell him about Marseilles or details of the chase because if Victor were caught he would certainly babble about the map. And it was hers now, the only legacy Louis had left her.

She said, "I was unconscious much of the time, sir— I can think of nothing."

"Too bad." He went to the door again. "I will see you again very soon." He bowed formally and opened the door.

The funeral took place two days later, with only three persons present as mourners. Lieutenant Bricard had brought her in a cart to the churchyard and stood behind her as a priest read in Latin and French. The body, in a plain wooden box, was lowered by three workmen, the ropes pulled up and earth tossed down. Midway through the simple service Becky fell to her knees, unable to contain her tears. She had never been so alone, so unhappy.

Afterward Bricard took her back to the little room.

His men had not been able to track down the brigands, he said sorrowfully. They had apparently disappeared into thin air; he thought it likely they had separated to rejoin later. It made their apprehension almost impossible.

He lingered in the room, inquiring about her future plans. When he learned she had none, and only the small amount of money found on Louis's body, he said he had influence in certain quarters. If she was interested in employment he might be able to suggest something.

"But I cannot speak French."

"Yes, that is a detriment, but perhaps it can be overcome. Many people in France speak English, as I do myself. I traveled in Britain as a young man and studied there for several years." He smiled. "I wished to become a doctor."

"But you became a policeman instead!"

"I soon discovered that medicine bored me. I was happier out in the open chasing thugs and smugglers." He smiled at her expression. "I am naturally inquisitive."

The money Louis had left was not nearly enough to buy passage on a ship; she said she would be grateful to him if he could help with employment since she must save enough to pay for her fare home. He promised to return soon with more information.

She was able to stitch together the ripped clothes, and when it stopped raining she went out to buy food. There was a street of small shops nearby and, though she had to point to what she wanted, she got on well, and learned a few words in the bargain.

Several days after Louis's funeral she walked to the waterfront. There was a long, curving stone embankment that defined the harbor, no larger than the one at Canaan, she thought. A number of wood and stone jetties poked through the surf with their attendant small boats. Farther out a half dozen ships rocked at anchor with clouds of piping gulls wheeling about. It was a gray, cold day with a stiff breeze whipping up whitecaps in the bay, but the smell of salt water and fish nearly brought tears to her eyes as she thought of home. How far away it seemed. . . . Had Marie given birth yet? How she longed to be there to hold the little one.

How she longed to be there for the sake of her own child! Would her baby be born in France? It seemed likely. Lieutenant Bricard would probably find her a job as a tutor, at miserable wages. There was so little available, especially in a small town like Argenton. She might even have to become a drudge to support herself and the coming child.

As she walked along the embankment she recognized the flags of a dozen nations. Men eyed her but she ignored them, and went back finally to her little room. When she had the money for her passage she would somehow have to find out how to talk to the ship captains.

Lieutenant Bricard came to call on her late the next day. He sat in the chair and refused a cup of tea, saying he'd never acquired a taste for it. He had a friend, he said, an older man named Andre Bataille, who was an invalid and needed someone to look after him.

"He has a girl now," Bricard said, "but she is slow and a little stupid. Andrew says she is impossible to talk to."

"Does he speak English?"

"Yes, certainly. He lived for many years in Sheffield, where his father had an exporting business. Knives, I believe."

"What kind of work—I mean—is he unable to get out of bed?"

Bricard laughed. "No, he is up and about in a chair

with wheels. But he is nearing eighty-five and forgetful. Let me take you to see him tomorrow."

"He has no family?"

"He has a son, Theo, but he lives alone and complains constantly that Theo never comes to see him. I think he forgets how often Theo is there. However . . ." Bricard shrugged and rose. He went to the door. "I will come an hour before midday, if that is your wish?" His brows went up.

"Oh yes," Becky said with enthusiasm. "Thank you, sir."

She was astonished, when Bricard drove her in a one-horse carriage to the house, to see a mansion. It was situated on a rise of ground facing the sea and had extensive gardens, trees, and even a small stream of water that gurgled under the ornate stone bridge they crossed to reach the front door. Andre Bataille was obviously a wealthy man.

An ancient servant in dark blue and black opened the door, smiled to see Bricard and stared at her. Bricard ushered her inside, told the servant to run along and took her arm. They walked half the length of a polished hall where there were figurines and busts on pedestals, Grecian pots and tapestries on the walls. They went through a huge sitting room with a dozen chairs, divans and tables, into a small room with diamond-paned windows and an Oriental carpet on the floor. An old man in a velvet coat was feeding a parrot in a brass cage.

The man glanced around and smiled on seeing her. He was large and plump with bright eyes and wattles that shook as he turned to greet them. "Ah, Bricard! How nice to see you—and this is the young lady you mentioned?"

"Yes. Mrs. Boyer of Connecticut Colony in America."

"Your husband was French, Mrs. Boyer?"

"Yes, sir. Please call me Becky."

"Indeed I will." Andre indicated a chair. "Please sit, Becky. My, you're a pretty thing! D'you have any children?"

"No, sir."

"Bricard told me about your husband . . . a great tragedy." He touched her shoulder. "I am very sorry for your loss. Bricard, bring us a bottle of wine from the sideboard there—yes, the center door—the glasses are up above." He turned back to her. "I suppose Bricard has told you all about me?"

"A little, sir."

"Ah. Well, let me tell you what I require." He lowered his voice. "The girl I have now is impossible, simply impossible. I shall let her go immediately." He leaned forward and patted her knee. "As you see, I get about with difficulty. If this chair were not fitted with wheels I think I would go mad!"

Becky saw the wheels for the first time. They were about six inches in diameter, one wheel on each chair leg. Apparently one pushed the chair from behind. She had never heard of such a contraption, but obviously it worked.

Bricard came back with a bottle and three glasses; he put them on a small table and poured, handing one to her.

Andre said, "You look a strong child, Becky. D'you think you can push me about?"

"Oh yes, sir. But how do you go upstairs?"

"Simple." He laughed. "I never do! Haven't been upstairs in my own house in five years. I require you to push me, to feed and talk to me. D'you suppose you can do that?"

"What do you talk about, sir?" she asked cautiously.

He laughed and Bricard joined in. "About everything, child. Any and everything."

"I will do my best, sir."

"Oh, one thing more. You'll have to live here, you know."

"Yes, sir."

Bricard said, "What will you pay her?"

"Umm. I understand you wish to return to the Americas, is that right?"

"Yes, sir, to my family."

Andre nodded. "I know a number of captains. Serve me well, young lady, and I'll arrange for passage. How's that?"

Bricard said to her, "I'll look in on you from time to time, madame. We'll keep him honest."

Andre said something to him in rapid French and Bricard laughed. "He does not need a policeman to teach him honesty. Well, we will see."

"The police are a necessary evil," Andre said with a sidelong look. He reached out and patted her hand. "When will you come to live here?"

"At once!" Becky said eagerly, thinking of the hovel room she'd left.

"At once will do fine." Andre beamed. "Bring her things today, Bricard, and do an old man a great favor."

There was very little to move. Bricard carried her canvas bag, put it in the light coach and they returned to the mansion. This time she was introduced to the old retainer; his name was Voliner. In the kitchen she met the cook, Elda. Then Bricard took her upstairs to her room. It was large and airy with two windows, one facing the sea, one the garden; it had a fine large bed, table and chairs, even a carpet on the floor. The walls were papered with floral designs in light pinks and grays and there was an armoire in one corner. She felt like royalty.

Lieutenant Bricard left her to freshen up and was waiting when she came down. She ran to him, holding out both hands. "You are so kind—"

"You will be good for my friend," he said simply. He patted her cheek. "I will see you again. *Au revoir*." He went out and Voliner closed the door behind him.

Voliner spoke to her in French and when she smiled and shook her head, he beckoned and led her to the sitting room where Andre reclined on a divan, reading a book.

He looked up and smiled. "Ah, there you are. How you brighten up the room, girl. Come, sit here and tell me about America. I've never been there, you know. Are there really red Indians everywhere?"

The next afternoon, while she was reading to Andre in the book-lined study, the door opened and a tall, elegantly dressed man entered. He was about thirty, she thought, dark and rather handsome, with deep-set liquid eyes and a full mouth. His eyes went to her at once, widened slightly, and then he smiled.

Andre looked around. "Ah, Theo, come in." He spoke in English.

"How do you do, Father?" Theo's English was not as flawlessly accented as Andre's. He came across the room, his gaze still on her, and Becky lowered her eyes, not liking what she saw in his face. Theo had a distinctly predatory look, she thought. He seated himself opposite and continued to gaze at her.

Andre said to her, "This is my son, Theo. Theo, this is Becky, my new helper—is that the right word?"

"She's beautiful," Theo said.

Becky managed a smile. "Thank you, sir."

"So that's why we're speaking English. You're an English girl. How charming!"

"I'm from America, sir," Becky said.

"America!" Theo was astonished. "Wherever did you find her, Father?"

"Bricard brought her here. I'm surprised to see you, Theo."

"Why is that? Don't I pay my respects often enough?"

Andre shrugged. "When you think of it."

"Well, I've come on a matter of business." Theo produced a bundle of papers from under his coat, like a magician, and smiled at Becky. "Do you mind, mademoiselle, if we speak in French? These things are more difficult for me in English."

"Of course." Becky rose and left the room. She found a chair in the nearby sitting room where she could hear the murmur of voices. Andre had a small silver bell to ring when he wished her services.

Theo was closeted with his father for more than an hour and when he emerged she thought he looked a bit sour. Perhaps the business had not gone his way—did he want to borrow money? But he brightened when he saw her.

"My father is a lucky man." He came very close, smiling down at her. "Do you enjoy being with the very old?"

"He is very kind."

"He is more kind to some than to others." He sat down by her. Suddenly his arm slid about her waist and he pulled her close. Before she could object he was kissing her; his free hand wandered up from her waist to fondle her breast.

Becky was startled. Then she struggled in his arms to free herself, clamping her teeth together as she felt his tongue.

"*Le bon Dieu!* What a wildcat!" He let her go and moved away, smiling. "We shall be great friends, Mademoiselle Becky." He winked at her, rose and crossed the room quickly.

She stared after him, breasts heaving, her face red. Anger made her fingers curl into fists and she thought of a dozen dockside curses she'd heard, but bit her tongue at the last instant. Theo would only laugh at her.

The silver bell tinkled from the study and she got herself hurriedly under control. Lieutenant Bricard had said Theo was not a frequent visitor. Perhaps she would not see him again soon. She patted her hair, smoothed her dress and went to the study.

Chapter Twenty-Seven

Marie sat with her loom in a corner of the kitchen; her mother had been cooking fish and the room smelled strongly of it. She was alone and the loom was still, her thoughts far off. Wager was coming in the morning with a light wagon to take her away to Massachusetts to his sister's home.

Did she want to go? Of course it was sensible, in her mother's view, because no other course was open; she could not have the baby in Canaan. She understood that. She and David were not married.

David was at Belford. She'd seen it in a newspaper— she could not remember where she had read it—but she was positive. Something was keeping him from coming for her. Perhaps his papers, or whatever was necessary to discharge him from the army, were slow. She'd often heard her father speak of the slowness of the bureaucracy, their frustrating dependence on bits of paper.

Belford was not distant, maybe fifty miles to the west. David should easily be able to ride that far in a day or a little more. She thought about the note he'd written her, and wished she could put her hands on it. She'd looked for it a hundred times. How annoying to think she must have put it in the fire.

Her mother came home in an hour or two; she'd been to see Widow Riley, she said. The old woman was getting on, even more forgetful than usual.

"Have you packed your things, Marie?"

"Yes, Mother."

"And all the baby things?"

"Yes. They're in the seabag at the head of the stairs."

Maggie nodded and put a small log on the fire, then looked at her fondly. "We're going to miss you, child. I wish there was some way I could go along."

"I'll miss you too, Mother." She looked down at the loom, then put it aside. "Will Wager be here early?"

"Yes, probably at sunrise."

Maggie made tea and gave her a cup, then took another cup upstairs to Azariah. Marie went to the rear window and stared out. There was a tiny breeze that moved the small branches of the trees and the ground was dry. It had not rained for several days; the sky was gray with high clouds but now and then she could see blue as they parted. Rain was not likely.

A month past she had written a letter to David, asking when he was coming for her, telling him what her mother and Wager proposed—sending her off to Massachusetts to have the baby. She'd asked him to write at once, but he had not.

She'd given the letter to Brayton to post, and she still recalled the look on his face as he took it. Probably he thought her very forward to write, but she was to be David's wife.

The day went by with agonizing slowness. Junius came home from the boatyard, filled with chatter about a new ketch on the stocks, and Brayton came from the store long after dark, dead tired and eager to hop into bed.

Marie went upstairs while her mother and Junius sat in the kitchen, talking about the ketch. She went to bed, but she did not sleep. Her mind was filled with thoughts of David. It was now that she needed him, with the baby due in two and a half months.

The baby would be a boy, of course; it never once occurred to her to select a girl's name. She would call the baby Allen, a name she had always liked—with David's approval, naturally. Perhaps he ought to be called Allen David, but they could discuss that when she saw him.

After a time she heard Junius come upstairs to bed, and half an hour later her mother followed. The house grew quiet, gently creaking as the heat diminished.

She did not want to go to Massachusetts. Of course it was the proper thing to do, from her mother's reasoning, but she would miss David; he might well show up a day after she'd left in the wagon with Wager! He might be on the way even now as she thought about him.

It was odd that he hadn't come for her. Maybe she should go to him.

It was not a new thought to her; she had considered it many times, but now there was a compelling urgency. The next morning she would leave with Wager. She would be gone for months!

Months! She would not see David for months!

Marie sat up in bed. Wager and her mother had her best interests at heart, she was sure. But if she did as they wished, it would separate her and David. She needed him by her side when the baby was born.

She slid out of bed and began to dress quickly and silently. She drew on drawers and undershirt, three petticoats and her best black dress. Her blue cloak was wool, thick and warm; she tied it round her throat and took her heavy shoes, the same ones she'd muddied David's bed with.

She went quietly downstairs and paused by the front door to put on the shoes. Then she let herself out and stood on the stoop, looking at the sky. It did not look or smell like rain. She went down the steps to the street and began to walk quickly away.

The town was silent and still. Not even a dog barked as she reached Fort Street and crossed the wagon bridge. David would be surprised and glad to see her. He would find her a place to stay; she visualized a pleasant room in an inn, then supper alone with him. . . .

She left the town behind and very soon the overcast faded away and a bright, shimmering moon came out, helping her to see the road. She walked purposefully, her heart joyous. She was finally going to see him! She had stopped her hesitating and made up her mind. It was right. She knew it was right.

Despite the moon the night was dark and filled with shadows. Away from the town the silences were broken by ocean breezes and the far-off sounds of surf. She met no one along the lonely road, and to keep her spirits up she devised bits of conversation with David.

"Are you glad I came to find you?"

He said, "My darling, I am delighted! I cannot tell you how I have missed you!"

"It has been weeks."

"Yes, but I have been unable to get leave and my discharge papers have not arrived from London. Please forgive me."

"Of course. We're together now."

Then he would embrace and kiss her. . . .

She closed her eyes, enveloped in this dream, and stumbled in a rut and fell to one knee. She must be more careful! The moon was bright, but it cast so little light. When the trees closed overhead, blotting it out, she was in a shadowy tunnel and had almost to feel her way through.

Yet the miles fell behind her; she was used to walking, though not of late, and could easily walk a dozen miles a day without fatigue.

"I thought of naming the baby Allen."

"An excellent idea."

"And I thought of David for a middle name."

"Why not name him Howard, after my father?"

Was his father's name Howard? She halted, hearing

the sounds of crashing branches, heart in her mouth. But the noises faded away in the opposite direction. Obviously it was a small animal, afraid of her. She went on, looking about keenly, drawing the cloak tightly about her; she did not feel cold but its warmth was comforting. The sounds of surf receded as the road curved away from the shore and it became very still again.

"David, tell me you love me."

"Of course I love you! You are my life, my very existence!"

"Why did you not write when you left?"

"I *did* write, my dove! The day I left, that note must have gone astray!"

Yes, of course it had. She had told herself so a thousand times. The king's post was inept and careless; everyone complained about it.

She cocked her head, hearing a new and strange sound . . . then identified it. A stream—running water.

When she came to it the moon sent shards of pale light to pick out its surface. The road halted at the bank and took up again on the opposite side. It must be a ford. There was no sign of a bridge but of course there probably were not five bridges on the king's road in all of Connecticut. She could not expect one here over this tiny but fast-running stream.

There was no way to get across but to wade.

Grimacing, she pulled her skirts high and stepped gingerly into the water. The first step was a surprise. The water came up over her shoe and it was icy. With the second step she sank deeper, all the way to her knees. The far side seemed a mile distant! She took a third step and slipped on the muddy bottom. With a cry she fell in and barely regained her footing, soaked to the chin.

In midstream the current was fast. It chilled her to the bone and pushed her mightily, twisting her about. She flung out both hands as her feet were swept out from under her. In the next second the water closed over her head.

Wager borrowed a light wagon pulled by a single horse and drove to the Lynn home at sun-up. He had placed a straw mattress in the back, in case Marie wanted to sleep or rest on the way, and had rigged a canvas top against possible rain.

Maggie answered the door and he went in to the welcome fire; the kitchen smelled of roast meat, and Maggie gave him a cup of steaming hot tea. "How does the weather look?"

"It's clear," he said. "How's Azariah?"

"He had a good night and he's still sleeping." She went to the stairs. "I'll see that Marie's up . . ."

Wager sipped the tea, watching the flames. He would stay the night at his sister's house and drive back the next day. It would give them a chance to talk and at the same time ease the unfamiliar surroundings for Marie; she'd be nervous in the company of strangers.

"Wager!"

He turned, surprised at the tone of Maggie's voice. She stood in the doorway, hand to her throat.

"Marie's not in her room!"

"What!" He rose. "Where can she be, then?"

Maggie went past him to the rear door. "It's bolted on the inside." She stared at him. "Her cloak and heavy shoes are gone as well."

"You think she got up in the night—!"

"Wager—" She came close to him. "She's gone to find David."

"What—you mean Urfe?"

"Yes. Remember I told you she said she'd received a

letter from him?" At his nod she continued. "There was no letter, of course. It was something she'd dreamed—and believed. She thinks he's alive."

"But how can she?"

"She *believes* it. It doesn't matter if it's true. It's what she believes that's important."

"She just started walking!?"

"She must have."

He drank the tea in a gulp. "Then I'll go after her." He started for the door and Maggie called after him.

"I'll go with you."

"No. You stay here."

"I want to go. Let me get my cloak." She went to the stairs and Wager took her arm.

"You can do nothing at all. It's better you stay here. I'll find her and bring her back."

"I'll worry every second you're away."

"Then worry. But see to your family." He patted her hand and went to the front door, looked at her, clapped on his hat and went out.

It was a brisk morning and the horse wanted to trot. Wager hurried down Pearl Street, turned right onto Fort and across the bridge. What an incredible idea! Marie thought she could walk to Belford! Of course she might get a ride on a wagon. Who would think a girl would do such a thing!

He was well aware of Marie's belief that David Urfe was still alive. Maggie had told him often enough. Marie believed that he would come for her—and when he did not, she had gone to him.

That must be it. She had gotten up in the middle of the night and started walking.

He looked for tracks in the road and saw none that looked recent. The ground was nearly dry, however, and it would take an expert tracker to find her footsteps.

He met no one on the road, and did not expect to. In the best of times there were only a few wagons each week, and a handful of horsemen. People traveled very little. After an hour he walked the horse, then let it run again.

When he came to the stream he halted, let the horse drink and had a few gulps himself. Marie would be soaked to the skin crossing that.

He shook his head, got back on the box and urged the horse into the swift-running water. It came up over the wheels and splashed the sides. Part way across it pushed the wagon half around and he had to shout and use the whip to get up the opposite bank. There was plenty of run-off from the hills.

On the far bank he halted and looked back at the stream uneasily. Marie would have a time crossing that in the night. But of course she was a strong girl, though her belly was rounding, and she was determined. He slapped the reins and went on.

In two hours he came to a village straddling the road, and halted. Marie should have reached this far about sun-up he thought. He got down, tied the horse in front of the inn and went inside to ask if anyone had seen her.

No one had.

He asked along the street and found a man who'd been delivering fodder to the blacksmith before sunrise. "No one come along the road," he said.

If she'd gotten soaked in the stream she would surely have stopped in the village to get dry. Wager thanked the man and turned the horse and wagon around. Maybe she hadn't crossed the stream at all but had gone up or down it looking for a better place to cross.

It took another two hours to reach the stream again. He crossed the stream again, finding it slightly easier, then tied the horse to a tree branch and examined the ground, finding no footprints at all. What would a girl like Marie do when she came upon the rushing water? Would she cross or would she sit shivering under a tree—or would she walk up or downstream? She was certainly not in sight. He walked a short distance making sure.

But would she walk along the stream at night? He doubted if he'd do that himself. Maybe she'd waited for someone to come along and take her across; a man with a wagon perhaps. And if so she was far along the road, dry and happy, while he worried himself walking about the stream.

At the same time he had to make sure, now that he was here. Maggie would certainly look at him askance if he reported to her that he'd made no investigation of the stream—it *was* a barrier, after all. He sighed, shook his head and started upstream.

After an hour he halted. The rushing water allowed little chance of a crossing, except perhaps in broad daylight by a very agile and strong man with an axe to cut poles.

Wager looked upstream, saw no change and turned back.

The more he thought about it the more sure he became that Marie had found a way across, probably in someone's wagon. Travelers were few, but they *did* use the road. She had probably waited till daylight and someone had come along.

When he reached the horse and wagon again, he rubbed the animal's nose, told it to be patient, and started downstream.

It was slow going, picking his way through brushy tangles, and there were times when he had to veer away from the stream, which ran mostly straight in its headlong dash for the sea. After several hundred yards he was tired and the investigative spirit was going fast.

Why in the world would Marie come this way in the night? He stood on the bank, staring at the brown water, and decided he was on a fool's errand. She had waited for a wagon.

As he was about to turn back he noticed that the stream curved to the right another hundred yards farther on.

Wager paused, pulled at an ear and suddenly decided to walk that far. At least then he could tell Maggie he'd made an honest effort. He'd look at the curve, then go back and continue along the road. Sooner or later he'd come on her, even if he had to go all the way to Belford.

That decision made, he hurried to the curve—and halted.

She was lying half in, half out of the water, the cloak swirled over nearby branches, and when he looked at her, he *knew*.

With a cry, Wager ran to her, trampling into the brush to get hold of her arms. He pulled her out and turned her over, tears in his eyes. Her face was pale as his shirt, but her expression was calm, even peaceful. Her wet hair fell over her forehead. She was cold as ice.

He knelt beside her and cried, unable to stop the tears, thinking of Maggie. Marie was dead. She would take it hard.

After a bit he slid his arms under her and lifted her gently. It took forever to stumble back to the wagon, and when he reached it he laid her out full length in the back and covered her with a blanket. What a sad burden to carry home to her loved ones. How could he tell Maggie?

When he reached Canaan he drove immediately to the only undertaker in town, Doc Purvis Orne, and halted in front of the building on York Street, just around the corner from the main part of town. He got down and went inside.

Doc Orne came from the back when he rapped sharply on a tabletop. "What is it—oh, hello, Wager." Orne was a stooped, skinny man, middle-aged and bespectacled. He shoved the specs up and peered at his visitor. "You look skittish. You brung me business?"

Wager nodded. "She's out in the wagon. It's Marie Lynn."

"Oh, hell. I'd a lot sooner it'd been somebody else."

"Me too. Can I bring the wagon around back?"

"What happened to her?"

"I think she drowned." Wager went out and drove around the building as Doc pointed. He halted by the back door and unfastened the tailgate. Doc moved her arm.

"Rigor's startin' to set in. Let's get her inside."

Carrying her by head and feet, they went inside and put the body on a metal-topped table. The room smelled of chemicals and Wager was glad to step out into the air again. He told Doc where he'd found the body.

"There's something else, Doc."

"You mean her bein' pregnant?" Doc's face wrinkled.

Wager nodded. "Can it be kept a secret?"

"Don't her family know?"

"Yes, they know, but they don't want the town to find out. Maggie Lynn would be mighty grateful to you."

Doc scratched his ear. "Hell, if I told all the secrets I know this here town'd be on its nose. You'd be surprised, Wager. One time when I was an apprentice in Hartford we took in a woman, only she wasn't a woman at all! She was a man dressed like one and been livin' like a woman for half 'is life!"

328

"That's not possible!"

"Hell it weren't! I could tell you some others too—only I won't. Does Maggie know about this yet?"

Wager shook his head sadly. "I've got to go and do that now. You'll keep the secret, Doc?"

"I'll keep it."

It was the hardest thing he'd ever done, to tell Maggie that Marie was gone. But when she first looked at him, she knew the truth. She had been watching the street for the wagon and opened the door when he stopped in front of the house. Her face as she stared at him was a mirror of despair.

He climbed over the wheel and went up the steps as she stood in the doorway. She said, "You—found her?"

He nodded, took her arm and led her inside. He could hear Azariah coughing upstairs. There was no one else in the house and he drew her close, arms about her. He said softly, "She drowned in a stream, Maggie."

She sagged against him feeling weary and faint—she must not swoon away! His arms held her up and he led her to a chair; she sat, head in her hands. Marie! Lovely little trusting Marie—drowned! *Lord! You try us hard. Did You have to take her?*

Her face was wet with tears and Wager held her and let her cry.

After a bit she roused and looked at him. He said, "I left her at Doc Orne's."

She leaned against him, feeling the rough texture of his coat on her cheek. What would she do without him? She closed her eyes, feeling the strength flow back into her. He kissed her and she snuggled closer, then pushed away with an effort. "Tell me how it happened," she said.

Chapter Twenty-Eight

Sharon Quant was shocked by her father's statement that she belonged to Captain Styles if he would have her as his wife. Enoch saw the rebellion in her eyes and smirked.

"Y'll do as I say and nothing else. He's waivin' the dowry just to get you."

She thought of Morgan and faced him. "He's too old, Father. You're selling me like a sack of kindling!"

Enoch took her arm, turning her toward home. "Then cry if y'must. But it won't do you any good. My mind's made up. Come along."

She had never been able to talk to her father, and in this matter her mother had little to say. "You know he does what he wants."

"But, Mother! It's only business to him. He doesn't care at all what happens to me! Captain Styles is an old man—"

"Lord, girl, he's rich. Rich is better'n poor."

Sharon stared at her mother, realizing there was no help to be gotten here. She was cornered, stifled, a lamb to the slaughter, and all because her father thought it would help his business.

In her room she sat on the bed and stared at the dreary scene from the window. She had no money to go anywhere and she could not travel alone in any event. There was nothing she could do but marry him. And be miserable the rest of her life.

If only Morgan would come back quickly . . . She would go with him in an instant, anywhere he wanted to take her.

But Morgan did not come for her. Instead a big, hard-faced man in a dark brown coat and gray breeches called for her with a coach. His name was Sergeant Dyer—her father introduced them—and he saw her down the steps and into the coach. Dyer got in after her and sat opposite.

The coach smelled of tobacco. It had black seats and dove gray sides and ceiling with four small windows, the first real coach she had ever been inside, and it seemed very elegant to her. There was even a footrail, which she could almost reach with her toe. When Dyer got in she asked, "Where are we going?"

"To see Cap'n Styles, mum."

"And where will we see him?"

"In 'is quarters, of course." Dyer looked surprised.

"I see. And why did he not call himself?"

Dyer's lip turned down a fraction. "It ain't his way, mum."

She stared at him, wondering if Styles would feel contaminated by coming into her neighborhood, so he had sent this big capable underling. She had heard her father speak of Dyer, how overbearing and arrogant he was, and she could believe it, having seen him. His face was devoid of expression, with eyes like agates; he almost made her shudder. If the underling was stony and cold, what was the master like?

The coach made a number of turnings and she was quickly lost. The tiny window next to her was difficult to see out of and she did not know the city.

When the coach stopped she had no idea where she was. Dyer quickly opened the door and handed her out. He slammed it and the coach rattled away at once. She had an impression of a large red brick house, on a street of other large houses; then she was up the brick steps and into the foyer. The heavy door closed behind her with an ominous click and Dyer said, "Please go into the sitting room, mum. I'll tell the cap'n." He indicated the room, then mounted the stairs.

The foyer was dark, with velvet hangings on every side, a smallish square room that smelled of candles. She went through an arch into the sitting room, which reeked of tobacco. Apparently the captain and his cronies smoked a good deal. The room was large, with a huge fireplace of light brown brick with a large raised hearth and brass andirons. A fire was smouldering behind a fan-shaped screen; wisps of smoke escaped into the room and as she moved into the center she could smell it. The chairs were fabric and leather, the wall hangings were of a dark, velvetlike material and there were two portraits on the walls. The room was carpeted; there were small tables here and there, with a small stack of newspapers on one. At one end was a tall bookcase with leather-bound tomes.

Sharon sighed and seated herself on the edge of one of the leather chairs. The room was larger than any three rooms of the house in Canaan where she'd lived most of her life. She wondered if Captain Styles had many servants. There seemed to be no dust on any of the surfaces.

"Ah, my dear," said a voice and she turned. Styles came into the room and she stood as he grasped both her hands and kissed one.

"I'm so happy you could come. Please sit down."

She sat with a murmured "Thank you." He looked exactly as she'd seen him in the park, except that his clothes were different. He wore a coat and breeches of light blue faced with white, and a lacy ruffled shirt. She knew that the suit alone had cost more than her father made in a year.

Styles turned to Dyer, who stood at the door. "Get us something, Gideon, will you." Dyer nodded and disappeared.

She found it impossible to be comfortable; she was conscious of her clothes, her worn shoes, which she kept tucked out of sight as much as possible, and her hands. What should she do with her hands?

He did not seem to notice her lack of composure but chatted of the weather which, he thought, was gradually warming. Winter was drawing to a close, didn't she think so? Sharon said that she was certain spring was not far off.

She was relieved when Dyer reentered with a tray on which was a silver and glass carafe and two glasses. He put it on a small table between them. Styles pointed to the fire with a languid finger and Dyer knelt in front of it, removed the screen and built it up, poking and adding kindling till it crackled more cheerfully.

Styles poured and handed her a glass. "A bit of light wine, my dear. It's so refreshing."

She sipped it. It had a tang and a sweetness, not at all unpleasant.

He said, "Your father has informed you, I presume?"

She looked at him. "Of your intentions, sir? Yes, he has."

"And do you approve? No, I shan't ask you that."

Dyer got up from in front of the fire and went out to the hall without a word.

She was glad of the glass. She could hold it with both hands as she studied him covertly. He was much older than Morgan and much more worldly, of course. She wondered if he had been married before. Probably. The idea of going to bed with him repelled her, so she tried not to think of it. However, there was a look in his eye that seemed to bode ill for her and she glanced at the open doorway. But Dyer would probably not come at her call—if she called.

He finished the wine in his glass and poured more, then reached toward her with the bottle, but she shook her head. She did not dare let herself get light-headed. She sipped very sparingly, savoring the taste. Her father had often brought home red wine and occasionally she'd had half a cup, but it tasted raw, nothing like this.

She glanced at him and saw he was studying her intently, a half-smile on his thin lips. The smile made her feel uneasy and she wished there were someone else in the room—even Dyer.

"Would you like to see the house?" he asked suddenly, and rose, putting the wine glass aside. He reached for her hand.

Sharon avoided the hand and got to her feet, moving away, and she heard his chuckle.

"You're like a frightened deer. Did you think I would harm you?"

"No, sir," she said tightly.

He stood in front of her. "You mustn't call me sir. My given name is Jennet. My friends call me Jen. Wouldn't it be better if you were one of them?"

"Yes, sir." She bit her lip. "I mean, Jen."

He took her hand. "You're trembling!" He patted it, shaking his head. "What will I do with you? You must get past this unflattering reaction. It simply won't do when we get back to London, you know."

"London!" It was a surprise.

"You don't think I intend to bury myself in these colonies, do you? I return to London every year, and one of these days I shall go back permanently." He held her hand firmly and pointed her toward the hall.

London! She had never considered that! It was a world away and the idea of it frightened her. Would she be able to get through the social functions he would demand? She was a girl from the country, after all, who had never attended more than a church social in all its primness.

He seemed to divine her thoughts. "You will learn," he said condescendingly. "There are excellent teachers of the fashionable arts. In a few months you will be surprised at your progress."

There seemed no answer to that so she kept silent. Was he going to send her to school? What kind of a wife did he want?

He led her into the hall and up a set of stairs to the second floor. The stairs were carpeted, as was the upstairs hall, and there was statuary on pedestals in the corners; stern-faced men glared at her as she passed and she looked at them out of the corners of her eyes.

There were three chambers upstairs, as well as closets and a room for bathing. Styles showed them to her quickly, with a wave of his hand. "This is a room where I keep uniforms and other clothes, and this is a guest bedchamber . . ."

The large bedroom was square and not at all spartan. It had a dark, plain carpet on the floor and also a large white animal skin that looked very lush. The walls were draped in bluish-purple cloth that shimmered slightly and the huge four-poster bed was shrouded in a lacy curtain, the uprights ornately carved. The room smelled vaguely of perfume.

Sharon stood in the doorway in astonishment; the room was nothing like what she'd supposed, and Styles was obviously proud of it. He strutted across the room, swept back the bed curtain and invited her to feel the mattress.

She said, timidly, "I'm sure it's very nice . . ."

"Come, come, you're a grown woman!"

She advanced into the room, looking at the very expensive white furniture, which was decorated with floral designs. The oval mirror was not even wavy!

Styles came to her and smiled, lifting her chin with a finger. "You are a little deer, aren't you? Ready to run at the first sound."

She said properly, "I've never been in a gentleman's bedchamber before, sir."

He stared at her, then laughed, grabbing both her hands. "My dear, you will soon be mistress of this house! It is only one room in the house, I assure you. These are all inanimate objects. There is nothing here to harm you."

She felt him pulling her closer and resisted. He took a quick step, slid his arms about her and kissed her hard on the lips. She struggled, but he was very strong and did not release her for a full minute. He looked into her flushed face and said calmly, "You will be my wife in a matter of weeks, my dear. I advise you to get used to the idea."

She was about to reply when he kissed her again with the same fervor, this time moving her toward the bed. She felt the base of it on the backs of her knees, and suddenly he tipped her back and she fell onto the bed with him nearly atop her.

The kiss broke and he was suddenly grunting, trying to pull her onto the bed and yank up her skirts at the same time. Sharon yelped, rolled and slapped out with the edge of her hand, connecting with the bridge of his nose. Styles growled and swore, grabbing at her as she scuttled across the bed and rolled onto the floor. She was on her feet in an instant, running for the door.

He shouted, "Come back, you little witch!"

She stopped in the doorway as she realized he was not pursuing her. He was still flopped belly down on the bed, glaring at her, his hair awry and face red, holding his nose with his fingers.

In a growling voice he said, "I think you've broken my nose, damme."

Suddenly she wanted to giggle. He was such a ludicrous sight, all his aplomb and reserve gone; he was a skinny middle-aged man, pouting like a boy with a skinned elbow.

She said, "I'm sorry, sir. I didn't mean to—"

"Damme, stop calling me sir! I told you what my name was."

"Yes, sir—" She bit her lip.

Styles sat up and smoothed his hair, then looked at his hand to see if his nose was bloody; it was not and he sighed. He edged forward and sat on the end of the bed, pointing to the washbasin. "Get me some water—use one of those towels."

She ran to the basin, soaked the end of a towel in cold water and took it to him. He wadded it up and held it against his nose, still glaring at her. "D'you have any brothers?"

She shook her head.

"Where'd you learn to hit like that?"

"It was an accident, sir—I mean, Jen."

"It's swelling up, you know. I'll look a sight tomorrow."

"I'm very sorry."

He got off the bed, still holding his nose, grunted at her and went out and down the stairs. She followed demurely and went into the sitting room again as he pointed. He disappeared in the direction of the kitchen, and she heard him yelling for Dyer.

Sharon sat by the fire, watching the smouldering logs, angry red underneath and gray on top. So it was really all settled; she was to marry this popinjay with

337

the fancy bedroom. She must make up her mind to it, he'd said. That meant he'd come to an agreement with her father and she knew nothing would change *his* mind.

"Oh Lord, Morgan, where are you?" Tears came to her eyes, and she dabbed them away quickly. Was there any way she could get out of this corner?

Styles returned after rather a long wait, accompanied by the burly, hard-faced Dyer. The captain's nose was still red and a bit swollen—had she broken it? He said, "The sergeant will take you back now, my love." He came down hard on the word love.

Sharon rose quickly, remembering not to look too delighted at going. She gathered up her cloak, which Dyer had laid over a chairback, and slipped it on.

Styles said, "I understand you're teaching in a school."

"Well, not exactly teaching. I'm minding the children."

He fixed her with narrowed eyes. "You will give up the position immediately."

"What?" It startled her.

He said grumpily, "I believe you heard me. You will give it up."

"But why?"

He rolled his eyes. "Take her home, Dyer." He motioned toward the door. "There are times I can't abide these colonial ways, Sharon, my love. Please do as you're asked and let's have no quarrels."

She stared at him, open-mouthed. Give up her newly won job? What difference did it make to him? She felt Dyer's touch and turned to the door.

Styles said, "I'll see you presently, my dear."

She paused, looked at him, nodded, and went out.

How could she marry that man?

The carriage pulled up in front of the house as they

went down the steps. Dyer opened the door for her, handed her in and followed. As he slammed the door, he smiled. The only time she'd seen him change expression except to frown.

He said, "You hit 'im a good clip, miss. I think you broke 'is nose."

Her father was out when she arrived home. Her mother was in the kitchen, stirring a pot of something that smelled like stew, and sighed, looking at her.

"Now don't start in on me, girl . . ."

"Mother, how can I marry that man? He's horrible!"

Tabitha shook her head. "Talk to your father—if you think it'll help." She tasted the stew and continued stirring. "He thinks it'll make a change in 'is business. I told him it wouldn't but he won't listen."

Sharon draped the cloak over a chair back and sat dejectedly. "He told me to give up my job. He didn't ask—he told me."

Tabitha glanced at her daughter. "It's 'is position, girl, don't you know. A man like that can't have his wife-to-be in trade."

"I'm not in trade."

"It's the same thing to him."

"I don't want to give it up!"

Tabitha smiled. "There's the rebellion, dear. It'll do you no good in the long run, I warn. Y'might as well give in gracefully."

Sharon blew out her breath and glared at her mother. "Do you approve?"

"It doesn't matter if I do or not. It's settled, Sharon. Give in."

She wailed, "How can I give in to that—that fop!"

Tabitha shrugged. "Call 'im what you will, but he's rich. And I tell you that's better than—"

"Lord! Is money everything?"

339

Her mother turned around. "You're innocent, you poor thing. Of course it is! Lord God, the slavin' we've done these past twenty years because we had nothing. Maybe he's a fop—and maybe he isn't—but he'll dress you in decent clothes and you'll have enough to eat and you won't have to work your hands red and get old b'fore your time. Smarten up, girl. Know when you're well off!"

Sharon stared at her mother. Then without a word she picked up the cloak and went into her room and fell across the bed.

Chapter Twenty-Nine

Maggie walked home from the funeral on Junius's arm, accompanied by Brayton and Wager Tanfield. Azariah had been too weak to make the short journey. Half the town had turned out, she thought, including Wager's wife, Melanie. But Melanie had gone home with friends when Wager said he wanted to call on Azariah.

Maggie felt wrung out, with the long service and with the lies that had to be told. Marie had been ill, she explained to all who asked, and had wandered off in a delirium, not knowing what she was doing. It was a terrible accident and she begged them all to remember Marie in their prayers. And yes, she had received a letter from Becky, and she was in good spirits, living in New York. Of course she had received no such letter, but Wager had urged her into the lie, saying it was better that way than to contend with suspicion.

There were times when she felt her life was composed of too many deceptions.

At home she changed into a cap and apron and put the kettle on, then went upstairs to see how Azariah was. He was awake and eager to talk to Wager when he heard he was downstairs.

Junius soon went to call on Olive Yurman, and Brayton walked into the town, saying he needed the air.

Maggie made tea and took two cups to Wager and Azariah upstairs, then sat in the kitchen by the hearth.

Marie's passing left a void that she knew could never be filled . . . except with a terrible hurt. Of course she knew it was useless to speculate on why Marie had done as she did; it was also useless to castigate herself for not heeding the warning signs. Marie had obviously worked herself into such a state that reality blended with daydreaming and she was no longer capable of telling the difference. But none of that eased the pain.

Azariah had taken Marie's death even harder than she'd thought. Something had gone out of him—and she thought it curious that he no longer mentioned Becky. Did he believe her story about Becky working in New York?

When Wager came downstairs he embraced her at once. Then they sat by the hearth, hand in hand.

"I had a dream about Becky last night . . ." she said.

"What was it?"

"She was a little girl, toddling across a meadow. But there was something—I don't know what—in the trees at the far side and I ran out and grabbed her."

"Then what happened?"

"That's all. I don't remember anything else."

"Dreams don't mean anything," he said. He smiled, leaned over and kissed her cheek. "Anyway, you saved her."

"Lordy! I wish I knew where she is. I wish I knew where Morgan is!"

"You'll find out soon, and everything will be all right."

She sighed, looking at him. "Do you promise?"

He smiled. "Morgan can take care of himself and Becky has a good man with her. He'll bring her back safe."

"And married . . ."

"Yes, and married."

Maggie leaned against him. "I've had other dreams too, and some of them frightening. I thought at first it was because my family is so scattered."

"Frightening how?"

"An impending danger. A *something* I can't see or hear or smell. Something's out there waiting for me."

"No, it isn't."

"Yes," she said softly, "it is."

"Tell me what you mean."

She closed her eyes. "It's waiting to take Az."

Wager was silent, looking down at her. His arms slid about her, pulling her closer. She was right, and there was nothing anyone could do about it. He had been shocked, on seeing Az for the first time in slightly more than a week, to see how greatly he'd deteriorated. Wager laid his cheek on her dark hair and stared into the fire. Soon they would be returning to the cemetery to pay their last respects to Az.

Enoch Quant was furious to learn that Captain Styles expected him to pay a good part of the wedding costs. It was his daughter, after all, Styles said in his supercilious way, and he *was* waiving a dowry.

He might have said he was marrying far beneath his station, but he did not, merely inferred it, so that Enoch could not miss the point.

Sharon was distressed because the wedding date was so close. When he announced it to her, Enoch had been drinking and he winked and smirked, saying that Cap'n Styles was fair wild to get her into bed. Legally, of course.

Her mother was not a bit of help. "Don't you go forgettin' us, girl, now that you're going to be rich." Tabitha's fingers rubbed together. "If you've a mind you can put a little something by for an occasion, eh?"

"You mean money?"

"Lord! 'Course I mean money! What a dense one you are sometimes, Sharon. He'll give you money, what's it to him? You've only to ask. He knows you got nothing."

The hardest thing was to tell Miss Preston that she could no longer come to work. Miss Preston would easily get another girl, but it was the job that was important to Sharon. She had gotten it by herself and kept it because of her industry. It was a measure of her worth—in her own eyes.

Miss Preston leaned her large breasts on the desk and stared at her with displeasure. "You can no longer come to the school?"

"I'll leave today, ma'am, if you don't mind."

"Dammit, girl! I want a reason!"

Sharon backed away a step, afraid of the glowering expression. "I—I'm going to—get married."

"Married! God! You told me you had no young man!"

Sharon squeaked, "I don't, ma'am . . ."

"Then who in God's name are you marrying?"

"My f-father picked him, ma'am. I had nothing to say in the matter."

"Oh." Miss Preston leaned back, her mouth curving down. "Your father, ay? I expect he picked a stonemason."

"No, Miss Preston. I'm terribly sorry. I enjoyed my work here and—"

"Who did he pick for you?"

"A man n-named Styles."

"Oh? What does he do?"

Sharon took a breath, feeling faint. "He's a—" She bit her lip and could not look at Miss Preston. "A—a British officer."

"Jesus God! A lobster!" Miss Preston's fist hit the

desk hard. "Your father must be a nitwit! Throwing away a precious girl like you on a Britisher!"

Sharon nodded, unable to speak. She edged toward the door.

Miss Preston got up heavily, came round the desk and grabbed her wrist, pulling her close. "You've been a charming addition to our staff, Sharon dear. I hate to see you go." She hugged Sharon and kissed her cheek.

Sharon struggled free, smelling stale perfume. "I h-hate to go, Miss Preston." She got the door open and ran out.

Enoch bought her a new pair of shoes, a hat and a basket of white and yellow flowers. Her mother's old wedding gown, that had been handed down twice, was made over for her and fit rather well; her mother had been young and slender when she'd married Enoch. Sponged and ironed, the gown was hung in the air for several days to get the musty, packed-away odors out.

On the day chosen, Sergeant Dyer came for her and her parents in the same coach; Tabitha carried the wrapped gown and the new shoes and they rattled away to Captain Styles's quarters.

Sharon felt that her life was ending. Her new existence would be something less than life and barely more than passing over. She managed to stifle the tears, determined to put on a brave face; she would cry later when it didn't matter. She was a pawn in a larger game and it hurt to think about it. She could not look at her father, though he spoke sharply to her, even with Sergeant Dyer in the coach.

"See you mind your manners and don't make a scene. You hear me?"

"Yes, Father."

"Don't take on with the girl, Enoch," Dyer said.

"She'll do fine enough." He actually chuckled. "If she's a mind she can always bop 'is nose again."

Tabitha clucked her tongue, staring sidelong at her daughter.

Enoch said, "Thass what I mean, damme."

"He got over it," Dyer assured him.

It was the middle of the afternoon when they arrived and stepped out of the coach. Sharon pulled the cloak tightly about her; she was colder than the weather gave reason. Her veins seemed to run ice water and she knew herself to be frightened. She was about to enter into a strange new world and it made her fearful, as much as Captain Styles himself did. She looked longingly at the coach that rumbled away toward the stable in the rear of the house. She gazed at the street, stretching in either direction. Then her father took her arm roughly and turned her toward the steps.

Inside the house she was hustled up the stairs into a bedroom with her mother and Sergeant Dyer. Dyer leaned in to say they had best hurry, that Cap'n Styles hated to be kept waiting. He closed the door firmly.

"Get out of those things," Tabitha said, opening the bundle she'd brought. She laid the dress on the bed, smoothing it with her hands while Sharon undressed, then put on the new shoes. They pulled the wedding gown over her head and Tabitha adjusted it, pulling and tugging while Sharon stood silently, regarding herself in the mirror. She looked like a criminal about to lay her head on the block, she thought. She felt much the same.

With the dress settled to her satisfaction, Tabitha told her to sit, then combed and fussed with her hair, retying the ribbon. Sergeant Dyer knocked on the door. "Come along . . ."

Sharon said, "Mother, I *hate* this man."

"I know," Tabitha said in a more gentle tone than she'd used in a long while. "Shall I tell you a secret?"

"What?" Sharon turned.

"Only days after we were married, I hated your father." She put down the comb. "Come on. They're waiting downstairs."

There were a dozen people in the sitting room; it had been cleared of most of the furniture, and three musicians were playing quietly in a corner. Sharon had an impression of women in silk and officers in glittering uniforms. The buzz of conversation hushed as she entered and stood in the doorway. People moved back and she saw Captain Styles and a black-suited minister on the far side of the room.

Her father appeared from nowhere and took her elbow. Sharon was startled to see him and realized at once that he had been drinking—he reeked of rum. He was in his Sunday best and she was startled to see that even his boots were polished. He leered at her. " 'Tis a glorious day . . ."

Words came to her lips but she stifled them. She felt icy again and was surprised to see approving looks on the faces of the nearest women. The music changed and her father juggled her arm. "Here we go," he said, and pushed her in front of him.

She walked across the room to Styles, the bouquet of yellow and white flowers brushing her chin. She felt herself moving without conscious thought, almost as in a dream; he was suddenly beside her, smiling broadly and the music stopped. She stared at him. It was all unreal. None of it was the way she'd imagined as a girl. He took her hand and she looked at the hairs on his wrist, and the minister began to speak.

In a moment a ring was thrust onto her finger and

she looked at it numbly. It was gold, with delicate etching, and it fitted her loosely. The minister asked her a question and when she did not answer at once, Styles nudged her. She nodded, trying to get the words out. The minister resumed speaking and in the next moment Styles pulled her around and kissed her.

The clamor startled her. People applauded, chattered and laughed. A woman kissed her cheek, then another and another. She saw her mother across the room, sniffling into a handkerchief.

She was married.

She was in the upstairs bedchamber, alone with Jennet Styles. He said, "Get undressed, my dear."

She picked at the ties and he came across the room, his shirttails flapping, turned her around and fumbled at them. His fingers were rough and she felt the strings pulled and yanked—then he pushed the dress down over her shoulders in a sudden flurry of excitement, baring her snowy breasts. She yelped as he tumbled her to the bed onto her back. In a minute he was half atop her, mouthing her nipples. She pushed him away and he growled like an animal, "You're my wife!"

In the next moment he ripped the dress off her and flung it across the room. With horrified eyes she saw him claw his breeches off. Then he jumped at her and she screamed. He slapped her face and she began to sob.

It did not stop him for a second.

Chapter Thirty

It was Sunday afternoon and the sky was blue with lacy white clouds on the horizon. The sun sparkled on the waves. A stately three-masted ship glided silently eastward a mile or more out, and a covey of brown-sailed boats heeled with the breeze only a short way past the rolling surf. Junius walked with Olive Yurman along South Beach Street, wanting to take her hand, knowing she wanted him to.

He told her about the boatyard, the thing most on his mind, and how it was becoming difficult to hire men to work there.

"Why is it?"

"There aren't enough men trained in boatbuilding in a little town like Canaan." He indicated the full-rigged ship. "I'd like to build ships too, one day."

"Isn't that too ambitious?"

"I don't think so. There's a demand, you know." He glanced over his shoulder; they were walking eastward and there were only a few houses in sight across the fields. He slid his hand toward hers and curled his fingers about it. Olive smiled as he squeezed.

"I've enlarged our rope and sail loft," he said, "and made room so that soon we'll be able to work on three boats at a time. And Jeremiah Chace has ordered another schooner."

"Another schooner!"

"Well, the *Annora*'s been very successful. Mr. Chace

says she's faster than lightning and the redcoats have nothing like her." They were out of sight of the last houses now and he pointed toward the beach. "Shall we go that way?"

She looked back and nodded. "I promised Mother to be home well before dark."

"The sun's high," he said. "We've got hours." He stepped off the road into the weeds and they made their way across the sloping field toward the booming surf. Olive held her skirts out of the dirt; it had not rained for a week and the ground was dry, almost dusty, with green grass sprouting everywhere. They followed a natural curve and swirl of the land and came out onto the narrow beach with the sharp tang of the sea in their nostrils and the sounds of screaming gulls just offshore, fighting for scraps of fish thrown by boys on a passing yawl.

Hand in hand, they walked along the beach, which was littered with driftwood; the town was far behind and nothing lay ahead for a long distance, save a few fishermen's huts clustered about a pier a few miles farther on.

Junius halted and drew her close immediately. Her arms slid about his neck and they kissed. Once again he was startled by her eagerness and in a moment had to break off the kisses to gulp air. When he suggested they sit on the sand she quickly assented. He removed his coat and spread it out and she plopped down, arranging her skirts, smiling at him as he sat by her.

In a moment they were lying full length, arms about each other, caught up in an excitement they could not deny. It was the first time they'd been entirely alone with no one likely to intrude.

He kissed her lips, her neck and moved to her breasts, kneading them through the cloth. When he began to untie the bodice she stopped him. "I don't think we ought to do that, Junius . . ."

"There's no one here to see us!"

"It's not that . . ."

"What is it, then?"

"I—I don't want you to undress me."

"I wasn't going to—"

"Mama says it isn't proper for a man to see a girl with—I mean—undressed."

"Not even her husband?"

Olive shook her head. "Not even him."

He was surprised. "You mean your father's never seen your mother undressed?"

"She says no. It isn't decent."

"But—but they must do something in bed! They had you, after all!"

"Well, that's different—I suppose." Olive did not seem sure, he thought; but it was obvious her mother had been talking to her severely since they'd been seeing each other. He knew what was considered "proper" and "decent," but he also did not believe everything he was told. It seemed to him that there were times when those stifling restrictions ought to be put aside.

However, Olive would not budge. She seemed to be eager as ever for his kisses, but nothing else. He was able to caress her with his hands now and then—it seemed to him she either forgot or could not stop him—but she would not permit him to undress her, even to the waist.

It was difficult for him; the ache their closeness caused in his loins would not go away, and after an hour he rolled onto his stomach and they talked. He was sure that she did not share her mother's feelings exactly, hinting that after they were married he might undress her—but not until.

He immediately discussed the marriage they had only talked of in generalities in the past. It would not be seemly, of course, to announce their betrothal so soon after his sister's funeral, but they would do it before summer, and perhaps be married in the fall.

Olive was enthusiastic, saying she would love to be married on her birthday, which was September eleventh. She would immediately begin preparing for the event. She had her mother's carefully laid-away wedding gown, which could be sponged and ironed and altered to fit her. The ceremony would be held at her home, of course, and Junius must get her a ring.

Junius walked home with her in quite a different frame of mind, listening to her making plans. He had not realized she was such a planner. Maybe Brayton could help him get a ring. She thought the clothes he usually wore to church would barely pass muster for this occasion, but not his shoes. He really ought to buy a new pair, she said, and get a haircut.

Maggie met Wager in the upstairs room in Widow Riley's house on the following Wednesday. She was able to get away when Azariah was feeling slightly better, saying she would only be an hour in town.

She was there before him, saw him safely through the kitchen and soon after was in his arms, feeling an urgency that surprised her. The recent events had tightened her nerves and worry had worn them thin. She needed him desperately, and when she undressed and crawled under the blankets, his touch set her on fire.

When he entered her she gave a great sighing moan, and locked her heels around his ankles. Her long dark hair, unfettered by ribbons, swirled under her head; she held him tight against her breasts, feeling his heartbeat as he moved with her. A wandering shaft of sunlight came in the window near them with dust specks dancing along its trail and she watched them languidly, feeling her body relax, seeming to expand under Wager's caress.

She had gone into the relationship with Wager, wondering how long it would last because of the terrible restrictions, and the consequences if they were ever found out. The guilt she'd once felt was largely dissipated; Wager helped her to be strong, to suffer Marie's tragedy, to bear up under Morgan's absence and Becky's flight with Louis. Without him she might not have withstood the trials.

The bonds that kept them apart still existed and might never be broken, but she knew in her heart that she would soon be free—a thought that brought guilt with it. Az could not last much longer, a terrible thing to contemplate. But it was so. She would be free, but not Wager.

It was a bridge they might one day have to cross, but not now. Now she reveled in his lovemaking, giving herself over to the ecstasy that he brought her, to the precious release that made her strong.

Chapter Thirty-One

Becky settled into the routine of Andre Bataille's house very quickly. Her duties were light and pleasant; Andre was a man of constant cheerfulness; despite his infirmity he never allowed himself to complain about his own state. Now and again he was sarcastic toward Theo, but she could overlook it. In her estimation Theo deserved what he got.

Andre slept in a large blue and white bedchamber, in an ornate four-poster that he said had been in his family for generations, as the house had. Voliner helped him out of bed in the mornings, helped him to dress and get into the chair, then pushed him to the dining room for breakfast, where she met him.

At his insistence they ate breakfast together, which Voliner told her had not been the case with her predecessor. After breakfast she pushed him outside where he could enjoy the morning sun. The weather had moderated and the rains were past; spring was invading the land with fragrant promises.

On occasion she read to him, or they talked, mostly about America. When she deplored the British oppression in the matter of colonial manufactures Andre said gently that all nations pursued nearly the same courses in their dealings with colonies; even the Romans had done it. Perhaps it was not fair, but it had precedent.

"Mind, I take no sides," he said, "but fact is fact."

"Hateful fact!"

Andre smiled. "I suspect the British will relent in time. They are not stupid."

"There is talk of self-rule," she said. "Some say we must break away from Britain."

"That will never happen. The American colonies are too close, bound by blood ties to the mother country. Such a thing is preposterous. It would be bad for both."

"It would mean war, I suppose."

"Let us not talk of war this glorious morning. Why don't you begin to learn French, would you like that?"

She clapped her hands. "I would love it!"

"Very well. We'll start with the names of things. This is an armchair." He patted the chair in which he sat. "We call it, *un fauteuil.*"

"Un fauteuil."

"Excellent!" He beamed at her. Indicating his coat pocket, he said, *"La poche."*

"La poche."

Touching his waistcoat, he said, *"Un gilet."*

"Un gilet."

He pointed to the ground. *"La terre."* He looked upward. *"Le ciel."* He indicated the sun. *"Le soleil."*

As she was about to reply, Theo's voice said, "What is this—school is in session?"

Andre craned his neck. "Theo! What are doing here so soon after your last visit?"

Theo smiled at her. *"Vous avez un bon accent.* You have a good accent, mademoiselle."

"Thank you."

He looked at his father. *"Mon cher Papa, ne vous fachez pas."*

"I'm not angry!" Andre said, "only surprised. For you to call twice in a month is suspicious."

Theo shrugged, smiling. "May I sit down?"

"Yes, of course."

Becky watched him pull up a chair and fish for a cigar, his eyes on her. "You are learning the language, mademoiselle?"

"Why not?" Andre demanded.

Theo's eyes rounded. "Please do not jump on me, Papa. I only asked a question." He beckoned to someone at the door of the house.

Becky said, "Perhaps you have business to discuss alone?" She rose, but Andre motioned her to sit.

"No, we have no business."

Voliner came hurrying out with a coal in an iron tray and Theo lit his cigar, puffing smoke, nodding to Voliner. "My father is not in the best of moods this morning."

"That is nonsense," Andre exclaimed. "I am in a perfectly good mood. Is that not true, my dear?"

"Yes, sir," Becky said, keeping her eyes averted from Theo.

"Then I stand corrected," Theo said magnanimously, waving his cigar. "Perhaps I am interferring . . . ?" He rose with a little bow.

Andre regarded him morosely. "We were getting on very well without you."

"Then I willl take myself off." He bowed to them again and strode away to the house, glancing at her.

Andre craned around to watch him enter the door and shook his head. "He does get on my nerves, you know. Can't help it. He always did, since he was in school. He was a troublemaker as a child. Most annoying."

Becky tried to change the subject, pointing out a full-rigged ship out at sea, sails billowing and white as summer clouds. Andre put both hands up, cupping them around his eyes. "*Un navire a voiles,*" he said, "a sailing ship." He glanced at her, "But you are tired of this game, eh? Perhaps we should go inside. It is a bit chilly. . . ."

She pushed him into the house and after a bit Voliner brought them chocolate and hard, round cakes which Elda baked once a week because Andre was so fond of them.

Theo stayed for the midday meal, making himself agreeable; even Andre could find no fault with him. In the early afternoon Andre went into his bedchamber for an afternoon nap. And when Becky went upstairs to her own room, Theo followed her.

She did not realize he was there until she tried to close the door. He smiled and pushed his way in, closing it at his back. "I cannot stay away from you, mademoiselle."

"I do not want you here!"

"Ah, but this is my house—or it will be very soon. Would you turn a man out of his own house?"

"It may be your house, but it's my bedroom." She backed away from him. "Your father—"

"Hush! Let us not speak of my father." He came close, smiling. "You are beautiful, *chérie*—"

"Please do not call me that!" How could she allow anyone ever to say that to her again?

He was surprised, but continued to approach her, arms at his sides, but curled into claws that moved slightly as if he ached to grab her. The long slanting light came in the window and brightened his face so that she saw each fleck of his dark eyes ringed with black, brows arching upward in a fashion she could only think of as devilish.

"You must go at once!" she said sharply and felt a pang of fear for the first time. Would he dare attack her in his father's house?

Silently he continued to advance, very near now, so

that she could feel his harsh breath. His smile reminded her of the cat who approached a bird in the grass.

She took a step backward, hand at her throat, and overturned the small square dressing table stool. Losing her balance, she clutched wildly at the table, feeling herself falling. Her head struck the table a stunning blow —she felt the pain of it—then nothing.

Slowly she came to her senses. She was lying on the bed, nearly naked, with Theo between her thighs, grinning down at her.

Azariah was lingering. Maggie could see it quite clearly, even though she was with him every day. She had long ago moved out of the double bed and taken to sleeping in a cot on the far side of the room to allow him more freedom; she often found him in the mornings with his arms spread wide.

The doctor came twice a week with his watch and his knife-thin mouth. He took Azariah's pulse and looked in his eyes and shook his head each time. Maggie was sorry to see him at the door. He could do nothing, suggest nothing, and he did it with a pomposity she found nearly unbearable. He told her what she already knew, and had probably known long before him, that Azariah was dying.

Azariah knew it too. He never spoke of death to her, and did his best to be as cheerful as she, but he knew. She could see it in his eyes.

She never tried to hide it from Junius and Brayton. Junius spoke with his father daily, telling him about the boatyard, discussing his problems, and Maggie sometimes thought it kept Az alive. He looked forward to the evenings when Junius would come home. It was different with Brayton; not that Az cared less for his younger son, it was just that the boatyard meant so much to him.

Az also was pleased when Wager came by to sit at the foot of the bed and relate the gossip along the waterfront and smoke a cigar. Az had given up smoking because it choked him so, but he loved to smell the aroma.

Every day Maggie brought him tea between meals and sat with him and it was on a beautiful spring morning, when she opened the windows so he could breathe the wine-like air, that he asked her to sit on the edge of the bed instead of the chair. When she did, he took her hand and held it tightly.

"It's been a different kind of year, Maggie . . ."

"You mean the children growing up?"

"I mean for all its happenings . . . and poor little Marie . . ." There were tears in his eyes and he made no attempt to brush them away. "Is there no letter from Becky?"

"No . . . but I expect one soon."

"She's got your strength, Maggie. I don't fear for her. I think they're all strong, in their ways. Even Marie had a fortitude we didn't know she had . . ." His voice trailed off. "I wish Morgan would come home. I want to see him before—" He closed his eyes.

"Morgan will be home soon," she said brightly, "you'll see. There isn't a charge against him and as soon's he learns it he'll be rapping on the door."

"Yes . . ."

"Do you want to rest, dear?"

"You've got three strappin' sons to care for you, Maggie. And the finest friend in the colonies."

She felt his hand close tighter on hers. He said, "I mean Wager."

She looked at him then and saw something she'd never thought to see, and she realized in that instant that Azariah *knew*. He had known for a long time, and said nothing but in his own way understood. Her heart was beating wildly—could he feel it as he held her hand? She tried to speak but could only nod.

Azariah closed his eyes, sighing deeply.

In a little while the pressure of his fingers lessened.

Chapter Thirty-Two

Waking, Becky screamed and heaved, twisting her body. Theo was dislodged and rolled off her, growling at her to shut up! Did she want to wake the dead?

She pulled a blanket up to cover herself. He had lifted her from the floor onto the bed, then undressed and raped her!

She was nearly speechless with rage.

"You've been had before," he said sourly. "Don't take on."

"Get out," she said between clenched teeth. "Get out!"

He pulled his clothes on, some of his cockiness returning. She watched him, hating his every movement; she was only a servant to him, of course, someone to do with as he chose. Had he also raped his father's other servants? Surely Andre did not know.

He put on his coat and went to the door, turning to sneer at her. "Keep your mouth shut."

She glared at him and he went out and closed the door.

Then she heard the shout, sounding like Andre's voice.

Sliding from the bed, she wrapped the blanket about her and opened the door. Andre, sitting in his chair was at the foot of the stairs with Theo halfway down. Andre's face was red and angry. He was shouting at his son in French. When he saw her he paused, took a breath and demanded of her, "What did he do to you?"

Becky leaned against the door, feeling the throb of the bump on her head. She did not look at Theo. "He—he took my clothes off."

"And did you allow him to do it?"

"No, of course not." She touched the bump with her hand. "I was—I was unconscious."

"The girl is lying!" Theo said loudly. "She invited me into her room."

She looked at him then, with disgust. "You are a pig—as well as a liar." She went into the room and closed the door. She heard more shouts as she bathed the bloody bump and patted it dry. Then she dressed and in a bit Voliner knocked on the door and gave her a square of paper. It read:

Please come downstairs. I wish to talk with you.
A.

She followed Voliner down the steps and found Andre in the sitting room with his parrot. He said, "Please sit down, Becky. Theo has gone." He looked at her head and motioned her to come closer. "That's a nasty bump—how did it happen?"

She told him the circumstances as he pressed his lips together tightly. He said, "I am terribly distressed at this, Becky. I have known for a long time that Theo is unable to keep his hands off females, but I did not suspect he would rape one of my servants in my own house. I must make this up to you."

"It is not your fault, sir."

"Perhaps it is. I have been too easy with him."

"What will you do?"

"With Theo?" Andre sighed, pressing his hands together tightly. "At the moment I have no idea. Perhaps I will discuss it with Bricard." He brightened. "But that is for me to decide. At the moment we must do something for you. I have already sent a message to my shipping agent and expect a reply in the next day or two. We are going to put you on a ship for America."

Becky was astounded. "On a ship!"

He nodded. "I will be very sorry to lose you, my dear, but as I said, I am in your debt—and I always pay my debts, one way or the other."

It was three days before Andre's agent sent a note to him and Andre showed it to her as they lunched together.

"The brig *Emily Stringer* is in the harbor, bound for Boston. When she pulls up anchor, my dear, you will be aboard."

Becky stared at the bit of paper; it was difficult to believe she would soon be going home—to Canaan. She sat with tears in her eyes as Andre chuckled. He said, "We will get your things together and I will ask Bricard to put you on board. Is Boston far from your home?"

"Probably a hundred and fifty miles. But there is a coach, I believe."

"And do you have the fare?"

"I—I think so." She brushed the tears away and smiled.

Becky packed her few belongings in the canvas bag and Lieutenant Bricard came to the house the following morning, in civilian clothes, which made him look oddly out of place. He belonged in the uniform, she thought. He explained that he did not wish the captain or the ship's crew to get the idea that she was being expelled from the country; the presence of a policeman might get that rumor started. Andre said it was kind of him.

Her parting from the old man was emotional. Though she'd known him only a short time he had become dear to her. His eyes glistened with tears as she kissed him goodbye.

"Get her out of here, Bricard," he said, dabbing at his eyes. "*Adieu, adieu* . . . remember me, Becky."

"I will never forget you." Bricard hurried her through the door, across the little bridge and into the waiting coach.

He said little during the ride to the waterfront, allowing her her thoughts. She was going home . . . without Louis, but with his child inside her.

It was cold on the embankment and she pulled the old cloak more closely about her shoulders as Bricard dickered with a boatman, then helped her down a half-dozen stone steps, awash with surf, into the small boat. He sat beside her on the sternsheets as the boatman pulled toward the two-masted ship that Bricard pointed out.

The ship was loading casks from a barge as they approached, men shouting, lowering a huge net to be loaded with the brown hogsheads, then hauled up to the deck. The boatman tied on aft of the work gang and shipped his oars. They were expected, she saw, and a rope ladder came falling down from the rail. Bricard steadied it and she went up slowly, her hands grasped from above. She was swung to the deck by two grinning seamen. Bricard followed with her canvas bag and a young officer showed them to her cabin, one very much like the tiny room she and Louis had shared on the voyage from America.

Bricard put the bag on the deck beside the bunk and handed her an envelope. "Your passage is paid, mademoiselle, and Andre instructed me to give you this."

With surprise she opened it. Money!

He said, "It's for your needs, and stage fare."

"But—"

Bricard smiled. "He can afford it, I assure you." He

doffed his hat. "I wish you a pleasant journey, Becky."

She rushed into his arms, tears rolling down her cheeks again. "You have been so kind—"

"Now, now—this is a day for happiness, not tears!"

She bit her lip, dabbing them away. "I'm foolish—"

"Not at all." He smiled and opened the cabin door. "Some day perhaps you will come back to France, and if you do, remember my name."

"Of course."

"Then *au revoir*, mademoiselle."

"*Au revoir*, Lieutenant."

He smiled and went out. She put the envelope into the bodice of her dress, drew the cloak tightly about her shoulders and climbed the companionway to the deck. The anchor was aboard and the ship began to heel under topsails as she headed for the open sea.

She was going home.

She was going home!

SPECIAL PREVIEW

THE SAVAGE HEART

by Arthur Moore

The following scene is excerpted from the first chapter in the second novel of a compelling new series from Pinnacle Books, Inc., *The Strong Americans**, by Arthur Moore. Here is the powerful and passionate saga of The Lynns, a proud Colonial family torn asunder as they dare to follow their hearts, defying the limits of their loves, in search of their impossible dreams.

*Copyrght © 1981 by Arthur Moore

Chapter One

The Atlantic, 1762:

The brig *Emily Stringer* was a month out of Argenton, France, bound for Boston in the American colonies, when the skies darkened and a cold wind came driving from the north. Becky Elise Lynn, her dark hair firmly held in place by a cotton kerchief, stood near the helmsman watching the green seas break over the prow.

She was not yet twenty, graceful and lovely, though her clothes were more coarse than fashionable and there was a sadness about her hard to define, others thought. She said nothing about herself, however, gallants like Sam Garnet, a fellow passenger, did their best to draw her out.

In a matter of weeks she would be home in Canaan, a seaport town in Connecticut, and the thought caused a lump to rise in her throat. She had left home to go to France with Louis in the middle of winter and now it was spring and she was returning after Louis's tragic death. But she would have his child. How could she tell her mother that she and Louis had never married? Somehow it would have to be said.

Becky turned at a touch on her shoulder and looked at Captain Hiram Eames. "You'll have to go below, Miss," he said, indicating the blowing sea. "Can't have you washed overboard . . ."

Men were stringing lines along the deck for safety and others were hurrying aloft to shorten sail. She thought of the tiny cabin, stuffy and dark and pleaded with him to allow her to remain in the chartroom until he finally relented. The chartroom had two small windows looking forward, and though the room was unheated it was better than the cabin. She pulled the old cloak tightly about her shoulders, fingers automatically straying to the place where, so long ago, she'd sewn the bit of paper that Louis valued so much—and had died for.

The winds brought rain and it quickly became necessary for the men to reef sails again; the ship plunged on at a fraction of the speed it had been making. Becky heard Captain Eames order the cook fires doused; then he changed course, heading into the wind instead of running before it.

The storm stayed with them all during the night and was even more violent the next morning when Becky struggled out of the confining bunk, pulled on her outer clothes, shoes, and cloak and made her way up to the chartroom again. The ship rolled and plunged, throwing her against the bulkheads and she soon had a number of purple bruises. Storms pass, as she'd heard her father and brothers say many times; they would wait this one out.

At midday the storm hit with fury and the rains lashed at them, beating against the windows like furious strangers demanding to be let in. The sea became dark and moody, heaving and tossing gray wavetops at the brig, and the wind howled through the rigging. The sky was black, streaked here and there with an ominous yellow, turning steely where the lightning flashed through it.

In an hour Captain Eames ordered the ship hove to and struggling helmsmen strained to keep her turned into the wind. Cold meat and bread were issued to everyone who could eat—there were only six passengers aboard—and Eames assured her that the brig was a stout ship and would easily ride out any storm.

But later she saw him in the ratlines with a glass to his eyes, searching to westward, and she wondered what he feared.

While she watched him, the charthouse door slammed open and shut and Sam Garnet came into the cabin. Becky had met Sam in the first hour of the voyage and he had been attentive every day since; he knew some of her situation—what little she'd told him—and he'd been unfailingly polite and pleasant. He was a tall man, perhaps forty she thought, with a good-looking ruddy face. He appeared strong and capable. He had large hands and a thick neck like a workman, but his speech was soft and his words well chosen.

He was surprised to see her. "You ought to be in your cabin."

"I have permission to be here."

Sam smiled and shrugged in defeat. "Of course. The cabins are small—"

"And smelly."

He laughed. "And very dark. I'm quite sure you'd be unhappy there."

Becky looked at him sidelong and nodded. There was a wooden ledge running the length of the two windows, a convenient place to hold onto with feet braced wide. One could stand upright against the most fearful rolls. The ship's timbers creaked alarmingly and when a particularly large wave crashed aboard, the ship shuddered. There were times when Becky thought they were lost. But the brig always righted herself though she seemed a clumsy sailor, slow to answer the tiller.

Through the window she could see that the ship had only a wisp of sail set to keep pressure on the rudder; the masts vibrated and the ratlines were as taut as the strings of a violin. She peered at the boiling seas, gray and bearded with foam as they heaved and rolled as far as the rain-shrouded horizon. It was cold and cheerless and every fearful wave that swept down upon them towered above the masts. Becky was sure they'd be engulfed and smashed to bits. But each time, while green seas came aboard and swept away everything not tightly lashed down, the ship managed to shake free, groaning and protesting. Lightning played a frightening counterpoint to the icy rain and Becky ducked her head when it cracked, seemingly just over their heads.

When she went below decks, finally, everything was in turmoil. Cargoes had shifted and men struggled, shouting and swearing horribly as they attempted to bring order out of chaos. Becky hurried up to the charthouse again, her cheeks burning.

Sam Garnet brought her a bowl of cold meat and beans, all that was available, he said, but she ate it gratefully and drank from a bottle he had slung about his neck.

During a lull she opened the door and stepped over the coaming to the deck. Icy mists and low clouds swept over the ship, a hand's reach high; the wind gusted like a live thing, tearing at her clothes and beating savage blows on the hull. A sudden flurry of hail drove her inside again as lightning flickered and thunder crashed, mauling her ears.

His face clouded, Sam entered to yell at her, angry that she'd ventured onto the deck. "Not even the hands are out there!"

"I came inside," she said calmly, but feeling anything but.

"I'm sorry I shouted," he said, apologizing, "but it's a terrible storm and I was afraid for you." He barred the door. "Please don't do that again."

"Storms pass," she said and heard him grunt. It was gloomy in the charthouse and when he saw her looking at the lantern, Sam produced flint and steel and spent a dozen minutes getting sparks to smoulder into a grudging flame. The candle-lantern was suspended from the ceiling by a thin chain and it swung with the movement of the ship, making ominous shadows on the bulkheads.

It was a long night with no sleep for anyone. Becky huddled in a corner of the charthouse, cold and miserable but out of the wet. Sam Garnet went out once and returned with two blankets, folding one about her. The storm, he reported, was still blowing with no sign of letting up, and Captain Eames looked worried.

By morning she was tired and her mind sluggish; it was an effort to think. The night had been noise-filled and her dreams agonized, all of them violent. She saw in horrible clarity the expressions on the faces of the men who had attacked her and Louis and the way in which he'd been shot in cold blood. It seemed to press upon her time and again, the same terrible scene acted out inexorably—and there was no way she could escape it. It was her fate to witness it over and over, until she woke sobbing.

When she pulled herself to the windows, monstrous green seas, mottled with gray, surged over the plunging prow and came seething across the decks to crash against the superstructures. Becky ducked away as the ship rolled, wearily struggling from the troughs of the waves to the crests and down again. Sam waited for a lull and went out to hurry back with more cold meat and bread.

"They're damned worried," he said, indicating the afterdeck where Captain Eames and his officers gathered.

"Are we in danger—really?"

He shrugged. "It's the worst storm I've ever seen."

"Have you sailed much?"

Sam smiled at her. "A bit, yes. I know a storm when I see it."

Becky studied him when he looked away. He was a trader, he'd told her; it was a word that could cover a multitude of enterprises. He looked like a man who was used to fending for himself and it was impossible to tell if he were poverty-stricken or well off. His rough clothes did not reflect wealth, but then he was traveling, not in a drawing room. She wondered if he had a cargo aboard the brig.

One of the ship's officers, a man named Hammond, slammed into the charthouse, oilskins dripping, and stared at them with round eyes. He was pale and breathing hard as if he'd run a long distance. He looked pinched with cold, and scared.

Sam asked hopefully, "Is the storm letting up?"

"Jesus, Lord!" The mate blew out his breath. "It's gettin' worse, if anything." He gave Sam a withering glance and pawed through the chart file, dragging one out. He rolled it up tightly and thrust it under the oilskins.

Sam took hold of his arm.. "Tell us the truth, man. How is the ship taking it?"

The man glanced to Becky then back to Sam. "It ain't the ship."

"What d'you mean?"

"The truth is—if you want it—we're gettin' close to shore."

"But by our last reckoning we were five hundred miles—"

The mate grunted. "That was two days ago and the wind's blowin' us west. You know what that means?"

"The coast of Maine," Sam said in a hollow voice.

"That's right. The coast of Maine." He glanced at Becky, opened the door and ran out.

Becky stared with frightened eyes. "He's afraid we'll be wrecked?" She knew about New England coasts, jagged rocks that tore the bottoms out of unfortunate ships hurled upon them.

Sam shrugged again, staring through the window. "They don't know our position. No one's been able to take sightings."

For the first time she felt dread. How terrible to be drowned among the rocks just when she was nearing home! She knew there was no chance to work the ship out to sea;

the men could not make sail in the freezing wind and even if they tried the gusts would tear the canvas out of their fingers—and maybe tear them from the rigging. A man lost overboard was lost indeed. No rescue boat could live a moment in such seas.

Sam turned. "Have you any luggage?"

"Only a canvas bag of clothes."

"No valuables?"

She shook her head, thinking of the paper sewn into the neckpiece of the cloak she wore. "Nothing."

He explained that it would be well for them to be prepared for any eventuality and went below to return with a large leather valise, which he said contained clothes and a few valuable papers. He put it to one side and continued to watch the waves.

Becky thought he was being foolish; if the ship were lost, he would certainly lose the baggage and, perhaps, his life. But she did not want to dwell on *that*. Thinking of the Maine coast was bad enough.

Toward evening Captain Eames tried again to get a sail unfurled with no success. A handful of men scrambled aloft but the keening wind would not permit them to stay. Becky peered upward at the tiny, struggling figures on the spar. They loosed a square of canvas and were sheeting it home when an angry gust tore it from them and flung it into the sea. Eames recalled them immediately as a huge, curling wave bore down upon the ship and crashed like thunder on the deck, causing the brig to stagger drunkenly. Becky was hurled aside and picked herself off the heaving deck, hearing Sam's muttered curses. When she looked through the window again all the men were down, safely, she hoped.

She spent another miserable night, thinking of the coming baby, snatching a bit of sleep here and there but wakened by the ship's violent movements too often and by the never-ceasing creakings. When dawn came at last, the storm still mauled them with even more fury, as if the gods of the sea were determined to crush and drag them down into the depths.

The foremast had splintered during the night and now leaned far to starboard, continuing to splinter as the wind played with it. Eames got men into the rigging with axes to cut away the lines and finally the mast fell, its awful weight slewing the brig broadside to the heaving seas. The men hacked furiously to cut the remaining stays and lines and all at once the mast dropped away with a huge scraping sound. The ship seemed to sigh in relief and began to right itself as the helmsmen hauled on the wheel.

The mast came free as another great wave was on them. The ship yawed ponderously, the bow lifted, and the wave passed by without doing harm. The wind and rain continued, slashing at the windows so that Becky could not see out. The storm increased. One towering wave after another attacked; crushing seas broke over the deck and the tired ship rolled and creaked in agony.

Sam dared not go out of the cabin as midday approached, saying it was unsafe to set foot on the decks, so they listened to their stomachs grumble. Becky huddled in a corner, wrapped in the blanket as the ship plunged and twisted.

Men came and went through the inboard door of the cabin, each bringing salt sprays with him till the floor was inches deep with icy water and Becky had to stand. In the afternoon Captain Eames entered, wearing a long, soggy coat and hat. He looked drawn and tired, his face gray with fatigue. They were being driven ashore, he told them, and nothing to do about it.

"It's my duty to warn you," he said. "Make whatever preparations you can."

"You mean prayer?" Sam asked, and his lip curled.

"If prayers will help, sir."

Becky asked, "Is there no chance at all, Captain?"

He looked at her with a trace of a smile. "I've been at sea for near fifty years, ma'am, and seen damned few miracles, excuse my frankness. But a miracle is what we need now. Perhaps your friend will pray for one." Eames opened the door and stepped over the coaming.

In two hours the ship struck.

There was a terrible shock, a smashing, tearing roar as the port side was hurled onto the waiting rocks. Becky was thrown down; her head hit sharply and she felt dazed. Fear for herself and the baby within her seemed to paralyze her mind. Dimly she heard Sam cry out and felt herself lifted. He placed her hands on the ledge and she hung on desperately, feeling the ship heave up and swing round with a terrible creaking and thundering of timbers. Through the window she saw the splintered deck and the mainmast shattered below the crosstrees. It slewed across the deck toward the jib and came to rest as the ship shuddered and a huge wave broke along its length with white water surging to engulf the charthouse.

Becky heard herself screaming. One window pane was smashed to bits and water poured in. The door was torn from its hinges and Sam grabbed for her. She flailed in his arms, yelling in anger and fright as he pushed her out of the cabin. He thrust her to an upright, shouting for her to hold on, and she wrapped her arms about it as another icy wave surged over them and receded, leaving her breathless.

The ship groaned and muttered like a thing in the grasp of a deadly trap, wounded and in agony. There were mysterious crashes from below and booming voices that sounded like cannon shots but could not be. Sam yelled to several seamen but they either did not hear him or ignored him. He shouted something about climbing aft and Becky nodded. The stem was under water; the only way to go was aft. She started to follow him and was suddenly buried by a bursting wave. Gray water held her fast for a moment, shook the ship, and smashed its way past. She came up spitting water, as sore as if she'd been pummeled by fists.

Sam yelled again and she went after him as he climbed over timbers and gained the afterdeck, which slanted sharply. Rain pelted her and the furious wind tore at the precious cloak, trying to rip it away.

Sam clung to a bulwark and beckoned and she managed to get to his side, able then to view the entire ship. Its destruction was complete. The rocks had broken her back and everywhere was the awful litter of havoc, spanks, and splinters, bits of broken spars and wrecked cabins. She could see some of the cargo, cabin furniture and pans from the galley; all were swept away by the eddies. There was a roaring, growling sound beneath her feet as if a huge sea monster were eating and tearing at the ship's vitals. A number of sailors, looking like drowned rats, crawled over the wreckage, but she did not see any of the officers or other passengers. The sea boomed, smashing into the black rocks, and the wind howled like a crazed thing, driving the hard rain into their faces.

Waves burst continually along the hull and she glanced

toward the dark shore unable to see details. She looked down; murky water surged upward all at once then fell away with frightening speed as the ship groaned. Nothing could live in that maelstrom.

Sam pulled at her sleeve and began working his way toward the aft rail; she followed him, her heart in her mouth. She'd had little time to be afraid and now it hit her that this was where she would die. Perhaps someone would find her body washed ashore and notify her loved ones . . .

"Hurry up!" Sam yelled. Then in the next second, shouted, "Hang on!"

Becky grabbed the bulwark with both arms as the wave broke over them and wrenched at her body, twisting her around. It tugged savagely but she hung on and the wave retreated, hissing and snarling in defeat. The sea had no intention of allowing them to escape. The rain seemed to increase in fury, nearly blinding her. The chill wind whipped and sawed, making progress almost impossible. She had to inch her way along, never daring fully to let go with even one hand. She saw Sam reach the end and turn to shout something—then another wave hit with the force of an erupting volcano; it seemed to explode, then took them with it, ripping her hands from the rail tumbling her about unmercifully. She felt herself unable to breathe, her lungs near bursting with the need for air.

She struck bottom and was shoved into the sand, then battered as if by a hundred angry clubs, wrestled about till she knew she was drowning, submerged in a racing smother of water.

Then suddenly Sam pulled her up. Her head was free and she gulped air! The waves rolled her along and she saw Sam's face turned toward her and felt his hand clutching her. Stones scraped her and she was unable to think—but she was breathing! A wave bumped her, shoving her rudely and she got to her knees. She was on a sandy beach! It was dark as pitch; the rain drummed and the wind snatched at the billowing cloak.

Sam shouted her name and she turned. He came out of the white water like a sea god, stumbled to her side and fell to his knees. "We made it! We made it ashore!" He seemed astonished.

Becky looked about, able to make out that they were in a frothy circle of beach with serrated rocks on every side.

The raging seas broke over the rocks with a thunderous roaring, and farther out, she could see the broken stumps of the *Emily Stringer*'s masts and the dark silhouette of her battered hull.

She was certain that if she had not followed Sam to the afterdeck she would never have been swept to this beach. And he had pulled her head out of the fury of surf and hauled her ashore. He had saved her life.

Captain Eames's miracle had occurred.